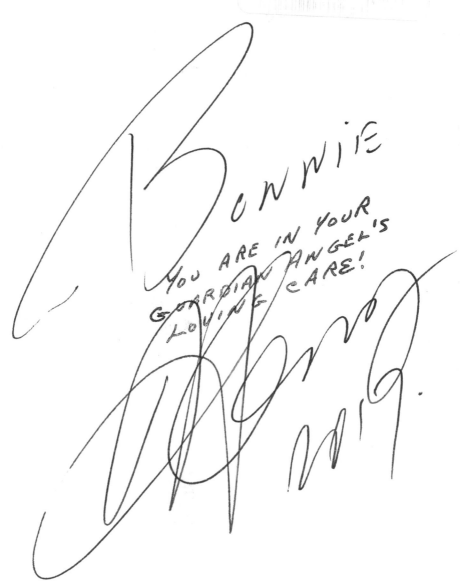

Bonnie

You are in your
Guardian Angel's
loving care!

WHAT READERS ARE SAYING ABOUT

PEWTER ANGELS

BOOK ONE in THE ANGELIC LETTERS SERIES
by
HENRY RIPPLINGER

"… What a beautiful tale you have spun. I was completely lost in another world every time I opened your novel and I never wanted it to end."

DEANNA

"… A lifelong and avid reader, I have consumed thousands of novels. Never has one been more delicious than *Pewter Angels*, and for the first time in memory I could not resist a second helping. Indeed, I read it twice, each time more than satisfying."

WENDY

"… I literally could not put it down! It was an amazing read, so heartfelt, it made me cry in parts!"

JEN

" I cannot wait to continue this amazing saga. To think in this day and age you wrote a story that keeps the reader glued to the pages and there is no foul language, no vulgarity—just a spell-binding story about life: things that affect us all and a belief system that is available to all who choose to see beyond. Thank you for reawakening the beliefs I have had since I was a child, for reminding me to call on my angels and trust in my God."

ELAINE

"… Wow!! You immediately got my attention and it was very difficult to put the book down; it's absolutely amazing how you pulled me right into the characters' lives and emotions. What an ingenious way to teach young people high morals, values and integrity. This book feels more real life than fiction—excellent job. Can't wait for the next book."

HILDA

"… It's been a long time since a book has taken me away on a journey that stimulated so many emotions on so many different levels."

DARRELL

"… I [have been] a social worker since 1987 and family counselor in private practice. As a mother of five children I appreciate my two older teens being able to read the book and be validated for their choices and beliefs just as the characters [are]. I will be recommending your book to all faith-based parents I see in my practice and to young people alike."

MARLA

"… Thank you for such a loving and caring book."   CAULETT

"… I couldn't put it down and could truly feel every moment of it. It is such a loving, Spirit-filled book, full of true humanity and wonderful life lessons."

ELLA

"… I just finished reading *Pewter Angels* and I absolutely loved it. What great insight and wonderful life lessons to live by! Thank you for sharing your talents and your spiritual wisdom."

WENDY

"… I have to let you know that this is the first time in a long time that I have been drawn into and lost in a book to the point of smiling, blushing and laughing out loud.… I know there are things I should be accomplishing today but find myself being drawn with eager anticipation to explore more of a world where humanity and the celestial meet."

JOAN

"… I absolutely loved it. It is in my top 10 books of all time!"   HOLLY

"… Awesome, awesome book!!! I bought *Pewter Angels* for our daughter. She reported that she read it faster than any book she'd ever read, then passed it to me, and I also couldn't put it down."

HELEN

"… I believe I have never enjoyed reading a book as much as yours."

DAISY

"… This is the most amazing book I have ever read! I go to bed at night thinking about Henry and Jenny. I can hardly wait for the next book to come out. Thank you so, so much for the beautiful story. You have made me a believer in Spiritual connections."

LYNN

"… I can only say thank you—thank you for such a wonderful read. [Your] book to me was like a warm blanket on a cold night, a meal with friends that one never wants to end, a beacon of light in the dark. I wanted to read and read—but at the same time I did not want the book to end. I fell in love with this book and the people inside…"

JAYLEIGH

"… You promised me a page-turner but you forgot to mention I would be reading a riveting novel that would capture my heart. It's hard to believe *Pewter Angels* is your first novel."

CYNTHIA

"… Bravo! *Pewter Angels* is a definite page-turner. From the first paragraph to the last word, I was one with the characters. Each one 'got under my skin' and compelled me to live and breathe with them."

CINDY

"… I simply loved it! The story was set in what many consider a simpler time, but it is really a timeless story with timeless lessons."

CHRISTINE

"… Thank you for writing a book that made me want to be a better person, not only for myself and my family, but in the eyes of God."

KAMLA

"… The characters are so much of my heart and soul that I'm swept away into their lives and journey."

SUSAN

"… It is rare that you find such a lovely book to read. I loved the wisdom of Mr. Engelmann, and we should all be so lucky to have someone like him in our lives."

DARLA

Please write to Henry at: **henry@henryripplinger.com** or visit *www.henryripplinger.com* for more information about Henry's work and art. We would love to hear from you!

ANOTHER ANGEL OF LOVE

"ANOTHER ANGEL OF LOVE"   H.M.A. IPPLINGER/20XI

Also by Henry Ripplinger

THE ANGELIC LETTERS SERIES
Pewter Angels

OTHER WORKS
If You're Not from the Prairie…
(Story by David Bouchard, Images by Henry Ripplinger)

Coming soon from Pio-Seelos Books:

BOOK THREE OF THE ANGELIC LETTERS SERIES
Angel of Thanksgiving

THE ANGELIC LETTERS SERIES

Book Two

— ✴ —

ANOTHER ANGEL OF LOVE

1959-1963

HENRY K. RIPPLINGER

Library and Archives Canada Cataloguing in Publication
Ripplinger, Henry
Another angel of love / Henry Ripplinger.

(The angelic letters series ; bk. 2)
ISBN 978-0-9865424-2-8 (pbk.)

I. Title. II. Series: Ripplinger, Henry. Angelic letters series ; bk 2.

PS8585.I565A65 2011   C813'.6   C2011-902279-6

TRUE LOVE (from High Society)
Words and Music by COLE PORTER
© 1956 (Renewed) CHAPPELL & CO., INC.
All Rights Reserved
Used by permission of ALFRED PUBLISHING CO., INC.

Author photo: Bruce Vasselin, Designer Photo
Cover concept and design by Henry K. Ripplinger
Cover production by Brian Danchuk Design
Page layout by Heather Nickel

Pio-Seelos Books
Ph: (306) 731-3087, Fax: (306) 731-3852.
E-mail: henryripplinger@imagewireless.ca

Printed and bound in Canada by Friesens Printers
First printing May 2011
Second printing November 2011
Third printing September 2012
Fourth printing April 2013
Fifth printing June 2013

*This novel is dedicated to the memories
of my mom and dad, Philomena and Christian,
whose love and friendship are deeply missed.*

ACKNOWLEDGEMENTS

FIRST, THANK YOU to my wonderful wife, Joan, for forty-nine years of marriage. You have always supported me in my endeavours; thank you for reading, assisting with the editing and being a sounding board. You truly are *Another Angel of Love.*

Thank you to my daughter, Tracy Jacknife, for reading *Another Angel of Love*, for your helpful suggestions and for always being there for me.

To my other daughter, Jody Ripplinger—a very busy mother!—thank you for your initial edits of *Another Angel of Love* and for your insightful suggestions as well. Your attention to detail, grammar and smoothing out the rough edges is much appreciated!

To Darlene Oakley, my editor in the early stages of this manuscript and the one who first suggested that one huge volume should be a series, I extend my sincere appreciation.

To my editor, Heather Nickel, who skillfully edits my work in such a way that retains my voice and writing style, and makes my writing the best it can be, I express my sincere thanks.

Once again, my heartfelt appreciation to my entire team for

your intuitive wisdom, sensitivity and honesty in helping to make this series touch the minds and hearts of its readers.

And finally, I acknowledge the presence of the Holy Spirit and my guardian angel for their inspiration and constant guidance; my spiritual mentors guide both my life and my pen.

PREFACE

IT IS SAID that within each of us is a story to tell. For years, I must admit, it has been my heart's desire to write a novel. For the longest time I thought it was just wishful thinking, an illusion or fantasy I was nurturing. Over the years, I started several stories that never went anywhere except into my drawer and then fizzled away in the recesses of my mind. And yet, I have long known that if one has a dream, a burning passion in his heart, that someday it will come to pass. Never would I have envisioned, however, the wonderfully creative way it would come about. How, one day, an unbelievable occurrence would eventually transform a fantasy into reality.

The "occurrence" tugged away at me for days, months and then years, begging my attention. Seeking understanding, I spoke of it to family and friends but I was so focused on the event itself that I missed the underlying significance of it all. It wasn't until I found myself in the sunroom of our farmhouse one sleepless morning in June 2005, watching the sun near the edge of the earth, that the deeper meaning of the occurrence came to me. As the rising sun brightened the room in which I sat, it also seemed to illuminate my mind. Insight, previously obscured in the shadows of my psyche, bloomed and intensified as dawn spread out across the prairie sky. As I traced the occurrence back to its beginning, I finally realized how it was a testament to the enduring miracle of love. Immediately, an overwhelming, almost feverish rush to write my story welled up inside me, and I began.

Without any outline or any knowledge of how to write a novel, I picked up a pen and scribbler on the end table and simply began to write. For two weeks, I wrote almost non-stop until my wrist and hand gave out. Then I purchased a laptop computer—the best investment of my life—and continued to write as fast as my fingers could type. Corrections could be made in an instant. Paragraphs moved here and there with incredible ease. The thoughts began to flow. It was as if during all the years I had been thinking about the occurrence, ideas had been incubating in my mind, stored, packed, imprisoned inside, until the writing process released them like a gusher, exploding and spilling onto the pages.

Sentence followed after sentence almost effortlessly as the scenes unfolded in my mind's eye. I relied not so much on my intellect as I wrote but rather on my imagination, ablaze as it was with imagery and thoughts. I began to write an outline, a list of chapters that would take me from beginning to end. It was like going on a journey, and I was tracing out the map where I wanted and needed to go to reach my destination.

Characters came alive and I followed them and their lives; we talked and laughed and cried together. They took me in directions I never would have thought of on my own … they led and I followed. This resulted in more chapters. My map expanded as twists and turns in the road came from nowhere and everywhere and from deep within. As the weeks of writing progressed, the vision before me became clearer and richer. It was like watching a movie. All I had to do was write down what I saw before me on the screen of my mind.

Incredibly, three years to the date I started writing, when all was said and done, a huge book of over 1000 pages was in my hands. Once the editing process began, even more pages were added, strengthening the story and dividing it into five parts and timeframes. The result is a chronicle of love and adventure in the lives of two people, whose story shows us how angels and the heavens are intricately involved in our lives and that miracles happen when we follow our hearts.

As I look back on this experience, I am still amazed by the effortlessness with which the story emerged, as if the chapters, their order and all the key elements were guided, predetermined—or perhaps more accurately—inspired.

The writing of this book also answered another prayer long held in my heart. As a teacher and then a high school guidance counsellor, it was always my aspiration to write a self-development book. From an early age, insights and understanding of human behaviour came naturally to me, and my study of psychology and counselling in university further added to my empathetic abilities.

Writing this novel utilized those aptitudes. Through the lives of the characters, I could infuse values and principles to live by and show how the choices we make determine our happiness. I wanted to demonstrate the importance of living our lives in the now so as to carry out our life mission to love and serve our Lord and others. These teaching and counselling skills were indirectly at work while I also re-examined my own life and the direction I was going. Ultimately, I realized that lessons are more effectively absorbed intellectually and emotionally when revealed through a story; my novel had simultaneously become my self-development book.

The story began in Regina, Saskatchewan in the 1950s—the place and time of my own coming of age—though I have taken liberties with the details of its places and events. But though this book is a work of fiction, the occurrence that motivated it was something I experienced personally. My initial intention was to simply write about the occurrence; what resulted was a work of fiction that took on a life of its own. As I'm sure must be the case for many writers, my own life experiences provided the ideal backdrop for the story and moulded the development of the main character to the extent that it was inextricably woven into the fictional narrative.

I firmly believe that God has a plan for each one of us. The desire to write was planted in my heart long before the Lord had me experience the occurrence. Fortunately, I finally listened to His calling to do so, to carry out His plan. I think the Lord knew that as I began to realize the underlying love associated with that event, the power of that love would draw me into the wonderful world of writing and give witness to love's beauty and ever-enduring wonder. And, just like the warm prairie summer sun eventually ripens a crop of golden wheat for the harvest, so too, as the seed of this story took root, warmed and nourished by the timeless love of two people, "The Angelic Letters" series grew and blossomed. You and I are its reapers.

Henry K. Ripplinger

"God causes all things to work together for good to those who love God, to those who are called according to His purpose."

ROMANS 8:28

"Trust in the Lord with all thine heart;
and lean not unto thine own understanding."

PROVERBS 3:5

"As the heavens are higher than the earth, so are my ways higher than your ways, and my thoughts than your thoughts."

ISAIAH 55:9

"All God's purposes fulfilled in due time."

MARK 1:15; GAL 4:4

"I will give you the treasures of darkness, riches stored in secret places, so that you may know that I am the Lord, the God of Israel, who summons you by name."

ISAIAH 45:3

PROLOGUE

A THOUGHTFUL MAN ONCE said that perhaps the greatest teaching a man can take to heart is to put God at the centre of his life and trust in His divine providence. This insight shows great wisdom and I have lived long enough to confirm its truth. To live a hundred years one sees much, learns much and experiences much. I cannot count the times I have witnessed our Lord change lives and circumstances when the faithful pray to Him. Many times I have seen this in my own life, but even more so in the lives of those so close and dear to me. Unfortunately there all too many unaware of the tremendous workings of God's sovereignty available to them, and as a result find life at times a struggle, frustrating and lacking peace.

"Divine providence" are words unfamiliar to many and, to be fair, their meaning eludes my full understanding as well. But it is a learning vital to our well-being as it is always at work for our benefit. And so I will do my best to explain what I understand of this mighty power.

The providence of our Lord is how our almighty God orchestrates, coordinates, if you will, through natural processes and without interfering with man's free will, all things on Earth to achieve His perfect purpose for the salvation of all mankind.

In the endless outworking of divine providence, God draws together millions of details and circumstances to achieve His will each day. It is the way He works and controls the daily course of human events, decisions and actions. And He does so out of love not only for me but for all His children in the entire world!

This is a miracle of the first order, far greater than a one-time cure we sometimes witness when one is instantly healed of cancer or one's sight is restored. Yes, it is a marvelous, wonderful, occurrence of the Lord's hands when He sees fit to intervene divinely to accomplish His will and purpose, but it is nothing compared to what is done in the seen and unseen world by our Lord and His angels.

You see my friends, life is like a big puzzle, and at the best of times we are fortunate to hold one or, at times, perhaps several, of the pieces. We scurry here and there in search of other pieces that might fit in and make us happier, richer and more satisfied, and thus complete the puzzle of our lives.

But most often the struggle is in vain.

If only we could have this, achieve that, possess her or him in our lives then all would be well and good. Yes, granted, at times a piece fits and some joy and satisfaction comes our way, but most often we go around in circles trying to fit a round piece into a square hole, a red colour where a blue is warranted, an interior piece to an outside edge. We try and try to make the pieces fit in our search for happiness only to find that what we thought would finally give us peace and joy yields only more heartache, frustration, emptiness and unrest.

The Lord, however, sees the whole puzzle at all times—even when it changes as the result of prayer or influence or a thousand and one other factors that continually affect the lives of His people. He is all knowing, all powerful and can bring good out of any situation; He can create possibilities when all seems bleak and lacking in hope.

Belief in God's providence prepares us as we encounter new challenges or trials. It gives us peace of mind because we know God is at work with His helpers even when we are in the shadows and feel alone. We walk by faith and not by sight. We know and trust that God will bring us out of the darkness.

So the sooner we place our Lord in the center of our lives and trust Him with all our hearts, *that* is when we start to see the whole picture and not a tiny snapshot of what we think is best. We finally begin to complete the puzzle of our lives, to fit into the plan that God has for each of His children.

So important is this teaching that I believe it is the other reason the Lord allowed me to return to the land of the living after my brief trip to the other side. During those precious few minutes my protector Zachariah allowed me to see his guidance, protection and love, not only in my life but also in the workings of other guardian angels in the lives of those so very close and dear to me. When I returned it was my purpose to make others aware of our celestial protectors through the undying love story in the lives of my closest friends. The more we are reminded or made aware of our angels, the closer our relationship with them becomes, and soon they are our best friends and allies, our unseen link to our Creator.

But there was also another vision I absorbed in the single moment Zachariah allowed: God's divine providence so clearly and wonderfully at work in the lives of my dear friends.

Imagine watching a movie sped up so you can see the plot develop almost instantly and, equally swift, the resolutions to the problems that arise. What would normally take two hours to understand took only minutes. I understood in very short order how each person dealt successfully or perhaps unsuccessfully with the issues in their lives.

In similar fashion, imagine having access to an omnipotent mind outside of time, one that can see and understand in a single thought the entire lifetime of not only you but of others close to you. Imagine the myriad pieces of the puzzles of everyone's lives coming together in the blink of an eye and faster.

Imagine, if you will, knowing everything *now*. How the angels prompted them to do this or that, how this person influenced some choices or their heart was softened by the Holy Spirit to be receptive to the Lord's will or how the meeting and separation of my dear friends was but a detour for the Lord to work out even greater possibilities than the ones they imagined or wanted or prayed for.

But I get ahead of myself! Ha, ha... a carryover from my trip to the other side is this desire to share and reveal the story more quickly. But we must re-enter time and slow it down for us to really see and appreciate how the divine providence of the good Lord works.

This is what the Lord wants me to share with you. So come, leave the lofty thoughts to the theologians and philosophers. We are simple people, let us go back outside and sit under the sun and rest awhile on the old grey crates while I share more of the tenderhearted love story of the lives so close to my heart.

You will soon see, as I do, that it is best to put our sovereign Lord in charge of our lives and trust in Him. It is the only way you will ever see the pieces come together to complete the puzzle of your life.

CHAPTER ONE

O N JULY 6TH, 1959, two days after his eighteenth birthday, Henry awoke, thinking about Jenny for the second year in a row. It was three years to the day since he'd first laid eyes on her. He remembered it vividly. Jenny Sarsky had walked past his house on her way to Mr. Engelmann's store; they had met in the store, and the moment he gazed into her eyes he'd been completely smitten. It had been love at first sight; the yearning in his heart for Jenny as strong now as it had been then.

When they'd walked home together, she'd said, "Quickly, hold my hand!" as they rushed across a busy avenue, the touch of her warm palm sending an electrifying surge through his body. He would never forget the wonderful phrase Jenny had said so often that summer. *Quickly, hold my hand*, Henry softly repeated to himself as he lay in bed recalling it all: their summer together, walks, dates, secret notes, a bike ride at the park— then her sudden departure.

That day at the park…they had almost made love. In a way, he still regretted that they hadn't, although he knew stopping had been the right thing to do. And then there were those guys who'd dragged her off one night … he still hoped to find out what had really happened.

He knew if he stayed in bed dwelling on it any longer, he'd just grow despondent and self-pitying. It had happened to him a year ago. Memories had flooded his mind and heart so intensely that for days after he could think of nothing but Jenny. At Mr. Engelmann's suggestion, he'd started meditating and praying every morning to help him get through it. Henry had seen how it had helped his mentor cope with and accept his wife's illness.

Henry was glad for summer holidays. It had been a good year; he'd finished Grade 11 with excellent grades and had loved his art class. He had been elected president of the student council and gotten along well with most of his classmates. Even though most other eighteen-year-olds had finished Grade 12 that June, Henry still had a year to go. He and Jenny had that in common too—something they had discovered during one of their first encounters. And then, as often still happened, Henry's mind and heart unwittingly filled with memories of her. He wondered how she would be spending her summer…if she was enjoying high school in Ottawa…if she ever thought about him…Henry caught himself before thoughts of Jenny brought on the heartache that inevitably followed.

Today, he reminded himself, *I'm starting full-time at Engelmann's Grocery.*

As much as Henry liked school, he also loved working for Mr. Engelmann and would be working full-time for the next two months. They'd had incredible success over the past two years. Business had more than tripled and was flourishing in all aspects. Henry loved the challenge of the business and the opportunity to make it a success, but he loved the talks he and Mr. Engelmann had out back behind the store even more, sitting on the old weathered crates under the warmth of the sun.

Mr. Engelmann was one of the wisest people Henry had ever met. Mr. Engelmann must have been a great teacher back in Austria and influenced the lives of many young people. Although the Engelmanns had every reason to be bitter about what had happened to them and their families during the Second World War, they weren't. Mr. Engelmann always said, "Regardless of where we find ourselves in life, regardless of our circumstances, it's what we *do* with life, how we *live* it—and ultimately how we *serve* that is the important thing."

And serve they did. David and Anna Engelmann had dedicated their lives to the service of others. It was evident every day in the store. For Mr. and Mrs. Engelmann, selling groceries was simply a way to reach out to others. They lived modest, humble lives. They never talked about or boasted of their education or knowledge. No one even suspected they were both university graduates and had probably forgotten more about worldly affairs than most people in the neighbourhood even learned in a lifetime.

Indeed, Henry was privileged to know Mr. Engelmann. If it hadn't been for his mentor's help in dealing with Jenny's sudden departure, Henry was almost certain he wouldn't have been able to cope. The loss he had felt, compounded by never hearing from her again, would have been too much to bear without Mr. Engelmann's support, care, empathy and advice.

He stretched out, then scratched his head, tugging the sheet up. Summer holidays meant they'd have more time to talk. On school days they had to wait until after the store closed for the day, but then they talked over the counter for however long it took. "You can't share your heart in a hurry," was a phrase Mr. Engelmann often said.

In summers past, either Mrs. Engelmann or Mrs. Schmidt tended to the store so he and Mr. Engelmann could go out back with a soda pop and talk about life. At times Mr. Engelmann used big words and referenced famous psychologists or psychiatrists: Eric Fromm, Abraham Maslow, Ivan Pavlov, B.F. Skinner, Victor Frankl, Sigmund Freud, Carl Jung and Carl Rogers, to name a few. He and Henry compared different schools of thought regarding conditioning, Gestalt psychology, existentialism, rational emotive therapy and behaviour modification.

Mr. Engelmann would say, "It's not the person's name or who said it or the school of thought that is important, but rather the lesson on life that is taught."

Henry clung to Mr. Engelmann's every word as if it was the last he expected to hear. Mr. Engelmann had a way of explaining the most complex thoughts and topics in a simple and straightforward way that somehow always applied to whatever difficulty Henry was facing. In the end, it usually had to do with making choices based on values, and those in turn seemed always to relate to the values and principles of the Bible.

"It's all there, Henry. It's very important to read the Bible every day so you stay focused on what is really important in life. All the psychologists, philosophers and psychiatrists in the world haven't really discovered anything new. They are simply relating what has already been taught from the beginning when our good Lord walked the earth and showed us the way, the truth and the light."

Who, passing by, seeing a young man and an old one sitting out back on a weathered crate behind a grocery store, would ever think that such knowledge was being discussed and passed down?

Henry stretched again. It was only six in the morning and the thin cotton curtains on the window couldn't keep the rising sun from flooding his bedroom with a soft light. *Time to get up and pray.* It always started his day off right. Mornings were so peaceful, and because it was summer and he didn't have to worry about school, Henry actually looked forward to getting up early.

He rolled out of bed, dressed and went to his desk. He read a few chapters of the Bible then sat quietly with his eyes closed. He was getting better at emptying his mind of all thought and found it very relaxing. The first step was to focus on his breathing. It brought him into the present moment.

Mr. Engelmann would say, "We need to think about the past at times, and also of the future, but to fret and worry about it constantly is a waste of life. Living in the now means living a focused life, an undivided life and a full life. The more we can live in the present, the more aware we become of our true selves and our ability to serve others."

Presently, the stillness was broken by the sound of his mother in the kitchen, getting ready for the day and planning meals. He decided to go down for breakfast.

Henry passed his father in the hallway. "Have a nice day, Dad."

"Yeah, you, too, Henry. You're up early."

"Yeah, I couldn't sleep anymore and I'm anxious to get to the store."

"Well, I'm glad you like your work."

Henry didn't respond because he knew his dad didn't really care for his own job. He wished his dad could find something else. It must be awful to go to work every day and not enjoy it. How trapped and unfulfilled it must feel.

"What would you like for breakfast, Henry?" his mother asked when he appeared in the kitchen.

"Oh, corn flakes and toast will be fine."

He looked forward to sitting and chatting with his mom for awhile. The sun beamed through the east window of the kitchen, filling the room with peace and warmth. It complimented the love he and his mom felt for each other.

They chatted about the day ahead, her gardening and her desire to find some part-time work. He sensed a loneliness in his mom as they talked and he knew it had something to do with his dad. His parents' relationship hadn't been the same since his father returned home after running off with another woman. Henry wanted to talk about it at some point but felt he had already thought too much about life for one day.

He stepped outside. It was going to be another warm one. The sky was clear, not a cloud in sight. A lone jet climbed high above him, leaving a long double trail of white vapour that converged into one wide streak and dissipated into the cerulean sky. He took in a long breath of fresh morning air. Many of their neighbours had already turned on their sprinklers before the water demand got too high, reducing the pressure to a trickle. It hadn't rained in days, and homeowners were putting a heavy strain on the city's tenuous water supply. Henry reminded himself to put the hose on Mr. Engelmann's front lawn as he walked between the houses to get his bike.

Henry waved to Mr. Weichel, who was always up and out working in the yard if the weather was nice. Mr. Weichel's garden and the flower bed in his front yard were the nicest on the block.

And there was Mrs. Kartush, watering her petunias.

"'Morning, Mrs. Kartush," Henry yelled as he sped past her. He didn't know if she'd heard him; her hearing was starting to go. Henry loved the people in the neighbourhood, and because of his job he knew almost everyone. They were mainly European in origin, hard-working and God-fearing. They helped each other out whenever they could. Henry felt a strong sense of belonging.

Mr. Engelmann was always downstairs in the store by seven-thirty and usually had the front door unlocked by eight in anticipation of Henry's arrival. When he entered the store that morning, however, the front door was unlocked, but the lights were still off and Mr. Engelmann wasn't down yet.

Henry went to the back storage room and flipped the light switches to both the back and front parts of the store, bringing a bit of life to the old building. It was unusual for Mr. Engelmann not to be in the store already. He hoped his mentor wasn't sick. Perhaps Anna needed his attention; she hadn't been well again lately.

In tenth grade, Henry had started visiting Mrs. Engelmann in her bedroom on occasion. On his first visit, he'd found her resting in an ornate antique canopy bed, her face as pale as the lacy white sheets. Anna's parents had owned such a bed, and when she'd seen one like it in an antique store, she'd told David she just had to have it. So they had purchased the bed, along with two end tables to go on either side, a dresser, chest of drawers and two lamps. The end tables didn't match the other furniture but they seemed to fit because they were antiques and elegant in their own right.

Since that first time, Henry had visited Mrs. Engelmann a lot. He liked talking to her. She was as wise as Mr. Engelmann, but softer spoken, preferring to listen. Henry often worried about her health, and hoped his visits cheered her and weren't too strenuous. Mr. Engelmann was very protective of his wife's need to rest and she didn't often come down into the store anymore.

Over the months, Mrs. Engelmann had conveyed to Henry how much she and her husband enjoyed having him around and what a blessing he was to them. Once, she had told him they thought of him as a son. Henry often felt like the Engelmanns were his parents too and he loved the time spent reading the Bible to her.

When nine o'clock came and went and Mr. Engelmann didn't appear, Henry knew something was wrong. Obviously, the old man had been down at some point because the front door had been open, but for some reason, he hadn't stayed downstairs or turned on any of the lights. Yet he didn't want to intrude on the Engelmanns' privacy, especially if Mrs. Engelmann was having one of her bad days.

The phone rang, startling Henry.

"Engelmann's Grocery, how may I help you? And good morning to you, Mrs. Neaster. Yes, it's a beautiful day. Sure, we can deliver that. Two pounds of salami, a loaf of fresh French bread and a pound of butter. Anything else, Mrs. Neaster? Do you need it before lunch? Okay then, we'll deliver it sometime today. Good-bye."

Henry replaced the receiver and left the order for Mr. Engelmann. Mr. Engelmann always knew how each customer preferred their meat cut. The sun streamed in, making the dust motes dance and Henry remembered the front lawn. He went to water it, hoping Mr. Engelmann would be down by the time he finished.

A half-hour later, Henry was back inside. But Mr. Engelmann was still nowhere to be seen. There was no choice but to go upstairs and find out what was wrong.

The staircase was dimly lit by the south-facing window. It was usually brighter up here, especially by this hour of the morning. The blinds must still be closed. Not a good sign.

Henry always worried that he would be intruding or might startle Mrs. Engelmann by going up there. But at that moment he was more afraid than nervous.

"Mr. Engelmann," he called out in a low whisper. After a moment, he repeated the call again, a little louder this time. There was no answer. Henry climbed up a few steps and peered into the dim light, trying to see. He wondered if he should call the police.

But then, it might be nothing. Maybe Mr. Engelmann had just gone back to bed after opening the store for him. He'd never done that before but he *had* been awfully tired lately.

Henry summoned up more courage and climbed a few more stairs. Once again, he called out for Mr. Engelmann but didn't receive a response. At the top of the stairs, he looked around. All the lights were off, and as he had assumed, the blinds on the window underneath which Mr. and Mrs. Engelmann usually sat and read were closed, only allowing a dim frame of light to seep in around the edges.

He gazed down the hall and saw a soft glow in the bedroom doorway. He wondered if he should go in. He was sure the Engelmanns were just sleeping. But even so he had to wake up Mr. Engelmann, didn't he? He'd be mortified if he slept the morning away while Henry worked alone downstairs. Henry imagined Mr. Engelmann's ruddy face next to his wife's pale one. What a contrast. The image only added to his growing anxiety.

Henry tiptoed down the hall, not really knowing why since he had every intention of waking Mr. Engelmann anyway. He neared the doorway, hearing nothing but the pounding of his heart. Perspiration rolled down his back. Finally, he reached the doorway and dared to peek in—and the image in front of him was forever imprinted in his mind and heart.

Mr. Engelmann sat in a chair beside the bed, holding Anna's still hand in both of his. His head was bowed. Anna's eyes were closed. Mr. Engelmann's curved back heaved slightly. He was sobbing, the tears silent. Henry knew then that Mrs. Engelmann was gone. He stood there, half in and half out of the doorway, frozen, unsure what to do.

A chill trickled down Henry's back as if all the warmth had left the room with Anna's spirit. Slowly, he drew close to Mr. Engelmann and put a hand on his shoulder. As he did, Mr. Engelmann's sobbing increased. Mr. Engelmann took one hand away from Anna's and placed it on top of Henry's. In the peace and stillness of the moment, they mourned their loss.

Henry's heart went out to Mr. Engelmann. He had loved his wife and would miss her so much. Henry knew he would really miss their visits; he'd loved her like a second mom. Actually, now that he thought of it, he was surprised he wasn't crying, too. Maybe he was in shock. He couldn't keep his eyes off Mrs. Engelmann. He'd never seen someone who'd just died.

Mrs. Engelmann looked perfectly peaceful, a soft smile on her face and a gentle glow on her skin. She finally looked at rest. She had been ill for so long. She should have been in the hospital, but Mr. Engelmann had refused, insisting on carrying the responsibility of looking after her day after day himself. He had never complained, only loved his wife and served her until the end. Mr. Engelmann had told him it was an honour to look after Anna, and often commented how she cheered him up when everyone thought it was the other way around.

Suddenly Henry remembered the store was open and unattended. He had no idea how long he'd been upstairs.

"Mr. Engelmann," he said in a low voice, "I better go back downstairs."

"Yes, yes, go ahead," Mr. Engelmann whispered back. He patted Henry's hand then took Anna's again. "Thank you, Henry."

Henry backed out of the room, a picture seared in his mind's eye: Mrs. Engelmann still under the sheets, the warm glow of the lamp caressing her face; Mr. Engelmann behind the light as if in the shadows, weeping and holding her hand, giving it his warmth; and the wooden cross on the wall above them, the bronze sculpture of the Lord reflecting the light. It was He who was at the centre of their lives, at the heart of their marriage. It was He who helped them carry their burdens, and it was He who united them now.

Henry was deeply moved by the beauty of that moment, by a love shared even in death. He felt the urge to draw what he'd seen, to paint it, freeze it on canvas. Why would he think such a thing at a time like this? He bumped into the doorway, startling Mr. Engelmann and himself. Slowly he turned and made his way to the light coming up the stairs from the storage room below.

Downstairs, the phone jangled. He ran towards it, but it stopped ringing as he got there. He was glad. He wasn't ready to talk to a customer just yet. He looked around the store and was grateful no one had come in. He decided to sweep the floor and restock the shelves. He'd wait for Mr. Engelmann to tell him what more he should do.

He was concerned about Mrs. Engelmann, though. Surely she couldn't stay in the bedroom? How was Mr. Engelmann going to get her out of there? Henry thought about the funeral. His mind buzzed with questions. Who would Mr. Engelmann want as pallbearers? Would Mr. Engelmann have to go buy a coffin? Where would the funeral be held?

It's so complicated to die.

Then Mr. Engelmann appeared in the storeroom doorway. He looked tired and sad. His eyes were swollen and his shoulders slouched a little more than usual. His glasses were so smudged they looked frosted over, as if he'd just come in from the cold. He wore the same sweater vest he usually did. He could afford a new one and maybe a nicer one, but he was satisfied with what he had. He was comfortable, liked things simple and saw no need to change.

Mr. Engelmann walked towards Henry, patting his shoulder as he passed. When he got to the front door, he turned the deadbolt above the doorknob to the right until it clicked and locked, then flipped the sign, which Henry had turned to OPEN when he'd come in, back to CLOSED. Mr. Engelmann slowly walked back to Henry and put his arm around his young partner's shoulder. "Come, Henry. Let us go sit on the old crate out back and feel the morning sun on our faces for awhile."

As they emerged from the back of the store, they squinted against the bright sun. They sat down side by side as they had done so many times before.

Fully expecting a conversation about loss and death, Henry was surprised when Mr. Engelmann began talking about how he had first met Anna, how he'd known from the beginning she would be his wife. He talked about her qualities, charm, mannerisms and looks, all the things that had attracted him to her. He talked about their life, marriage, honeymoon, first apartment and first home. He talked about their trials and sorrows, including the fact that they could not have children. He talked about their love of theatre and music. He talked about how they'd gotten out of Austria during the war and come to Canada. Mr. Engelmann told Henry his life's story, passing on the legacy to the only son they had.

Mr. Engelmann finished shortly after noon, ending with how they'd bought the store and the plans they'd had, some of which had not turned out. In a sense he was reliving his life with his chosen mate, not regretting a minute of it. If there were any regrets, it would be that his time with Anna hadn't been long enough. Mr. Engelmann was deeply in love with her.

Henry could relate; it was how he felt about Jenny.

They sat in silence, each in his own thoughts. Henry thought of Jenny and how he had wanted her for his wife. He envied Mr. Engelmann for having married his true love.

"Well, Henry, you can sit for awhile longer if you wish. I have things that need to be done."

When Henry came back into the store, Mr. Engelmann was on the phone to the funeral home. When he hung up, Henry asked if they should open the door to customers.

"No, today is a day for mourning, Henry. It is Anna's day. We respect her passing today. I am not interested in making money or carrying on any other business than what I have to do now. When the ambulance comes, let them in, Henry, and show them the way upstairs. I am going up now, to get Anna ready. You stay here, answer the phone, and tell people we are closed and why. Do the same for anyone who comes to the door. Tell them we will be open again tomorrow but will be closed on the day of Anna's funeral."

As Mr. Engelmann turned to leave, he added, "Maybe phone Mrs. Schmidt and tell her to come in for awhile today, and for sure tomorrow because I won't be here for most of the day. I have many things to do and many preparations to make."

As Mr. Engelmann headed upstairs, Henry remembered Mrs. Neaster's phone call. "Mr. Engelmann, Mrs. Neaster phoned when I got in this morning and placed an order for salami, bread and butter. I told her I'd deliver it today. Should I phone and tell her that we can't right now?"

"No, no, if you promised her it would be delivered today, then we must honour your word." He walked over to the meat counter, took out the salami and cut the meat the way he knew Mrs. Neaster liked it, then wrapped it first in wax paper then in coated brown paper. He wrote the weight and price on the out-side of the package then laid it on top of the glass display case.

"Here, Henry, finish the order and take it to her this after-noon when you can."

So Henry phoned Mrs. Schmidt and explained to customers who called or knocked on the front door about Mrs. Engel-mann, telling them the store would re-open the following day. Many wept as soon as Henry told them. He'd never realized how much the community loved Mr. and Mrs. Engelmann.

Besides their visits, Henry's most vivid memories of Anna were of her constant kindness and sincerity, and the fact that despite the obvious pain her cancer inflicted, she never com-plained about it. She had always wanted to help in the store, even towards the end when Mr. Engelmann insisted she rest.

Henry had always liked it when she was able to come down to the store, though; she brought with her a sense of peace and an aura of simple elegance and charm.

A tapping at the front door startled Henry from his recollections. The ambulance had arrived. He opened the door and held it while the men entered, carrying a cot between them. He led them upstairs, calling up to Mr. Engelmann that the ambulance men were there. When they arrived at the bedroom door, a teary Mr. Engelmann greeted them and swept a hand towards the bed.

It was still hard for Henry to believe. Mrs. Engelmann looked as if she were asleep. Her arms lay on top of the covers, her hands now holding each other naturally.

"I thought I would leave her nightgown on," said Mr. Engelmann, breaking the silence.

"That's fine," said the first man who entered the room. "They'll dress her at the funeral home, if you have clothes you want to send along. You can stay if you want, or you can wait downstairs while we get her ready."

"No, no, I will stay."

It was evident that it bothered Mr. Engelmann to have to share the sanctity and privacy of his bedroom with other men.

The first attendant walked to the other side of the bed and reached for the covers, gently sliding them from underneath Mrs. Engelmann's arms, and slowly lowered the sheets, making certain that he wouldn't expose her unnecessarily. But Mr. Engelmann had anticipated this and had prepared her so that her modesty was preserved, her gown pulled down as far as it could go, wrapped snuggly around her ankles and tucked in underneath. All that showed were her tiny feet, tight together and pointing straight up.

The man removed a heavy vinyl plastic bag of olive green from the case he'd been carrying. He set the bag down on the white bedspread beside Mrs. Engelmann and unrolled it in the space where Mr. Engelmann would normally sleep. The bag had a long zipper in the middle, running its entire length. He opened it wide and then motioned to the second man. They leaned over to the far side of the bed and slid their hands underneath Mrs. Engelmann. Henry worried they were off-balance, but Mrs. Engelmann was so frail and light they had no trouble lifting her and placing her into the open bag.

Mr. Engelmann gasped as the first man took hold of the zipper and slowly pulled it up over Anna's face, closing out the last image that Henry and Mr. Engelmann would ever have of Anna in her bedroom. It seemed a cruel thing to do and yet it was necessary. Henry went over to Mr. Engelmann and put a hand on his shoulder.

They both stared at the cold plastic bag. It seemed so wrong for such a warm, loving person to be sealed inside it.

The ambulance attendants tucked their arms underneath the plastic bag and shifted it towards the other side of the bed, making room to set down the stretcher. Clearly they'd done this many times before. They laid the stretcher on the edge of the bed beside Mrs. Engelmann and shifted her onto it, then buckled up the straps, pulling very hard to make them tight so they wouldn't lose her going down the stairs. The first man nodded to the second and they lifted the stretcher.

Under Henry's hand, Mr. Engelmann tensed as Anna's body left the bedroom.

MR. ENGELMANN STOOD motionless. The ambulance men had left with Anna's body and Henry had followed them out. As the bag holding his wife went past him, he had almost reached out to touch it, but seeing her placed inside had been bad enough without adding the memory of the feel of her body through its cold plastic.

He stared at the empty bed for a long time, then walked over to the bed and sat down where his wife had lain. He put his hand on the white sheet, hoping somehow to still feel her warmth.

He felt only cold emptiness.

He missed her already. How would he survive without her?

He leaned back and tried to lay down so that he covered the spot where Anna had been. He rested his head on her pillow, trying to fit it into the slight depression left by her own. He looked as still as Anna had. He closed his eyes, thinking to dream of her, but found himself praying instead…that the Lord might take him this day, too.

CHAPTER TWO

"GOOD MORNING MOM," Jenny said as she bounced into the kitchen carrying her diary.

"Well, it's about time you got up. Just in time for lunch rather than breakfast."

"I *did* wake up earlier and had every intention of getting up—then I drifted back to sleep somehow..."

"You must have been overtired from helping the grounds-keepers yesterday."

"I love working outside...perhaps I should be a landscaper instead of a librarian."

Edith smiled, poured another cup of coffee and sat down at the table. "Thought of something special to tell your diary?"

"Yes." Jenny turned to her mother and opened her mouth to tell her today was an unforgettable anniversary but thought better of it. It was just too upsetting for her mom and especially her father to know how much she still loved and missed her first love, Henry.

"I—I'm planning to go out to the gazebo and...well, yes, there *are* a few things I want to share with my diary," Jenny winked at her mother, hoping she'd get the hint that it was private.

"Want some lunch first?"

"No, just a glass of orange juice."

Jenny closed the fridge and sipped the tangy liquid as she gazed at the flowers outside. "It's just so beautiful here, Mom. And I love the transformation spring brings."

"I love it too, Jenny. Of all the homes we've had this certainly is the most beautiful, with the loveliest surroundings...especially compared to the small yard we had in Regina." Edith glanced at her daughter hoping the mention of that city wouldn't stir memories best kept buried.

Jenny returned her mother's gaze and smiled in an attempt to hide the thoughts she had entertained only moments earlier too. As soon as she opened the sliding patio door several butterflies, attracted to the blooms near the house, flew into the kitchen.

Edith quickly reached for the dish towel on the counter to shoo them out.

"It's okay, Mom, they'll leave on their own."

"Jenny, don't start that again," Edith said curtly as she made her way over to the door already waving the checkered cloth.

As soon as Jenny stepped out onto the patio the butterflies followed. Edith rushed to close the door behind her.

As EDITH WATCHED her daughter stroll down the path her expression turned from one of condemnation to puzzlement. Many times when Jenny was a child she'd had to drive these silly thoughts of butterflies and angels from her daughter's mind. "What nonsense," Edith muttered. "To think that angels turn into butterflies...and she even had her father convinced of it too!"

Edith remembered the night it had all come to a head. Ted had gone into Jenny's room to kiss her good night, and as he opened the door he'd thought there was a glow in the room. At first he thought it was just his little girl's natural radiance— Ted had always maintained Jenny loved being out in the sun so much she absorbed it into her bright smile and fine blond hair so she glowed a little herself. But there *had* been a kind of soft light. Hovering above little Jenny, her eyes wide with delight, were three colourful butterflies. "Look, Daddy!" she'd exclaimed, "The angels are singing to me."

Ted had stood at the door, dumbfounded, blinking to clear his vision. But there they were. And like Edith herself had just a few minutes ago, Ted went to shoo the intruders away as well. But as he approached, he told her afterwards, the butterflies began to flit away, disappearing out the open window into the night...except for one. He could just make out the deep violet-coloured butterfly nearly blending into the growing darkness, fluttering ever so gently near his daughter's face. She seemed mesmerized, a stray golden strand fell forward into her eyes as she watched the butterfly's dance. Ted edged still closer and the tiny winged creature flew up on top of the bedpost nearest the wall and perched there as if guarding its charge.

Afterwards, Ted had said it was surreal but wonderful. And instead of being concerned or annoyed by their daughter's over-active imagination (*Or* his, *for that matter,* Edith thought) he had simply been compelled to say, "Yes, they *are* beautiful, sweetheart" and kiss his daughter good night. He left feeling, he'd said, strangely elated.

Edith shook her head as she recalled it. *Ted is so much like her*, Edith thought, *two peas in a pod*. She hadn't believe a word of their nonsense and for the next week she'd visited Jenny's room each night to tuck their little girl in herself, doing her best to nip these flights of fancy in the bud. There was a time and a place for storytelling and imagination, but for Ted to en-courage these—these *fabrications*...

As Edith gazed at her daughter now, however, she had to ad-mit Jenny *did* have a way with butterflies. She had seen it before and now here she was again with the tiny creatures dancing about her, seemingly guiding, protecting...maybe even loving? her daughter.

Then, "Oh my, that's a pretty blue one flitting above her head."

For the first time since her own childhood oh, so long ago, Edith was momentarily filled with wonder.

THE SUN WAS already high in the sky and its hot rays warmed Jenny almost instantly as she strolled along. Carlos and his crew were unloading new sod to repair the grass that had suffered winter kill. Carlos saw her and waved. His broad, friendly smile revealed brilliant white teeth set against chocolate brown skin. Jenny held up her diary, waved it and grinned back.

The stone path wound around a small fountain before splitting into three. Jenny took the one that meandered to the south side where the gazebo waited. The faint smell of the dusty miller lining the pathway tinged the air, but the mix of wildflowers and herbs surrounding the gazebo intoxicated her. Her spirits lifted as she entered the scented space, the fragrance of the mixed bouquet wafting around her. The aroma soothed her and complemented the memories of Henry she'd had since she woke that morning.

Three years ago today she'd met him and each thought of that special meeting wrapped her in a warm embrace. If only these memories carried the reality of Henry's touch, of his strong arms around her.

Jenny took another sip of orange juice and set the glass on the railing circling the gazebo, settling herself into the swinging bench that hung from its rafters, the sun breaking through the latticed roof to land on her golden hair, making it glisten like tinsel.

Jenny opened the diary to read what she'd written last year on this date. The words touched her heart even more today. Last year she'd penned a prayer of hope and love inspired by the closing sentence of the last letter she'd written to Henry, the one that contained the pewter angel: "Even though we are far apart, you are forever in my heart."

A tear fell on the page as she softly whispered the poem once more.

The star of the east we both can see,
its bright rays your warmth caressing me.
I long for evening on this special day,
for the star of the east to gleam my way,
to fill my heart through our star
with all your love, though from afar.

Jenny ran a finger over the words and smiled. How true the poem was. Each time she gazed at the star in the eastern sky, she felt enveloped by its shimmering rays as if Henry were there, holding her. She felt certain the star was guarded by an angel, its rays always felt so warm and comforting.

She gazed at the wildflowers and the butterflies flitting about them, touching each flower as if kissing its petals. A glowing butterfly came to rest on the hand holding the pen and Jenny felt prompted to add to the poem she had just read:

I'll always remember the day we met,
into your arms I was easily swept.
'Twas your eyes drew me, clear and bright,
into the depths of your heart with pure delight.
Oh, dear, sweet Henry, on our anniversary day
I send an angel just to say
I'll love you forever, come what may.

Jenny gently raised her hand and the snow-white butterfly fluttered away.

She closed the diary and pushed against the wooden floor, setting the swing into gentle motion, tilting her head up to catch a ray of sun. She closed her eyes and smiled, once more reliving July 6, 1956, the morning she'd met the love of her life.

The instant the store door had opened and Henry stepped in to Engelmann's Grocery, she'd been drawn to him like a pin to a magnet. She loved his cute boyish features, could see the man he would become—that awkward transition of out-of-propor-tion growth, yet in Henry it was endearing. His dark brown hair was thick and disheveled as if he were in a perpetual race with the wind, the latter clearly winning the battle. She loved his ruddy complexion and wide, gentle smile.

Jenny had watched him from behind the groceries, peeking between glistening bottles of detergent. Henry walked hesitantly into the store and peered down each aisle. She moved over slightly, holding her breath, heart fluttering. Henry had come around to the other side as if looking for someone. Jenny moved yet again, watching—hiding. A grin had grown on her face.

Then the store owner had bellowed out, "Henry, are you looking for the young lady who came in a few minutes ago?"

Me? she'd wondered.

Even now Jenny's heart raced at the thought. She'd muffled a screech as Henry's face reddened to fire and he'd turned so quickly he hit a pyramid of salmon tins, scattering them in all directions.

She'd felt sorry for him then. Still, it *had* been her chance to meet him.

Jenny had slowly emerged from the end of the aisle to kneel down and help him pick up the tins. She'd handed him one, asking if she could help.

Henry hadn't looked up. *Did he even hear me?* she'd wondered. Then he'd raised his eyes and Jenny was drawn into depths of dark green. *My gosh, he's so handsome!*

Henry looked down silently, embarrassed. Jenny had instinctively known he was shy—and she'd loved it. She'd picked up more tins, eager to help him, eager to look into his eyes again.

And then it had happened…

She'd turned to look at him and their gazes locked. They rose to their feet as if lifted, as if she and Henry had been transported into another world. An electrical energy flowed between them, setting her heart ablaze. She had been helpless to withdraw. If it hadn't been for a distant voice, calling, she would have gazed into Henry's eyes forever…

"Jenny? Jenny! Are you listening?"

"Yes…yes, Mom. What is it?" Jenny struggled to come back to the present.

"James is on the phone," her mother called. "He can't take you to the movies tonight—something's come up and his father needs his help. He can take you tomorrow, though—he wants to know if that's okay."

"Tell him that'll be fine. I'll call him later."

Jenny looked down at her diary and shook her head. *Why do I keep drifting back to Henry?* She was sure it had something to do with that first meeting. But it was the incredible summer that followed that sealed her fate. Jenny shook her head once more as if trying to dispel her thoughts. *I can still feel the wonderful, indescribable sensation of looking into Henry's eyes…why can't I feel that with James? Oh, Henry, why haven't you written back to me?*

Tears welled in her eyes as she opened her diary and stared at the blank, cream-coloured page. After a long, thoughtful moment, she wrote:

July 6, 1959

> *I love James' dark, jet-black eyes, how they dart and flash when he speaks of his dad's business and how he will improve it. I was attracted to them that day we met in the cafeteria. But they lack the warmth and care of Henry's eyes. With James, his eyes reveal an eagerness for opportunity, constantly in search of any advantage by which he might gain or make profit. He says he loves me but does he really? And how do I really feel about* him?

"Oh Henry, why have you not written," she muttered again.

She had a feeling their special connection would never leave her. Tears fell on the page. Grabbing the top outside corner, she ripped the page out of the diary. *This is so unfair to James...* *Henry must have lots of girlfriends by now. I just have to move* *on too.*

"*Buenos dias*, good afternoon, *Señorita* Jenny. A wonderful day to enjoy the sun."

Jenny quickly brushed away the tear rolling down her cheek as the gardener bent to pull a weed from the flowerbed. "Why yes, Carlos, it *is* a beautiful day."

"There must be many celebrations going on today. I've never seen so many beautiful butterflies. Look how many flutter over the wildflowers. But how can they not, the flowers are all so lovely."

"Yes, I am admiring them too. That was interesting what you said though, Carlos—what do you mean there must be many celebrations today?" Jenny asking, still thinking of her own anniversary.

"Ah, yes, our people believe *las mariposas*—the butterflies— bring messages from loved ones as a reminder of their parting. My mother sends her love to me on the wings of a butterfly. I know it's her because the butterfly is always yellow and lands only on a freshly budding rose. It happens the same every year. This morning the petal had a drop of water. Santiago said it was dew but it's too late in the day for that. I know it was a tear from my mother's eyes. When she was alive she always cried when she was happy. It is three years today she went home to the Lord. Look how beautiful and happy the butterflies are," Carlos said, gesturing at the wildflower patch. And then almost as if reading Jenny's heart, Carlos added, "Perhaps you are celebrating a special day too?

Jenny looked at the smiling gardener in amazement, he had read her thoughts exactly!

"And look at the beautiful blue butterfly here!"

Jenny looked down and slowly moved her hand closer to get a better look at the small creature that had alit there. It made her think of Henry. Blue was his favourite colour. She smiled; perhaps Henry too was sending a message of love on the wings of a butterfly. Sunlight glowed through its gossamer wings. As Jenny studied and admired the depths of its colour, thoughts of Henry surfaced again. Thoughts of Henry were never far, it seemed. She felt Carlos's gaze on her and pink tinged her cheeks. She looked up and caught his tender smile.

"Is it a special friend you think of?" he asked in a soft, low voice. "A beautiful butterfly sometimes appears following the departure of a loved one. It is an expression of love and comfort to the one who remains behind."

The thought was soothing.

"I've loved butterflies ever since I was a little girl," she told him. "I enjoy their graceful beauty and their beautiful colours, but there is something special about them…" Jenny's words trailed off and she started again. "They seem to be such a—a spiritual side of nature. Do you think that's possible, Carlos? Oh, it's probably silly of me to think that."

"Oh no, *Señorita* Jenny, butterflies remind us of the beauty of love and of our loved ones, like my mother did today. Perhaps that blue butterfly was sent to you as a reminder that someone special loves you. Look how it has stayed with you…does it remind you of someone, *señorita*?"

"Why yes, it does," Jenny said, surprised he'd guessed. "It reminds me of a boy I once knew and—I miss him very much." Jenny was surprised to find herself sharing her feelings this way with an almost total stranger. Yet there was something comforting about Carlos, as if he understood and saw into her heart.

"Loss takes time to heal—perhaps *la mariposa* comforts you like my mother does me. It is good that you recognize the butterfly as a gift of love. I can see in your eyes you love this boy too."

Jenny blushed. "It's that obvious, is it?"

"*Si*. You know, I loved my mother very much. She comforts me to this day. Even in the winter here she sends an angel to me on the wings of the butterfly! During the coldest months when the snow is piled high and the temperature well below freezing the yellow butterfly like a ray of sunshine hovers and taps at my bedroom window."

"Really? I've never heard of butterflies coming in the winter."

"*Si*. There is much we don't understand and have to take on faith. Nature is intended to sooth our hearts and replenish us, to give us spiritual food each day. It is only natural that our good Lord uses nature and its creatures to comfort us in this way; they know how to serve our Lord perfectly."

Jenny studied the gardener, amazed by this conversation.

"My, my, *Señorita* Jenny, that blue butterfly surely has a message for you. It stays so long! But me, I better be off. The grass will not grow if I do not plant it soon!"

Jenny watched him walk away then looked down again at her hand, lifting it closer to her ear, listening for the flutter of its wing, the whisper of its song, letting it touch her with love.

She lifted her hand higher. "I love you too," she murmured, and watched as it flitted away, its blue wings blending quickly into the sky so that it disappeared almost instantly.

Comforted beyond her understanding, Jenny didn't allow herself to doubt any of it, not even for a single moment. It all felt so right. Perhaps the butterflies she had seen over the past two summers had carried messages of love she was unaware of. She was glad Carlos had mentioned the possibility. His words still lingered in her mind. Yes, perhaps Henry's angel had sent a message of love.

Jenny took in a deep breath of air, the scented air turning her attention to its source, the wildflowers. Nature and its bounty reminding her of her lost loves; butterflies and angels sending Henry's love and now the wildflowers bringing thoughts of her little girl, Camilla. It was the scent and sight of wildflowers that had helped heal her heart after giving birth to her daughter. Right from the start when her father had asked the garden staff to sow a garden patch for her with wildflower seeds, Jenny had loved the excitement, anticipation and unpredictability of what would bloom and grow so freely. No matter what flower appeared, it complemented the garden and she was exhilarated by the wildness and freedom of it all. She just knew that the spontaneity, gaiety and beauty of each flower that grew would blossom in the heart of her little Camilla as well. She could see Camilla so clearly, growing, unfolding and budding into a wild-flower, the most beautifully free of them all.

The garden patch blurred before her as memories overtook her again. How her heart ached to see and hold her little girl.

Camilla was two years old now and Jenny would never forget May 24, 1957—the day her little angel was born. Jenny wondered what she looked like and who she took after. The only memory she had to hold onto was the fleeting moment she'd seen her daughter dangling from the doctor's hand before she was whisked away by a nurse to her adoptive parents.

Without telling anyone, Jenny celebrated her daughter's birth on the 24th of each and every month. A yearly birthday was too long to wait; even the monthly idea wasn't enough. Oh, she wanted to shower her child with gifts and love each day. Yes, every day would be a birthday if she could arrange it. Her little girl would be walking and talking by now. She would be calling someone else mommy and daddy.

Oh, Jenny, sometimes you torture yourself too much…

While Jenny's heart ached with thoughts like this, she accepted these feelings as part of her life. Not that acceptance had been easy or accomplished without buckets of shed tears. Spending as much time as she could in nature, feeling the presence of her guardian angel, gave her strength and hope and saved her from spiraling back into loss and depression.

It suddenly dawned on Jenny why each time she thought of either Henry or her child she was reminded of the other. It was only natural, after all, Henry had been there the night Camilla was conceived—in fact, she thought of him as Camilla's father, not the terrible boy who had pinned her down.

If only Henry were *the father, things would be so different now.*

Jenny closed the diary, got up and made her way to the flowerbeds surrounding the gazebo. She snapped off a tall white daisy near the base of its stem, whispering softly to the wildflower as if it were Camilla herself. "And good afternoon to *you*,

Señorita Camilla. Are you playing out in the sun today? All dressed in dazzling white like this flower, I bet."

Jenny smiled at the beautiful daisy but it wasn't the flower that brought the tears. In her mind's eye, she saw her daughter in a pretty white sundress, hopping and singing amongst the wildflowers, chasing butterflies.

Yes, thought Jenny, *my little girl is truly the prettiest and most free of them all.* She brought the daisy to her ear, fully expecting to hear its song as well.

JENNY STROLLED BACK to the house still holding the daisy, basking in its sweetness. She passed Carlos and his co-worker replacing the dead grass with fresh new sod.

"Still enjoying God's creation, *señorita*?"

"Yes, I am, Carlos—I can't seem to get enough of it."

His wide smile widened further. "It is a good addiction to have."

"I see you've added another wildflower patch on the east side of the grounds. The flowers there are really lovely."

"*Si,*" he said. "It was your father's suggestion. He knows how much you like them."

"That was thoughtful of him. I do love the carefree charm of the garden, the waves of orange-coloured poppies scattered with red and blue flowers."

"The blue flowers were your father's idea, too. They are called Baby Blue Eyes like the colour of your eyes. Your father wants you to be happy; he loves you very much."

"That is so sweet of him. Thank you for seeding them."

"You are most welcome, *Señorita* Jenny."

"Oh, by the way, what's the name of the plant with the dark green leaves that grows between the walkway stones? It gives off such a wonderful fragrance."

"That is thyme. The herb releases its odour when you walk on it. Crushing the plant releases the fragrance."

"That's wonderful, Carlos. What a great idea to plant them there. I won't be so careful to avoid stepping on them now!"

"That is their service to you, *señorita*. We cannot deny them a part of their beauty and purpose."

"I never thought of it that way…that's wonderful."

"You have a blessed day."

Jenny looked at the gardener on his knees in the soil and nodded. *He has such a wonderful outlook,* Jenny thought, *and his voice sounds as if he were singing all the time.*

She became conscious of the diary in her hand. It felt heavier somehow, even though only a few words had been added today. Her two loves. And James. *Where does he fit into all of this…?* Once again Jenny's thoughts trailed off.

Just before she went back inside, she turned to survey the new wildflower patch once more. The dots of red flax punctuating the Orange California poppies were nice but it was the Baby Blues that sparkled and gave the garden its life. Perhaps that's what her father wished for her, to see the sparkle in her eyes once more.

CHAPTER THREE

T HE NEXT DAY was crazy. There was no other way to describe it. Mrs. Schmidt and Henry were run off their feet. While Mr. Engelmann was making funeral arrangements, they filled orders and answered innumerable phone calls. At times the store was so packed Henry was unable to get to the shelves to fill orders. People talked about Anna's death and the funeral. Many hoped that their husbands or wives could get off work to be able to attend. One customer said that her son would be flying in from Toronto to be there.

All their suppliers phoned, too, asking if they could provide food or drink at the hall after the funeral. Somehow the mayor of the city got wind of Mrs. Engelmann's passing and phoned to pass on his condolences and to inquire about the funeral. Mr. Mahoney, the tax man who had given Mr. Engelmann the ultimatum three years earlier to put the store up for sale or pay taxes in arrears also phoned, asking when the funeral was. Even Henry's dad, who didn't know Mrs. Engelmann very well, said he was going to try and get off work to come. Henry was overwhelmed by it all.

By the end of the day, Mrs. Schmidt and Henry were exhausted. Mr. Engelmann returned to the store around five o'clock. He still looked weary, but surprisingly not as tired as the day before. They filled him in on how busy the store had been and the many people who had called and expressed their sorrow. Mr. Engelmann was touched by it all and didn't know what to say.

"When *is* the funeral?" Henry asked. "There are so many people asking."

Mr. Engelmann looked at Henry, and Henry wondered if he'd even heard the question.

"I was planning on having it Friday." He hesitated as if to give it some additional thought. "Perhaps Saturday would be better. I didn't expect there would be so many who would come. Perhaps having the service on Saturday would let those attend who might not otherwise be able to get off work on Friday. Yes, yes, Henry, tell everyone the celebration will be Saturday."

"You mean funeral," Henry corrected.

"No, Henry, it will be a celebration."

Henry looked at him, puzzled. Mrs. Schmidt had the same look of bewilderment on her face.

"When someone dies," Mr. Engelmann said, "we celebrate their new life with the Lord in heaven." He stifled a yawn. "Well, good night, Mrs. Schmidt. Good night, Henry. Thank you for all you did, today. Henry, please turn out the light and lock the door on your way out."

Mrs. Schmidt and Henry looked at each other, unsure what to make of Mr. Engelmann's comments.

Just as Mr. Engelmann turned to go there was a rap on the door. Eddy popped his head in. "You still open?"

"Yeah, Eddy, for a minute. Out of smokes?"

"Naw."

Eddy stepped in and made his way over to Mr. Engelmann. He stopped about a yard away and looked the weary store owner right in the eye. "Hey, Mr. Engelmann, me and Pop heard the missus passed on. Folks say she was a good woman. I come to say we're sorry for your loss."

Mr. Engelmann nodded and a gentle smile grew slowly on his face. "It's good of you to come, Eddy, to tell me that."

Mr. Engelmann extended his hand and Eddy leaned forward to take it. He nodded to Mr. Engelmann, then turned to Henry, shaking a cigarette out of its pack. "Some of the boys are coming over Friday for a few beers and a card game. Wanna come?"

Henry looked at Mr. Engelmann then back at Eddy. "I can't make it, Eddy. Mrs. Engelmann's prayer service is tomorrow night."

Eddy lit his cigarette and waved the match out. "Yeah, maybe some other time, Hank. See ya." He nodded towards Mrs. Schmidt and then at Mr. Engelmann.

As HENRY WALKED home, he wondered how Mr. Engelmann felt about going up to the apartment knowing the love of his life wasn't there anymore. Mr. Engelmann had told him this year would have been their thirty-fourth wedding anniversary. How empty and alone Mr. Engelmann must feel. Henry wondered where Mr. Engelmann would sleep that night, if he would change the sheets, and how it would feel not to have his lifemate beside him. He imagined the bed would feel terribly cold and empty.

It was Jenny leaving so suddenly; in a way, she too seemed dead and gone. He'd mourned her absence for months after she'd first left, and even now, three years later, the loss could still catch him off guard. What sorrow Mr. Engelmann must be going through. Life could be good but it could also be cruel. Thoughts of Mrs. Engelmann's death, Jenny's moving away, and his mom and dad's loneliness tumbled over in his mind.

The sun was just beginning to creep towards the vast prairie horizon, filling the sky with a spectacular array of colours that usually ignited a sense of awe and peace within Henry—but not tonight. No amount of colour could penetrate his sadness and fear. What was it like to die… and what did Mr. Engelmann mean about celebrating Mrs. Engelmann's new life in heaven?

Henry decided he would have to talk to Mr. Engelmann more about that.

THE FOLLOWING DAY was even busier at the store. Mr. Engelmann worked part of the time, helping Mrs. Schmidt and Henry fill orders and answering phone calls and questions. About mid-afternoon, Mrs. Bueralli arrived and slipped up to Mr. Engelmann's living quarters. Mrs. Bueralli was the local seamstress and Mrs. Schmidt and Henry guessed she was altering Mr. Engelmann's suit for the funeral.

Henry wondered how Mr. Engelmann would look in a suit. For as long as he could remember he'd only seen Mr. Engelmann wear black slacks, a button-down shirt and his checkered vest. The only thing that ever changed as far as Henry could tell was the shirt. Henry wondered what he would wear himself. At the funerals he'd attended so far everyone had dressed in black. But since he didn't have a black suit that fit him he'd have to think of something else.

About an hour later Mrs. Bueralli came down, muttering and shaking her head as she passed Henry at the counter.

"Is anything wrong?"

She looked him up and down. "Oh, *Santa Maria*, he's stubborn! I don't like the colour."

"What do you mean?" Henry asked.

"You'll see," she said as the door slammed shut behind her.

Prayers for Mrs. Engelmann were to be held that Friday at the funeral home. Most ceremonies held there usually consisted of a brief service and a homily by the parish priest. Mr. Engelmann had decided on an open casket viewing to allow people to say goodbye to Mrs. Engelmann. Henry wondered how she would look after three days of being dead.

Again around five o'clock, Mr. Engelmann came downstairs. Henry wondered what he'd been doing up there for most of the day. "Were you sleeping?" he asked.

"No, Henry," Mr. Engelmann said, "I was reading for most of the day and preparing for Anna's farewell. There are so many scripture verses Anna liked. And there are so many I like, too.

It was difficult for me to decide what the priest should read tomorrow night and the day of the funeral."

"I see." Henry was going to ask Mr. Engelmann what he meant about celebrating Mrs. Engelmann's passing but then thought better of it. Mr. Engelmann had enough on his mind and Henry would understand as the events unfolded.

Mr. Engelmann interrupted his thoughts. "I get a lot of peace just praying and reading God's Word. Someday perhaps you will understand."

"I think I do now."

Mr. Engelmann looked at Henry and smiled. "I'm sure you do...I'm sure you do."

THE NEXT DAY, Friday, Henry opened his eyes at about five-thirty, wide awake and unable to get back to sleep. He thought about the funeral and about the prayers scheduled at the funeral home that night. His mom had told him he should wear his black dress pants, a white shirt, one of dad's black ties and his navy blue sweater. As Henry pictured himself in it, he told himself it would be okay.

Henry pushed himself out of bed and went to his desk, taking out a few sheets of paper to make a sign for the front door of the store:

CLOSED TODAY
CELEBRATING ANNA ENGELMANN'S LIFE
ST. MARY'S CHURCH

Henry was certain Mr. Engelmann would approve.

He was about to put an extra sheet of paper back into the drawer when he recalled the scene in Mr. and Mrs. Engelmann's bedroom. As the image hovered in his mind, he picked up a pencil and started sketching. The drawing that took shape beneath his hand showed Mrs. Engelmann lying in her bed with her eyes closed and Mr Engelmann leaning towards her on his chair, holding her hand. Part of the bedside table lamp was visible, giving the image a source of light and shadow. Henry shaded Mr. Engelmann's face as he remembered it, forlorn and grieving. He sketched the large wooden cross on the wall, centred above their bed.

Before Henry put the pencil down, an idea came to him. The wings of a guardian angel formed on the page to gently enfold Mr. Engelmann, the angel directly behind the old man, his arm resting across Mr. Engelmann's shoulders, comforting him in his sorrow. And then Henry wondered about Mrs. Engelmann's spirit and her guardian angel, her guide in life…and death?

There was a motherly-sounding rap on his bedroom door. "Henry, are you up? It's almost eight o'clock."

"Yes, Mom, just finishing something. I'll be right out." Henry looked at the drawing again. He felt very good about it. He had captured a special moment in time, honouring a love not even death could weaken. Someday he would paint it.

When Henry joined his mother in the kitchen for breakfast, he showed the sign for the store to his mom. She said it was fine but didn't know if the word "celebrating" was appropriate. When Henry explained to her what Mr. Engelmann had said the other day about celebrating a new life with God in heaven, she reconsidered.

"Maybe it's okay, Henry."

When Henry arrived at the store, Mr. Engelmann was up and preparing the day's cash as he usually did. Henry was glad to see him there. Things seemed to be returning to normal.

"Sleep well?" Henry asked, thinking a split second after he said it that maybe it was a rude question.

But Mr. Engelmann responded readily enough, "Yes, yes, I did. I have everything planned and ready. The casket has been purchased. I talked to Father Connelly and he has agreed to everything I requested, and so I'm ready to celebrate my Anna's new life."

"Oh, that reminds me, Mr. Engelmann…" Henry reached into his carrying case, "I made a sign to put on the front door. Is this okay?"

Mr. Engelmann looked at it and beamed.

"Yes, yes, that will be just fine. I'm glad you thought of it. It completely slipped my mind." And then he added as an afterthought, "Only one more thing—the prayers tonight start at seven so I think we should close the store early today. Four o'clock would be good, no? That will give us all time to get ready, have supper and think about what we want to say."

Henry wasn't exactly sure what Mr. Engelmann meant by that but he would find out soon enough.

As usual, the grocery was very busy, but around quarter to four the store emptied. Most people knew of Mrs. Engelmann's passing by now and those who could planned to attend the prayer service.

Henry knew he needed to get going, too. But as he headed out the door, Mr. Engelmann called him back.

"What is it, Mr. Engelmann?"

"I have something for you. I forgot to give it to you yesterday. Wait here a minute." He disappeared into the storeroom, his footfalls echoing up the stairwell and then back down. He reappeared holding a brown paper bag. "This is from Anna. She asked me to give this to you after she went to see her Lord."

Henry took the bag. "What is it, Mr. Engelmann?"

"It is her Bible. She wanted you to have it."

"Oh!" Henry was surprised. "Th thank you. Uh, are you sure you don't want it?"

"No, no, she wanted you to have it and so do I. I have my own and it's marked the way I like. There's one more thing. You will see that there is a little note from Anna to you. Be careful when you take it out because it marks a passage she wants you to read at the mass tomorrow."

Me? "Uh, yeah…for sure, Mr. Engelmann. Which passage, do you know?"

"When you get home tonight, you will see. It was her favourite. Now go and get ready for prayers. I will see you there, yes?"

"Of course, Mr. Engelmann."

Chapter Four

Henry and his parents arrived at Speers Funeral Home at about quarter to seven. They thought they would be early, but many people were already there.

Mr. Engelmann, still wearing his black slacks and vest, shook hands with everyone as they entered. There were no tears in his eyes. Instead, he was smiling and cheerful. The only thing that had changed since Henry last saw him at the store was that he was wearing a clean white shirt and a dark navy tie, and that his glasses were clear for once.

His father shook Mr. Engelmann's hand. "Sorry for your loss, David."

"Thank you, Bill."

The funeral chapel was already packed when they entered. The only seats left were in the second last row. Henry was disappointed. He had hoped—and wanted—to be up front to see it all. Just after they were seated, a funeral attendant approached and asked if they were the Pedersons.

"Yes, we are," Henry's dad replied.

"Mr. Engelmann would like you to sit up front with him. He

doesn't have any family and considers you folks to be his closest relatives. Would that be satisfactory?"

"We'd be honoured," Henry's father said.

The attendant held out his arm for Henry's mother. As they walked up, people turned their heads; as hundreds of eyes fell on Henry, he felt important and nervous at the same time.

The coffin rested at the front of the chapel. As Henry and his parents drew closer, Henry could see the outline of Mrs. Engelmann's face, though it was partially obscured by some sort of white netting and by the edge of the coffin itself. Before he could see the rest of her, the attendant let go of his mother's arm and stood in front of the pew, resting one hand on the rail and motioning to Henry to go in and be seated with the other. Henry's father squeezed in first, then his mother and lastly him, leaving enough space for Mr. Engelmann on the end.

As they waited for the service to begin, he tried to discreetly peer into the coffin at Mrs. Engelmann, but the only thing he could see at that angle was the sheer white net above her face. On either side of the casket stood two wooden plant stands, white, each holding a simple but beautiful bouquet of assorted flowers. Another modest floral arrangement lay atop the closed bottom half of the casket.

The casket was nothing like the elaborate oak caskets he had seen some of his relatives buried in. There was no gold trim or brass handles. It was made entirely of clear light pine; it didn't even look varnished. Henry knew Mr. Engelmann could afford more. Why would he go with such an inexpensive casket for the woman he loved so much? Wasn't the casket a symbol of how much you cared for the deceased? Mrs. Engelmann's coffin was a—a *pauper's* casket; it would rot away in weeks! Would it even support the weight of the ground on top of her? Henry was certain most of those gathered must be feeling slightly ashamed of Mr. Engelmann and sorry for his wife. Henry was embarrassed for him at the thought.

When the organ finally started, it wasn't a familiar funeral hymn. It wasn't even mournful. It sounded more like some type of classical music. Perhaps baroque? It was very pleasant to listen to, anyway. Rather than setting the stage for tears, it was more likely to encourage foot-tapping. It sounded like the music Mr. Engelmann often turned on in the store.

Henry had expected—and figured everyone else had, as well—Mr. Engelmann to come down the aisle at any moment accompanied by a funeral attendant, but once again Mr. Engelmann surprised them. The door to the right of the podium suddenly swung open and Mr. Engelmann appeared. He walked to the pew where Henry and his parents sat, faced the congregation and gave a brief nod of greeting, almost like a conductor greeting an audience before a performance. This was completely outside of the norm for him; it was almost like a celebrity coming on stage and was so unlike Mr. Engelmann, who shunned any kind of showiness most of the time. Henry wondered what else Mr. Engelmann had in store.

After a moment Father Connelly emerged also. He walked over to the podium and cleared his throat. "Good evening. It is so nice to see so many of you here to share in prayers for Anna Engelmann. I am sorry there is not enough room for everyone in the chapel but the funeral director has turned on the speakers in the foyer so everyone can hear and participate.

"We will not say a mass this evening as we sometimes do. A Low Mass will be celebrated tomorrow at St. Mary's Church, beginning at ten a.m. Following the mass you are invited to the Regina Memorial Cemetery to attend Anna at her final resting place.

"After I say prayers for our dearly departed, there will be a procession to the front at which time you may say goodbye to Anna and offer a parting prayer. After the viewing, Mr. Engelmann would like to speak to all of you, and following that any of you who knew Anna are welcome to come forward and say a few words of remembrance."

Father Connelly moved behind the altar and opened a large red book. "Please stand."

For the next fifteen minutes, Father Connelly said prayers

and gave a blessing over Anna. Walking over to the podium, he reached into an invisible pocket in his black robe and pulled out a folded sheet of paper. After a pause to unfold it, he began to talk about Mrs. Engelmann, her life as he knew it. He recalled some of the chats they'd had during their visits over the years, as well as the ways she had helped both the parish and community. Perhaps most impressive of all had been her service of care and kindness to the customers at the store.

Henry had often wondered why Mrs. Engelmann spent so much time talking to people who weren't really her friends. But now that he thought about it, maybe she thought of them as her family—the only family she and Mr. Engelmann had.

When he had finished, Father Connelly gestured the congregation to come forward. "We will now form a procession starting with the front rows and going to the back until everyone who so wishes has paid their last respects to Anna. We will then be seated and Mr. Engelmann will say a few words. The ushers will direct the procession for the viewing." As Father Connelly returned to his seat, the classical music Anna had so loved started up once more.

Mr. Engelmann went up first. He stopped at the casket, reached out his hand and put it on top of Anna's. He bent to kiss his wife then, wiping a single tear, walked around to the other end of the pew.

Butterflies fluttered in Henry's stomach as he moved slowly towards the open casket.

"Oh, my gosh," he whispered.

Mrs. Engelmann was wearing a wedding dress. The net he'd seen earlier was a veil flowing down the sides of her face onto her shoulders. She looked very beautiful. So peaceful. Her skin held a luminous glow and a bit of rouge coloured her cheeks. Her hands were folded over her chest near her heart and, as if to complement the pose, the wooden cross of a rosary rested within them, the beads intertwined between white, delicate fingers.

Henry looked down at Mrs. Engelmann. This was the last

time he would see her. He didn't know what to say to a dead person. Could she even hear him? He had often kissed her cheek at the end of their talks, but he didn't know if he wanted his lips to touch her dead body now.

Finally, he murmured, "Goodbye, Mrs. Engelmann. I really liked you. No—I loved you. You were so kind and generous. I'll miss you." For the first time since her death, tears welled up in his eyes and Henry was filled with such a oneness with Mrs. Engelmann. Without even thinking about it, he leaned over and kissed her cheek. It felt warm and soft, not cold and lifeless as it should. Somehow at that moment life and death merged, rising above the reality of what normally was. As Henry straightened, he noticed a little drop near where he had kissed her. Quickly, with the tip of his finger, he smoothed away the tear he had left behind.

Henry walked back and sat next to Mr. Engelmann, who put an arm around him. Henry sat with his head down and sobbed quietly. He couldn't understand how Mr. Engelmann could be so strong and show no sign of tears.

It seemed the entire congregation wanted to pay their respects as those from the foyer followed those from within the sanctuary to the front of the chapel. When Henry looked back, it was impossible to tell where the line ended.

Henry swivelled back around and stared at the coffin. As the procession continued, he realized how stuffy the chapel had become. He looked up at Mr. Engelmann; beads of perspiration dappled his forehead. The air grew staler as the heat and breath of the large gathering became nauseatingly close, pressing in on him. Henry began to feel sick, like he wanted to throw up. Suddenly there was a commotion behind him. He turned to see that an elderly lady had fainted. The two people on either side of her held her up as a third waved a booklet in front of her face. A few moments later, she revived.

One of the ushers rushed to open the windows on the north side of the chapel. Another set up a fan in front of the door

Father Connelly and Mr. Engelmann had come through earlier. Within minutes a cooling breeze wafted through the chapel.

It took over forty-five minutes before the procession ended and the service had already lasted almost an hour and a half when Mr. Engelmann finally rose to speak. He peered out over the rim of his glasses and surveyed the congregation.

He paused for the longest moment.

"Anna, I'm sure, is very pleased and happy to see you all here tonight…and so many people. My, my…she has so many friends." Looking at Anna's coffin and then back to those assembled there, Mr. Engelmann continued, "Lying here before us is Anna's mortal body. The one we knew and spoke to while she was with us. However, Anna's spirit, her soul, the one the good Lord gave her when she was conceived in her mother's womb, still lives on and, I believe, is here with us this evening. I believe she is looking down, surrounded by a choir of angels, and is very pleased and happy at what she is seeing. She touched so many people's lives while she lived in service for the Lord. Many may ask, 'What can the owner of a small grocery store do that is all that important?' No job is unimportant if it is done in service of others for the Lord. Look around you. We are all witness to a simple life, very well lived."

A couple of "amens" rose from those gathered.

"I don't need to list Anna's accomplishments, and she would be upset if I stood up here in front of you and did that. All any of us need do is look into our own hearts and it will be clearly evident, if you encountered Anna, what she has done for you."

Once again Mr. Engelmann glanced towards his wife.

"I know it is the custom to buy as nice a casket as one can afford. This is the casket Anna wanted. She picked it out herself a long time ago. She has been ready to meet her Lord for a long time, and we openly and freely talked about it. Yes, Anna liked this casket, and a similar one is waiting for me.

"We are simple people. We came into the world with nothing and we go out the same way. From dust we were created and to dust we shall return. The only difference between life and death is the split second when we move from an earthly life to a heavenly one. Our mortal bodies are only temporary, a stage of the eternal life our Lord offers us, along with the free will to choose how we will live it.

"Over a lifetime we make thousands of decisions. We decide to live for the Lord or to live for ourselves. Hopefully, we choose wisely in the short time the Lord gives us so that when we leave we will make our final home with Him. Anna chose wisely. She was a good wife, a good friend, a good comforter, a good woman. She was a soldier for the Lord in every way. Many a time I would have chosen poorly, my vision clouded, but Anna's example and soft words always steered me to the right path.

"In the end, this is what we are here for. To serve and to love each other. And Anna has served and loved. This is her legacy. This is what she has left behind. What greater richness and treasure could anyone leave behind than a love for her fellow man?"

Mr. Engelmann paused. "Anna is wearing a wedding gown. This is the same gown she wore at our wedding thirty-four years ago in Austria. She was so beautiful; I can see her walking down the aisle towards me as if it were yesterday. So full of life, so happy, so radiant. She glowed with an aura of light as only angels in heaven do. How fortunate a man I was then, and how fortunate I am today, to stand here and tell you of the happy life we lived.

"There was never a day my Anna and I ended without a kiss or a hug. Any anger or disagreement disappeared with the setting sun. Each new day was a new beginning for Anna and me. We were both wise enough to practise what the Lord said, 'Do not let the sun go down on your anger.' He knows we should not fret or worry over yesterday. Today will have enough cares of its own."

Mr. Engelmann paused again, scanning the faces of the crowd. "Anna loved the Lord with all her heart, soul and mind, and she loved her neighbour as herself. She obeyed to the letter the two most important commandments that our Lord gave us. Even though she was married to me, she was first and foremost married to the Lord. She was His bride long before she ever met me. And so, my friends, I see it only fitting that my Anna wear her wedding gown. I had my Anna for thirty-four years and now she will see her groom in heaven. 'The eye has not seen, or the ear has not heard, what is in store for those that love the Lord.'

"Right now my Anna is experiencing the treasures heaven has prepared for her. She is looking down on all of us right now, loving and thanking us for being here together as one family, paying our respects to her for being such a worthy child of God.

"Before Anna passed on she gave me a letter to read at her funeral. I was going to read it tonight, but it is getting late. I will read her farewell letter to all of you at her funeral tomorrow."

He paused long enough to acknowledge all those in attendance, then finished, "Thank you so much for being here tonight. Anna and I love you all."

Mr. Engelmann returned to the pew and sat down as Father Connelly retook his place behind the podium.

"Thank you for those thoughtful words, David. Our prayer evening is now over. However, as I mentioned earlier, David has asked me to provide time to anyone who wishes to make a comment or tell a brief story about their relationship with Anna. You may do so now."

From somewhere in the middle of the chapel, a lady rose and worked her way towards the front. She was dressed all in black and wore a black veil over her face so it was difficult to tell exactly who she was. Father Connelly greeted her and assisted her to the podium. He leaned forward into the microphone. "This is Mrs. Leibel."

"You may not all know me," Mrs. Leibel began. "More than fifteen years ago my husband Tony passed away, leaving me with our young son. Johnny was a good boy but he had a lot of problems, especially at school. When he was sixteen, the other kids teased him about all the acne he had on his face. I told him not to worry about it, that he would soon outgrow it. One day I came home from buying groceries at Engelmann's and I found my Johnny dead in his room. He had taken his own life. First Tony left me, and then our son John."

She paused to steady her voice, then went on. "The first

person to come over and see me was Anna Engelmann. She helped me through the funeral and for days after prayed with me to accept this awful thing. What I would like to share is how Mrs. Engelmann always remembered my son from the day it happened until now. She always sent me a note or phoned me on the anniversary of Johnny's death. She would tell me she had offered up a mass for Johnny, and then together we said a prayer.

"While most people forgot a week or two after the funeral, Anna never did. She always remembered. She knew I would be grieving, especially on that day. She knew a mother never forgets her children and what happens to them. She was always with me in my grief, sharing my sorrow and heartache, encouraging me to go on and accept what had happened and to ask the Lord for healing." Mrs. Leibel's voice cracked and tears came to her eyes. Father Connelly moved to go to her, but then she spoke again.

"I remember as if it were yesterday. A few years ago, two days before what would have been Johnny's eighteenth birthday, I was feeling very sad..." Voice trembling, she added softly, "I missed my Johnny so much. Anna took me into the back room of the store, and there among all the boxes, she sat me down on one of the sturdy boxes..." with a small smile, she said, "I was heavier then—and she knelt down in front of me and prayed to the Lord with all her heart. I remember her saying to Jesus that she would not get up until he delivered me from the awful anguish I had...and at that moment a healing and calmness I have never known came over me. The Lord granted me peace. He filled my heart with a spirit of forgiveness for what Johnny had done, and He freed me from the anger I had towards God Himself for allowing such a thing to happen.

"From that day to this, I have been at peace. All that I could give to Anna was a hug. And that was all she ever wanted. I could see a great joy in her eyes and knew how happy it made her to see me at peace. As Mr. Engelmann said, Anna was a soldier for the Lord." Mrs. Leibel nodded and dabbed at her nose with a handkerchief as she stepped away from the podium.

A well-dressed young man got up from his seat. He walked confidently up to the microphone and adjusted it as if he did so all the time.

"Hello, my name is Irvin Goronic. Before I moved away I lived on the north side of Victoria Avenue on Atkinson Street. Many of you may know my grandmother who lives just a block away from the Engelmanns. One day Mrs. Engelmann was alone in the store. Mr. Engelmann was either away or upstairs, and I thought I could easily steal a chocolate bar. Thinking Mrs. Engelmann wasn't looking, I put it in my pocket, pretended to look for something, then made my way to the door. Before I got there, however, Mrs. Engelmann called my name.

"When I turned, Mrs. Engelmann was already standing behind me. I will never understand how quickly she got there. She put her arm over my shoulder and asked, 'Irvin, did you forget to pay for that chocolate bar?' I remember to this day how my face burned. 'Oh, yes, I did forget, Mrs. Engelmann,' I said. But then I didn't have any money to pay for it.

"Then she told me to come with her. I can tell you, I was worried! We walked back into the storage area, and like Mrs. Leibel before me, she sat me down on an old box. I thought for sure I was going to get the strap. But Mrs. Engelmann just sat on the box next to me, looked me in the eyes and spoke words I'll never forget:

"'You know, Irvin, taking things that don't belong to you or that you don't pay for is stealing. Stealing is dishonest. It's not only a sin, but more important, you are putting shame on yourself. If you do it once, you will do it again, and each time you do it, you are forming a very bad habit that is a black mark against your character. I can see in your eyes Irvin, you are a good boy. You have such a nice, honest face. I would like to see that the inside of you is even nicer than what I see on the outside. Do you understand?'"

"I could only nod. Then she said, 'If at any time you want a chocolate bar, I want you to come up to me and say, "Mrs. Engelmann, could I have one? I don't want to take it dishonestly." And I will give it to you. Here, Irvin, I will give you this chocolate bar as a gift because I know from now on you are going to be an honest young man.'

"I remember asking her if she was going to tell my parents. She told me it was just between us. I was hesitant, but when she nodded at me, I put the chocolate bar she had given me into my pocket and walked out into the store. As I got closer to the front door, I suddenly stopped and went back to the candy display and put the chocolate bar back on the shelf. And when I left Mrs. Engelmann caught up to me and put her arm around me again. 'See, Irvin, I was right. You are a very good and honest boy. I am so proud of you.' And then she gave me a hug.

"I'm twenty-four and I have had a lot of hugs in my time, but I will never forget the warmth of the one Mrs. Engelmann gave me that day."

Like Mrs. Leibel, Irvin's eyes welled up with tears. "Whenever I came into the grocery store," he went on, "Mrs. Engelmann always greeted me with a big smile, as if it were meant just for me. And when I walked up and down the aisles, getting things my mom asked me to get, she'd often turn her back or go into the storage room. She was telling me she trusted me and that I didn't have to be watched. She taught me to be honest from the inside and not from the outside.

"Before I leave, I want to say, from the day Mrs. Engelmann gave me that hug, and because of the way she treated me in the days that followed, I have been an honest man. In fact, my company trusts me so much I am the youngest executive officer they have ever appointed. I had to come back today to pay my respect to the Engelmanns for helping to form my character."

As the young man stepped down from the podium, silence fell upon the congregation, except for the odd sniffle. It was broken when Mr. Engelmann began to clap. Others joined in and soon the entire congregation was clapping. Such an upbeat display of emotion was unprecedented at a prayer service!

And so it went, one person after another standing and sharing what Mrs. Engelmann had done for them. It didn't even seem like a prayer service anymore. People clapped, laughed and cried with joy.

Henry's favourite story came from two boys he knew. They told about the store's squeaky floorboards and how Mr. Engelmann used the sounds to keep track of them. They would deliberately go to different parts of the store and squeak all the boards at the same time, totally confusing Mr. Engelmann. Everyone laughed, even Mr. Engelmann. But Mrs. Engelmann had walked up and down the aisles to keep them on the straight and narrow. They were glad they had stopped doing it out of respect for both Mr. and Mrs. Engelmann, not wanting to add to their troubles when she became ill.

Although others wanted to share, it was almost ten-thirty by the time Father Connelly decided to end the service. He came to the podium and just as he opened his mouth to speak a dismissal, he stopped and stared down the aisle. "Perhaps just one more remembrance before we conclude the service," he said.

Everyone turned and no one was more surprised than Henry to see Gary coming up to the mike. Henry's eyes stayed glued to his best friend as he made his way to the podium. *My God, he's brave.* Henry's heart went out to his friend. He was so overwhelmed by his friend's courage at getting up to speak, goosebumps spread instantly across both forearms.

Gary threw a furtive glance at Henry, nervously adjusted the microphone and then spoke.

"For most of the evening I've wanted to come up and tell you about Mrs. Engelmann but was too afraid, too nervous about talking in front of such a large crowd. But then I remembered what she told me one time: 'Never be afraid to stand up for what you believe…your guardian angel is always with you, ready to lift you up. I knew then I had come up here because I believe Mrs. Engelmann was a very holy person filled with peace. She has been such an example to me in believing and having faith in God. During the summer when I worked for the Engelmanns I saw time and time again how, in spite of her illness, she helped others—always through the power of Jesus. I have witnessed people healed and transformed after a visit with her. Her example and her strong faith in Jesus instilled a love for Jesus in me too. I decided I want to help people like she did, and several times we talked about me maybe going into the priesthood. I'm still not sure what I want to do but this I know: because of Mrs. Engelmann's example I want to commit my life to the Lord. I have good parents and I love my mom, but Mrs. Engelmann was like another mother to me…"

Tears came to Gary's eyes and he paused to regain his composure. He tried to express his sorrow that she was gone but was overtaken by emotion. After a few moments, Mr. Engelmann stood and began to clap. The congregation followed and Gary stepped down from the podium.

As everyone left, they talked about the prayer evening and how different it had been from what they were accustomed to. It had been more like a family get-together where everyone recalled the times they had shared together. And that was exactly what Mr. Engelmann had wanted—a celebration of Anna's life with family and friends.

As Henry walked to the car with his parents, he noticed Gary ahead heading home. "Dad, I'll meet you and Mom at home in fifteen minutes, okay? I'm going to catch up with Gary and walk home with him."

"That's fine, Henry," his dad said.

"Hey Gary, wait up!" Henry hollered as he ran down the street. When he caught up to Gary, Henry put his hand on his friend's shoulder and patted it.

"Geez, it is good to see ya, Gary. I didn't know you were coming to the funeral."

"I didn't know either until the last minute. One of the teachers drove in to Regina after dinner and I was able to catch a ride in with him. I'll go back to Notre Dame in the morning. I just wanted to be here for one of her services."

The boys walked in silence for almost a quarter of a block

before Henry broke the silence. "That was real nice what you said about Mrs. Engelmann. I was close to her too."

They were quiet for a moment then Henry suddenly turned to his friend. "What Mrs. Leibel said tonight was so true. I was there in the store when it happened. I was getting stock for the shelves and Mrs. Leibel and Mrs. Engelmann were each sitting on a box, praying. Suddenly Mrs. Engelmann slid off the box, got on her knees and said, 'Jesus, I will not get up until You deliver Agnes from the awful burden of anguish she carries for her son.'"

"So what happened then?" Gary stopped and looked at him.

"I'm not kidding, Gary—it was almost like electricity filled the air! I couldn't get off the ladder to take the stock to the front of the store if I wanted to. All of a sudden Mrs. Leibel began to cry and a sort of radiance came into her face. And I just knew something good happened to her right then." He added, "Ever since that day Mrs. Leibel never looked so sad again. It was just like she said tonight."

"It's really too bad about John. I remember the guys teasing him about his pimply face. It sure bothers me when kids tease others. We can be so insensitive and look what it can lead to."

Henry nodded. "Yeah, the guy hung himself. Geez, we all just want to be accepted more than anything and it makes me crazy that people try to make themselves feel better by making someone else feel worse. I try to stop it whenever I can."

"Me too. But, yeah, you're right about Mrs. Engelmann, Hank. I was in that storeroom many times and heard her on the phone comforting someone. It sure touched me what she was doing. She was such a holy person. "

"So, you're really still planning to go into the priesthood?"

"Yeah, maybe. This past year Father Murray was talking quite a bit about this lady in India. She's a nun who started up Missionaries of Charity—her name is Mother Teresa. Jane and I were thinking that maybe we would try to go there for a year or two before pursuing a vocation."

"Wow, that sounds like some adventure, going all the way to India!"

"Yeah, that's why Jane and I thought we should spend the summer preparing by visiting hospitals, care homes, and working in the Salvation Army and places like that."

"You seem so sure about what you want to do. It's the first time I ever heard of anybody our age doing something like that."

"Well, Mrs. Engelmann influenced me a lot. I'm sure going to miss her."

"So, I guess you won't be working at the store this summer?"

"Maybe the odd Saturday if you need me. Jane and I have our plans pretty well set. And, as things turned out, we both received scholarships that will pay for our tuition at Notre Dame next year, so it's not so critical that we get jobs this summer."

"It looks like the Lord is looking after you and preparing your way."

"That's what Jane and I think...we want to carry out His will."

Henry looked at his friend and was at a loss as what more he could say about all this. His friend showed such maturity and confidence in his purpose.

"What about the military? Being a chaplain, I mean? Are you still thinking about that?"

"I know my dad wants me to do that, but I don't know any more. Being around fighting and war just sort of bothers me. I think we should be learning about loving and understanding each other rather than killing each another. My dad and I argue about it all the time—I guess we just have different views."

"I think I know what you mean, Gary. Still, *someone* has to defend us against other countries...well, you know, take Russia, for instance—they're always talking about nuclear bombs."

"Yeah, my dad says that all the time, 'peace is maintained by a show of power and force.' I understand that but I think we also need to be peacemakers. God is the greatest power and the answer to world peace. Look, Hank, all through history wars have dominated the scene as people attempt to rule the world. And it'll never change until we learn to get along, accept each other's differences, love each other, pray for each other—you know. Just think what would happen if everyone started praying for peace."

The thought boggled Henry's mind. He could see the difference between Gary's way and his dad's. While Gary's dad had faith in man, Gary was growing to have trust and faith in God and His power to bring about peace. And what was more, it was giving him such confidence, security and purpose. Gary had anchored himself to something bigger and stronger than he was. Henry had seen something similar in his mother and for sure in the Engelmanns. He couldn't get over how his long-time friend was changing, how much he seemed to have grown and matured beyond his years.

"My dad says I don't live in the real world, that I'm too soft and weak. He hoped that a strict school like Notre Dame would straighten me out, toughen me up."

"Geez, what do you say to him? Do you get into big fights?"

"Well, I tell him Notre Dame *has* strengthened me. They've taught me that love, prayer, belief in God and following God's will is where the real power is, and that strong people with that kind of purpose in mind are needed to carry it out. And yeah, we used to get into arguments but not anymore. I used to get so defensive, so hurt by his comments I'd stay mad at him for days."

"I think I would too, Gary."

"But I realize now that I am a child of God, and what He created is good. We're *all* good, Hank, and just because we have different points of view doesn't make any of us better than the others."

"You've really thought this out."

"My ethics teacher at Notre Dame said relationships can be healed silently. Just trust in God and prayer can accomplish far more than attack and argument. There's a lot more peace in the house since I've started doing that. And its allowing me to understand and accept my dad where he's at. Someday, I hope he'll let go and understand and accept me too."

For the first time Henry felt a twinge of envy at his friend's growth, at how he had matured and become so strong within himself in such a short time. He was reminded of Mr. Engelmann saying that how we live our lives can have tremendous influence on others. He could feel Gary's example like a hot iron searing into his heart.

Henry broke the long silence. "Well, hopefully it will all work out between you and your dad."

Gary turned to him. "And what about you, Hank? Did Jenny ever write to you? I've been praying that she would."

"No, she hasn't. But I have a plan, though; I've been working on it a long time and I'll finally be able to carry it out this year. Soon I'll know what happened."

Gary nodded thoughtfully. "I'll continue to pray for you both. I'm beginning to see the power of prayer and the power in letting go and letting God take over."

Henry looked at his friend and then down at his watch as they reached the streetlight at the corner. "I'd like to share my plan with you, Gary, but it's getting late and I still have to prepare for a reading at tomorrow's mass for Mrs. Engelmann. Maybe I'll write to you about it. Thanks for praying for us."

"Yeah, well, let me know—that'd be great."

"It was sure good seeing you, Gary."

"Same here, Hank."

The boys did their secret handshake as they had so many times over the years. The love and friendship between them seemed to brighten the rays of light from the street lamp for a moment before they turned and went their separate ways.

Back on his block, Henry walked past his house to where Jenny once lived. The lights were all out in her old house, but for Henry the light of his first love still lingered, so much so that he half expected to see Jenny come out the front door. His hand brushed the top of the gatepost. He looked down, hoping against hope for another note fastened with an elastic. But there was nothing there except a sliver of peeling paint, a sign that time had passed and deterioration had set in. He felt like an angel with only one wing and wondered if Jenny ever felt the same. If only they could hold each other once more, they would be able to soar.

He flicked the peeling paint with a forefinger, patted the post and walked home.

HENRY QUICKLY BRUSHED his teeth, got into his pajamas and sat at his desk, curious as to which scripture Mrs. Engelmann wanted him to read at the funeral tomorrow. He stared at the brown paper bag on the edge of his desk, thinking Mrs. Engelmann's Bible deserved to be held in a jeweled box or something that somehow indicated its sacredness. He was impressed once more by how completely unpretentious the Engelmanns were, just plain simple folk living such a profoundly rich life.

Henry reached for the bag and slowly pulled out the burgundy leather Bible. He still couldn't believe she'd wanted him to have it. The cover was worn, its edges well-thumbed, yet it struck him as having been tenderly cared for. The book felt warm, almost as if Mrs. Engelmann had just let go of it. He recalled reading to her from it when he visited. It had always felt good in his hands. Mrs. Engelmann had loved this Bible so much...and now it was his. He'd treasure it always.

A plastic bookmark and a white piece of paper stuck out from the top of the gilt-edged pages. Henry opened it first to the bookmark and saw an underlined passage: Isaiah 26:3 "Thou wilt keep him in perfect peace, whose mind is stayed on Thee."

Yes, Mrs. Engelmann's mind was always on the Lord. Even in her pain, she was in peace.

Henry's eyes wandered to the bookmark he held in his hand. When he turned it over, he discovered it had a guardian angel prayer written on the back, the one he'd said almost every night since he'd met Jenny. "Angel of God, my guardian dear..." Amazing! He'd never have dreamed Mrs. Engelmann would've known that prayer. On the other side of the bookmark was a beautiful angel with long, flowing golden hair hovering over a boy and girl walking across a high bridge, hand-in-hand above a deep canyon, water gushing and crashing into the rocks below them. The boy and the girl reminded Henry of him and Jenny. They were holding hands, the guardian angel watching over them, protecting them. How Henry wished Jenny were here with him now. He could almost feel her hand in his. But just as Mr. Engelmann would no longer hold the hand of his beloved wife, Henry feared he'd never hold Jenny's again, either.

Before reading Mrs. Engelmann's note, Henry opened the front cover of the Bible. At the top of the page were the names of two people, below them were the names of another two, and below that was Mrs. Engelmann's name. Under her name, written in German, were the words *Wir lieben dich.* It was signed *Mutter und Vater, 12 June 1914.*

Henry was surprised to see his name on the opposite page: *To Henry, whom David and I, in our hearts, adopted as a son.* A rush of love swept over him. He was so close to the Engelmanns. According to the names listed, Mrs. Engelmann's Bible had been handed down for three generations. Henry felt privileged and blessed to receive it as part of Mrs. Engelmann's family and carry on the tradition.

He sat back and took a deep breath. The Bible was such a beautiful gift to him and yet he wished he could share it with Gary. Henry knew his friend's bond to Mrs. Engelmann was just as special. Gary would have loved to receive this as well.

Henry read Mrs. Engelmann's inscription again. He really felt like he *was* their adopted son. He remembered one morning in particular during one of his visits to Mrs. Engelmann's room. She'd often had the Bible open and by her side facing Henry, a mute request for him to read the chapters the book was opened to. That morning, just as Henry had been about to read, Mrs. Engelmann had softly placed her hand on top of his own. "You have been like a son in our lives, Henry. We are so grateful your parents have allowed you to share your life with us."

There had been tears in Anna's eyes when he glanced up at her and, unsure what else to do, Henry had begun to read, hearing his voice but more conscious of Mrs. Engelmann's hand on his than what he read. He had felt her love in that moment and he hoped she had felt his love for her in return. "Your voice is so clear and strong Henry," she had often said, thanking him over and over for reading to her. Henry was beginning to see how both Mrs. and Mr. Engelmann helped him feel good about himself; always building up his self-image.

When Henry left after these visits, he always turned the Bible back around and laid it on her lap so she could continue to read. That morning, he'd hesitated for a moment and then bent down to kiss her cheek. She'd smiled and thanked him for coming. After that, every time Henry visited he would kiss Mrs. Engelmann goodbye as naturally as if she'd been his own mother. Henry felt that love between them surge through him now. He was nervous about getting up and reading in front of a bunch of people—based on the turnout at tonight's prayers, the funeral was likely to be packed—but he promised himself that tomorrow he would read to the best of his ability. He thought of how Gary had gotten up and spoken so boldly about Mrs. Engelmann. Tomorrow he would do the same. He would read for Mrs. Engelmann.

Henry sat up, straightened his back and opened the Bible to the scripture Mrs. Engelmann had marked with a short letter. Tears trickled down his face even before he began to read:

Dear Henry,

By the time you read this, I will be with the Lord. All of my life this Bible has been my constant companion and guiding light. I pray that it will guide your path, too. You have been such a blessing to David and me. We prayed many times for a child when we were young, but I accepted long ago that the Lord's plan for our marriage didn't include children. What a surprise that so many years later, our prayer was finally answered: the Lord had given us you! We didn't realize it right away, but the more you came into our lives, the more we grew to love you and consider you our son. You will never fully realize how much you have helped us and the joy you have brought into our lives.

Thank you for all the times you came to visit, the talks we had and those precious times when you read the Bible to me when I was too tired and weak to read on my own. You have a wonderfully expressive voice and I have often repeated in my mind the words you read long after you left.

I have asked David to give you my Bible. It's the one possession I have treasured most in my life. It has been in our family for a long time. And because we consider you part of our family, David and I both feel this Bible should be given into your care. Treasure it always. It is the key to heaven and the source of great blessings.

I would make a last request of you, Henry. Would you be so kind as to read St. Paul's letter to the Corinthians, Chapter 13, verses 1 to 13 on love at my funeral mass? I so love the way you read it to me and I would like you to read it one more time for me as I leave this earthly life.

May God bless you always,

Love, Anna

Henry could barely read the last paragraph. He wiped his eyes with his fingertips and read the passage Mrs. Engelmann had requested. After reading verses one to thirteen, Henry realized that St. Paul's letter to the Corinthians perfectly described Mrs. Engelmann. Suddenly, the scripture Henry had heard many times before came to life. He understood it all so clearly. He could hardly wait to share his insight the following day.

"What a beautiful gift," Henry murmured as he closed the Bible and crawled into bed. He pictured Mr. Engelmann getting into bed, thinking of and missing his Anna. *It must be so strange and feel so empty.* Mr. Engelmann surely understood completely how Henry felt without Jenny. And Henry felt Mr. Engelmann's loss anew. How he must be feeling…the ache in his heart, the loss, the sorrow…how much he missed Anna… how much Henry missed Jenny.

Henry rolled over and began praying to his guardian angel for comfort. That his protector would fly to Mr. Engelmann and to Jenny and send them his love. Yeah, both Anna and Jenny were angels, both so beautiful. Mrs. Engelmann is in heaven with her angel tonight and Jenny's is protecting her, watching over her like the pewter angel inscription I sent her promised. He wondered if Jenny was in bed thinking of him now too. He tried to visualize Jenny curled up in her bed and he lay beside her, his arm around her, holding her. He prayed that sleep would take him soon lest his heart would surely break. He prayed for Mr. Engelmann that sleep had overtaken him as well. The bed beside him was all too empty now.

JENNY LOOKED OUT the car window at the bright full moon reflecting on the hood of James' shiny black sports car. It was almost midnight and they had just returned from the city after seeing a movie. Jenny always felt uncomfortable when James dropped her off at home late at night. It was usually then that James did his best to get physical. To ward off his advances Jenny did her best to distract him with what was becoming a recurrent complaint.

"Sometimes I wonder if we're going steady at all," she said, glancing at him now. "You phoned almost a week ago to ask me to the movies and yet you broke our date twice before tonight."

"Sorry, Jen, Dad's not feeling well and someone has to look after the business."

"Well, it's not like you have a small store or something. Your dad's business is huge and he has lots of people working for him. That's what corporations have executives *for*, James. My father trusts his staff to look after business affairs all the time."

"But Jenny, the guys Dad has working for him don't know *anything*. I feel like I shouldn't even start university—maybe just take over right away. I'd have that place humming in no time."

Jenny rolled her eyes and looked down. James placed a forefinger under her chin and raised her head until her gaze met his. "Look, Jen, I'm sorry. I'll try to keep my dates with you in the future."

James looked tenderly into Jenny's eyes, then kissed her. "You're so beautiful, Jenny." He put an arm around her shoulders and drew her in, raising his other hand to place it on her shoulder and then slowly letting his fingers trail down over her breast. Jenny quickly pushed his hand away. James kissed her once more then tried again to touch her breast.

Jenny pushed herself away from him. "I told you before, James, I don't want to do that."

"Come on, Jenny. Everybody does."

"Well, that's their choice. I want to wait until I'm married."

"You can't be serious!"

Jenny turned to face him. "Yes, I *am*." She looked down at her hands in her lap and an uneasy silence fell. In the wake of the rape, Jenny also didn't want to conceive another child until she was married and secure in a relationship, one in which she could raise a child with a man she loved. Her thoughts naturally turned to Henry and the day they'd almost made love. It was Henry who had stopped. It was he who had realized it was important to wait. From that moment, Jenny had decided to remain chaste until she was married.

Oh, I felt so safe with Henry!

"Jen?" James asked, but she didn't hear him. "Jenny? What's wrong? It always seems like your mind is elsewhere when we're together. And it's something else besides this sex thing. What is it?"

Jenny kept her gaze lowered, tears beginning to surface. She said nothing. She knew James was frustrated with her, tense because of her unwillingness to go further than kiss. She had hoped things would be better now that he was going into his first year of university and not in high school anymore.

"Is there someone else?"

Jenny shook her head, wiping away a tear. "No," she whispered, "no, there isn't." For a long time Jenny had been afraid that James would sense the love she still had for Henry. That he would see it in her eyes or sense it in her touch. That it wasn't he who excited her but rather the memories that lay just beneath the surface. Jenny was afraid to look at James—he knew.

"Who is it I remind you of Jenny? I remember when I first met you in the cafeteria you said I reminded you of someone. You seemed thrilled at the time. And yet I always have this feeling that I'm competing with some unknown guy."

James reached out and gently took hold of Jenny's chin, tilting her head towards him until their eyes met once more.

"Just tell me, Jen. Who is this mystery man?"

"Oh, it's no one, James, just a friend I had the summer we were in Regina before we moved here." Jenny felt his fingers stiffen under her chin. She didn't want to rouse his jealousy and get him upset. "It's really nothing."

But James knew better and Jenny could tell that he did. Even in the darkness of the car she could visualize the red flooding James' neck and face, his veins swelling. She'd seen it many times when he was around other guys who liked to flirt with her. Jenny took hold of his hand and tried to comfort him, to reassure him he didn't need to worry. But James persisted.

"So, tell me about this guy from all those summers ago. What's his name? How old is he?"

"James, it's really nothing—"

"What do you mean, 'nothing'? He's with us all the time! At least tell me *something* about him so I know what I'm up against!"

Jenny looked at her boyfriend and in the dim light tried

to read on his face if it was okay to indulge in sharing what weighed so heavily on her heart. Would he understand?

"It's Henry—"

"Henry who?" James wanted to know, his voice rising slightly, demanding.

Jenny tensed and a cold chill ran through her. Still, she continued. "Henry Pederson. You see, when Dad was transferred to Regina from Vancouver we moved in three doors down from his house. I met him a few days later and we became good friends over the summer. He was from the farm and a real nice guy. In the fall we started Grade 9 at the same high school and then, two weeks later, Dad got transferred here."

James dark eyes flashed "So, do you keep in touch with this lover boy?" His voice was curt and razor sharp. Before Jenny could answer, the interrogation continued. "Do you write him? Does he call? Does he write you?" James peppered her with one question after another, wanting to know where he stood as quickly as possible and trying to decide just what he'd have to do to correct this situation and ensure his position in her heart.

"No!"

James relaxed slightly but wanted more assurances. "What do you mean, 'no'? Surely you must have written one another?"

"Yes, I did write him. Many times in fact, but he never wrote back, not one letter…not once."

James relaxed still further. "Not one?"

"No. Not even one."

"Some friend…but then, what do farm boys know."

"Actually, James, Henry was very sensitive and a real gentleman—there must be *some* reason why he hasn't written."

"Yeah, sure there is. He found someone else, Jenny. That's the only explanation and the sooner you accept it, the better for all of us."

Jenny sighed. "Yes, I know, James. You're right. That's why I told you it was nothing."

"So you're just peeved he hasn't written you."

She nodded. "I guess that probably has a lot to do with it."

Jenny knew James' jealousy wasn't a good thing and that she should be upset with him, yet she *did* feel guilty about letting her thoughts stray to Henry so much and comparing him with James. *Perhaps James' sensitivity is justified, well...to a degree anyway.*

"I'm really sorry if I've given you the impression I'm not being attentive to you, I must admit my mind does wander at times...I'll try to be more devoted..." Jenny trailed off and winked at James

But he was having none of it. "Look, Jennifer, you're with *me* now so move on—get over him."

"I have...I am, James. Really, you're overreacting."

"I don't know, Jenny, you seem to be in another world all too often. Sometimes I think I don't know you." His voice softened and he looked into Jenny's eyes, "I'm very sorry for what I did earlier, it's just...I love you so very much, Jenny."

And after a long moment, Jenny replied, "I love you too, James." *I think.*

Their lips met and Jenny made every effort to keep her thoughts on the boy who held her tight in his arms.

JAMES DREW HIS lips away from Jenny's and looked long and hard into the eyes of the girl he wanted to possess more than anything. He wanted to make certain there wasn't anything that could take her away from him. It was obvious she liked this Pederson, missed him and maybe even loved...he couldn't finish the thought. A deep surge of loathing slammed his guts. Revulsion for his competitor cemented in the core of his being. He was the envy of every other guy at school, and was constantly being challenged by guys phoning his girl at all hours. If it hadn't been for Jenny's lack of interest in any of them it would have driven him mad. *But this guy seems different to her; I'll have to keep a close watch.* If only he could lock her up some place, away from everyone. The name "Henry Pederson" reverberated irritatingly in the confines of his flaming consciousness and with every echo he despised it all the more.

CHAPTER FIVE

THE PEDERSONS ARRIVED almost an hour before the start of the service and easily found a parking space in front of the church. Since Henry and his dad were pallbearers they headed to the back of the church to meet with the funeral director, while Henry's mother, Mary, entered through the front door. An usher greeted her and led her to where Mr. Engelmann waited. She took his hand in support.

St. Mary's Church held 750 people, and when Henry and his father and the other pallbearers walked in, the church was almost filled to capacity. For a simple grocery store owner with no immediate family to have so many people come to pay their respects was unbelievable. Mr. Engelmann and the funeral director followed behind the casket as it was carried to the front of the altar, and everyone took their seats. As they walked down the aisle, heads turned to get a glimpse of the widower. Those who had not attended the prayer service the evening before were surprised, however, by Mr. Engelmann's expression and attire, both of which seemed more suitable for a wedding than a funeral, and murmurs were heard throughout the church as the congregants tried to make sense of it. But anyone who had been with Mr. Engelmann twelve hours earlier knew that this was not going to be an ordinary funeral and smiled warmly through their tears as Mr. Engelmann made his way down the aisle. Mr. Engelmann's light tan suit—adorned with a single, bright yellow carnation in the lapel—and his genial smile were a sharp contrast to those dressed in traditional black, their grief deeply etched on their faces.

When Henry saw what Mr. Engelmann was wearing, he was immediately reminded of the day he'd met Jenny. He had fallen asleep waiting to take her to Balfour High School to pick up registration forms and had a dream which still haunted him to that day. In the dream, Henry, as Prince Charming, came upon Jenny—who lay sleeping on a bed of white daisies in a vast field of wildflowers. As he approached her, anticipating the touch of her lips on his, she suddenly disappeared and in her place was an older man wearing a tan-coloured suit with a yellow flower in the lapel. *Was it Mr. Engelmann?* But he hadn't even really *known* the Engelmanns back then. Unbidden, the rest of the dream came rushing back: a faceless figure in a black cloak held him back from getting to Jenny and the man in the tan suit... the thought sent quivering coldness down his spine now the way it had then, despite the warm air in the church.

About halfway down the long aisle of St. Mary's, the organist began playing "The Lord of the Dance." Hardly a tune to be played at a funeral. By the time Mr. Engelmann was seated, the mood in the church had shifted from mournful to something approaching jovial.

While Father Connelly inwardly cringed at Mr. Engelmann's choice of song, his clothing and demeanour, fearing it would offend some attendees, he nonetheless greatly respected both Mr. and Mrs. Engelmann and had agreed to honour their rather unusual wishes for her funeral. He started the mass by making the sign of the cross. Ten minutes into the ceremony, it was time for Henry's reading. He was very nervous. He wanted to get up and run away. Mr. Engelmann patted him on the knee and whispered, "You will do fine."

Peace and confidence settled over Henry by the time he reached the podium. He vowed he would do the best reading for Mrs. Engelmann that he possibly could. As he looked over the congregation, he prayed for strength and help for him to read well. He remembered last evening how Mr. Engelmann had looked over the crowd and waited until he had everyone's attention. Henry, too, looked over the crowd, met Mr. Engelmann's warm gaze, then spoke.

"Before I do the reading, I would like to tell you about the wonderful gift Mrs. Engelmann left for me. She gave me her Bible." Henry lifted it up for everyone to see. "When I opened it up last night I found a note she'd left for me, requesting that I read one of her favourite passages on love. I feel very honoured to be reading it now for her and for you, from her Bible."

Henry looked again at Mr. Engelmann, who smiled and nodded.

Henry read verses one, two and three of 1 Corinthians as they were written, but when he reached verses four through seven he replaced the word "love" with Mrs. Engelmann's name. As he had read the scripture the night before, it occurred to him that although Mrs. Engelmann had been a simple woman running a humble grocery store, she lived her life like a saint. Mrs. Engelmann gave meaning to the words of 1 Corinthians 13. She was a living embodiment of love, a clear example that it was possible to live by God's Word. At first, saying "Anna" out loud felt odd on his lips; he had always called her "Mrs. Engelmann," but once he started, it flowed.

> Anna is patient and kind; Anna is not jealous, or conceited, or proud; Anna is not ill-mannered, or selfish, or irritable; Anna never kept a record of wrongs; Anna was never happy with evil, but was happy with the truth; Anna never gave up; Anna's faith, hope and patience never failed...Anna was love.

When Henry finished verse 13, he added, "During the times I spent with Mrs. Engelmann she always reflected these very words. I always left her presence feeling I had gained so much more than what I tried to offer by my visit. On one occasion, after I had read this very passage to her, Mrs. Engelmann said to me, 'There is no hope without love. There is no forgiveness without love. We will never be able to serve the Lord or our neighbour without love. Love your Lord with all your strength, soul and heart. Love your neighbour as yourself. Live by this commandment, and you will be a king and inherit all the worthy treasures on earth and in heaven.'"

Henry walked back to the pew and sat down between his mother and Mr. Engelmann. Mr. Engelmann patted Henry's knee and whispered, "Well done, Henry."

His mother placed her hand on his, on the one that still held Mrs. Engelmann's Bible, and patted it.

After Father Connelly read from the Gospel of John, he told them how happy he was to see so many people and welcomed all the newcomers. He added a few words about Mrs. Engelmann, repeating much of what he had said the night before at the prayer service, then called on Mr. Engelmann to say a few words.

All eyes were on Mr. Engelmann. As he approached the altar, he knelt and bowed his head before the crucifix hanging behind it. After a brief prayer he made his way to the podium, unfolded a letter he had taken from his suit jacket pocket, and with a gentle smile on his face, slowly surveyed the people before him.

"Thank you, from the bottom of my heart, for coming today to celebrate Anna's entrance into heaven. Long before Anna passed on, many an evening we would sit and talk about meeting Jesus. It was as casual as if we were talking about what opera or movie to see. We have no fear of death. Death is as much a part of life as life is a part of death. We are all born to die. From the moment we are conceived, our days are numbered. It is what we choose to do between that is important. If you have lived a Godly life, there are no worries or concerns. Death is simply the key that unlocks eternal life for us in which there is no longer pain or suffering, only pure joy.

"For the longest time, I wished that I would be the one to go first. But with her illness, it was better that she went, and I am happy for her. She deserves to be with the Lord, to have His love and presence before I do.

"But I, too, am ready. Like Anna, who is wearing her wedding gown to meet her groom, I am wearing my wedding suit. We both thought it fitting to wear our wedding attire to celebrate our passing from this life to a new life with Jesus in much the same way we celebrated when God joined us together in marriage. And when I too die, I want to wear this same suit— although it may need some alteration if I put on a little weight. One quick cut down the back is all it would take, and no one would be the wiser as I lay in the coffin." Mr. Engelmann smiled, and the congregation chuckled.

"In any case," he went on, "before Anna died she wrote a brief letter that she wanted me to read to you today:

Dear Brothers and Sisters in Christ,

As many of you know, when David and I left Austria in 1942, we left behind our homeland and the few relatives who had survived the war up to that time. Since then, we have made our home here, and you have all become our family.

Please don't cry for me now that I have gone on to be with the Lord. I would rather have you smile and be happy that I lived here in the neighbourhood, and that we have become friends, to be grateful for our visits, and the good and sorrowful times we have shared.

All of us must someday leave our friends and go through the door to be with the Lord in eternal life. It is not a sad time but a happy one. It is a time to celebrate and cherish the memories we have shared and let them live on.

Let the love we shared blossom and give fruit to all those lives we touch with ours. Someday soon we will all be together with the angels and saints in heaven, giving praise and glory to our Lord.

May God bless you and may my memory and love be with you always.

Love, Anna

Mr. Engelmann folded the letter, slid it into his breast pocket and patted the outside. Henry knew it would forever be by Mr. Engelmann's heart. "Anna made one more request," Mr. Engelmann said. "All the songs you hear today, Anna wanted sung. And before Father Connelly leads us in Holy Communion, I would ask Margaret Tearhorst to come forward and sing 'Amazing Grace.' Anna always loved to hear Margaret sing and often said the Lord blessed Margaret with the voice of an angel."

Margaret came down the aisle to stand in front of Anna's casket. Henry waited for the organ to play an introduction, but there wasn't one. After Margaret finished the first verse it was clear that musical accompaniment was unnecessary. The notes soared to the rafters in Margaret's clear, strong voice, and each word carried such a melodic flutter he wished it would go on forever. As Margaret sang the fifth verse, "And, when this flesh and heart shall fail, and mortal life shall cease; I shall possess within the veil, a life of joy and peace," shivers tickled Henry's spine, and there wasn't a dry eye in the church.

As Margaret retook her seat, Mr. Engelmann began to clap. Others followed, until the entire congregation was on its feet in a standing ovation.

During communion, many stopped to say goodbye to Anna for the last time on the way back to their pew.

When the mass was over, Father Connelly blessed the casket one more time. The funeral director walked up and began to lower its lid until Mr. Engelmann whispered something to him. The director raised the lid and moved away, allowing Mr. Engelmann to step forward. Mr. Engelmann stood there and looked at his wife for a long moment. He bent over and kissed her. He put a hand on top of Anna's and patted them. For the first time in public, tears rose in his eyes.

After Mr. Engelmann's final farewell, the funeral director closed the casket. Father Connelly reminded the congregation they were welcome to gather in the church hall for lunch and refreshments. Those who wished to attend the graveside ceremony could return to the hall right after the internment. The service concluded with "Come and Go With Me to That Land," a sprightly contrast to "Peace is Flowing Like a River" and "How Great Thou Art" the organ had played during communion.

When the choir started to sing, the congregation joined in. As they sang people clapped to the music, swayed back and forth, and danced on the spot. By the time the pallbearers, led by Father Connelly and the altar boys, had escorted the casket out to the waiting hearse, the congregation was in a cheerful mood, out of character with what most people would consider a normal, solemn funeral. It was almost as if they were happy Anna had died and gone to heaven. But, Henry knew Mrs. Engelmann was looking down on all this and just a-lovin' it.

Because Henry and his dad were pallbearers, they got in the limousine with Mr. Engelmann and watched the people spill out onto the sidewalk. He didn't see one person without a smile on his or her face. They greeted each other, shook hands and talked about the service. Henry had never seen people mingle and talk to each other like that after a funeral or even after a regular Sunday mass. It was almost as if people's inhibitions had been exchanged for a spirit of love.

When Mr. Engelmann had settled himself in the seat next to them, the funeral director signaled the hearse to start what would become almost a half-mile long procession. Other drivers who had stopped out of respect for the deceased must have become impatient as car after car streamed by. Henry was certain they must have thought some dignitary had died.

"Thank you, Henry, Bill, for doing this last service for Anna," Mr. Engelmann said.

Henry's dad just nodded. Though he said nothing, Henry knew he was feeling it all very deeply.

The breeze was soft. Birds chirped and flower petals fluttered gently on this beautiful prairie summer day, their sweet, natural perfume filling the air. Mrs. Engelmann was surrounded by all the things she loved—her friends, her loved ones, the glory of nature. What a perfect place in which to be put to rest.

At the graveside, Father Connelly waited until the hundred or so people had gathered then nodded to the funeral director to open the back of the hearse and slide the casket out. Henry, his dad and the other pallbearers took hold of the rope handles and carried the casket to the grave, weaving among the tombstones until they reached the site.

On either side of the grave, they positioned the casket over the opening and began to lower it onto three straps that spanned the opening in the ground. All of a sudden, Bill slipped on the vinyl tarp surrounding the hole and fell partially in! Fortunately the middle strap caught him squarely between the legs, preventing him from falling further—though it was undignified, to say the least. The crowd nearest the grave let out a gasp. Those farther away rose on their tiptoes or moved from side to side to see what had happened. Henry almost burst out laughing at the horrified look on his dad's face. He had to quickly divert his attention to rebalancing the casket in order to maintain his composure.

The funeral director rushed over and pulled Bill out. Once his feet were firmly planted on the tarp, he took up his position once more and they lowered the casket successfully onto the straps, letting go with a silent sigh of relief.

Father Connelly then spoke as loudly as he could, trying to project his voice so all could hear his final prayers and blessing.

Mr. Engelmann stood behind Henry and his dad, and as Father Connelly read the prayers, Henry moved until he stood beside Mr. Engelmann, who slipped an arm around his shoulders.

At the Father's signal, the altar boys removed the lid of a small brass container suspended from three chains. Father Connelly took a spoonful of ashes from the container, emptied it on the casket and said, "From dust thou wast made and unto dust thou shalt return." He bowed his head, focusing his eyes on a prayer in the book an altar boy held open before him. After reading it, he blessed the casket and gravesite by making the sign of the cross. "In the name of the Father and the Son and the Holy Spirit."

Mr. Engelmann slid his arm from Henry's shoulder and went over to the casket. He removed the carnation from his lapel and set it on the casket next to the ashes. Then he knelt and kissed the pine box, the wood warmed by the bright sun overhead. He patted it several times as a last farewell. As he stood, a heavy tear splashed onto the pine box and rolled over the side into the depths of the grave below. A part of him would be with Anna forevermore.

Mr. Engelmann turned and walked away, the final image of Anna beneath that pine cover difficult to dispel from his thoughts. He headed right to the hearse, not looking back. The crowd stepped aside to make room for him. Most looked on with compassion, while others reached out in support and comfort to touch him as he passed by. Mr. Engelmann's final quiet goodbye and the long, lonely walk back to the limousine was perhaps the saddest thing Henry had ever seen.

WITH THE FUNERAL over, David knew the next and hardest phase had already begun. He would return to an empty house. He would no longer have the support of friends or the distraction of the funeral. He would be alone. Even though Anna had been bedridden, at the end of each day he'd had someone to come home to, someone to talk to, someone whose presence he could feel even when she slept. But with Anna gone, the only thing awaiting him upstairs was a lonely and lifeless room.

The pain hit him as he sat in the limousine, the tinted windows shutting out the light he needed at that moment to revive his sinking spirit. After a whispered word to Bill and Henry, Mary slid into the limousine beside him and placed a hand over his. They sat in silence as the vehicle's engine sprang to life. The driver pushed a button and the sunroof slid open above them. Slowly the shiny black car meandered through the cemetery, periodically stopping for people crossing the road.

The sunlight through the trees alternated light and shadow, dappling the glow through the open sunroof as they passed under the thick canopy of elm trees lining the lane, helping to distract Mr. Engelmann. The warm summer breeze wafted over him like a soothing massage. He closed his eyes, rested his head against the high back seat and allowed himself to drift, welcoming nature's healing balm. Soon they would be back at the church hall, and for the last time that day, he would have to put on a brave front. He wanted it all to be over. He ached to be alone so he could let go and mourn his beloved Anna. Thankfully, the next day was Sunday and a day of rest. The store would be closed and he would have at least a day to contemplate his new life...alone.

As MR. ENGELMANN's limousine left, Bill pulled Henry aside. "Son, there's something I want to show you, and something I want to talk about."

"Don't you think we'd better be heading back to the hall?"

"In a moment; the other limousine isn't quite ready to go yet. There's something I want you to see. I saw it as we carried Anna's casket to the gravesite."

Without the parked hearse to guide them through the maze they had carried Anna's coffin through, Henry's father had to stop and read the tombstones.

Henry followed, baffled.

In the distance, Henry watched a tractor with a long arm and a scoop at the end of it wend its way up the lane, probably towards Anna's grave. Once the hole was filled and the sod replaced, Anna's gravesite would look like everyone else's, lost among the multitude of those who'd gone before her. Only a brass marker or granite stone would let the world know that Anna Engelmann had lived until 1959.

"Here it is," his father called out. He had been weaving in and out of tombstones for almost five minutes and was about quite a number of yards off to the right from where they had started. Henry walked over to his dad, following his father's gaze to the words chiselled into a granite tombstone:

JACOB STEVENS

1873-1946

ETERNALLY I ASK FOR FORGIVENESS

As they stood there under the warm afternoon sun, partially shaded by the leaves of the large tree overhead, Henry's mind settled on the word "forgiveness." *That's* what his dad wanted to talk about.

He didn't look up at his father but kept his eyes on the tombstone. Henry guessed he was about to hear a confession of some sort—and he wasn't really sure he wanted to hear it—but he waited until his dad was ready to talk, as Mr. Engelmann had done so many times with him.

"Seems like this man did something he wasn't proud of to ask for forgiveness in such a bold, public way, don't you think?"

"Yeah," Henry said, "wonder what he did?"

"I don't think it really matters. I read it earlier and I guess all the things that were said yesterday and today made me think about my life, and what I needed to do."

Henry was going to ask what he meant by that but decided to remain silent and listen like Mr. Engelmann always did when he was trying to sort out and express something important and personal.

"Son, I did a terrible thing to Mom and to you. I'm not proud of it. I'm ashamed, as a matter of fact. And like I said, when I read this inscription, it struck me hard that I need my family's forgiveness and that I need to set our lives straight again. I made a mistake, son, a huge one, and I'm very sorry for what I did. I failed, both as a husband and a father. I broke my wedding vow to your mom, and my commitment to you as a parent…I can't explain to you why I did it, and in the end it doesn't matter. There's nothing that can justify what I did. Whether it's my job, the need to get away from the daily coldness in the plant, some escape—no…"

His father's voice had become dry and crackly. Henry could feel the sorrow and regret in the sincerity of his words.

"I guess I don't want to be like this Jacob fellow here and have to ask for eternal forgiveness, Henry. I want and need your forgiveness now, when we are alive. I promise I'll never do such a terrible thing again. You'll never have to question my trust and loyalty to Mom or you ever again. I want this thing to be over once and…" here he began to cry, "I need you to forgive me."

No other words came and he broke into sobs.

By then, tears had filled Henry's eyes as well. He turned to his dad and before he could speak, his dad grabbed him and wrapped his arms around him. Henry returned the hug, and it wasn't anything like the lifeless gesture he'd given his father the night he'd returned from Vancouver.

Catching his breath, Henry said, "I forgive you, Dad…and I love you."

His father's grip tightened around him. It was the closest Henry had ever felt to his father.

The words Mr. Engelmann had said to Henry several times before, that good can come even out of tragedy, echoed poignantly in Henry's mind as he and his father embraced one another among the tombstones. From seemingly terrible things in life the most wonderful moments could arise when people trusted the Lord. From Anna's death, his father's infidelity, even the trials of Jacob Stevens, came new life, renewal…forgiveness.

As they walked back to the paved road, the black limousine slowly approached. The funeral director's assistant was waiting. Henry understood then that his dad had asked the man to wait after the burial service. The assistant stopped the car just ahead of them and got out of the limousine.

"Thank you for waiting for us," said his father.

"My pleasure, sir," he replied, with a nod. "It's a beautiful day."

Henry looked out the window at the cemetery before leaving the grounds. For most of his life, he had considered a graveyard to be a fearful place, a place where ghosts rose from the ground to walk or float around at night. But that day left him with a new image. A cemetery was a place of peace, a placeholder marking the end of one's earthly journey, the end of pain and suffering—and the beginning of a new life with God.

CHAPTER SIX

ON SUNDAY, THE day after the funeral when Henry and his parents arrived for the ten o'clock mass, Henry spotted Mr. Engelmann sitting about seven rows from the front, but there were no other seats around him. He would have to wait until after the service to talk to him.

Somehow the High Mass seemed anticlimactic compared to the Low Mass for Anna the day before. Following the service, people approached Mr. Engelmann to express their condolences and offer their help in any way they could. Mr. Engelmann nodded politely and moved from one parishioner to the next. Finally, Henry's mother had the opportunity to talk to him, and Henry, standing nearby, noticed Mr. Engelmann's eyes were red and puffy. *Last night must have been very hard on him.*

His mom asked if he would come over for supper that evening.

"Thank you for the invitation, Mary, but I would like to spend today at home. Perhaps next Sunday. I would very much like to come for supper then if the offer is still open?"

"Yes, of course, David."

"Good, I will look forward to a home-cooked meal."

MONDAY MORNING, HENRY awoke and glanced at his bedside clock. Nine-thirty—he'd slept in! His father had already left for work when Henry entered the kitchen.

His mother had her hands in the dishwater, scrubbing the roasting pan from Sunday dinner.

"It sure was good to sleep in. I really must have been tired," he said as he sat at the table.

"Yes, I could see you were."

"How are you feeling today?"

"Oh, a little tired myself, I guess. When you head off to work, I may lie down and have a little nap before you come home for lunch."

An uncomfortable silence settled between them and Henry knew something was bothering his mom.

"Is everything okay, Mom?"

"Oh, yes…" After a considerable pause, she asked, "What did you and Dad talk about after the funeral?"

Henry thought about her question, trying to decide how much to tell his mom. Would it upset her to know that his dad had asked for his forgiveness? Maybe she had forgotten most of it and he would only be reminding her of the hell she'd gone through. *Tell the truth*, he thought. "Truth is always the best policy," Mr. Engelmann would say.

"You know, Mom, I don't think I've ever been closer to Dad than I was on Saturday."

"Why?" she asked. "What happened?" She looked at him for a moment, but then turned back to the sink and stared at the dirty dishes.

"I hope this doesn't upset you, but Dad asked me to forgive him for what he had done. He told me he felt so ashamed for hurting you and me, and vowed he would never do such a thing again."

After another long silence, Mary asked hesitantly, "Did he tell you why he did it?"

"No, not really. He kind of hinted that it had something to do with his work. I don't think he likes his job. Maybe he just wanted to get away. I really can't say. But one thing I do know is that I've never seen Dad like that before. He cried a lot, and I know he felt very sorry for his mistake. I forgave him, Mom, and told him I loved him." And as Henry said the words "forgave" and "loved," tears welled up in his eyes.

His mother remained silent, her back still to him. Henry couldn't read her and didn't know if he'd upset her.

"Have you forgiven Dad?"

There was another drawn-out silence, then, "Yes, I have."

"Have you really?"

"Yes!" she snapped, offended by his persistence.

Once again, Henry considered whether it was better to drop it or keep the issue alive. And, once again, Mr. Engelmann's advice popped into his mind. "Always talk things out. Avoiding problems is very unhealthy. They will fester like a dormant volcano, ready to erupt when you least expect."

"Mom," Henry said cautiously, "I don't think you really have forgiven Dad."

Now Mary turned and faced him. She was crying. "How do *you* know how I feel? How can you say such an awful thing?"

Henry paused, knowing her anger was superficial. He allowed his gaze to turn towards his parent's bedroom. Her eyes followed his.

"Henry!" she blurted. "That is between your father and me and doesn't concern you one little bit!" Her face was red, but Henry didn't know if it was because he had looked at their bedroom or because he was challenging her on the twin bed set-up. Henry could feel the anguish his mother held inside, the hurt like knives piercing her heart. The pain she must suffer every day… and Dad carrying that burden…and me. He clearly understood what Mr. Engelmann had told him on several occasions. *Unwillingness to forgive holds you in bondage and those around you as well.* What his dad must be going through…*yeah, it* is *almost as if the entire family is trapped in an invisible prison.*

When she didn't say anything else, Henry stood and put his arms around her. She fell into his chest, sobbing.

"You've been hurt so much, Mom; I understand. I only felt a little of what you do. I love you, Mom."

After a few minutes, her sobbing subsided. Henry patted her on the back. "Are you okay, Mom?" When she nodded, sniffing, he added, "I'd better be going. Mr. Engelmann will wonder what's happened to me. I'm usually there by eight-thirty and it's almost ten now. I don't think I'll be home for lunch today. I'll just grab some salami and a bun or something at the store."

Mary didn't look at him. "Yes, you better get going." She turned and sank her hands into the dishwater again.

"'Bye, Mom, see you later."

As Henry biked towards the store he mulled the conversation over. Was his mom as ready to forgive his dad as he was? He wished she could let go like he had done at the cemetery. Henry had thought he'd forgiven his dad after he talked with Mr. Engelmann about it when his dad had first left, but realized after the funeral that he hadn't really. He felt at peace now, like a huge weight had been taken off his shoulders. He felt so free.

When Henry arrived at the store, Mr. Engelmann was on the phone taking an order. He already had a stack of orders for Henry to deliver, and the store had to be restocked. After being closed all day Saturday, today was going to be busy. In a way Henry was glad—it would help Mr. Engelmann keep his mind off his loss.

ON THURSDAY MORNING before Henry arrived, Doug, the Co-ca-Cola rep, stopped in on his weekly call to follow up with Mr. Engelmann about any repairs he needed done to the coolers. A week earlier he'd mentioned to Mr. Engelmann that the service man had suffered a stroke that left him paralyzed on the left side. He wouldn't be coming back to work for a long time, and if he even did, he probably wouldn't be able to do that job anymore. The company was looking for a replacement but in the meantime they had to hire an outside repair service if the equipment needed attention.

"So, Doug, have you found a replacement service man yet?"

"No. One of the Coke executives wants to hire his brother-in-law, but that would go against company policy."

David wasn't sure why but he felt compelled to find out more. "What are the qualifications for the job, do you know?"

"Well, whoever we hire needs to know something about machinery and be handy, for one thing—although Coca-Cola will send the right candidate on a three-week training program. Why do you ask?"

Suddenly David knew what had prompted him to pursue the matter. "Henry's dad!" he exclaimed.

"What about Henry's dad?" Doug asked, bewildered.

"Henry's dad is the man for the job."

"How's that?"

"Well," Mr. Engelmann said, pausing to think of a persuasive response, "Bill Pederson is a kind, personable and dependable man. You know how hard-working and smart Henry is. Well, who do you think he learned it from?" Mr. Engelmann paused only long enough for Doug to come up with the obvious answer. "He looks after all the machinery at the plant where he works. When something breaks down, Bill usually gets the equipment working before the company has to call in an outside repair service. After awhile the company had so much confidence in Bill's know-how they asked him to do all the repairs." David looked squarely into Doug's eyes and summed up his pitch. "He's a good man, Doug."

"I see," the cola rep said, and David knew he'd sold him. "Well, why don't you ask him to put in an application? I'll drop one off here on Monday if you think he'd be interested."

"I'm going to their home for dinner on Sunday and I'll ask Bill then. I'll get back to you Monday morning, one way or another."

"All right, thanks. See you, David."

David had to coach his heart rate to a slower pace after Doug left. *Bill would be perfect for that job.* He knew Bill didn't like working in the plant or the conditions there, especially during the winter. From what Henry had shared with him, perhaps one of the reasons Bill had left with that other woman had something to do with his job. David was looking forward to his visit Sunday evening with Bill and Mary more than ever. He would pray and call Father Connelly to say a mass that it all work out for the best.

He could hardly wait for Henry to come in. They had been very busy lately and seemed to be getting even busier. Customer loyalty was at its peak. So strong was their customer base, they'd even heard that if some of the children of their regular shoppers went elsewhere, they would get a scolding from their mothers! The store even gained a modicum of fame as a tourist attraction. When friends of their customers came to visit, they were brought in and told of the friendship and service they received from the grocery that remembered everyone's birthday!

"Not like those big stores that are starting to pop up," they would say and beam proudly.

Still, David was concerned what would happen when Henry went back to school in the fall. He was going into Grade 12 and needed time for his schoolwork and student council business. Mrs. Schmidt was good but not as quick or efficient as Henry. And David found that he didn't have the energy to carry the store himself—he missed Anna dearly.

Maybe it's time to sell. The bigger stores would take over eventually, he knew. Safeway was only three blocks away and they were already underselling him. They bought in much bigger quantities than he could. If it wasn't for the fact that he provided such good service, he would have lost a lot of business to them.

But, what would he do without the store? It was his whole life. But now that Anna was gone, things weren't the same anyway. Maybe…just maybe, he should sell.

Chapter Seven

A N HOUR AFTER her search began the phone book was still missing. She plunked herself onto a chair in the kitchen and quizzed herself about where she possibly could have left it. Had she thrown it out with the old newspapers and magazines last week? But the weight would have given it away. Well, if she couldn't find it, she'd just have to phone information to get the number for Simpsons-Sears.

As she sipped her coffee and flipped through the catalogue looking for shirts for Henry, it occurred to her that the phone book might be in his room. She had checked everywhere else.

Coffee in hand, Mary went down the hall to Henry's bedroom. And there it was, sitting on Henry's desk. *Who would Henry be phoning?* She sat at his desk and scanned the rows of names. Then she noticed a pencil wedged between the pages at the back of the book. Mary opened it to that spot and saw a light pencil mark under the words Trans-Canada Airlines and a circle around the airline's phone number.

She knew she hadn't made those markings—the only time she'd needed flight information was when Bill was coming home from Vancouver. Peter had given her all the information she needed. Those had to be Henry's marks…but why?

Then an idea came to her, and the more she thought about it, the heavier her heart grew. Henry still missed Jenny. He was going to try to find her. *Could he really be planning to do that?* He'd never mentioned a word or even hinted, and yet…

The bottom drawer of Henry's desk was slightly ajar and Mary's motherly instincts told her to open it. Inside was an envelope that looked like it contained a lot of money. Reluctantly she reached down for it and set it atop the desk. Worry for her son outweighed the guilt she felt for snooping through his things.

Mary opened the envelope. There were easily several hundred dollars in it, along with a folded sheet of paper, *a letter?* Maybe he'd already found Jenny and was planning to meet her somewhere. She took the page out and slowly opened it.

- *July 1960: find and visit Jenny right after Grade 12 graduation.*
- *Get a map of Ottawa.*
- *When I arrive, call Mr. Sarsky at his office and make an appointment to see him. Mackurcher and Co., 1854 Lyon St., Ottawa.*
- *Save up money for an airplane ticket. Cost?*
- *Call the YMCA to see if rooms are available. Save up money for a hotel room.*
- *Save up money to spend while there and to take Jenny out.*
- *Make a reservation and buy the plane ticket. Also make hotel reservations for July 2-6. Be there for our anniversary.*
- *Save money to buy Jenny a ring.*

Mary could barely read the last item. She reached for the tissue in her apron pocket and dabbed at her eyes.

She hadn't known Henry still felt so strongly about Jenny. How had he been able to keep it from her? Perhaps he knew it would bother her to know how he still felt. He wanted to carry the burden alone.

Mary wept. She felt helpless. What could she possibly do? Suddenly she realized she couldn't let Henry know she had discovered his secret. Their trust would be at risk.

She marvelled at his determination, though. He must have phoned TCA to see how much the flight would cost. *That* was why he had the phone book. Mary glanced at his plan again impressed by what he'd already considered and astonished once more that he'd kept it from her. All this time she thought he'd had forgotten about the girl. That he'd moved on. Mary shook her head and wiped her eyes again.

As she folded Henry's note, a teardrop fell onto the bottom corner of the page. She dabbed at it with the tissue, but it didn't go away. It would disappear once it dried, she thought. Mary carefully tucked Henry's plan back in its envelope the way she had found it.

As she reached down to put it back in the drawer, she saw several pamphlets about things to see in Ottawa along with a map of the city. Mary couldn't believe Henry's initiative. He must have visited the Chamber of Commerce or some tourist company to get that information.

She slid the drawer almost closed the way it had been. She knew Henry's keen attention to detail and didn't want him to suspect she'd been there. And so, rather than taking the phone book back with her to the kitchen, she quickly looked up the number for Simpsons-Sears, wrote it down and placed the phone book on Henry's desk as she'd found it.

In the kitchen she poured herself a fresh cup of coffee and sat at the kitchen table. It explained so much. *This* was why Henry wasn't going out with other girls. They phoned him all the time, and he always came up with one excuse or another. Perhaps he felt he was too busy, too. Working for Mr. Engelmann, keeping his studies up and being the class rep took a lot of time, but he still needed to go out. And what if Jenny was no longer interested by the time he finished Grade 12? He would have wasted so much of his life when he could have been enjoy-ing his high school years.

Mary's heart churned with anger at Jenny's parents, who were responsible for cutting off all communication between Henry and their daughter. Oh, she understood they were doing what they considered to be best for Jenny but she wondered if there was another reason.

As she sipped her coffee she realized that the only thing she could do was pray that it would turn out for the best.

Mary looked up at the crucifix hanging above the doorway. "Dear Jesus, I never realized how deeply my son still misses Jen-ny. How he's made a plan to help him cope, to give him hope and strength to appear strong. Keep him from further hurt. Protect him and…please help him fulfill his heart's desire. It is in Your hands, now."

CHAPTER EIGHT

D AVID ENGELMANN KNOCKED on the door just before five on Sunday. He had been looking forward to this visit all day. As Henry opened the door and welcomed him inside, Mr. Engelmann revelled in the heavenly aroma of pot roast, onions, carrots and potatoes. Also mingling in the air were the scent of baked bread and the unmistakable baked cinnamon smell of apple pie.

"You're in for a real treat tonight, Mr. Engelmann."

While the meal finished cooking, they all retired to the living room. They talked about the weather, Henry's schooling and Mary's desire to get a job once Henry finished school.

When Mary excused herself to tend to dinner, David decided to bring up the job with Coca-Cola. "Speaking of jobs, I have something that might be of interest to you, Bill."

"What's that, David?"

Mr. Engelmann looked at Henry and said, "Well, you know Doug, our Coca-Cola rep?"

"Yeah, sure," Henry replied, "he got our sign for us."

"Yes, yes," said Mr. Engelmann. "Well, he told me their service man has had a stroke and is paralyzed. He can't work there anymore." Mr. Engelmann looked at Bill. "They're looking for a new man for the job. I mentioned to Doug that you might be interested in the position. I think they pay well. They also have a company van and good benefits." He paused, allowing what he had said to register. "I told Doug I would mention it to you."

After a brief pause, Henry's dad asked, "What sort of things does the service man do?"

"He repairs fridges and compressors when they break down."

"I know I can fix the machines at the plant, but fridges are different."

"Doug said Coca-Cola would pay for three weeks of training for the right person. And, come to think of it, I remember the last service man telling me the company also has an ongoing training course during the winter when things slow down a bit."

Bill was quiet as he pondered the prospect.

Henry had to bite his tongue to keep from shouting at his dad to "go for it!" He figured it was best to stay out of it.

"Where do you apply for this position?" Bill asked, casting a glance David's way.

"Doug said he would drop off an application form at the store on Monday if you expressed an interest."

Henry's dad shifted in his chair. Things were moving a little too quickly. "Let me think on it for a bit."

"It's up to you, Bill. But I have to let Doug know one way or the other in a day or so."

The men jumped to their feet when Mary announced dinner was ready, the smells wafting through the house having whetted their appetites. Later, as Mary served Mr. Engelmann a steaming piece of apple pie, Henry noticed him undo the buttons of his vest.

"That was the best meal I have had in a long time, Mary," Mr. Engelmann said. "Anna was also a good cook, but the last few years she could not stand long and made small meals that took only a little time. If you don't mind, could I take a piece of that apple pie home with me? I'll have it with my bedtime cup of tea."

"Absolutely!" said Mary, clearly pleased that Mr. Engelmann had enjoyed himself.

After dinner, they headed into the living room to relax, digest and wash everything down with a cup of tea. No one said anything for a few moments.

Then Bill spoke. "You know, David, that job at Coca-Cola sounds interesting. Maybe I should apply or at least talk to this Doug fellow."

"Yes, yes. Well, I will phone Doug in the morning and let him know you are interested. I'll send the application home with Henry after work tomorrow night."

"Sounds good. Thank you for your trouble."

"No, no—no trouble at all. Glad I can be of some service."

They chatted a little while longer and Mary suggested they play cards, but Mr. Engelmann declined, saying he needed to head home and wanted to work off his dinner with a walk.

"Thank you so much, Mary and Bill, for having me over tonight. I appreciate it very—"

"You're most welcome and please come over again next Sunday," Mary said. "We'd love to have you. We appreciate all that you've done for Henry."

"Well!" said Mr. Engelmann, clearly delighted, "next Sunday would be fine, just as long as I don't become a nuisance!"

"I'm sure that will never happen. Oh, just a minute, your pie!" Mary rushed into the kitchen and returned a moment later with a wedge of apple pie in a brown bag. "Here, make sure you have it tonight, while it's real fresh."

"I promise—in an hour or two, I will be ready."

Mary hugged Mr. Engelmann, then he extended a hand to Bill and then Henry, wishing them all a good evening.

He took the stairs slowly and headed down the walk. Mary, Bill and Henry watched him trudge along.

"He seems so tired," said Bill. "I'm worried he won't be able to look after that busy store much longer."

"Yeah," Henry said, "And *I'm* worried about how he'll manage once I go back to school. He really misses Anna."

"Maybe I can help," said Mary. "Do you think he'd like me to work at the store?"

"Are you sure you want to?" Bill asked. "You really don't have to work, you know. We can afford for you to stay home."

"Oh, I know that, but I need to think of something to do, especially when Henry goes back to school. Besides, I think it would be interesting to work at the store. How do you feel about that, Henry?"

"I think it would be great! You'd be a big help to Mr. Engelmann and I wouldn't have to worry so much about him. I don't like to see him alone. I'll mention it to him tomorrow and see what he says."

MR. ENGELMANN CALLED Doug at eight o'clock the following morning and asked him to drop off the application form on his way by. About half an hour later, Doug walked in.

"'Morning, David," he said, as he approached the counter. "Here's that application form. But remember I told you that one of the executives was trying to get his brother-in-law the job?"

"Didn't you say that was against company policy?"

"That's true, but you know how it is. Things don't always go the way they should, you know."

"Well. As long as Bill gets fair treatment and an equal chance at the job, that's all I ask. He's a good man. Your company will be proud to have him."

Doug chuckled. "If he's anything like his son, we'd be lucky to have him. I'll do my best. Can't promise anything, though."

"And I can't promise that the Coca-Cola sign hanging out front won't be changed to Pepsi-Cola, either," Mr. Engelmann quipped.

Doug laughed. He knew Mr. Engelmann was teasing; there wasn't a manipulative bone in the man's body. But as Doug left the store, Mr. Engelmann's comment simmered. Engelmann's Grocery sold a *lot* of pop. Doug's local branch manager had even attended Anna's funeral and was very impressed by the huge gathering. It was obvious Mr. Engelmann had a lot of influence in the community. People in the neighbourhood tended to follow his judgment.

If the store sign *were* to change, it would have a substantial effect on their local sales. Doug knew Mr. Engelmann would never do what he had joked about, but his superiors didn't know Mr. Engelmann the way he did. He just might mention the sign when he gave them Bill's application.

A little spicy food for thought never hurt.

It took until Wednesday evening of that week for Mr. Engelmann and Henry to catch up with all the orders and get things back to normal. They couldn't believe how closing for just one day had affected the lives of so many people.

After receiving the application from Henry Monday night and much hemming and hawing, Henry's father had finally filled out the two-page application for Coca-Cola.

Mr. Engelmann and Henry were sitting on a couple of boxes in the back storage room when Henry remembered the filled-out form in his bag. "Here's that application form. Dad decided it wouldn't hurt to try."

"Oh, that is good to hear! I was hoping he would take this opportunity. Doug is here first thing tomorrow morning. I will make sure he gets it."

Henry gulped the last third of his bottle of Orange Crush.

"Oh yeah, we've been so busy I also forgot to ask if you'd be interested in having my mom work for you. She's looking for a job and is real organized and very quick."

"Yes, I remember her saying she was interested in finding a job. That would be very good. I need help, especially with you going back to school at the end of August. To have your mom here would be a blessing."

Chapter Nine

I CAN'T BELIEVE YOU finally took a day off, James," Jenny said as they finished a game of tennis at the country club.

"See? I *told* you I wasn't all work and business. We Hamiltons know how to have fun too."

Jenny rolled her eyes. "Well, I'm so happy you're enjoying the summer; it's half over and I can't think of the last time you spent a day in the sun. That was a great game you played."

"Once the Hamiltons learn a skill, Jen, they never forget it."

Jenny gazed at her handsome but vainglorious partner and shook her head. "James, I think you're given to vaunting,"

"What the hell does *that* mean?"

"You don't understand it because modesty never was one your virtues." Jenny smiled at his bewildered look. It was true. He was totally unaware of how conceited he was.

"Oh, if you mean I'm being boastful, well, I don't see it that way at all, Jen. It's self-assurance, confidence in your abilities—surely you can see that?"

Jenny laughed, bouncing the ball against the ground with her racket. "You're too incorrigible for words!"

"There you go again! Hitting me with library words I'm not

114

clear about. If I spent all my time reading books like you do I'd sound like a dictionary too," he sputtered, defending his ignorance, or perhaps more accurately, his lack of command of the English language. And then, finally thinking of something to support his position, he quickly added, "Some of us have to work and run a business and keep the world spinning, you know."

Jenny stopped and stared at James, shaking her head again slightly. He certainly was sharp financially, but socially—well, he had a lot of rough edges. "Honestly, James...well, anyway, I guess it's about the only way I can keep the upper hand with you. Come on, let's have some lunch."

Jenny took James' hand and led him to the clubhouse. She had to hide a smug little smile; she'd finally found another one of James' weaknesses—but this one was to her advantage.

Jenny's father, Ted Sarsky, had just returned from the branch office in Calgary. Sales there were down and the minute he'd walked in, Ted could tell that the manager there simply wasn't capable of fulfilling his role. And it had gotten worse from there. The key people under him were no better. Ted shook his head. If only he himself had been more on top of things he'd have known sooner that the branch lacked the staff to secure the contracts the company so desperately needed. Ted was going to have to make more trips, not only to the branch in Calgary but to all of them across Canada.

The company needed his leadership. Competition was getting keener and tighter; too many contracts were slipping through the cracks and the board was aware of it. But the energy and inner drive he used to have had been gone for awhile now. He was up half the night with these damn angel dreams and at work he was confronted again and again by the angels' fleeting appearance across the sky in the painting that hung in his office.

Ted glanced over at the painting now and was glad he'd thought to cover it with a large towel brought from home this morning. He couldn't bring himself to take it down—what would the angels do to him then? No, covering the painting was the best solution. But he was somewhat embarrassed when Elaine came in and saw it draped over the expensive painting like so much laundry.

"Oh my, Mr. Sarsky, why have you covered that beautiful painting? Surely you're not tiring of that peaceful landscape already?"

Ted struggled to think of something to say.

"The glare of the sun off the varnish was bothering my eyes yesterday, so I covered it."

Elaine looked at him, puzzled. How could that possibly be? He wasn't even in the office yesterday, or for the entirety of last week for that matter. He'd just got back from Calgary. Still, it was probably best not to question him; he'd had enough worries of late.

"I need your signature on these three letters, Mr. Sarsky," she said instead. "Could you please sign them right now? The mail is going out shortly and I want to have them ready."

Ted took the letters from Elaine and picked up a pen. He wished she wasn't there, watching him. To make matters worse, she leaned closer, waiting for him to finish. As slowly and deliberately as he could manage, he began to sign the letters.

Elaine noticed the trembling of his hand immediately.

SHE WAS BEGINNING to understand why her boss had started to confine himself more and more to the office instead of being out in the field where he should be. There was *something* about that painting Ted didn't want to see. She remembered how once before she'd come in to find him with his nose right up to it, talking to it. It was almost as if he were hypnotized by whatever he saw there. *She* couldn't see a darn thing.

She had picked up a brochure about alcoholism a long time ago and still remembered the symptoms: shaking, tremors, memory loss and hallucinations were listed under the more advanced stages of the disease. Oh, how she wished she could help him. He'd been such a strong, capable leader when he'd first started—and then last Christmas everything rocketed downhill. Elaine was certain whatever was bothering her boss had something to do with those letters, too. She picked up a clean sheet of paper and inserted it into her typewriter.

Those damn letters. She couldn't get them out of her mind.

As SOON AS Elaine left his office Ted rushed to the liquor cabinet and poured himself a drink. He was caught between a rock and a hard place. If he went out into the field like he knew he should, the staff would quickly become aware of his condition; when he'd been in Calgary, he could hardly wait for the end of each day so he could get back to his hotel room and have a drink. And yet if he didn't check up on the branches, he knew darn well the company's bottom line would continue to slide. He'd always expected his staff to be accountable and now he himself wasn't; he'd always maintained high standards, but his job performance and that of his staff were now well below the norm. It was just a matter of time before he was called on the carpet. It was all so stressful.

Ted returned to the cabinet for another drink. Maybe if he relaxed he'd see things more clearly. Heaven knew he had to do *something*, and quick. He pushed the empty glass away.

How could I have let things get so bad?

He went back to the desk and took out a stack of paper. He needed a plan. His attaché case was in the way of the paper and he shoved it aside but still there wasn't enough room. It was the spark that ignited a simmering mountain of emotion. What was left of his patience unraveled. Frustrated beyond belief, he let the volcano erupt and with a mighty swing sent the briefcase flying across the room, striking the heating register below the large window with a clang.

Outside, the peaceful Rideau Canal flowed on.

There was a gentle rap at the door and Elaine peeked in, "Is everything okay? I heard a crash."

"Oh. My briefcase just fell on the floor."

Elaine's eyes wandered to where Ted's briefcase lay next to

the heating vent, its lid dented and half broken off, a ream of paper strewn across the floor.

TED FELT RUSH after rush of embarrassment after Elaine closed the door. Never in all the days of his life had he lost control. *What's happening to me?* Rather than feeling relieved after letting off a little steam, he felt more deeply ashamed than ever. Every fibre of his being yearned for a drink and he would have gotten up for another if it weren't for the fact that he felt suddenly depleted. He was exhausted; totally emotionally drained. He fell back into the burgundy leather chair and in a matter of minutes sank into a reverie, a censored state in which he projected the responsibility for his wrongdoings more on his wife than on himself. After all, he'd just been following her orders…

It had all started out innocently enough: two young teenagers meeting and experiencing the usual "puppy love" syndrome. But from there it quickly spiralled out of control. Edith feared the worst about her daughter's relationship with the boy down the street and made every attempt to discourage and restrict their meetings—all to no avail. Their relationship was stronger than even she suspected.

Jenny's farewell to Henry the evening they'd left for Ottawa still haunted him. Edith had been utterly cruel, the way she'd stripped Jenny from Henry's arms, then decided to stop all communication between them. Jenny had trusted him to mail her letters to Henry, and still believed that he had. But it was all Edith's idea to destroy them. He'd just done as she'd told him. But to lie to his daughter time and time again when she asked if he was sure he'd mailed them was killing him.

Then there was that box of letters from Henry. Rather than allowing those tender written words to reach his daughter—who had prayed daily for a letter from her boyfriend—at Edith's insistence, he had ordered them destroyed. The image of those letters consumed by a blazing furnace fire cycled endlessly through his mind beside Jenny and Henry's sad farewell.

The only consolation was his decision not to destroy the two

Christmas letters with identical pewter angels tucked into each envelope. Perhaps it was a supernatural warning or simply an attempt at quelling some of the guilt of his previous actions. Or maybe he was asserting his fatherly role in some small way. Whatever it was, something had prevented him from sentencing those final angelic letters to the same fate as all the rest. For once he had stood his ground and defied his wife's wishes. In all this, he finally had done something to be proud of.

But whatever satisfaction he had felt died as Jenny's pregnancy became obvious. The circumstances surrounding the conception of her child and the pain of seeing his daughter's anguish at giving the infant up for adoption tore him apart.

How he wished things had been different and that Jenny had kept the child she'd given birth to. He would have been a grandfather, Edith a grandmother, and he knew Jenny would have been happier. Maybe they would even have grown closer as a family. But it hadn't happened; Edith didn't want to have anything to do with raising another child. That was her right, but ordering the destruction of the letters was *not* and the ensuing deceit shredded his innards. The guilt was so deep, he ached from the overwhelming power of it.

Try as he might to suppress it, the truth continued to surface as often as those angels flitted across the painting. It was like trying to hold a balloon under water. He had no stamina for this, and the increasing pressure of his work sparked alcohol binges, and *everything* was compounded by the stress of concealing his guilt and denying his problems.

At first, sleep was his only respite. It no longer provided a safe haven, though. Even now his mind was filled with a vision of the box full of Henry's letters being thrust into the fiery flames of the furnace that Ted feared the most. No longer was his secretary assigned to the messy deed; in his dreams he himself held the envelopes to the flames. He had to take full responsibility—even though his wife had initiated it. And the boy's letter to him, pleading that he take Henry's heartfelt words to Jenny, had been seared into his consciousness; there was no escape.

Every time Ted had the dream the box turned darker and blacker, making an inscription on it stand out in stark relief. And now he saw that it was his name, glaring at him like the inscription on a tombstone.

For him, the box itself no longer held merely the letters of a lovelost boy, no longer held simple sheets of paper, their words of love consumed by the furnace fire. It was his very *soul* he was thrusting into this self-inflicted hell. He could feel the scorching burn of his misdeeds. He alone would be judged, held accountable for his actions. The pain was so excruciating, so unbearable he could no longer bear up under it. He began to scream—and once again there was an urgent rap upon his door.

Elaine hurried in to see the company president in the throes of some sort of attack. She rushed to his side, trying to help him, to save him from whatever it was, but there was nothing she could do. Ted looked at her without seeing, his face filled with agonizing fear and dread and...bewilderment?

What the hell is going on?

Elaine and Ted stared at each another in confusion. Finally Elaine broke the standoff.

"Mr. Sarsky, I—I think you must've had some sort of nightmare."

It was the only conclusion his faithful secretary could come up with to justify why she was standing there with one hand on his shoulder and the other clutching a metal letter opener as if ready to defend her leader to the death.

Ted shook his head. Slowly it came to him that Elaine was right. "Elaine, I think I have to take the rest of the day off—and maybe the next few as well. I guess I've been working too hard. I need to think about what's best to do."

Silently each agreed that those few words were probably the most honest he had said to himself in a long, long time.

CHAPTER TEN

A FTER THE FIRST week or so while things got back to normal, Mr. Engelmann began to spend more and more time upstairs. Henry and Mrs. Schmidt more or less tended to the store. If Henry had a problem or question about ordering goods, he would go upstairs where he would often find Mr. Engelmann sitting in the chair Anna used to occupy by the south window, reading the Bible. Mr. Engelmann was grieving his beloved wife and the only way he could cope was to immerse himself in the Lord.

It began to make sense to Henry. Mr. Engelmann had shown so much strength when Anna died, only the odd time had he seen his mentor cry. At the start, Mr. Engelmann had been enthusiastic about Anna going to heaven and all, and being united with Jesus, but her absence was catching up with him now, the loss of her daily love and support. He needed time to heal, to adjust, to accept; he needed the Lord more than ever.

Henry and Mrs. Schmidt felt the loss in the store too, the grace and charm Mrs. Engelmann brought into the store, her easy way with customers, her wise words. And with Mr. Engelmann spending so much time alone upstairs it seemed like the heart of the store was gone.

It was hard to move forward for all of them—day in and day out people came in saying how much they missed Anna, constant reminders that Mrs. Engelmann was gone. And without Mr. Engelmann there to talk with and comfort their friends and neighbours, Henry felt, for the first time in the years he'd worked for the Engelmanns, that sadness filled the store.

One afternoon when Mrs. Schmidt was in and the store wasn't too busy, Henry went upstairs to find Mr. Engelmann sitting in the tattered old armchair, the bright light streaming through the window onto his face. His Bible lay open on his lap and he had dozed off. Henry went into the kitchen and brought back a chair, set it beside his beloved teacher and sat down to wait. He wanted to reach over and touch Mr. Engelmann's hand to comfort him but was reluctant to wake him. Sleep was good for him, Henry thought, an escape from the sadness in his heart. Many nights Henry too couldn't wait for sleep to come, his mind and thoughts so filled with Jenny.

The sun had moved and its rays were beginning to inch their way across Henry's face now too. The warmth was soothing, healing. In a way it was kind of like sitting out back on the old grey crates, basking in the sun and letting it's hot light dry the many tears shared as a result of the talks they had.

Henry had received so much help from Mr. Engelmann and he wished he could help him now. Henry knew when he hurt, his teacher hurt, and so it was the other way around as well. It was then that Mr. Engelmann's own words came to mind: *When all the words or knowledge in the world don't help in times of trouble and grief, what is it that most—if not all—of us do?* And so Henry prayed for Mr. Engelmann, that Jesus would fill his beloved friend with peace. It was a selfish prayer; Henry knew praying was the only way he could feel peace himself. As he prayed in the silence of the sun-filled room, Henry drifted into a peaceful slumber himself.

PERHAPS IT WAS the coolness that both men felt; the sun had long since gone on its journey into the western sky and no longer warmed the air. But perhaps more than that it was a growing awareness of each other's presence that caused them both to stir.

Mr. Engelmann woke first and did what Henry had wanted to do earlier; he reached out a hand and placed it upon his beloved adopted son's.

Henry woke, thinking that if he shared how much the customers missed Mr. Engelmann it might help him to get going again. "You know, Mr. Engelmann, the customers sure miss you. They already miss Mrs. Engelmann terribly, and your absence from the store only makes their loss feel greater."

"Yes, yes, I am aware of that Henry. It seems I just don't want my mind to be filled with anything else but my Anna. She was the love of my life, along with the Lord. It is so hard for me to let go and allow the thoughts of daily living to steal away even one of the precious memories I have of her."

"But she's still here in spirit, isn't she?"

"Yes, of course. I feel her with me all the time but I miss seeing her in the store and coming up to see her at the end of the day."

"I understand, Mr. Engelmann, how alone you must feel."

Mr. Engelmann nodded and went on. "As ill as she was, she would still smile and greet me with a kiss. And occasionally, Henry, when her illness gave her a brief respite, she would have dinner prepared and waiting, with soft music and only a candle to illuminate our meal. She was always young at heart and no amount of pain or suffering could snuff out her romantic spirit."

Geez, it must be so hard for Mr. Engelmann to come up to an empty apartment and eat alone.

Henry placed his other hand on top of Mr. Engelmann's trying to let him know how sorry he was, how much he cared. Mr. Engelmann squeezed Henry's hand, then slid his own from underneath it to wipe the tear sliding down his cheek.

He nodded several times before he spoke. *"Ich vermisse meine Anna, Heinrich.* I miss her deeply."

Henry nodded, feeling the older man's sorrow but didn't know what more words to say; he could only hope that simply being here helped.

The silence was broken by Mrs. Schmidt softly calling his name. Henry checked his watch. 6:05. *Geez, I better close up the store!* "I have to go close up, Mr. Engelmann. Do you want me to come back up after?"

"No, that's fine. Just turn out the lights and lock the store. Thank you for coming up. I will see you tomorrow."

Henry was reluctant to leave. He so wished he could do something to help. But Henry understood loss. *You don't get over it, ever. It just has to weave into your heart somehow… enough so that you can go on.*

The next day and the next, Henry came up again. Each time Mr. Engelmann shared a little more about Anna and his loss. Henry had heard much of it on the day Anna died when they had gone out back and Mr. Engelmann shared the story of their courtship and marriage. But he didn't mind. He just let Mr. Engelmann talk and he listened, much the way his mentor did when Henry was hurting. It had always helped to be heard and Henry hoped it would help Mr. Engelmann now too.

And then came a day when Henry arrived at work to hear music playing in the store. It wasn't his favourite, it was the classical kind Mr. Engelmann and Anna liked to listen to. But when Henry saw his teacher behind the counter ready for whatever the day would bring, Henry liked that music more than ever before.

THE FOLLOWING TUESDAY, Henry took the day off to visit with Gary and his friend Jane. Henry planned to pick them up at the Salvation Army and together the three of them were going out for dinner and a movie. There was a new restaurant called A&W they were dying to try out.

Henry was early; he wanted to know what his friends did at

the Salvation Army. Gary and Jane and several other workers were just finishing serving meals to men of all ages. Some wore old, ill-fitting clothes and yet many were well dressed. Some looked young and capable; Henry wondered what on earth they were doing there when they seemed perfectly able of working and fending for themselves. And his friends were serving them yet! Still, the Salvation Army was there for those who needed it.

Gary had told him that at the end of the month when most of the men received their government support cheques the kitchen slowed right down for several days as many of them would buy liquor and go on a three or four day drinking binge. Then, when their money ran out, they'd return for another handout. Henry hadn't understood it then and now, seeing how capable some of them appeared, he wondered if he could stand there with an open heart and serve them as Gary did.

Henry turned his gaze to Jane. He'd liked her from the first moment they'd met. She was a gracious, gentle girl with clear hazel eyes much like Mr. Engelmann's, with that same kindly shine that seemed never to go out. Her light brown hair was mostly hidden beneath the kerchief she donned most days. There was no sign of any cosmetic on her face. She always wore long-sleeved blouses or sweaters and heavy stockings so that as little of her skin as possible was revealed. But despite her modesty in dress, Jane was a very beautiful girl with a smile that instantly put others at ease.

All the workers wore small wooden crosses around their necks. They were there to serve Jesus. Once again Henry wondered if he could do it, devote his life like that. He watched Gary and Jane dish out meals to the last of the men in the line. They looked good together and Henry thought they would make a great husband and wife team. And yet, according to Gary, they were each married to the Lord and seemed content just sharing a deep friendship.

Gary was talking to one of his co-workers as he took off his apron. The other worker seemed to be motioning him and

Jane to go ahead and leave. Gary patted the man's shoulder and came to greet Henry.

"Hi Hank," Gary said, beaming and giving Henry their special handshake. "Jane'll be along in a minute. So, how are you doing?"

"Pretty good. Things are starting to get back to normal at the store but it's not the same without Mrs. Engelmann."

"For sure, it wouldn't be, Hank. She was the kindest person I ever knew. People loved her—and Mr. Engelmann too, of course—but there was just something special about her that gave the store heart. Know what I mean?"

"Perfectly, Gary, I feel exactly the same…Oh, hi, Jane."

Jane made her way towards them, a radiant smile on her face. She pulled the kerchief from atop her head, allowing her hair to drop and hang loosely on her shoulders in soft curls. She carried a small Bible in her other hand.

"I don't know about you two, but I sure could go for one of those frosty root beers I keep hearing about," she said.

"Yeah, me too—let's go," Henry agreed.

A&W WAS CROWDED when they got there but after a short wait they managed to get a spot at a picnic table out front.

"Geez, some place, huh?" Henry said as the three gazed around and took it all in.

"Just look at that line-up of cars! They must be making a killing here," Henry said, his business instincts buzzing.

"I can hardly wait to try one of their apple pies," Jane chimed in. "And their onion rings are supposed to be really good, too."

"You know, we're lucky we got this table, we'd have waited forever in the car," Gary said.

"Having people drive up and eat their meals in the car means they can get them through faster and serve more people; must be how they keep the prices so low," Henry observed. "In fact," he said, checking his wallet, "dinner's on me."

They got their orders and Henry couldn't wait to dig in. That's when he noticed Jane and Gary had joined hands and were each holding one out towards him. *Geez, they're going to pray—here?* Henry sort of glanced to the side to see if anyone in the line-up was watching, then took their hands in his.

Gary and Jane bowed their heads and Gary prayed, "Bless, oh Lord, these thy gifts which we are about to receive through Your goodness and bounty."

"Amen," Jane said.

Henry mouthed the word, a red-hot flush heating his cheeks.

"Thanks for treating us, Henry; it looks great! Let's dig in," said Gary as he unwrapped his double-patty Papa Burger and took a huge bite. The others did the same.

Afterwards, they took in a great movie at the Broadway The-atre. *Ben-Hur*, it was called. All three thought it was an amazing film. It had been three years since Henry had had such an enjoyable outing.

WHEN HENRY CAME in to work the next day he could tell right away his boss was nearly his old self again, at least on the outside. Mr. Engelmann's eyes twinkled as he asked about the movie night.

"It was *such* a great movie, Mr. Engelmann—I heard it was the most expensive movie ever made, and did it ever pay off! That Charlton Heston can really act—I'll bet he gets an Academy Award—and there's this chariot race…you know, I'd really like to see it again. Why don't you come with me?"

"That would be a real treat, Henry; I haven't been to a movie or out to the theatre in years. Anna and I used to go all the time when we first came to Canada, but the demands of the store made going out an expense we couldn't often afford, and then Anna got so ill…" his words trailed off for a moment, then he quickly brought himself back to the here and now. "I'd love to see the movie with you, Henry, just name the day."

When Mrs. Schmidt got in around ten, Mr. Engelmann surprised him by suggesting they go out back and have a soda pop. "It's a beautiful day, we should enjoy it a bit."

Henry opened two Dr. Peppers and carried them outside,

sitting in his usual spot to wait for his mentor. Shortly after, Mr. Engelmann joined him and the two settled in to talk.

After Henry had enthused a little more about *Ben-Hur,* the topic shifted to his friends, Gary and Jane, and their work at the Salvation Army. He told his teacher what he'd observed there; how many of the men were young and seemed quite capable of working. It didn't seem right to Henry that they could use their social aid cheques to buy booze and go on binges, and then go there to be fed. It would really bother him to serve them if he knew they were doing that. *How could Gary and Jane serve them every day and not expect more from them?*

"If it were me, I'd tell them to get out there and get a job like the rest of us!" Henry finally exclaimed.

"Yes, yes, it seems like they are taking advantage of young Gary and Jane, using them, no?"

"Yeah, that's it *exactly*, Mr. Engelmann," Henry said, his voice rising in indignation. "I don't see how catering to those young men helps them at all. What good deed are my friends doing?"

"They are serving their Lord by serving His children and do-ing so unconditionally and lovingly, Henry."

Henry turned to his mentor, puzzled.

"They are there to serve them, Henry, not to judge them. Perhaps it is their hope and prayer that these men come to Christ. Someday they may go out and find work, but it is not for your friends to place any judgment or expectation on those they serve. If they did, they would strip them of the little pride and self-respect they have left. Many would stop coming and perhaps get into even greater trouble. These men need to be loved—just as they are. Remember, Henry, flowers grow so beautifully only because they are exposed to lots of sunshine and nourishment," Mr. Engelmann winked.

But it immediately dawned on Henry that this was exactly how Mr. Engelmann accepted him. He'd always felt free to ex-pose his faults and weaknesses and never had to be defensive. In Mr. Engelmann's care and guidance he never felt the shadow of judgement or blame.

"It's always easy to judge, Henry," Mr. Engelmann went on. "What we see on the outside cannot reveal the secrets of a man's soul. What is the saying, 'Never judge a book by its cover'? The story inside may be completely different from what we expect. Each of those men has a story, something that brought him to this point in his life. If you were to walk in the shoes of one of those men for a day, if you had access to his past, to his story, I'm sure you would get down on your knees and thank the good Lord that you've had a good upbringing and a secure, loving home to go to each night.

"It is for the Lord to judge, he sees into the hearts of each of us." Mr. Engelmann took a sip of his drink and shifted on his seat, settling more comfortably into the warped slats of the crate. Henry liked it when he did that. It was a sign that his mentor was in no hurry to get up and go back to work.

"I remember something my father shared with me one time after he heard me unkindly criticize someone else. I will never forget. He asked me to point my forefinger at him as if to make some judgment. When I did, he asked me what my other three fingers were doing."

Henry looked down at his hand and pointed his finger, only to quickly realize the other three fingers pointed back at himself. Mr. Engelmann didn't need to say anything more. Henry simply nodded and hung his head. He recalled the scripture he'd read just the other day: "Judge not lest ye be judged."

They sat for a bit with their faces tilted slightly toward the sky, taking in the warmth of the sun, then another thing that had puzzled him from time to time entered Henry's mind. It had bothered him last night at A&W.

"Why are we afraid to talk about God or pray in public, Mr. Engelmann? Last night I'm ashamed to say I was very embarrassed when Gary, Jane and I held hands and prayed before we ate."

Mr. Engelmann nodded, "Yes yes. *Es ist traurig, aber wahr.* Sad but true, Henry. I have witnessed it many times in my life. Merely mention the good Lord in a conversation and suddenly there's discomfort in the air, as if it's not acceptable to discuss God or exhibit our love for Him."

Henry nodded in agreement.

"To pray to God and show our love for Him is both a private and public matter. Unfortunately for many of us, we do only the former and sometimes not even that. First, the Lord asks us to acknowledge Him and give witness of our faith before men. Many times I have told you we need strong people in this world, strong people who are rooted firmly in the Lord's Word. They stand out like a beacon and have tremendous influence over others. Their faith is contagious. Perhaps at the restaurant last evening others witnessed your boldness and were reminded of their Lord. It may have even brought someone back to Him. We will never know what our actions of faith do for others and so we must not be afraid to show our commitment to the Lord. He should be forever in our hearts and on our lips, as much as the air we breath. It is the way we work with Him for the salvation of the world."

Mr. Engelmann smiled at Henry. "If I were to give you a gift of $50 out of the goodness of my heart, I could just see you jumping up and down thanking me. You would readily tell others of my generosity and how good and kind I am, no?"

"Well, yeah—for sure, Mr. Engelmann."

"Henry, look around at all creation. The heavens and everything in the earth…all its beauty! Everything in the world, including you, was created by the Father. Surely this is worth more than a $50 bill? Is it not right that we should give thanks to Him for everything continuously? *Nothing* is ours! It all belongs to Him and yet we so take it for granted or don't even acknowledge it; we think the world is ours and many work so hard to possess it—even hoard at times."

Mr. Engelmann's eyes had not left Henry's but now his gaze carried a sternness. "When we stand before Him naked, all the possessions and treasures we have accumulated in our lives don't mean a thing unless used for His service. It is how we acknowledge Him and His children He will consider and reward.

How kind and loving were we? Did we give our brothers and sisters food and drink? Did we share our wealth? Did we forgive and, like our friends Gary and Jane, did we acknowledge Him and thank Him for the limitless bounty He has given us?"

Henry stared at his teacher, taking his words to heart in all seriousness.

"Henry, if you do not acknowledge your Lord, when you show up at the pearly gates He too may say to you, "I do not know you.""

Henry was speechless; his mentor spoke with such truth and clarity. It always cut right to his heart.

As they got up to go back to work, Henry looked down at his hand and again pointed his finger. Just as Mr. Engelmann had never forgotten his father's lesson, Henry too, would always remember.

He'd be a little more careful in judging others in the future.

CHAPTER ELEVEN

THE NEXT FEW weeks whizzed by as Henry busied himself getting ready for school and keeping up with the ordering, maintenance, accounting, government forms, stocking and restocking associated with the business. Mr. Engelmann and Henry had to put in a lot of extra hours every day.

Henry went out with Gary twice more before school started. It was all they could work into their busy schedules. Gary and Jane were not only working a lot at the Salvation Army but during the evening they visited care homes and hospitals as well. Henry was amazed at his friends' commitment to serve the poor and comfort the sick and shut-ins.

Eddy often came into the store to chat and buy smokes until he got a job at Simpsons-Sears working in the warehouse. His uncle was trying to get him a job at a brokerage firm so he was filling in time until then. Henry and Eddy hung out a few times and were becoming better friends as well.

For the last four Sundays, Mr. Engelmann had had dinner with Henry and his family. With each visit he was more relaxed and soon it felt like he'd always been coming for dinner on Sundays. Henry liked having him there, being part of his family.

Henry noticed that his father started treating and speaking to him more like Mr. Engelmann did. When Henry walked into the living room with something to say, his dad would put the newspaper down and give him his undivided attention. Henry liked this change a lot, and it made him realize again how important it was to be a good role model, or better yet, to live a life based on good values. Without even meaning to, Mr. Engelmann's choice to live that way had affected Henry's entire world.

The same week Henry started school, his mom started working for Mr. Engelmann. She liked working at the store and soon became friendly with most of the customers. When they learned she was Henry's mother they went on and on about what a good boy he was and how well she had raised him. Henry wasn't surprised to find her favourite part of working there was cleaning, dusting and washing down the shelves—the place had never been so clean. With Mr. Engelmann's permission, she also tidied up his living quarters and did some of the laundry and ironing. Henry immediately noticed a change for the better. All at once, Mr. Engelmann no longer resembled an unmade bed.

About a month after Mr. Engelmann had passed along Bill's application to work for Coca-Cola, Henry's father received a call for an interview, scheduled for the following Saturday morning. In the days leading up to it, Henry was glad to see his mother helping his dad prepare by asking him questions and being a sounding board for ways Bill might answer. They didn't know their son was sitting on the floor just inside his door, listening to them. He liked hearing his parents work together.

At the store on Saturday, Henry and his mother could barely concentrate on what they were doing. It was already noon and they hadn't heard from Bill yet—Henry figured he and his mom were more anxious about the interview than his dad had been. Shortly after one o'clock. Bill walked in. Mary was just finishing with a customer but could hardly focus, her eyes on her husband. Henry also stared at him, and like his mom, tried to read from his dad's face whether or not he'd gotten the job. When Mr. Engelmann came in from the storage room, he stopped and stared at Bill, too. The customer Mary was serving looked from one to the other in total confusion. It was as if they'd all been frozen.

Finally Mary burst out, "Well? Did you get it? Don't keep us in suspense!"

His father struggled to put a sad look on his face as if he thought to tease them with bad news, waited for one of them to respond, then couldn't help but let a huge grin split his face.

"I got the job!" When their cheers subsided, he added, "They're sending me to Toronto for three weeks of training."

"When do you start?" Henry asked.

"I'll give my two weeks' notice at the plant on Monday and when I'm finished, they'll send me to Ontario—by plane, even—and they'll pay for all the expenses while I'm there."

Henry had never seen his dad so excited.

"I'll have another week of training when I get back, too; I'll be driving a company van that I can bring home at night."

"Oh, Bill, that's wonderful," Mary said. "I'm so happy for you!"

Mr. Engelmann shook Bill's hand. "I knew they had enough sense to pick the right man."

Hesitating for only a moment, Henry went over to his dad and gave him a big hug. "That's great news, Dad."

"And that's not all. Can you believe it? My starting pay is five hundred dollars more than I make right now, and after my six-month probationary period is over, I even get ten shares in the company!"

"Wow!" Henry said.

"Oh my, that's wonderful," his mother said again.

Mr. Engelmann just smiled.

"Thanks, David, for helping me get the job," Bill shook Mr. Engelmann's hand again.

"*Pfft.* I had nothing to do with it. They just knew you were the best man for the job."

"Maybe so, but without your help I might never have even gotten the interview."

"How is that?" Mr. Engelmann wanted to know.

"After the interview, Doug told me you were a mighty persuasive man. I didn't quite understand what he meant, but I know he thinks very highly of you."

Mr. Engelmann smiled. "You got the job, that's the main thing. Tomorrow when I come for supper—oh my, here I am inviting myself even before I have been asked. How rude of—"

"Of course you're coming for supper!" Henry's mom said, rushing to Mr. Engelmann and putting her arms around him. "You're one of the family, aren't you?"

"Yes, yes, of course I am, thank you." After catching his breath Mr. Engelmann added, "Anna and I received a bottle of wine a long time ago and were saving it for a special occasion. Unfortunately, we never had the opportunity to open it and I know Anna would want me to celebrate with you. Tomorrow when I come, I will bring it, and we will toast Bill's new position at the Coca-Cola Company!"

So anxious had they been to hear from Henry's father that they'd all but forgotten Mrs. Peters, who'd been waiting at the counter all this time. Mary turned towards Mrs. Peters, ready to apologize, but Mrs. Peters had gotten so caught up in it all, she took Henry's father's hand and congratulated him as well.

Henry knew his mom was excited for his dad because she had trouble concentrating on her work after that. He wished she had given his dad a big hug, though, but then thought perhaps he was being too sensitive.

That night at suppertime, his father gave them all the details of the interview and the questions they had asked.

"There was only one I wasn't sure how to answer," he said.

"What was that?" Henry and his mother asked almost in unison.

He looked at them very seriously. "The one where they asked if I wanted a paid holiday in Hawaii or Paris." He laughed.

Henry's mom gave his dad's shoulder a smack and rolled her eyes. "Oh, Bill!"

It was good to see his parents kid around with each other.

The following Monday, Bill gave his notice at the plant. Management offered him a raise equal to what he'd been offered by Coca-Cola, but he declined. He'd needed a change for a long time now and was looking forward to the new challenge.

THE FIRST THREE weeks of school passed quickly. As student council activities ramped up, Henry had meetings with the council, the teacher advisor assigned to the group, the principal and the vice-principal. He spoke at a student assembly and talked with students who expressed concerns or ideas about the school. It all started to interfere with his job and Henry began to feel the pressure of trying to do too many things.

As Saturday neared and his dad prepared to fly to Toronto, it occurred to Henry that Jenny wasn't too far from there. He considered asking his dad to call Mr. Sarsky to see if he could get Jenny's address or phone number, but thought better of it. His dad had lots to worry about without adding Henry's agenda. Besides, Henry had a feeling he needed to be there in person.

On Sunday night just as Henry, his mother and Mr. Engelmann were finishing dinner, the phone rang. Henry's mother jumped up.

"That'll be Bill. He said he'd try to call. Hello? … Everything's fine, Bill. How are you doing? … Yes. Was it as good as my cooking?" Mary looked over to Mr. Engelmann and Henry and winked. Their back-and-forth carried on for another few moments. From what Henry could make out, his dad was talking about busy streets, the weather and the restaurants he'd been to. Then his mother told him what was going on at the store, that Mr. Engelmann had hired a new delivery person because Henry was getting too busy in the evenings.

"Well, I'd better go," his mother said, "this is probably costing a fortune—oh, the company's paying for this call, too!" She laughed into the phone. Then she said something Henry liked a lot. "I miss you, too, Bill. Yes, I love you, too. Yes, he's right here. Here, Henry."

Henry jumped up and grabbed the phone.

"Hey, Dad, how's it going? What's it like in the big city? … Oh yeah? … Oh yeah? … And how was the airplane ride? Wow! So, when do you start training? That's good. Oh, he's fine." Henry turned to Mr. Engelmann and smiled.

"Yeah, okay, I will. Sure, I'll look after things. Don't worry. Take care, Dad. Talk to you next Sunday. Okay, 'bye."

CHAPTER TWELVE

"OH, JENNY, I wish I were like you!" Tammy said as the two girls walked down the school hall after the last bell. "You're on student council again, you're popular, you're pretty... no, you're *beautiful*—the guys fall all over you."

Jenny looked at her friend and smiled. "Really, Tammy, I think you're exaggerating just a bit! I do love being secretary on the student council, but you can run to be on it too—I sure don't do it alone. And I see how the boys look at you too!"

"But look how attractive you are—slim, tall, a chest that most of us girls would die for—you've got it all, Jen. Bubbly, great personality, I could go on and on."

"Please, Tammy..." A bit overwhelmed and rather embarrassed by her friend's praise, Jenny faltered.

"Girls should hate you and be so jealous, yet everyone likes and wants to be your friend. You just take everyone as they are...I've never heard you say anything mean or put anyone down."

"But, Tammy, I do speak my mind when there's something or someone I disagree with."

"You do it in such a nice way, though! You might disagree but you never make anyone feel bad when you do. We all just flock around you and look up to you. I'm so glad you're my friend."

"Oh, Tammy, I appreciate what you're saying but, really, we are who we are and I don't think I'm any better than anyone else. Maybe it's because I'm 18, a year older than most of the rest of our grade, maybe that's what appeals to some of the boys. But really, I'm not comfortable with all the attention; I'm only interested in James."

"What about that other guy, that artist boy you always talked about at the pajama parties? Wasn't he the one you sent that angel ornament to?"

"Boy, you sure have a good memory, Tammy—that was ages ago. You're right, I did write him—lots, in fact—but he never wrote back, not even once. I'm sure he dumped me for someone else, someone he could see every day."

"Aw, Jen, I doubt it. There must be some other reason."

"Well, that's what I keep telling myself. But I don't know. Besides, I'm getting to like James more all the time so I guess I'm moving on now too. I know my parents will be a lot happier if I do. For awhile there my dad was really upset and worried that I kept writing Henry even though he never wrote back."

"Henry! *That's* his name. He must have been pretty special for you to fall so head over heels for him. You could have any guy here, Jen, and yet you wanted to be true to him."

"Well, there was this, this special *connection* between us. Almost…magical." Just the thought of the moment she'd first looked into Henry's eyes filled her heart with indescribable warmth.

As they left the school, Tammy suddenly stopped and turned to her best friend. "There's something I want to tell you, Jenny—" but before Tammy could share what was on her mind several other girls burst through the door behind them.

"Hey, Tammy, Jenny," said their friend Janice. "We're going to Pete's Soda Shop for a coke. They've got Elvis' "Big Hunk O' Love" in the jukebox and I've gotta hear it. I just can't sit still when I hear his music."

Tammy looked at Jenny, "Sure, let's go. I'll talk to you about it some other time. That Elvis is pretty dreamy; I still can't believe they drafted him."

Jenny grabbed hold of her friend's hand and swiftly stepped down the stairs to the sidewalk, her buoyant persona almost floating ahead like an angel.

Jenny parked the car in the garage and went into the house through the kitchen. No one was in the there. Then she heard her parents arguing in the living room.

"You're drinking too much, Ted. At least three before dinner and now you're at it again!"

"Oh, relax. It's not that much and there's barely any alcohol in here, most of it's mix."

"Hardly. More like it's the other way around."

The living room fell silent. Jenny suspected her father was drinking too much as well. Sometimes when she greeted him at the door after work, he staggered taking his coat off and the smell of liquor was very evident.

"It's those damn letters. I'm sure I see them flying around the office."

"What on *earth* are you talking about. Those letters were destroyed over two years ago, Ted. Surely, you're still not on that guilt trip?"

Jenny wondered what they were talking about. Must be something to do with correspondence at her dad's office. She didn't want her parents to know she'd heard them arguing and so she quietly stepped back to the kitchen door, opened it, then slammed it shut.

"Hi Mom, I'm home!" she hollered loud enough to be heard in the living room. Jenny hurried into the living room, hoping they'd stop fighting now that they knew she was home. Her mother was sitting in an armchair near the fireplace, her father was standing, his elbow resting on the fireplace mantel, swirling the ice around in the drink her mother had been complaining about.

"I wish you'd phone when you're going to be late for dinner."

"Sorry, Mom, Tammy and I went to the Soda Shop after school and we were listening to some of the latest hits. I had fries and a coke so I'm not very hungry. Think I'll take a shower. I'll maybe make myself a sandwich in a bit, so don't worry about me."

"Your father and I had salad and chicken casserole. I left it in the oven. It should still be warm if you'd like that."

"Sure, sounds great, Mom." Jenny turned to her father and made her way to his side. "Hi Dad." She kissed him on the cheek. "You're home early."

"I had a meeting on the south side earlier this afternoon. Rather than go back to the office I thought I'd come home early so we could all have dinner together for a change—"

"And here I wasn't home…sorry, Dad."

"'S'okay, honey, I was just teasing." Ted winked at his daughter and took a sip of his drink. "How's school going?"

"Great. Although I may have to drop out of drama club, things are so busy with student council."

"Now, that would be a real shame, honey. You did such a wonderful job last year as Dorothy in *The Wizard of Oz*. I was so proud of you."

"That was two years ago, Ted, not last year," Jenny's mom's correction was sharp. "But Dad's right, Jenny. You're a natural actress—maybe it would be better to bow out of cheerleading or the library club until after Christmas."

"That might be an idea. I'll think it over and see how things go in the next week or so."

As Jenny turned to leave, Edith said, "Oh, by the way, James phoned. Sound like he wants to take you for dinner on Saturday evening."

"This isn't getting serious, is it? You're seeing quite a bit of that young man," Ted winked at his daughter.

"Hardly," Jenny muttered under her breath. Aloud she said, "I'll be down later for some of that casserole. Thanks, Mom."

TED WATCHED HIS daughter leave the room and head for the stairs leading up to the second level. The light coming in the windows of their grand foyer lit Jenny's wheat-coloured hair, making it spark with flashes of gold. She was growing more beautiful all the time. Ted just hoped she felt as beautiful inside.

Jenny did a good job camouflaging her feelings, he thought. She seemed buoyant and bubbly to most, but Ted could tell even in the conversation they'd just had, that the sparkle that came from deep within, that gave life to everything Jenny did, just wasn't there. It'd been gone since they'd moved here. Then the baby...and those letters. Destroying those damn letters was the biggest mistake of their lives.

Ted lifted the glass to his mouth, savouring the last swallow before making his way to the liquor cabinet in the dining room. He quietly poured himself another, hoping Edith wouldn't hear him and took it into the kitchen to drink. He stood at the patio doors and looked out on the beautiful grounds. A small brown box of gardening tools on the patio table reminded him of the box of Henry's letters. God, would they never stop haunting him! Awake or asleep, it seemed there was no escape from his deeds; his conscience plagued him incessantly.

Ted shook his head. *What were we thinking? How could we have done such a foolish, terrible thing.* The alcohol was starting to get to him. He took another gulp. He couldn't obliterate his conscience fast enough. He swallowed the rest of his drink.

And that boy, James, I don't know about him. Edith likes him, but I wouldn't want him in my company. Oh, he's a very ambitious young man—maybe too ambitious. Not that ambition is all bad. I just know I'd have to watch my back with him. But at least Jenny's going out with someone; *at least she's going out, not locking herself in her room.*

Ted snorted as he thought about how Edith had been so worried about Henry, wanting to protect Jenny from him. *She'd better be more concerned about James.*

He drained the last of the drink. The maple tree near the patio had already begun to lose its leaves. As he looked closer, he saw white and pink objects dangling from each of the tree's branches. Ted looked again, then blinked. The leaves had been replaced by letters! And zooming down from the top of the tree were two pewter-coloured angels heading right for him.

As JENNY SAT under her mom's big blow dryer, curlers in her hair, a trial run for when James took her out to dinner. If he didn't cancel again. She wondered what it was Tammy had been about to tell her. Oh, well, they'd talk tomorrow.

Her thoughts drifted to the argument her parents had had. Destroying letters didn't sound good; something about the finality of it was troublesome. Jenny hoped her father hadn't done something wrong at work. She wondered if these letters had something to do with the fact that he was drinking so much.

Under the hum of the dryer, Jenny closed her eyes. "Dear guardian angel," she whispered. "Please help Daddy with his drinking and make sure he doesn't destroy those letters he was talking about. I don't want him to get into trouble."

When her hair was set, she walked over to the window and stared outside. The sun was sinking and off at the edge the window Jenny could just make out the star of the east. She felt the warmth of Henry's love surround her. Softly she murmured:

> *Angel of God, my guardian dear,*
> *to whom His love commits me here;*
> *ever this day be at my side*
> *—and Henry's...and Mom and Daddy's—*
> *to light and guard, to rule and guide.*
> *And...James too.*
> *Amen.*

CHAPTER THIRTEEN

"WHEW!" ELAINE EXCLAIMED, sliding the last folder into its proper place. The filing always took longer than anticipated and now that it was done, she looked forward to getting back to the novel she'd started the other day. Filing complete and Mr. Sarsky away at a two-day conference, there'd be nothing coming her way for the next few hours.

Elaine strongly identified with the heroine of the story she was reading—a thirty-two-year-old woman who takes over her father's company, much to the chagrin of company insiders—and could hardly wait to finish. Elaine felt her own talents and abilities far exceeded the job she currently held. She was already doing most of the work Mr. Sarsky should've been doing, and yet receiving a salary that was only a fraction of his—and no recognition other than the occasional thank you he offered. Elaine knew she possessed both the attributes and leadership to get the company back on track and was frustrated with the "ol' boys' club" for not recognizing her talents.

Elaine had tried to help Mr. Sarsky confront his drinking problem. She'd put an empty bottle of whiskey on his desk at night, left his liquor cabinet open and set a half-full glass of whiskey on a side table in the office to alert him that others might notice his drinking and that he should stop, at least at work. Unfortunately, the tactics had not deterred him at all; in fact, his drinking had actually *increased*, perhaps his way of trying to overcome the fear of being found out.

As Elaine settled into her novel, the phone rang. The blinking extension told it was Alan Peakan, chairman of the board.

"Good morning, Mr. Peakan. If you're hoping to speak with Mr. Sarsky, he's away at a conference. He'll be back tomorrow morning, however."

"Actually, Miss McIntyre, it's you I wish to speak to—can we speak in confidence?"

"Certainly, I'm the only one in the office at the moment."

"I've given considerable thought as to whether I should call you or not. But my fondness for Mr. Sarsky and concern for him made the decision for me. This is something of a delicate nature, you understand."

He paused. Elaine knew what was coming next but decided not to volunteer anything. "What can I do for you?"

The man sighed. "I'm in the very uncomfortable position of having to ask you if there's anything going on in the office that may perhaps not be in the best interest of the company."

"What exactly do you mean?"

Mr. Peakan paused again, obviously weighing his words. "Some of the board members have noted that Mr. Sarsky doesn't seem himself lately. He doesn't appear well…and perhaps his inattention due to this is the reason for the loss in sales over the past year. Are you aware of this, Miss McIntyre?"

"Yes, I've noticed on occasion that Mr. Sarsky doesn't seem well. His is an important job and it carries a lot of stress."

"We are aware of the pressures of the president's job, and also that, in the end, he must accept responsibility for the health of the company. But I, or rather the board, was wondering if there was something more specific ailing Mr. Sarsky that you might be aware of, a contributing factor to the sharp decline in the company's net profit? I ask this in Mr. Sarsky's best interests, to help him, of course."

"Of course, Mr. Peakan. I fully understand."

And before Elaine could offer an answer, Mr. Peakan added, "Do you think a few days off to rest would suffice or would his condition require a more lengthy remedy?"

How much more could the man say without coming right out and accusing Mr. Sarsky of being an alcoholic? She knew the company was faltering. Her job and those of hundreds of others across the country depended on sound leadership. Yet her loyalty was so strong that not even the risk of losing her job made her waver. Elaine knew they were trying to get some hard evidence that Mr. Sarsky had a drinking problem, but she was not about to add fuel to the fire.

"Mr. Peakan, I'm very glad you and the other board members are so concerned for Mr. Sarsky's well-being. You're aware there's likely something amiss and, of course, have the company's welfare at heart. I am confident that the board will remain on top of this matter and do whatever is necessary to improve the company's bottom line. With that, I really have nothing further to offer at this time."

Mr. Peakan didn't respond for a few moments. "Thank you, Miss McIntyre, I appreciate your loyalty and your commitment to the president. Perhaps I shouldn't have put you in such a precarious position. I assure you this will not affect your employment at Mackurcher and Company."

"Thank you, Mr. Peakan."

"I, or rather the Board, thought you might be able to shed a little light on the matter. In any case, I trust you will keep this conversation in confidence. I don't wish to add to Mr. Sarsky's concerns."

"Of course. I will keep this conversation in confidence as I would any I hold with Mr. Sarsky."

"Thank you, Miss McIntyre, for your time. Good day."

"Goodbye, Mr. Peakan."

How easy it would be to expose and dethrone Mr. Sarsky

in such a way as to reveal her talents, abilities and clear insight into how the company should be successfully operated. If she were ruthless, she could quickly point out what the problems were and where Ted was failing—and just as quickly offer the solutions. She could have outlined her vision and listed the steps she would take to realize her goals. It was the perfect opportunity to make a strong case for herself, but she was a person of integrity. She had morals and compassion. She would never take advantage of or hit a man when he was down, especially her president. Her position as personal secretary carried with it a commitment she remained loyal to.

Elaine sipped her now cold coffee and settled back to read her book, nodding in approval each time another trait of the heroine was revealed: how she inspired others to share her vision, made them feel part of the challenge and shared the victory. Executives who had first questioned the heroine's abilities dug in and worked much harder than they normally would have. *Money is only one motivation,* the heroine said at one point.

"That's right," Elaine agreed. *Personal satisfaction, achievement, recognition and glory are clearly the impetus for team success. A leader must always be vigilant to keep those elements alive.*

Although the novel's heroine had many fears, she never allowed her doubts or personal problems to interfere or even be known. And when she was confronted by an obstacle, she strove all the harder and persevered until success was achieved.

Elaine could clearly see how Ted had lowered the bar of success at Mackurcher and Co. He was no longer setting the example, his vision and communication were no longer clear. Incompetence had crept in, and mediocrity had stuck its ugly foot in the door. Elaine was getting worked up thinking about it all. If only she was given the chance, an opportunity to take control for three months, say, or six, the board would see the company's shares skyrocket to a height the likes of which the stock exchange had never before witnessed.

Frustrated, beads of perspiration formed on her brow. She felt so handicapped. When you could see the problem—and, just as clearly—the solution but were restricted from action, it affected the spirit. Elaine took a deep breath and exhaled slowly.

As she continued to read, it felt like the author knew her inside out. Like the heroine in the book, Elaine usually wore a two-piece suit. Today it was a pinstriped number in banker grey. Under her jacket was a snow-white blouse with a soft collar that folded over the jacket's lapels. The woman in the book was blond and Elaine's hair was dark brown. Both women, however, combed their hair straight back and wore it folded into a tight bun.

Elaine and the heroine were each attractive and sophisticated. Each wore glasses revealing lively, intelligent brown eyes. Both were tall, shapely and exuded an air of efficiency and authority as they went about their work. And both were economical in their speech, precise and to the point.

Elaine read on, admiring the woman's intelligence, perception, punctuality, competency and orderliness, recognizing those attributes in herself as well. She put the book down. She looked like a president and certainly had the abilities to act as one. And yet here she was, realizing that ambition vicariously through the life of some heroine in a work of fiction.

The only consolation, if there was one, was that she was, in fact, fulfilling the responsibilities of a company president. Indirectly, she had power and authority. She had learned the subtle skill of advising her bosses without seeming to. So in a sense, she *was* at the top.

She sighed. That was all well and good, but all the fantasizing in the world wouldn't change things at Mackurcher and Co. They had a problem and unfortunately it was at the top, the most vulnerable spot, where any damage could be fatal.

She had lied to Mr. Peakan. She knew what was bothering Mr. Sarsky. Those darn letters. When her boss had first arrived, he was decisive, quickly assessing his staff and placing them in positions where they could be most effective. He'd created immediate positive results and she'd agreed with his decisions. What normally took months if not years to notice in others—

people's motives and weaknesses—Ted had seen almost instantly. *If only he could see his own, now.* His instincts had been remarkable. Better than her own. Within weeks, morale had improved and sales immediately increased.

Unfortunately, it was this very man who was now the cause of the company's even steeper decline. His leadership capability had taken a nosedive right after he'd ordered her and Michael to destroy his daughter's and her boyfriend's letters.

Elaine had few regrets in life, but a big one was that she hadn't read at least one of those letters before they'd been burned.

The phone jangled her out of her thoughts and she realized she'd read the same paragraph ten times.

"Good morning, Mackurcher and Company. How may I assist you?"

"Hello, Elaine, this is Mike from down in the basement."

Elaine straightened in her chair. "Yes, what is it, Michael?"

"I was just cleaning out the furnace room after they took the old boiler out and I found another couple of those letters. They must have slid underneath when all those letters fell out of the box that day."

"Oh my!"

"Do you want them? Or do you need to watch me throw them into the furnace like last time?"

Unbelievable! She'd just wished she'd read one of those letters! But as the opportunity stared her in the face, she wondered if it was really the right thing to do. Was something trying to tell her this chance might be used to Mr. Sarsky's benefit, maybe even the company as a whole? What should she do? She should tell Mike she'd be right down to get them. But what if Ted somehow found out somehow she had them?

Oh, things were so complicated when people weren't straightforward with each other!

"Elaine, are you still there?"

"Yes…yes, I was just deciding whether or not I needed to come down there. No, Michael, I don't need to come down. I know you'll deal with the matter immediately and ensure the letters are destroyed. I appreciate it very much that you let me know."

"Well, I thought I'd better. I'm sure Mr. Sarsky would be very upset if they got lost or weren't destroyed like he wanted."

"Yes, Michael, Mr. Sarsky would be very upset and concerned. I'm very glad you found them. Please burn them straight away and ensure that there are no others."

"Yes, ma'am."

And that's that, she thought, glad not to have to go downstairs to the dingy basement. She felt for Michael, having to work in such a gloomy environment day in and day out. About now he'd be going into the hot furnace room, the new boiler blazing away as he tossed the letters in. Her memories of watching him burn the others still lingered in her mind. How he'd struggled to pick up the letters that had slipped out of his grasp and thrust them into the leaping flames of the furnace. She could still see the sweat carve its way through the dust and grime on Michael's face like rivulets forming on a dirt road in a rainstorm.

Distracted, Elaine got herself a fresh cup of coffee, then returned to her desk and picked up her novel, but the thought of those letters ricocheted through her mind. Doubt gnawed at her. *What would it hurt to read just one if I gained some insight that might help Ted—and the company?* Maybe she'd find out why such an outstanding leader had faltered so quickly.

Before she could rethink it again, Elaine picked up the phone and called down to the basement.

"Hello."

"Michael, it's Elaine. I was just thinking about those letters again. Perhaps it would be best for me to see them after all. I'll be right down—"

"Elaine, I…I…burned them."

She almost cried.

"Thank you, Michael."

CHAPTER FOURTEEN

IT WAS LATE and the rehearsal for *Hamlet* hadn't gone that well. With only two weeks to go, Mr. Johnston was displeased with the lack of commitment of several of the actors. Jenny was glad she had studied her lines and hadn't added to his aggravation—at least not today. As she made her way down the hallway to the parking lot she noticed Tammy sitting on a bench near the door, staring out the window. "What is she still doing here?" Jenny muttered as she slowed her pace and quietly made her way towards her friend.

Tammy was so absorbed in thought she didn't notice Jenny coming until her friend put a hand on her shoulder.

"What are you still doing here, Tammy? It's almost five. Did you miss your ride?"

"Robert and I had a fight. I was just about to phone home and have Mom come get me."

"Oh, Tammy. I'm sure it'll be okay. Tell me what it was about."

Tammy turned to her, the silent tears sliding down her cheeks becoming a waterfall, her sobs audible.

Jenny studied her friend. This was something more serious than a little spat.

"Tammy, what's wrong?" Jenny sat next to her troubled friend and tugged her in for a hug. Jenny had never seen Tammy look so distressed. "Tell me what's troubling you...can I help? Has it got something to do with what you were going to tell me the other day?"

Tammy nodded. "I don't know what to do Jen...I—I'm pregnant. The doctor confirmed it yesterday." With that Tammy's crying escalated into an almost uncontrollable hysteria.

Jenny was momentarily paralyzed and didn't know what to do or say. Flashes of her own pregnancy swept across the screen of her mind. So much pain and heartache. The rape, thoughts of abortion, feeling the baby kick in her womb, growing to love her even before she was born, the adoption, the absence of Henry's support and love. Other than the social workers and medical staff, only her parents knew of her baby's existence. Jenny had never shared it with any of her friends. Now she wondered if she should tell her best friend that she understood exactly what she was going through.

Compassion welled inside her and she began to stroke her friend's shoulder, though she remained silent. Gradually the heaving subsided and Tammy made a considerable effort to speak calmly through her tears.

"If only Robert wanted the baby, but he doesn't. He doesn't! He...he thinks we're too young and that our lives would get too complicated. That it would interfere with his basketball scholarship and that it would mess up my academic one too. Who knows if they'll even let me finish Grade 12!" Tammy stopped for a moment and took a tissue out of her purse. She went to wipe her nose but instead burst out again, "He—he wants me to have an abortion! Oh Jenny, what am I going to *do*?"

Jenny knew in her heart it would be a terrible thing to do and that her friend would regret that decision for the rest of her life. Tammy was alone in this just the way she had been. Only she still felt that if Henry had known he would have supported her. She considered what to say. There was only one thing she could.

"Tammy, there's something I want to share with you that I haven't told anyone. My parents are the only ones who know."

Jenny slid her arm from Tammy's shoulder and held both hands in her lap, as if cradling the swollen belly that had once held her daughter. She turned to face her troubled friend.

For a moment Tammy forgot herself and sat up, sensing her best friend was going to share something that would help her. She wiped her nose and the solitary tear hovering on her lashes, looking right into Jenny's eyes.

"Tammy, you remember the boy I met in Regina the summer before I started Grade 9?"

Tammy nodded. "Henry. You thought he would be an artist someday and he's the one you sent the pewter angel to back then."

"Right," Jenny said. "What I wanted to tell you was that during that summer, one night on the way home after Henry and I went to a movie, some boys in a car attacked us and took me to the park."

Now it was Jenny's turn to cry. Just the thought of that night sent tremors through her body. Jenny reached out and took Tammy's hand. "Tammy, I was raped by one of those three boys…"

"Oh, *Jenny*…!"

"I didn't realize it until after Christmas when I noticed I was gaining weight. At the end of January I learned that I was pregnant."

"Oh, Jenny," Tammy said again, squeezing Jenny's hand. "What happened? Did you have an abortion?" Tammy's eyes were wide, searching Jenny's face for an answer she wasn't sure she wanted to hear.

"At first I wanted to—I didn't want anything to do with that drunken oaf! But Tammy, I quickly learned to love the baby growing inside me. It wasn't it's fault. It didn't ask to be born— and the thought of destroying it, a live little baby, became unthinkable."

Tammy was puzzled. "So when did this happen, and where's the baby now? I never saw that you were pregnant."

"Remember in the spring of Grade 9 when I told you I had mononucleosis…?"

Tammy nodded and Jenny went on. "The baby was small, and I hid my belly under big sweaters, but I got more and more tired and my parents thought it best for me to stay home. On May 24, 1957, I gave birth to a little girl. I named her Camilla."

Tammy could barely believe her ears. "Oh, Jenny! Where is she?"

Tears rose in Jenny's eyes and for a moment she couldn't speak. "I…I don't know. I gave her up for adoption. I was only in Grade 9, too young to raise a baby and …" Jenny was going to tell her about Henry, how if he'd known and written to her she felt certain she would have kept the baby. But Henry never wrote…and Tammy had enough on her plate, Jenny knew, without burdening her with old heartaches, especially now. "I was just too young, Tammy—but I think about her every day. And I'm so glad I didn't have an abortion—I only saw Camilla for a moment before they took her away, but she was beautiful."

"But Robbie says it's just a fetus—he says it isn't really anything until it's born."

"Oh, Tammy, he's *wrong*. When you feel it flutter inside you, you know it's a real little baby. And the doctor can hear its heartbeat even before that. Remember Mrs. Torrence, our English teacher last year? Her baby was born premature and had to be put in an incubator for several weeks, but you saw the pictures she shared with the class. Your baby is growing now too, Tammy, and I believe a baby is a baby as soon as it's conceived."

"But, Jenny what would I do with a baby without Robbie? I'm only seventeen…"

"Have you told your parents yet?"

"Oh *God*, no, they'll have a fit. I'll never hear the end of it from my dad. When I'm not home on time he grounds me. I know how worried he is I'll get in trouble. And now he's right."

Tammy could barely get the last word out before the tears started again, fear etched in her face.

"Tammy, first you have to tell your mom. I'll drive you home right now and we'll tell her together. After all, I have all this experience," Jenny added, "so because of Camilla, maybe I can help. Besides, the sooner you get it over with, the sooner we can start to deal with everything. I was terrified of what my parents would say too, especially my mother, but I was actually surprised by how supportive she was."

A watery smile lifted the corners of Tammy's mouth. How grateful she was for her friend. And there was even a small comfort in knowing that Jenny's perfect life wasn't so perfect. If Jenny had survived an unplanned pregnancy, maybe there was hope for her too. "So you really think it would be a mistake to get an abortion? Robbie thinks he might be able to get someone to do it so we could keep the whole thing a secret and avoid the shame—and having to tell our parents."

"Oh, Tammy. It's not so easy to get an abortion. In my case, because of the circumstances, I could have had one, but—but Tammy!" Jenny blurted. "I really believe in my heart that you'd regret it. I believe from the moment of conception a baby has a spirit and a soul. I believe God sends each of us a guardian angel who stays with us from that moment on.

"I think of Camilla every day—and I just know that one day we'll meet again. And *that's* what got me through it, that's what kept me going, Tammy, and still does. If I'd had an abortion I don't think I could've lived with myself; to take my own little baby's life would haunt me for the rest of mine. At least this way I know she has a good home and that one day we'll be together again. I just know my guardian angel is going to make it all work out."

Jenny blushed a little then; she'd gotten so passionate about it she had spoken aloud her innermost belief. She didn't know if Tammy would understand the close relationship she had with her unseen helper—and didn't want her to criticize it.

But Tammy didn't seem to take it in; her thoughts were

mired in practicalities. "But Jenny, if I decide to keep it and Robbie doesn't support me, I don't know if I can make it. And what will all our friends say when they see my belly growing... oh! it's mortifying even to think about!"

"Most of that is just fear, Tammy, of something that's bigger in your head than it is in reality. Things will work out. They did for me, didn't they? And I'll be at your side the whole time."

Footsteps echoed down the hall. The girls turned to see the principal approaching them.

"My gosh, girls, why are you both still here? I'm just about to lock up." When he came closer and saw that both girls had been crying he added, "Is something the matter?"

"Oh no, Mr. Thompson," Jenny quickly replied, "just some boy/girl problems. We were just leaving."

Bracing themselves for the coming confrontation, they went out together to face whatever came next.

CHAPTER FIFTEEN

A WEEK AFTER MR. Engelmann had mentioned to Henry that he was thinking about selling the business, a tall man dressed smartly in a brown houndstooth suit entered the store. He exuded an air of importance which was softened by a friendly smile. He stopped short of the counter and introduced himself as Jim Webster. Mr. Engelmann shook his extended hand and responded with his own name.

"Mr. Engelmann, I'm representing a company interested in learning if the property your store sits on and the adjacent lot are for sale.

"Well, possibly. What would they do with the store?"

"It would probably be torn down."

"But what about all my customers?"

"They would go to another store. Safeway is only a few blocks away."

"For many of my customers, three blocks is like three miles."

"Well, I'm sure something could be figured out. There's a solution for everything."

It was clear to Mr. Engelmann that this Mr. Webster was very serious.

"How much is your client offering, do you know?"

"Well, Mr. Engelmann, unfortunately your building here isn't worth very much; we can easily hire a real estate firm to do an appraisal, if you like. But your business itself is another matter. We know you've built up a large clientele, and I'm sure it's become quite profitable for you. Perhaps if we were to go over your financial statements for the last two or three years, we could arrive at a fair figure."

"Oh, I will have to think about that. My business is my business. I don't like anyone to come in and look at my books."

"I understand, but how else can we determine the value of your store?"

"I'm not certain I want to sell. If and when I do, I will think about what I want."

"That's just fine, Mr. Engelmann. Would you be willing to meet again, say in about two weeks?"

Mr. Engelmann looked at the man in front of him, so smooth, so polite and so agreeable. He had to be cautious and think the entire matter through very carefully before making a decision. "Yes, yes, that will be fine. Yes, come again in two weeks. I might have an answer for you then."

But as Mr. Webster headed for the door, Mr. Engelmann knew two weeks wouldn't be long enough. "Mr. Webster, better make that a month. I am very busy for the next little while." He hoped the delay would disappoint him and he would go away.

"That's fine. A month it is." The door banged shut behind him.

He needed to discuss this with Henry and Mary; he needed a sounding board. *Oh, Anna, if only I could talk to you too!* Mrs. Dance's son was a real estate lawyer who could, perhaps, provide counsel. And he himself would naturally have to review the accounts. As a plan began to formulate in his mind, Mr. Engelmann relaxed against the wall behind the counter.

ON SUNDAY EVENING, a week before Bill was to return home, Mr. Engelmann sat down with Henry and Mary for their usual dinner. After everyone had helped themselves to roast chicken, mashed potatoes, gravy and creamed corn, they resumed the discussion they'd been having since Mr. Engelmann had arrived.

"Well, David, if you sell the store what would you do?" Mary wanted to know. "You're too young to retire."

"And where would you live?" Henry added.

David chewed a succulent slice of chicken, then swallowed.

"Yes, yes, I have thought about all these things and haven't found the answer yet, but I know the Lord will help me sort it out. I'm worried about all the old people we deliver groceries to, though. Who would do that if we close down?"

"They'd have to go to Safeway or maybe have their children get their groceries for them," Henry said.

"Yes, but most of their children are grown and gone. Many of our elderly customers are all alone and sometimes are too achy with arthritis to get out. They need someone to bring the groceries to them."

"What about a taxi service?" Mary suggested.

"Oh no, they would never pay for a taxi. Too expensive."

And so it went, back and forth, for several minutes until Mr. Engelmann laid his fork and knife on the table and stared at a spot between Mary and Henry with a strange, far-off look.

"What is it?" Henry asked.

Mr. Engelmann was quiet, then he whispered, "Maybe, just maybe, I might have the answer."

Henry leaned closer. "What is it? What's the answer? The answer to what?"

The vacant look on Mr. Engelmann's face dissolved into a warm smile and his eyes sparkled. He shook his head as if to clear it.

"Oh, it is just a thought," he said, taking a sip of water.

"What is it?" Henry pressed.

David picked up his fork, about to take another mouthful.

"Mr. Engelmann, you have to tell us what it is," Henry said, exasperated. "You...you just can't leave us hanging here."

But Mr. Engelmann only smiled and filled his fork with potatoes. "It's just an idea. Way too early to tell. It's something I alone will have to think on."

"But…but—"

"Now, Henry," Mary interjected, "David will tell us when he's ready."

"But, Mom, we're in this together—!"

The phone rang.

"That's your father," Mary said as she rose to answer.

As Mary talked to Bill, David took a moment to consider his brainwave. Henry and Mary might think it was crazy, but it was something he'd felt a tugging in his heart to do for a while.

"What?!"

David snapped out of his musings and noticed Henry paying rapt attention to his mother's conversation.

"Join you in Toronto? Oh, I don't think so—I'm too busy. I have work to do at home and at the store. And besides, we can't afford it right now. No, Bill."

"Go, Mom," Henry said.

Mary shook her head at Henry and waved at him to be quiet. Henry looked down at the table, stung. David knew there was more to her defiance than the household budget.

Mary turned to her son. "Do you want to speak to Dad?"

"No, it's okay. Say hi, and—"

Mary held her hand over the receiver and motioned for him to come and say hello.

Henry slouched over to her and chatted with his dad for a minute. While he talked, Mary sliced the saskatoon berry pie she'd made earlier. As Henry hung up, she brought three plates of pie out to the table. Silence fell over the room.

Henry stabbed at his slice of pie without eating.

"Is anything wrong, Henry?" his mom asked.

"Just feeling tired, I guess," then he looked at his mother and added, "I wish you had agreed to go to Toronto."

Mary blushed and turned her attention to her pie.

David looked from mother to son, caught in the middle of a deep-seated issue he'd no business being a part of. *So that's it.*

"Oh, there will be other times and right now we can't afford it." But she wasn't fooling anyone—least of all herself.

"Mary, this was a wonderful supper," David said to change the subject. He asked Mary to remind him to get the pumpkin order in that week for Hallowe'en, then questioned Henry about school. After a brief cup of tea with Mary in the living room and reminding Henry that he should concentrate on his schoolwork instead of trying to do everything, including making it into the store, David excused himself.

He used the walk home to plan out what he would do with the next phase of his life, without the store.

HENRY WASN'T ABLE to get in to work until the next Saturday. He usually walked to the store with his mother on the weekend, but she was going to meet his father at the airport at eleven so he walked alone.

Mr. Engelmann's characteristic whistle greeted Henry as he stepped into the store, a sure sign that he was happy about something. Henry was curious to know what was on his mentor's mind, but no sooner had he opened his mouth than a customer entered, starting another busy day.

His mother arrived around two, but it was so busy that Henry didn't have time to ask about his father. After spending much of the day in silence, Henry and his mother turned the lock on the front door at five-thirty.

As they said good night to Mr. Engelmann, his mother said, "We're looking forward to seeing you for supper tomorrow night."

"Yes, yes," he answered, "I am anxious to see Bill and learn all about his trip. And I may have something to share with all of you, too."

"What is it?" Henry asked.

"Tomorrow evening will come soon enough. We'll talk then."

The days were growing shorter now and winter was just around the corner. Henry and his mother walked into the cool breeze.

"Wonder what Mr. Engelmann's news is?"

"I was thinking about that myself," his mother replied. "We'll know tomorrow, I guess."

"What will you do if Mr. Engelmann sells the store?" He could hardly think about it himself, but knew he'd support whatever decision Mr. Engelmann made.

"Oh, I'll find something else. I may have to go downtown, though. It won't be so bad. We just have to be ready to go wherever the door opens."

Henry's heart sped up as they reached their front door.

His father emerged from the living room as they walked in. Henry rushed over and gave him a strong hug.

"Glad to see you home, Dad." Henry said, hoping his mom would follow his example. "How was the trip?"

"Fine, son."

"Did you like flying?"

"Yes, it's quite the experience, being way up there. I liked the take-off, but landing was a bit nerve-wracking."

Henry's mother pecked her husband on the cheek, then disappeared into the kitchen, saying, "I'll start supper right away; it won't take long—I put a chicken casserole into the oven before I came to the store this afternoon. Why don't you two sit in the living room until dinner?"

Henry looked at his father, the expression in his father's eyes echoing his own. Not quite the reaction he'd hoped for either. Obviously, she hadn't completely forgiven his dad yet.

Henry wondered if she ever would.

Chapter Sixteen

M R. ENGELMANN ARRIVED promptly at five-thirty, his whistle preceding him through the screen door. During dinner, David told Bill about the visit from Mr. Webster.

"Who do you think his client is?" Bill asked.

"I think it is Safeway. He never told me and I never asked, I was so surprised that someone had walked through the door to make such an offer. I am not even sure I want to sell the store yet. It has been so much a part of my life, and now that it is doing so well, it is going to be very hard for me to sell."

"I know what you mean," said Bill. "But maybe now *is* the time to sell—when your profit is at a peak."

"Yes, yes, you are right, of course. I know I have to sell. But it's almost like a child to me. It's so hard to give it up."

"We understand," Mary interjected, reaching over and touching David's hand.

"Do you have a price in mind?" Bill asked.

"I was hoping to get maybe around $40,000 for it. We didn't pay too much for the building."

"You should get an appraisal," Bill said.

"I called Mrs. Dance last Friday. Her son is a lawyer. I told her I have some business to do, and that I need some legal help and she said she would have her son phone me. Hopefully, I will hear from him soon so I can ask him all these things."

"Good idea," Bill nodded.

Mary opened her mouth to speak, then seemed to think better of it and rose from her chair to go to the oven. They all watched as she pulled out a lemon meringue pie, Bill's favourite dessert, the tips of the egg white peaks a perfectly browned mountain range.

The men wasted little time digging into their after-dinner treat.

Pie finished, Bill asked, "If you sell the store, where will you live? Have you got other plans?"

David looked at Henry, knowing he'd been waiting anxiously for this answer.

"Well...?" Henry prompted, leaning forward.

Excitement was written on Mr. Engelmann's face, his eyes sparkled. His smile grew into a broad grin. He raised his fork, a piece of lemon pie hanging precariously off the tip of it, and waved it around as if he were a conductor setting the beat to music about to begin. The words of his song would be sweet and soothing to their ears and hearts. He knew he had found the perfect solution. Now that Anna was gone, he would do what he was meant to do.

"Bill, Mary, Henry," he said, looking at each of them in turn. "Next spring when I leave my store and home—"

"Yeah?" Henry blurted, barely hanging on to the edge of his seat.

"I will be going to Gravelbourg. It's a small community about 250 miles from here."

"But why do you have to go away?" Henry's voice was steeped with disappointment.

Mr. Engelmann looked at his young friend reassuringly and put a hand on Henry's.

"There is a seminary there," Mr. Engelmann's voice rose, unable to contain or control his excitement any longer. The words of his music had reached a crescendo and had to be sung gloriously. "I…I am going to become a priest!"

They were all stunned. They stared at him, transfixed, mouths open. Then gradually, as if awakening from a coma, one by one they nodded their heads. Henry and Mary jumped up and smothered him with hugs. In the excitement, Mr. Engelmann's piece of lemon pie landed across Bill's nose and cheek.

They all laughed. Mary used the napkin beside her plate to wipe the pie from her husband's face. After settling down, David told them how he'd come to his decision.

"It came to mind last Sunday when I was here for dinner and we were talking about what I might do," David said.

"Yeah, I remember," Henry said, adding, "You wouldn't tell us anything."

David smiled, "Yes, well, that's because I wasn't sure myself. This past week, I went to see Father Connelly and talked with him about it. He thought it was a wonderful idea. He spoke with the archbishop, who told him he wanted to meet with me. Thursday afternoon was my meeting with the bishop. You may recall I was away for over two hours. He already knew a lot about me from Father Connelly, and had heard about Anna's funeral and said that I might be a little ahead of my time. In the end, he said they would send me to Gravelbourg for two years. When I finish, they will place me in St. Mary's Church as an assistant to Father Connelly until such time as I am ready to have my own parish."

"You'll be a wonderful priest," Mary said sincerely.

"Yeah," Henry said. "You'll be great. There's only one problem, though."

Everyone looked at him.

"What is it?" Mr. Engelmann asked.

"You're gonna have to give up your favourite vest for a black robe."

David looked down on his old red, blue and grey checkered vest, and they all laughed again.

Once the laughter died away, David pushed himself from

his chair. "Thank you so much for that wonderful dinner, Mary. You truly are an excellent cook. You are all so dear to me. You have no idea what it has meant to be part of your family. I love you all very much."

"And we love you too, David," Mary quickly responded.

Bill and Henry smiled in agreement.

Mr. Engelmann got up and made his way to the front door.

"Would you like a piece of lemon pie to take home?"

"No, Mary, thank you very much anyway."

"How about a drive home in the van, David?" asked Bill.

"Oh no, that's fine. I need the fresh air and a little exercise to work off this wonderful meal. The sky was clear when I came, so the moon and stars should be out. I like to think of my Anna beside me as we stroll under the heavens. It's hard to give up the romance of one's life, no matter how old you are," he said, winking at all of them.

Just before the door closed behind him, Henry called out, "Good night, Father Engelmann!"

David turned and smiled.

THE NEXT MORNING, the phone rang at eight-thirty.

"Good morning, Engelmann's Grocery."

"Mr. Engelmann? It's Joseph Dance. I'm a lawyer with Travis McKechan. Mom phoned and said you were looking for some advice, and that I was to get right on it or there'd be no apple pie on Sunday when I came for dinner," he said, chuckling.

Mr. Engelmann laughed too. "Pie or no, thank you, Joseph, for calling so quickly."

"Well, you and your wife have done a lot for the people who come to your store. Our family has talked a lot about the difference you've made to the neighbourhood."

"That's very nice to hear."

"Mom said you have some legal concerns. What can I do for you?"

"I would like to sell my store…and I think I have a buyer. A Mr. Webster came in last week; though he didn't say it in so many words, I think he might represent Safeway. There's one down the street. I suspect they want to buy me out."

"Did you settle on a price yet?"

"No, he just came in and said the company he represented was interested."

"I see," said Mr. Dance. "Unfortunately, Mr. Engelmann, I'm a litigator, not a real estate lawyer. If you're ever in trouble and have to go to court, I'm your man. But with mortgages, land title transfers, deeds and business sales, you need someone else. The good news is I know just the man who can help you. Johnny Balfour is an amazing man and one of the best negotiators I know. If anyone can get the deal done for you, it's him."

"I would appreciate it. How much do I owe you for your trouble?"

"Oh, there's no charge. You've both been so good to my parents over the years, especially your wife. She was a very close friend of my mother's. It's the least I can do."

"Oh no, I will pay," Mr. Engelmann insisted. "You are a busy man, I can't accept—"

"No, that's fine," Mr. Dance reiterated, with a tone of finality. "Don't worry about a thing."

Twenty minutes later the phone rang again. This time it was Johnny Balfour. After chatting briefly about Johnny's aunt and uncle who used to frequent the store, they got down to business.

"Joseph mentioned that this Mr. Webster approached you about purchasing your business on behalf of another company, is that correct?"

"Yes, yes, that is so. Mr. Webster never mentioned who he was representing, but I think it is Safeway since I am their biggest competitor in this community."

"I'll find out. Should only take a phone call or two. What do you think your business is worth?"

"Well, I didn't pay very much for it in 1944, but we have made improvements to the property and in the last three years, with the help of a very good employee, the business has improved immensely and has become very profitable. I also own the empty lot beside the store, which could be used for expansion."

"I see," said Mr. Balfour, "then what do you think you might want for the business?"

"Well, I've had a look through the financial statements and think it might be worth $40,000."

"Okay. What about good will?"

"What do you mean 'good will'? Do you mean how good I was to the people?"

"That has something to do with it. It means how much you have added to the business because of the service you provided."

"I think that's in the price I quoted to you."

"All right, we'll see," the lawyer replied.

There was silence for a few moments except for a rustling of papers on Mr. Balfour's end.

"Would you be agreeable to me looking after the negotiations with Mr. Webster? I assure you I won't let your business go for anything less than the figure you mentioned. In fact, I'll do what I can to try to get more. According to Joseph, the entire neighbourhood community are very loyal customers; you're likely doing significant damage to Safeway's bottom line."

"That may be so. And so I think they are trying to buy me out," Mr. Engelmann agreed.

"Unfortunately, I don't have time to meet with you, but if you'll allow, I'll put together a few people who can help assess your business's worth. All you need to do is ask Mr. Webster if he is prepared to meet with us at my office on…" more rustling of pages "…October 4, at eleven a.m."

"Yes, that would be fine. And where do we come to?"

"We're downtown on Scarth Street, across from Victoria Park, south of 12th Avenue," he said, giving him the address.

Mr. Engelmann jotted down the details and repeated it back.

"That's it. I'll see you, then—and don't worry about a thing, Mr. Engelmann. Leave it all up to me."

"Thank you so much, Mr. Balfour. How can I repay you?"

"Don't worry about that, either. There's no charge. It's all being looked after."

Mr. Engelmann was startled into momentary silence. He hadn't expected this. "B-but, by whom, Mr. Balfour?" he wondered aloud.

Mr. Balfour's smile was audible. "Think of it as a small acknowledgement for all you and your wife have done for the neighbourhood. I really must go now. I'll see you at my office on the fourth unless I hear from you otherwise."

He was dumbfounded by this good fortune—to think one phone call from behind his meat counter had brought instant results with such far-reaching consequences. One call from an east-end mother had set a network into motion that would gather together a very impressive team of professional people.

At the end of the month, Mr. Webster stepped through the door exactly when he'd said he would.

"Good morning, Mr. Engelmann. How are you today?"

"I am fine, Mr. Webster. And a good morning to you."

"Have you given any further thought to the matter of selling your store?"

"Yes, yes, as a matter of fact I have. I discussed the matter with my lawyer," Mr. Engelmann said, looking at the other man over his dark-rimmed glasses, more confident in dealing with Mr. Webster now that he had professional representation.

"That's good," Mr. Webster said. "And what were his suggestions?"

"He wants you to meet with us on October 4, if that's suitable." Mr. Engelmann fished a piece of paper out from under the drawer under the cash register and showed him the details.

"And your lawyer is…?" asked Mr. Webster.

"Johnny Balfour."

Mr. Webster's face paled, although he did his best to cover his reaction with a nervous grin. "My client's lawyer and I will be there," he agreed. "Have you settled on a selling price?"

"Yes, I have," Mr. Engelmann nodded.

"And, what did you decide?"

The phone rang.

"Excuse me just a moment, please. Engelmann's Grocery."

"Johnny Balfour here, Mr. Engelmann. Is Mr. Webster there yet?" the lawyer wanted to know.

"Yes, Mr. Webster is right here. He has agreed to meet with us at your office."

"That's good. Look, Mr. Engelmann, if he asks, don't tell him what you want for your business," Mr. Balfour said.

"Oh?" said Mr. Engelmann meeting Mr. Webster's gaze across the counter. "We were just discussing that—"

"Did you name a price?"

"Not yet."

"Well, don't. Please let me handle that for you. That's why I called. We'll talk about that at our meeting. Until then, please don't mention any dollar figures. You can tell him that I am handling all the business valuation on your behalf. All right?"

"Yes, yes, of course, if that is what you wish."

"Absolutely. I'll see you on the fourth of October at eleven."

"We will be there, Mr. Balfour. Goodbye."

Mr. Engelmann hung up and turned back to Mr. Webster, unsure quite how to broach things now. . .

"You were about to tell me the sales figure you'd arrived at," he prompted.

"Yes, yes, I was. But on the advice of my lawyer, I would like to keep that information to myself until we meet with him."

Mr. Webster stared at him, and David suddenly understood he had just foiled some of the man's plans.

"I see," he said.

"Thank you for stopping by, Mr. Webster," David said, injecting his voice with a confidence that was becoming more firm. "I will see you in a few weeks. I'm sure you can wait until then."

"Absolutely, sir," he said, a hint of desperation in his tone.

David had the distinct impression that Mr. Webster was not pleased with how the visit had ended.

"Good day to you, Mr. Engelmann."

CHAPTER SEVENTEEN

"HELLO? JUST A moment please…Jenny? It's for you, I think it's Tammy."

"Thanks, Mom. I was just going to my room—I'll get it up there, okay?"

Jenny dashed up stairs to her room and grabbed the extension, calling out, "Got it Mom, thanks—you can hang up," then spoke into the phone, "Hi, Tammy, is that you?"

"It's me. Jenny…oh, Jenny, I'm so nervous and afraid. I just don't know what to *do*."

"What's wrong, Tammy—is everything okay with the baby?"

"Yes, but my mom and Robbie are insisting that I have an abortion! Our family doctor refuses to do it and he's concerned that the fetus might be close to three months already."

"What do *you* want to do, Tammy?"

"Oh, Jen! To be honest with you, I'm just so confused. Mom says I'm too young and that this will interfere with my education and—and that it's my body and I have the right to make my own decision. And Robbie feels the same way; he's worried about his scholarship and says that getting rid of the baby would solve everything…"

"But Tammy, you still haven't said what *you* really want to do. Have you thought about adoption? There are lots of married people out there who can't have children and desperately want a baby."

"I know, but just the thought of walking down the hallway at school with a big tummy scares me to death. Can you imagine what everyone would say? And I know Robbie would be embarrassed beyond belief. I'm—I'm afraid he'll leave me if I don't do it." Tammy started to cry and Jenny listened, heartsore, unsure what to say to her friend. She knew what she would do, she would keep the baby for sure, but Tammy needed to make up her own mind.

Just as Jenny was about to speak, Tammy blurted, "Mom's been on the phone for the last two days trying to track down someone who will perform the abortion. She's talked to three midwives already. There's one in Toronto who will do it, but I don't know Jenny. I've heard there was one woman who started to hemorrhage and the midwife couldn't stop it. She was rushed to the hospital and the doctor on duty refused to treat her since he didn't want to be responsible for her death or any complications and she almost *did* die from an infection afterwards."

"If that's your choice, it would be best if it were done in a hospital," Jenny said quickly, "And by a doctor."

"Well, Mom wants to get a doctor too. She's been trying to reach this doctor in Montreal who has apparently been doing a lot of abortions, he feels it's a woman's right."

Jenny wondered how someone who took an oath to save lives could be such a strong advocate of destroying them.

"Gosh, I don't know, Tammy. Do you really think it's our right to…" Jenny didn't want to say *kill*, "well, you know, get rid of a baby."

"See, that's why I'm so *confused*, everyone says something different! Even my dad isn't sure. He says maybe it's best to keep it and give it up for adoption. I was surprised he said that, but he's worried about the whole procedure—that I might not be able to have children after or regret doing it."

"Listen, Tammy, I think you need some time to think this through. Why don't you come over on Friday night and spend the weekend with us? The grounds are so beautiful; the leaves are changing colour and it's so peaceful—you can sit in the gazebo and think about this away from all the pressure."

"I'd like that, Jenny. I hope there's time, everyone is worried about how old the baby is, and the sooner it's done the better. But yes, I'll come over tomorrow night."

"Oh, Tammy, you're my best friend and I really care about you—I'm keeping you in my thoughts and prayers every second. I know you'll decide what's best for you and your baby. And you know," Jenny added, "I could call the social worker who helped me sort things out with Camilla—I'm sure she'd talk to you about it."

"Yes, okay. Maybe that'd help," Tammy said, and Jenny could tell she was crying. "We'll talk about it tomorrow night."

"All right, Tammy. See if you can get some sleep—and try not to worry. Things will work out, I just know it."

As soon as Jenny hung up she went over to her bedside and knelt down. *Oh, dear Jesus, please help Tammy do the right thing. She's so confused and troubled. I know what she's going through. Please help Robbie to accept his responsibility and if he won't, dear Jesus, if you help Tammy decide to keep her child, I promise I'll help her look after it. Thank you for the guardian angel who has helped me so much, and let Tammy's angel help her feel the comfort of Your heavenly love, too.*

Tears came to Jenny's eyes and she lay her head on the bed.

The phone rang. Jenny picked up the extension to find her mother had already answered. Tammy was asking for her.

"I'm on the phone, Mom, I've got it."

The receiver clicked as Jenny's mom hung up downstairs.

"Hey, Tammy, is everything all right?"

"Mom says I can't come over tomorrow night and she doesn't want me talking to you anymore right now."

There was a long silence between the two friends and then

Tammy spoke again. "Mom got ahold of that doctor in Montreal. She's made an appointment for me to see him Monday morning. She's already called the airline and booked tickets. We leave at seven on Sunday night. Oh, Jenny, I'm so scared! I really wish you could come with me!"

Jenny didn't know how to respond. *I want to help Tammy but I'd feel like an accomplice to...to murder.*

Muffled voices broke the silence. "My mom says I have to hang up now. 'Bye, Jenny."

"'Bye," Jenny said faintly. She heard Tammy shout at her mother to go away before the receiver clicked. The sound of the dial tone resonated in her ear. Stunned and momentarily frozen by dread, she could only think that a developing little human being had just been sentenced to death.

Oh Tammy, I feel so sorry for you—and that poor little defenseless baby.

JENNY HARDLY SLEPT. It seemed to her that Tammy was being pressured to have an abortion and that her friend might do something she would wholeheartedly regret. Perhaps they could talk at school today. Maybe she could help her friend sort things out. Thoughts of Camilla flashed through Jenny's mind as she got ready for school. As her due date had drawn closer, she'd been so in love with her unborn child, she hadn't wanted to give her up. She too had felt pressured by her mother.

But Tammy wasn't at school. Jenny wanted to phone her but was worried that Tammy's mother would get upset and keep the friends apart. She'd already said Tammy couldn't come over that night.

Trying to distract herself, Jenny invited James over instead. They had finished watching Dragnet on the TV in the rumpus room and were about five minutes into a Lucille Ball comedy special when James noticed that Jenny wasn't laughing the way she usually did over Lucy's antics.

"What's wrong, Marjorie? You're pretty quiet."

"Please don't call me Marjorie, you know I prefer Jenny."

"But Marjorie *is* your first name and it sounds more sophisticated. Besides you should always go by your legal name. Dad says that all docu—"

"James, I like my middle name Jennifer better. I like being called Jenny, and I'm really not interested in what your dad thinks."

"Okay, Jennifer then. So what's the matter, you seem a thousand miles away. It's not that Pederson guy again, is it?"

"No, it has nothing to do with him. It's something else..." Jenny trailed off. She wasn't sure if she should tell him about Tammy, and yet James was her boyfriend. They were getting serious and *should* be able to share private matters with each other, right?

"Look, Jen, if this is anything to do with that Henry, I'll..."

"I told you, it doesn't, James!" Jenny was surprised James even remembered Henry's name. "It's something I've been talking about with Tammy. Something she shared with me..."

"So what is it? You can tell me." James looked hard into Jenny's eyes.

"Well, I suppose I can tell you, but you've got to promise it will be just between us."

"Yeah, yeah," he agreed, waving a hand to get her to go on. "What's the big secret?"

"Oh, James. Tammy's pregnant and she's going to have an abortion."

"So? That's her problem. What has that got to do with you?"

"She's my best friend! I'm so worried about her—I really think she might regret it. Plus, it's a serious procedure."

James shrugged. "If a doctor does it, it should be all right, shouldn't it? What's Robbie got to say?"

"He wants her to have it done. He's concerned about their education and—"

"Well, if he wants her to have the abortion, it's pretty much settled, isn't it. He's the father."

Jenny turned and slapped him on the shoulder. "Oh, you

men! It's Tammy who's carrying the baby and has to live with the decision. It's not just a man thing."

"Serves him right, though," James said after a moment's reflection. "If he'd used a condom, he wouldn't have this problem."

"James! That's not the point at all. Sex belongs in a marriage where two people give themselves to each other in love and commitment, and if a baby comes along it enters the world in a loving, secure home. Look what's happening with Tammy—"

"Well, I still think if Robbie had taken precautions this wouldn't have happened. If two people like one another, what's the big deal with expressing it physically?"

Jenny knew he wasn't just talking about Robbie and Tammy anymore. *Everything I just said to him about sex and marriage went in one ear and out the other.* The urge to have sex *could* be very strong, but once again she couldn't help but compare James with Henry. Henry had stopped when he could have gone on. *He wanted to protect my purity...he respected me.*

After a long, uneasy silence Jenny asked, "Would you be willing to adopt a baby, James?" She was thinking of her own little girl. Of Tammy's unborn child.

"No way. I wouldn't want someone else's kid. I'd want one of my own, especially a boy. Someone I could train to take over the business. But we've got lots of time for that."

"Is that all you ever think about? The business?"

"You know I'm living out my dream, Jennifer. Besides you, it's all I think about."

Once again an uneasy silence fell between them.

"And if it was a girl?"

"I suppose a girl could be trained too." And as an afterthought he added, "If she was as pretty as you, Jenny, it wouldn't matter to me." He winked at her.

Her eyes didn't leave James' for a minute.

What would he say if I told him about Camilla?

About the rape?

The thought sent cold shivers down her spine.

ALL DAY SATURDAY, Jenny couldn't stop thinking about Tammy. She tried phoning her but there was no answer. She went for a walk, seeking solace in nature the way she usually did, but feelings of foreboding followed her. She just couldn't shake the nervousness she felt for Tammy or the relentless thoughts bouncing around her head. She made her way to her favourite spot, the gazebo, and sat on the swing. How beautiful everything was. *How can nature be so peaceful and yet I still feel so troubled?*

Several of the garden wildflowers retained a hint of their summer colour, but most had already gone to sleep. She could smell the repose nature was settling into as it did every year. Fall reminded Jenny of the need for everything to die so it could renew its beauty. *If you never witness the trees and flowers in this state, you'd take their beauty in the spring and summer for granted. If it were light all the time without darkness, you'd even take for granted the sun. If you don't have a little sorrow in your life, you'd never truly appreciate the happy moments.* Under her breath, Jenny murmured, "Even though I gave my little girl up for adoption I do know the joy of giving birth to a new life… and I just know I'll see my little sweetheart again."

Jenny pushed against the wooden floor and set the swing in motion, thinking again how different James was from Henry. It was something at their very core. There was a softness and tenderness, a caring in Henry that she had always felt. She wished so much she could feel that way about James. *He's always so business-minded, so calculating, so…possessive.* At times like this, Jenny wondered why she continued to go out with him. And yet there was something in her that compelled her to accept him, to love him despite his shortcomings. It was a feeling she couldn't explain. It was just a very strong part of her nature.

I wonder what Tammy's thinking and doing right now. Jenny thought about driving over there and simply knocking on the door. She imagined Tammy's mother answering and slamming the door in her face.

Women have to be very desperate to abort their child, Jenny thought. She'd never have been able to live with herself had she done that to Camilla. There must be so many women out there who regretted their decision. Terminating the life within them before the baby ever saw the light of day, before even knowing if it was a boy or girl, what it looked like, how it felt in their arms, before knowing who it would become and what it might do for the world, before knowing the joy that could have been theirs. *Perhaps their one consolation is that their baby is in heaven, waiting for them, forgiving them.* If mothers asked, she knew Jesus would heal them.

Softly Jenny whispered:

> *Angel of God, my guardian dear,*
> *to whom God's love commits me here,*
> *ever this day be at my side*
> *—and Tammy's and her baby's.*

"I know the baby's guardian angel is already with her or him. Please protect it, and have Tammy's protector guide her to make the right decision…"

Oh Tammy, please call, the silence is deafening.

CHAPTER EIGHTEEN

"WELL, THAT WAS another fine dinner, Mary."

"And I'll say amen to that," echoed Mr. Engelmann.

"Why don't you all sit in the living room and I'll bring some apple pie and tea along in a few minutes?"

"The feast never ends in the Pederson household," Henry quipped.

"I'm impressed that you two men manage to keep as trim as you do with such a fine cook in the house. I'm already starting to bulge a bit just from coming over here every Sunday!"

"Nonsense, David, you look just fine," Mary said.

Henry and Mr. Engelmann each took a spot on the couch, leaving the leather arm chair for Bill while he turned on the television and waited for the picture to appear.

Henry smiled as he recalled the day his dad had come home with the black and white RCA Victor television. He'd spent part of his first paycheque from Coca-Cola on it. They were all so excited that Mary agreed to eat dinner in the living room that night just to watch the shows.

But it wasn't just the television that was new—his dad had changed since starting his new job. What a difference! He seemed like a new person. He smiled when he arrived home and Henry could tell how proud he was to park the Coca-Cola van in front of the house. Their neighbours were always asking what it was like to work for such a big company and whether he could drink as much free Coke as he wanted.

Henry had noticed something else, too. His dad actually talked about his work and the problems he was having, which mainly had to do with figuring out how things worked in his new job. He seemed to realize what a great counsellor he had in Mom, who used her insight to offer possible solutions. He'd finally stopped trying to face life alone, with just old thoughts bouncing around his head repeatedly. It all meant that the family was growing closer, but his parents still weren't close enough for Henry's liking.

"It sure takes a while for the set to warm up," Henry said now.

"I bet if you worked for RCA you'd have figured out a way to speed it up already."

Bill smiled and brushed off Mr. Engelmann's compliment and adjusted the TV antenna. There's a show I'd like you to watch, David. Have you heard of Bishop Sheen? He has a program every Sunday night called 'Life is Worth Living.' Now, *there's* a man who knows how to speak."

"Yes, Anna and I often listened to him on the radio, too. 'The Catholic Hour,' it was called."

"He reminds me of Superman the way he wears that cape and tosses it around all the time," Henry said, and then blurted out something else he sort of wished he hadn't, and yet… "He's started this slogan I like, 'the family that prays together stays together.'"

"Actually, Henry," Mr. Engelmann interjected, "Father Connelly told me it was an Irish priest named Father Patrick Peyton who started that slogan. But Bishop Sheen picked up on it and is certainly doing a good job of promoting it as well."

"Doesn't matter who started it, I agree with Henry," said Bill. "It's a good slogan."

Henry was surprised and pleased by his father's support.

But it wasn't Bishop Sheen on the air when the picture finally came on. Elvis Presley suddenly filled the screen, singing "A Fool Such As I."

"Mom, come quick! Elvis is on TV!"

Henry knew his mom had liked Elvis Presley since she'd seen him on the Ed Sullivan Show. But Ed had only allowed the singer to be seen from the waist up and this, well…Henry glanced at Mr. Engelmann, not surprised to see his mentor's eyebrows somewhere in the vicinity of his hairline.

Mary ran into the living room holding an empty cup and a damp dish towel, "Oh my gosh…oh my gosh!"

"That man's going wear his pants out from the inside," Mr. Engelmann quipped. Everybody laughed but their eyes remained glued to the screen.

"Looks like they're broadcasting right from his Army base in Germany," Bill said as the camera panned across an audience of U.S. soldiers and screaming girls. "And wow—look at that crowd—maybe your mom's *not* his biggest fan."

Mary blushed. "Really, Bill!"

But she stayed to watch, Henry noticed. He caught his dad's eye and motioned with his head to where his mom had perched on the arm of the sofa, clearly ignoring the dishes in the kitchen in favour of the famous rock 'n roller's hip-swinging gyrations. Bill waggled his eyebrows and Henry nearly laughed out loud. It was good to see his parents tease each other like this.

"Well, entertaining as this is," his dad said finally, "it's too bad we missed 'Life is Worth Living.' I was looking forward to watching it with you, David."

"I don't think it comes on until eight, Dad."

Bill checked his watch. "Another ten minutes. I think you're right, son. I guess we'll let your mom act like a teenybopper until then," he joked.

Mary swatted him with the towel on her way back to the kitchen. "Well, here we are! Hot apple pie," she said a moment later, balancing three plates.

As she handed them out, Elvis pulled a lovely dark-haired

young girl from the audience and began singing a song that made Henry oblivious to his parents, Mr. Engelmann and even his favourite pie.

Heart pounding as he thought of Jenny, he began to mouth the words to their favourite song as Elvis crooned "True Love":

While I give to you and you give to me
true love, true love
so on and on it will always be
true love, true love.

On the screen, the dark-haired girl gazed adoringly at Elvis, just as Henry used to when he was with Jenny. Henry's heart began to flutter as Elvis sang the next verse.

For you and I have a guardian angel
on high, with nothing to do
but to give to you and to give to me
love forever true.

"ISN'T HE A kick!" Jenny and her parents were watching Elvis shimmy and shake over the transatlantic broadcast. "I hope my friend Janice is watching—she'll flip!"

"What is the world coming to?" Edith murmured.

"I can't get over all those girls yelling and screaming. Just look!" Jenny exclaimed as the camera panned the audience, lingering on a beautiful young brunette.

"I have to admit his music gets you moving. I can hardly sit still," chimed in Ted.

"I can't get over how he shakes his legs and hips. You'd think they'd fall off," Jenny added with a chuckle.

The Elvis special was a good distraction, though it was tough to keep her mind off of Tammy. She'd called her friend again right after coming home from church but there was still no answer. Maybe Tammy and her parents had left for Montreal already. The thought of Tammy having the abortion twisted her stomach. It was the same kind of gut-wrenching feeling she'd had when she'd realized that she'd been raped that night in the park.

As if her mother had read her mind, Edith asked, "Have you heard from Tammy at all?"

"No, and it's driving me insane. I sure hope everything goes okay for her."

Edith didn't respond and neither did Jenny's father at first, but then he said, "It's quite a problem for her to be facing at such a young age." He glanced furtively at Jenny, then squirmed a bit and turned his attention back to the television set. Unhappy memories of her own pregnancy lurked in the room. Jenny knew her father hadn't wanted her to give up her baby. It was her mother who hadn't wanted the responsibility of raising another a child, and Jenny understood that. *But I would have.*

"Well, I think I'll head off to bed. I started that book, *Dr. Zhivago*, earlier today. Hope it'll keep my mind off Tammy." She kissed each of her parents on the cheek and began to make her way out of the living room.

But at the foot of the stairs she stopped dead in her tracks and turned around. On TV, Elvis Presley had begun to sing what she could only think of as their song, hers and Henry's. Memories flooded her mind as she listened to the lyrics of "True Love." Their first date. Going to see *High Society*, starring Grace Kelly and Bing Crosby. She definitely preferred Bing's version to Elvis'—she had the 45 on the record player in her room and listened to it all the time.

She smiled as she recalled the big oaf who'd sat between her and Henry at the movie theatre. She had so wanted to sit beside Henry and hold his hand. The two of them had missed the bus after, they'd walked home, holding hands, each remembering the song…

*For you and I have a guardian angel
on high, with nothing to do
but to give to you and to give to me
love forever true.*

"The song touching your heart, Jenny?" Ted asked, noticing his daughter at the doorway, her eyes filled with tears.

The reverie was broken. "Yes," she sighed, "silly me."

"Well, at least it's a more sensible song than the one about the hound dog," Edith opined.

"Yes, I guess it is. Well, good night again, Mom and Dad."

As Jenny started to climb the stairs to her room the doorbell sounded. In the living room her mother remarked, "Who on earth could it be at this hour?"

Edith and Ted came to the front door as Jenny opened it. Tammy stood there, eyes teary. She was trembling like a lost little lamb in the dark.

"Oh Jenny," her voice quavered, "I ran away from my mother at the airport and took a taxi here. I don't have enough money to pay the driver. Have you got fifteen dollars?"

Ted motioned Tammy inside, pulling his wallet from his back pocket. "Come in, Tammy. I'll deal with the taxi."

He slid outside past Jenny, who was already hugging her best friend. Edith stood in the foyer, not knowing what to do.

Tammy looked at Jenny's mom, "Oh, Mrs. Sarsky! Could I please stay here with Jenny tonight?"

Jenny turned to her mother as well, willing her to be compassionate.

"Yes, I suppose so. Where did you say your mother was? I'll have to phone her."

"I left her at the airport. She might have taken a cab home or waited for Dad to pick her up. She's probably already guessed I would come here."

"Well, go upstairs with Jenny and we'll wait for her to call. If we don't hear from her, I'll call your house in a half-hour or so."

"Thank you so much, Mrs. Sarsky."

Jenny put an arm around her friend and led her upstairs.

HEARING "TRUE LOVE" stirred such strong memories of Jenny, Henry had to excuse himself. Mary was still holding his apple pie, trying to figure out why her son hadn't taken the dessert.

"Thanks anyway, Mom. I'll have it later."

Henry said good night to his parents and Mr. Engelmann, and went to his room. He sat at his desk and relived one memory after another. The movie, the walk home, holding hands—and then Eddy's friends attacking them.

Henry did his best to pull his mind away from that awful scene. He was becoming good friends with Eddy and didn't want to go back to being mad at him, though he often still wondered what exactly had happened that night after Eddy's friends had taken Jenny to the park.

Soon he would know.

He opened the bottom drawer of his desk and glanced in. He almost had enough saved to carry out his plan. If only he could get Jenny's phone number or home address. He had Mr. Sarsky's work address and phone number. And he had a list of all the high schools in Ottawa and their phone numbers. He'd tried phoning a couple of the them but both had declined to either call a Jenny Sarsky to the phone or give out any home phone numbers. He tried to think of a way he might trick the school secretaries into giving out the information. If only he could create some emergency or other, but hadn't figured that part out yet.

He would, though.

He closed that drawer and opened the one second from the top, taking out the notes Jenny had left for him on the gatepost when she lived three doors down. He recalled the first time she'd put a note there. She'd done it to appease him for not being able to see him that night. He wished now that he'd never agreed to see her only every other evening. Her parents had been terribly concerned by how much they were seeing of each other. It hadn't made any difference to their feelings anyway, and the thought that he'd missed out on even a second of being with the love of his life saddened him to the soul. He began to read the notes, hoping Jenny's words of love would fill the void in his heart.

As soon as Jenny closed the door to her room she grabbed Tammy's hands and squeezed them. "Oh Tammy! You don't know how relieved I am to see you! What happened at the airport?" Jenny led her friend to sit on the edge of her bed.

"The look on my mom's face when I told her I just couldn't have the abortion is still stamped in my mind. I thought for sure her chin would hit the floor when I ran off," Tammy giggled a bit hysterically, but Jenny knew her friend didn't think it was the least bit funny and the choking laughter reverted to tears almost immediately.

Jenny inched closer and once again took Tammy's hands in her own, waiting until her friend's sobs subsided. When she finally looked up, Jenny saw that Tammy's brown eyes didn't have the lost, forlorn look they'd had the other day. They seemed clear, despite the tears. More settled.

"I'm so happy about your decision—but can I ask, what changed your mind?"

"The thought of the baby being scraped out of my womb and thrown away seemed so awful and—and…cruel. My mom kept telling me that it isn't anything yet, that it's a fetus just beginning to form and that I shouldn't call it a baby. But I told her it was and even *she* called it a baby in many of our discussions. But what you said to me the other day really hit home and I told Mom too. That the moment the baby is conceived it has a spirit, a soul and a guardian angel flies to its side. She said that was all nonsense but I know you're right. When any life begins it has a life force—how can it not? And an unborn baby has a soul right away. It doesn't get it after a month or three months or nine. It's a living spirit at its creation!"

After a brief moment Tammy added, "I hope it's okay. I told Mom about your baby and that you would never have an abortion and how much you miss your little girl, that you gave her up for adoption."

"Sure, that's fine, Tammy. I just hope it helps her understand." Jenny gazed at her friend with compassion. Tammy was being bombarded by every emotion there was and had still been able to make what Jenny knew was the best choice. Inwardly, she thanked Tammy's guardian angel for giving her insight.

"Was Robbie at the airport with you?"

"No, he came over to our house earlier today and we talked for a bit. He was glad I'd decided to have the abortion. I don't know what'll happen when he finds out I changed my mind."

That's the difference between James and Henry, Jenny thought. James would probably react like Robbie, but she knew Henry wouldn't. He'd be there for her, he'd never want her to destroy something they'd created together. The lyrics of "True Love" came back to her...*Oh where are you, Henry? Why haven't you written? I just know something must have happened, but what?*

She brought her attention back to her friend. "Tammy, I just want you to know that I'll always be here for you."

"I wish Robbie felt that way too. It would have been nice for him to come to the airport. The way he talks sometimes, I feel like he just used me. Do you and James do it, Jen?"

"James wants to all the time, but..."

"But you refuse, right? Oh Jenny, you're so perfect, always knowing what's best."

Jenny's grip on Tammy's hand tightened. "No, Tammy, I don't! When I was with Henry I wanted to, but *he* was the one who stopped at the last minute. *He* knew it was best to wait until we got married. At the time I fully believed that we would but then I left. Still, I hoped that someday we would get married... but he hasn't answered any of my letters so I guess his gallantry was all for nothing. But I have to say, too, that I understand completely why it's so important to wait to have sex until you're in a secure relationship and committed to each other."

"Yeah, look what's happened to me."

"Well, it happened to me too, Tammy. But there's so much more when you think about it. When you give yourself to each other, it's a precious gift, especially on your wedding night. And I know that if I give in to James it's all he'll want to do."

"That's what happened with Robbie and me. I didn't want to for the longest time, but he kept insisting that he loved me and I was afraid of losing him. I know lots of the girls do it, so I gave in too. I *do* love him, but once we started that's all Robbie wanted to do. He was forever taking me somewhere private in his car or to his place when his parents weren't home."

Tammy looked down, "I just knew this would happen. So many times I wanted to stop, but Robbie never would. I guess he never really listened to my wishes or concerns. He just wanted what he wanted."

"Don't worry, Tammy. I'm living proof that it's not the end of the world. And I'll be with you all the way."

"The baby's going to show soon, Jenny. I'll be so embarrassed and there'll be so much gossip and I know Robbie will just hate it. He probably won't have anything to do with me anymore."

"If that happens, Tammy, it's good for you to know now what the future with him might have held. If he won't support you now..."

"I'm so scared, Jenny, and confused by it all."

"I know. I felt the same when I was pregnant and I wanted Henry to be there. But he wasn't." Tears surfaced in Jenny's eyes.

"Are you sorry you gave your baby up?"

"Lots of the time I am, but I know I was too young and I know it was for the best. But I do miss my little girl so much and at times I think my heart will break. If only the rules weren't so strict and I could visit her...but then I guess they know what's best and maybe it would be too confusing for the child."

Jenny was quiet for a moment. "I've thought about it a lot, and even though I wish differently at times, I still think it was the best option. I talked to my social worker about it and she thinks it's best too. And if you want, I'm sure she'd be more than willing to talk to you too, Tammy."

Tammy nodded and then asked, "If you had to do it all over again would you give your baby up? You know, if you were my age?"

Jenny shrugged. "It's not important what I think, Tammy, it's what *you* really want in your heart that matters. If you've really decided to keep the baby and give birth to it, I think that's the best decision. You're carrying a precious human life and there are so many people out there who can't have children. And between now and when the baby is born, you'll have time to think about what's best for you. And whatever you decide, I'll be there for you through thick and thin. If you decide to keep the baby, I'll help you raise him or her. I'll do everything I can to help you."

Just then the phone rang.

"That must be Mom!" Tammy exclaimed. "I don't want to talk to her—I just can't!"

"I'm sure my mom will explain things. She's good at smoothing things over."

Ever so quietly Jenny picked up the extension and listened in, looking at Tammy and putting a finger to her lips.

"Oh, it's no trouble at all, Mrs. Anderson. She and Jenny are in Jenny's room and may even be sleeping already, they both were so tired … Yes, Jenny will drive her home tomo—"

Jenny hung up the phone and smiled at her friend. "It's okay. It was your mom and it sounded like she said you could stay. My mom told her I'd drive you home tomorrow."

"Oh, that's good! I just can't go home right now. Mom'll be so mad at me."

"You know, it might seem that way, but then again she just might not be. I was surprised by how my parents supported me."

Jenny paused, watching her friend stifle a yawn. It *had* been a trying day.

"If you like, I'll get you one of my nightgowns and there are new toothbrushes in the guest room. Do want to sleep there tonight?"

"I'd rather be here with you, if that's all right."

"Sure. Why don't you go get changed and I'll do the same."

Both girls stood up and Tammy gave her a quick hug.

"You're such a good friend, Jenny. I don't know what I would do without you."

ALONE IN HIS room, Henry turned out the light. He went over to the window and gazed up at the moon. Just below it was the brightest star in the sky, the star of the east. He could feel Jenny's love and he sent his out in return.

JENNY HELD HER friend close as they lay together in the single bed. Tammy didn't speak for the longest time, but Jenny knew she wasn't sleeping. She could feel Tammy's tears through the thin cotton of her nightgown and silently handed her friend a tissue.

Tammy wiped a tear from her cheek. Softly she whispered, "Last night, alone in our backyard and thinking of Robbie and what to do, I saw a dazzling shooting star streak across the sky. I once heard that if you make a wish right away the dust of the star's sparkle will settle in your heart and your wish will come true."

Jenny smiled at the thought. "Did you make a wish, Tammy?"

"Oh yes, that very instant. I wished with all my heart that Robbie would come back to me and that we would be married. I just know it'll come true."

"Oh, I don't doubt it, Tammy, not for one minute. Each star has an angel guarding it. Maybe the angel was telling you to believe in what you hope for."

"That's a beautiful way to look at it, Jenny."

"You know, the first bright star that appears in the eastern sky, that was our star, Henry's and mine. I still believe it. Sometimes it's as if I can feel it's angel sending Henry's love to me."

"Wow, Jenny, you sure must have loved him."

Jenny was quiet. Here she was, going steady with James and talking mostly about Henry. Tammy's next question went right to the heart of what she was feeling.

"Is there a wish you'd like to make, Jenny?"

Jenny took a deep breath, then told her best friend her heart's deepest desire. "I pray to my guardian angel about it all the time. What I wish for is to look into Henry's green eyes and kiss his warm, tender lips."

"You'd better not let James hear you say that."

Jenny chuckled, "For sure not. It's just that on the night we left Regina to come here, Henry came to see me off. I rushed to him to kiss him and look into his eyes one last time, and just as we were about to, my mother dragged me off to the car…you have no idea, Tammy, how I long for that last kiss."

"Well, keep your eyes open for a shooting star then, Jen."

Then all was quiet but for Tammy's soft sobs.

Jenny had forgotten to pull down the blind and the bright, full moon shone in through the window, the spark that was the star of the east not far below it. As always, she felt the rays of light enter her room and then her heart.

In her mind's eye, Jenny could see her and Tammy under the light of the heavens, each thinking of her baby and her first love, their feelings made clear by the sheen of the tears streaming down their soft, luminous cheeks.

Quietly Jenny hummed…

While I give to you and you give to me
true love, true love
so on and on it will always be
true love, true love.

For you and I have a guardian angel…

"Oh Jenny, you have the heart of an angel," Tammy murmured as they both finally drifted off into sleep, exhausted.

Chapter Nineteen

As Henry made his way down the hallway, he saw his buddy Travis coming up the stairs. Ever since the start of Grade 11 last year, they'd hit it off.

Henry still hung out with Timmy Linder occasionally, but they had sort of drifted apart, due in part because Henry had to rush home every day to work for Mr. Engelmann but also because they'd developed different interests and no longer had much in common.

Travis was a lot of fun and was in all of Henry's classes. He was one of those students who never seemed to study, yet earned straight A's. He was interested in art, didn't care much for sports and worked part-time at a shoe store downtown. The big difference between Travis and Henry was that Travis was girl crazy. Walking down the hall with Travis was like walking with a big dog in heat. Unfortunately, Henry didn't have much of a leash on him and at times Travis could be very embarrassing.

They landed at their lockers at the same time.

"Hey, Hank," Travis said. "Who ya taking to the Halloween dance?"

"Uh, I'm probably not going to go, Travis."

It's not like there was a shortage of girls interested in him. Girls were always flirting with him as they passed in the hallway. But Henry had decided a long time ago that Jenny was the one and only girl in his life. Someday they would be together again. And even if he wanted to find someone else, his schedule simply didn't allow it.

"Listen, Hank," Travis said, "I can get my dad's car for the dance, and my date has a friend who'd really like to go. Why don't you go out on a blind date with us? Julean promised me her friend is really nice, and very attractive."

"Oh, I don't know…"

"Look, all work and no play makes Hank a dull boy. Come on, it'll be fun. You never take the time for any enjoyment."

It was true. All he did was work, but he wasn't sure about going out with someone he'd never even met. "I've heard some pretty gruesome stories about blind dates," he said now.

"Aw, Julean wouldn't mess around like that. She said to say you'll be sure to like her friend. I won't take no for an answer."

"Well…okay," Henry agreed.

"Great! Lookin' forward to it." Travis nearly burst with excitement and smacked Henry on the shoulder, knocking him off balance.

"What are you going to wear? I mean, dress up like?"

"Oh right. Halloween dance. Geez, I don't know."

"Don't worry about it. It's still three weeks away. You'll come up with something."

The thought of having to dress up in some goofy costume for some date with some girl he didn't know sent shivers up and down his spine. Now he *was* spooked. He already regretted agreeing to go.

ON THE MORNING of the meeting at the lawyer's office, David Engelmann paced in front of the door, waiting for the car Mr. Balfour's secretary had said would pick him up. He had entrusted his entire future to a man he'd never met, one who had asked him to just "leave it all to me." He had no idea what he was supposed to say or do or might be expected to sign. *Just trust in the Lord with all your heart and lean not unto your own understanding.* The scripture came into his mind at that moment and he found it soothing.

"Is everything okay?" Mary asked as she straightened the magazines beside him.

"Yes, yes, everything is fine. I just don't know what kind of day the Lord has prepared for me."

"Well, be glad and rejoice, for this is the day that the Lord hath made!"

"Yes, yes, that is true. I will stand and accept the day as it comes."

"That sounds like a good plan. What time did they say they were going to pick you up?"

"The car is to be here at ten-thirty this morning."

Mary smiled at him. "Looks like the Lord has it in for you today. You're going to get real spoiled."

At precisely ten-thirty, a shiny black Lincoln pulled up in front of the store. For a moment, David thought the prime minister might step out.

"There's the car!" Mary exclaimed.

"Oh my. Mary, what shall I do?"

"Well, go out there and get in."

"Yes, yes, of course." And for the first time in his life, he asked, "Mary, how do I look?"

Mary took a deep breath and then another as she looked at him, giving him a chance to relax and do the same. "You'll be the most handsome and distinguished-looking man there." She kissed his cheek, then hugged him. "You'll be just fine"

He looked appreciatively into Mary's eyes and thanked her.

Mary made a little shooing motion and smiled warmly as he turned and headed out the door.

MARY RUSHED TO the window to watch David approach the car. A chauffeur wearing a black suit, white shirt and black bow tie stood smartly by its rear passenger door. She wondered if the chauffeur—who was looking straight ahead—had noted David's nervousness or that David's apparel was different from his usual clientele.

"Good morning, Mr. Engelmann."

"And good morning to you," Mr. Engelmann replied as he entered the car and sank into the tan leather seat.

The chauffeur closed the door and swiftly rounded the car to retake the driver's seat hidden behind dark tinted windows. After a pause, the Lincoln rolled away from the curb. Mary wished she could see the expression on Mr. Engelmann's face as he was whisked away like some highfalutin dignitary.

"YOU'RE RIGHT ON time, Mr. Engelmann," said Mr. Balfour's secretary. "Please have a chair over here."

As he sat down, David noticed a table littered with business and financial magazines. Since he had little interest in either, he sat back and gazed around the room instead. In one corner Mr. Webster waited beside another man. Mr. Engelmann waved hello. Mr. Webster appeared embarrassed by the gesture but reluctantly waggled his fingers in response.

David didn't have a chance to strike up a conversation before a buzzer sounded at the receptionist's desk. Miss Blane, according to her desk plate, said, "Mr. Balfour would like all of you to please join him in the boardroom."

All three gentlemen followed Miss Blane towards two tall burgundy doors. She turned the brass handles and swung both doors open.

Mr. Engelmann's eyes widened as he took in the spacious room. A wall of west-facing windows presented a scenic view of Victoria Park and the Hotel Saskatchewan. At the far end of a very long mahogany table sat several be-suited gentlemen.

Miss Blane directed Mr. Webster and his lawyer to their chairs then motioned Mr. Engelmann to follow her to the other end of the table to an empty chair between the other gentlemen.

Mr. Engelmann relaxed a little. Sitting there, he looked like the president of a huge corporation surrounded by an arsenal of highly trained professionals, experts in their fields ready to protect him. In fact, the looks on their faces suggested they would do their utmost to get the price he wanted for the store.

Mr. Balfour turned to Mr. Webster. "Mr. Webster, I presume?" At the other man's nod, he suggested, "Perhaps you'd like to introduce your associate?"

"Certainly. I'm Jim Webster and this is Reg Fuller, our lawyer." Mr. Webster indicated the man beside him with a nod.

"Good morning and welcome to you both," said Mr. Balfour. "I'm John Balfour, Mr. Engelmann's lawyer and this is Frank Watson, a chartered accountant, and Warren Thompson, a tax specialist," he said, indicating the men on Mr. Engelmann's right, then turned to the men on David's left. "Neil Sharp, a broker and financial investor, and finally Al Gregor, my legal partner. Al will be looking after the details of the actual sale, should we agree on a final purchase price."

David looked at each man. He'd never in his wildest dreams thought so many would be required in order to sell his small business. By the expression on Mr. Webster's face, David knew this sale already wasn't going according to the plan he'd had when he'd first set foot inside the store.

Mr. Balfour removed a stack of papers from his briefcase and laid one in front of David and each of his team, then slid a second package down to Mr. Webster and his lawyer. It stopped precisely in front of them as if Mr. Balfour had practised the move.

"If we can all turn to page one, please," Mr Balfour said. "You will notice that Mr. Watson has analyzed Mr. Engelmann's business over the past three years."

David realized that was when he had first hired Henry.

"It is significant to note," Mr. Balfour continued, "how the profits have steadily increased. Based on the financial records supplied by Mr. Engelmann's bookkeeper, this year, after salary to Mr. Engelmann and wages to his several employees, and including all other expenses, the business will turn a profit of just under $20,000. Mr. Watson further projected, based on past performance and the consistent increase in business, the net profit should easily increase to $40,000 over the next three years. And if Mr. Engelmann decides to expand into the adjacent lot, he can double the size of his establishment, make room for a parking lot and become a formidable force to other retail grocers."

"And then there's the whole matter of good will," Mr. Balfour went on. "Mr. Engelmann, as we all know, is a highly respected man in the community. The service and image he has established over the years is nothing short of entrepreneurial genius. A review of the graphs on page two detailing the increase in sales over the past three years shows a steady and sharp increase. It is just short of being vertical!"

Before Mr. Webster and his lawyer could speak, Mr. Balfour introduced the tax specialist. "Mr. Thompson, I understand you wish to make a few comments."

"If everyone would please turn to page four," Mr. Thompson directed, "you'll see we have reviewed Mr. Engelmann's income tax over the years and the financial statements of his business. You will note there are some tax-saving deductions we can make; however, the money received for selling the business would put him into a higher tax bracket and require him to pay significant capital gains. Mr. Engelmann's store was purchased at a very good price, and all maintenance, expenses and the building itself have been fully depreciated. As a result there will be significant tax consequences."

"So what are you saying, Mr. Thompson?" Mr. Balfour asked.

"Whatever price Mr. Engelmann asks for the store needs to be high enough to offset at least some of the money he will lose to Revenue Canada. If not, it would be better for Mr. Engelmann to keep the store open for another few years and reap the handsome profits that he would otherwise lose if the price were too low. It all depends on how badly Mr. Engelmann wants to sell his store at this time."

All eyes turned to Mr. Engelmann, looking for some reaction, but there was none. He knew they wanted him to say something profound, but in truth he really didn't know what to say. And he'd long ago learned that when you didn't know what to say, it was best just to listen.

Everyone's gaze returned to Mr. Balfour who then said, "I see. So, what do you believe to be a fair purchase price, Mr. Thompson?"

"Based on Mr. Watson's figures and analysis, including good will and capital gains, we have arrived at a bottom line figure." Mr. Thompson pulled a sheet of paper from his attaché case, wrote a figure down, then passed it forward to Mr. Balfour.

Mr. Balfour studied the figure for a few moments and passed it around to all the other members of his team. David had the feeling they were putting on a show for the benefit of Mr. Webster and his lawyer. They had known the amount they were going to ask for before the meeting even started.

When the paper finally arrived face down in front of him, David turned it over and nearly gasped aloud. His heart raced as he tried with all his might to maintain a poker face. He reread the figure: $75,000.

He had only paid $5,800 for the store, including the lot. Was it really worth so much?

Mr. Balfour's voice broke through David's shock. "Is the number satisfactory, Mr. Engelmann?"

The eyes of all those assembled, especially Mr. Webster and his lawyer, were glued to Mr. Engelmann, awaiting his response. A mixture of nervousness, excitement and disbelief swirled inside him, holding him speechless.

Reining in his emotions, he managed a, "That's fine."

"Good, as long as you're satisfied, Mr. Engelmann," Mr. Balfour said. He then asked that the paper be given to Mr. Sharp.

"Mr. Sharp, based on say 75 per cent of that figure, can you think of some investments your firm can make on Mr. Engelmann's behalf that will ensure a sufficient return for his retirement years?"

Mr. Sharp studied the figure for a moment. "A purchase of solid stocks—General Electric, Seagrams, Molsons, Imperial

Oil—have been performing very well over the past ten years and pay a good annual dividend, yielding a steady return of 10 per cent. While one can never predict with absolute certainty what the future holds in the stock market, these are solid stocks and should weather any disruptions, providing Mr. Engelmann with a reasonable return in later years."

"Fine," said Mr. Balfour. He retrieved the paper from Mr. Sharp, approached Mr. Webster, and placed the sheet in front of him and his advisor before striding back to his chair.

David wondered what their reactions would be. Mr. Balfour had handed the paper to Mr. Webster and his lawyer face down. By the time they turned the sheet over, Mr. Balfour had returned to his seat and was watching them.

Mr. Webster tried to mask his surprise, but David knew the figure was much higher than he had expected. Both Mr. Webster and his lawyer sat up, shocked, then leaned forward ever so slightly to have another look.

After a long pause, Mr. Webster said, "This is considerably higher than the offer we were prepared to make. I'll have to take this back to the company I represent."

Mr. Webster didn't have to say the name of the company. They already knew. He coughed, then asked, "Are there any other conditions to this sale?"

"Are there any other conditions to this sale, Mr. Engelmann?" Mr. Balfour asked. "For example, when do you want to vacate the premises? Will you leave the store's coolers behind? The drapes and things like that, you understand?"

By that time David had caught his breath and was prepared to speak. "Yes, yes, I understand. Thank you, Mr. Balfour."

He reached into his vest pocket and took out his own piece of paper. Mr. Webster and his lawyer leaned forward, anticipating another surprise. David slowly unfolded the paper, laid it in front of him and ironed the wrinkles out with the palm of his other hand. The tension in the room was almost palpable.

"Yes, I do have one important condition of this sale, Mr. Balfour."

"And that is?"

"I have a list of nine names. Each of these people has been a customer since I purchased the store in 1943. They have been faithful and loyal. They are getting on in age now, and many days it's too difficult for them to come to my store. Our delivery service was a godsend to them."

Mr. Engelmann looked down the long table at Mr. Webster. "You have never said, but I suspect I know which company you represent."

Mr. Webster didn't offer any sign of confirmation.

"I am glad it is Safeway interested in my store, rather than some company looking mainly for real estate. I know Safeway is a much bigger store than mine, but a big company has a big heart, too."

Everyone at the table smiled. Even Mr. Webster.

"The condition I ask for is that your company, Mr. Webster, look after these people until such time as they either pass on, go to a care home or are looked after by some member of their families. This is not too much to ask, and think how much Safeway will appreciate not only the business I had, but also the support and loyalty of my former customers." And then, like a seasoned negotiator, he added, "No amount of money can buy that kind of loyalty."

Everyone smiled or chuckled to himself. Even Mr. Webster had a bit of a twinkle in his eye.

"There is one more condition," Mr. Engelmann went on, seeing he had won his first battle. "I have made plans to go away for awhile next spring, and when I return, I will have another special place of my own. But until next spring, I need my home and store. The sale can go through at any time. However, the possession date cannot occur until next June. I want my store to be open this Christmas and I'll need time to tell my customers of the sale and also to clear out all my possessions. That is all, gentlemen," Mr. Engelmann said, as though he were the chairman of the board, concluding the meeting.

"Thank you, Mr. Engelmann," said Mr. Balfour, "Please leave that list of names with me."

Mr. Balfour looked down the table at Mr. Webster. "I will prepare papers to reflect today's discussion and have them sent over to your office first thing in the morning for your company's consideration. Are there any further questions or comments?"

"No, that will be fine, Mr. Balfour. I'll expect the proposal at my office sometime tomorrow morning, then?"

Mr. Balfour nodded, and with that, Mr. Webster and his legal advisor got up and left.

After David thanked his team profusely, Mr. Balfour led him to the reception area.

"Thank you, again, Mr. Balfour. I cannot believe such a thing has just taken place."

"You're very welcome, Mr. Engelmann. It was our pleasure. We'll be in touch."

Before Mr. Balfour returned to the boardroom he turned to his secretary, "Miss Blane, would you please escort Mr. Engelmann down to the lobby and have one of the commissionaires show him to the car?"

CHAPTER TWENTY

BLINDING SUNSHINE SPLASHED across David's field of vision as he stepped out of the building. The breeze felt good as it fingered its way through his clothes to cool his sweaty body.

"Oh, Mr. Engelmann!"

David turned to see the chauffeur who had brought him to the meeting.

"Mr. Balfour asked me to drive you home or anywhere you wished to go."

David just smiled and nodded. He'd never been so spoiled. "Thank you." The Lincoln sped off with him inside. He felt like a millionaire who had just closed the biggest deal of his life. The excitement revived a subconscious old habit and he reached into his vest pocket for the cigars Anna had made him give up a long time ago. But perhaps he could indulge just this once. David leaned forward to slide the shaded window aside and tapped the driver's shoulder.

The driver glanced up in the rear-view mirror. "Yes, sir?"

"Could you please stop at the next drug store? I would like to buy a cigar."

"Certainly, Mr. Engelmann. If I may suggest, sir, we just

passed the Trading Post. They specialize in cigars and are well known for their Cubans."

"Yes, yes, that would be fine. By the way, what is your name?"

"Douglas, sir."

"Yes, Douglas, that is an excellent idea. A Cuban cigar would be very fine."

Douglas turned the car, throwing Mr. Engelmann slightly off balance, and pulled up to the Trading Post. A few minutes later, David emerged with two cigars. He slipped one into his shirt pocket, then tore the plastic covering off the other. He wet the cigar with his tongue then bit off the end. He lit the cigar, took a few quick puffs to make sure it was well lit, then walked over to the car. Douglas stood next to the open back door. David climbed in, well aware of the stares of passersby.

They set off again and David turned so that he could look out the window. The back seat was large enough to comfortably transport six people. He pressed a button to lower the window and let in the warm fall air, leaning back a bit as he puffed away on the cigar. The world swirled around him. It had been over ten years since he'd stopped smoking. He imagined Anna watching him and immediately wished she were at his side.

If only Anna were here, enjoying all the pampering with him. He regretted that he and Anna had not taken more time to enjoy themselves. Somehow they had gotten caught up in the never-ending needs of the store and had not gone on many outings. Even if they had wanted to, they could never afford to get away. And then Anna had grown sick. Who would have taken care of the store, anyway?

Well, there was someone watching the store now. And even if it were only in his imagination, it would be nice for him and Anna to relax a bit.

David leaned forward and said, "Douglas, do you think Mr. Balfour would mind very much if we drove through Wascana Park on the way back to the store?"

"Certainly not, Mr. Engelmann."

The black Lincoln coasted through traffic, and David was

surprised how quickly they reached the park. Douglas slowed down to follow the scenic drive beside the lake, where several boats glided on the mirror-like surface. The image of the tall white sails with the Legislative Building behind them was reflected perfectly in the still water. *What a beautiful sight,* David mused, *how peaceful it must be to sail on the lake and enjoy the fall afternoon.*

Canada geese were feeding near the edge of the water and showed no sign of fear as the car crept by. An elderly couple sat on a bench, tossing bread pieces from a brown paper bag.

That should be you and I, Anna. We lived a good life, a godly one, but perhaps not a balanced one.

"Take time to stop and smell the roses." The old cliché, crossed his mind. Yes, it was all too much work and hardly any play. Yes, there should have been more roses.

As they passed the band shell, David recalled the times, many years ago, he and Anna had come to the park to listen to the orchestra—really the only thing they had done outside the store. On those days, they would walk through the park for hours and, after the music ended, stroll to the edge of the water, following it to the tiny shop in the boathouse to buy an ice cream. "Yes, it must have been over there," he mused, pointing with the hand holding the cigar. Visions of him and Anna walking hand in hand materialized beyond the curling cigar smoke.

Since Anna's death he had appreciated each day the Lord granted him more and more. When she had first died, he wished wholeheartedly for the Lord to take him too, but then he realized it was a privilege and an honour to spend another day serving his Maker.

Each moment, each breath must be acknowledged and used with thanks and purpose. The Lord had chosen his beloved wife to go home first. There was a reason the Lord was giving him a longer time under the earthly sun. There was work to do. Confessions to hear, babies to baptize, hearts to heal, lives to touch and sinners to save. Soon enough the night would come and his Maker would take his hand as He had Anna's and say,

"Come, it is time to go home. You have served well." He could see his Anna too, waiting, smiling, her hand reaching out towards him. "Come, David, and rest with me awhile."

Every now and then David noticed Douglas peering at him through the rear-view mirror, catching him reminiscing. He liked Douglas; he seemed like a good man.

The limousine was wonderful, but it was too spacious. Too empty. He missed his Anna deeply, ached to have her by his side, to share the joy of this day. To reap the rewards of their labour. To hold her hand. To tell her how much he loved her. David's eyes watered as he gazed out at the lake.

Unbidden tears spilled over, making rivulets in the weary lines of his face. By the time he had wiped them away, the lake was no longer there. They had gone through the park and were heading back towards the store.

"How quickly a holiday is over," David muttered.

"Would you care to go back through again, Mr. Engelmann?"

"No, that is fine, thank you."

As the car picked up speed, so too did the lazy fall breeze wafting through the open window, messing Mr. Engelmann's grey-white hair and swirling the smoke from his cigar. Mr. Engelmann felt like an eccentric tycoon as he sat there, legs crossed and fully extended, puffing away on a Cuban cigar. His shirt was clean but wrinkled like a crushed paper bag. Fortunately at least half the creases were hidden by his very comfortable, well-used vest. It all spoke of a man with a spirit rebellious of conventional approval. *What you see is what you get.*

"So this is what it feels like to be a millionaire," David quipped in an effort to cheer himself up. Douglas smiled at him in the rear-view mirror.

"You know, Douglas, I could really get to enjoying this."

Douglas nodded. His smile broadened.

By the time they reached the store, David had finished the cigar. Douglas jumped out and opened the door for him. David's brief escapade in the world of high finance and business, however enjoyable, was over.

"Thank you so much, Douglas. I liked that immensely."

"I'm glad you did, sir."

"Please, wait here a moment, Douglas, I wish to give you something."

"Certainly, Mr. Engelmann, but I assure you it's completely unnecessary."

"Just wait here."

Minutes later, David returned.

"Here, Douglas," David said, handing him a package. "This is the best salami in the city. I have it specially smoked."

"Why, thank you, Mr. Engelmann! I look forward to having it this evening at dinner."

"You're welcome, Douglas. And oh, by the way, here is something else." David reached into his shirt pocket and pulled out the second Cuban cigar. "Here, you better have this. Giving in once to temptation is more than enough. I've been spoiled amply for today."

The two men looked at each other. They were not millionaires; they were ordinary, average working people with just enough to get by. Each knew it wasn't money or a big car which made them important, but their unique character and desire to serve their fellow man.

It was this sense of each other that prompted each of them to extend a hand, carrying with the gesture a sincere mutual respect and understanding. Not another word was spoken, just a nod, and they both felt in that very short encounter a silent friendship had emerged.

AROUND TWO O'CLOCK the following afternoon, the phone rang.

"Engelmann's Grocery, how can I help you? Yes, this is he."

"Johnny Balfour, here, Mr. Engelmann, still remember me?"

"Yes, yes, of course, you did such a wonderful job for me at your office yesterday."

"It was my pleasure. Well, I just got a call from Mr. Webster..."

"Yes, yes, go on."

"They have accepted your price and all of your conditions. Congratulations, Mr. Engelmann."

"They are willing to pay $75,000?"

"That's right."

"This is unbelievable. I was sure they would come back with a lower price."

"I thought they would counter-offer, too," Mr. Balfour replied. "I guess they just wanted to get rid of you and were concerned you might change your mind or sell it to another buyer who might continue on with your business."

"This is unbelievable!" Mr. Engelmann exclaimed again. *If only my Anna were alive.* "How can I ever thank you for all you have done?"

"The pleasure is all mine. We'll look after the details and get back to you shortly. I'll send Douglas over with the papers for you to sign. Congratulations again. Goodbye, Mr. Engelmann."

David stared off into space as the dial tone replaced Mr. Balfour's voice. He was too stunned to move.

"Are you okay?" Mary asked, emerging from the storage room. She grabbed his arm and shook it. "David! Are you all right?"

Mr. Engelmann blinked and shook his head. "I just sold my store, Mary."

"What!" shrieked Mary. "What do you mean?"

"Safeway bought my store and paid a fortune for it. I cannot believe it. Please, come. I have to sit down. Get me a root beer and have a drink, too. Let us sit in the storage room for a few minutes. Have I got a story to tell you."

After Mr. Engelmann told Mary what had happened, she couldn't sit still. In fact, she jumped up and danced around the storage room. Then she grabbed him off his perch atop a box and danced him around too.

When Mrs. Schmidt came up from the basement and saw the two of them jumping around like two school kids playing Ring Around the Rosy, she shook her head and muttered, "They've lost their marbles."

THE FOLLOWING SUNDAY evening, Mr. Engelmann repeated the story for Henry and Bill over dessert. By that time he had told several people, embellishing it a little each time.

Overnight, everything seemed to have fallen into place.

"This has been a very busy week for me," David said as the clock in the living room chimed seven, "and I am all tired out."

"Yeah, it must be tough closing million-dollar deals and having a chauffeur drive you around all day," Henry teased.

Mr. Engelmann turned to Henry with a grin and shook a finger at him. "Never fear, your turn will come, Henry."

He and his parents walked Mr. Engelmann to the door.

"This has been quite a week for you, David, a very successful one," said Mary. "You solved two problems that usually take months and even years to sort out."

"I'm glad you sold the store, but I sure am going to miss it," Henry said. "I really enjoy working there."

"Well, Henry, someday I know you will be a highly successful businessman. You have a natural talent for it. Well, good night, Mary, Bill. Thank you for the wonderful dinner."

"You're welcome, David," Mary replied, kissing his cheek.

He shook Bill's hand and accepted Henry's hug then headed toward the store and home.

CHAPTER TWENTY-ONE

THE WEEK LEADING up to the Halloween dance flew by and kept Henry so busy that he hardly had time to work at the store. He'd decided on a Lone Ranger costume for the dance. He borrowed his dad's western shirt and old black hat, which his mother lined with masking tape until it fit just right then steamed it and reshaped it into more of a western look. Henry found a couple of old pistols he used to play with, but they had to enlarge the holster belt by several notches. Mary found a black mask at the drug store and an extra large red hanky to tie around Henry's neck. He didn't have cowboy boots and so would have to wear his black Sunday shoes instead. Not exactly worthy of the Lone Ranger, but it would have to do.

Henry left work around four that Saturday so he could shower and get ready. His stomach was clenched and his fingers fumbled with the buttons on his shirt as he thought about going out with another girl. He hadn't dated since Jenny. He imagined she would have dressed up as Cinderella or Snow White if he were taking her to the dance.

But those were fairy tales. And in a fairy tale, Jenny would have to remain. Tonight, he was stepping out into the real world, where Jenny could not be.

JENNY'S SHOES ANNOUNCED her arrival at the bottom of the stairs where James waited, eyes and mouth wide open. She lifted the front of her white Cinderella gown with her fingertips to keep from tripping, revealing her silver slippers. Her mother's alterations to her wedding gown had worked beautifully. Jenny's hair had been swept up and pinned at the back of her head, a white tiara glinting just behind her curled-down bangs.

"My God, you look ravishing, Jenny," James said, finally coming out of the spell she'd put him under.

"Thank you, Prince Charming!"

James bowed and made a broad sweeping motion with his arm, gesturing his princess to the door. "Your carriage awaits, my dear."

"Thank you, kind sir," Jenny stifled a giggle and curtsied.

She gasped when she saw the changes the body shop had made to the car to make it look like the pumpkin carriage of fairy tales. She knew he'd have been adamant that no lasting damage be done to his Chevy Corvette.

"But where are the white horses?" she jested.

"Under the hood, my love! All 230 of them," quipped James.

"Make sure you have her home before midnight," her mother called out just before James closed the door.

AT QUARTER AFTER seven, Travis pulled up in front of the Pederson home in his dad's 1956 Ford Fairlane and honked the horn until Henry came out.

"We'll pick up Julean first," Travis said as Henry jumped in, "and then her friend. I think Julean said her name was Lorraine."

Julean lived about two miles from Henry's place. Hers was a two-storey home with brick exterior, almost twice the size of his. Obviously, her parents had a lot of money—or at least more money than the Pedersons. When Travis pulled up, he hopped out, ran up the walk and pushed the doorbell.

When Julean stepped out, Henry gasped. She was dressed as Snow White, the same costume he had earlier fantasized Jenny in. Julean's dark brown hair was bobbed around her chin. She wore a blue blouse with puffed sleeves and a white collar, and a yellow layered skirt that puffed out below her waist. Her black patent leather shoes reflected in the streetlights. Henry couldn't take his eyes off her as Travis escorted her to the car.

Travis opened the door and handed her in. She thanked him as she slid into the front seat, glancing back at Henry as she straightened her skirt.

"Hi, Hank," she said. "I'm so glad you were able to come. Lorraine is so excited. She's a real sweetheart; I'm sure you'll like her. What are you going as? I can't tell from here."

"I'm the Lone Ranger."

She twisted around onto her knees and peered over the back of the seat. She looked Henry up and down. "You do look like the Lone Ranger. That's really cute, Hank."

Travis plunked himself behind the wheel as Julean sat back down and gave him directions to Lorraine's.

Lorraine's house, in contrast to Julean's, was a little smaller than Henry's. When Travis pulled up, Henry got out and walked to the front door, churning over what should he say, how should he act and why on earth had he agreed to go with her in the first place. Before another self-defeating thought entered his mind, the front door opened and Lorraine emerged, dressed as Florence Nightingale in a white nurse's cap, white blouse and long Victorian-era black skirt.

"Hi!" she greeted him, "I guess you're Hank—or should I call you the Lone Ranger all evening?"

"No, Hank will be fine." Henry was somewhat taken back by this girl. She *was* very attractive, Julean hadn't been kidding. Her straight brown hair fell below her shoulders, adding length to her already long, slender build. Her dark eyes sparkled as she spoke. A subtle shade of pink lipstick coated her lips. She looked like a beauty queen. Lorraine descended the front stairs and stood in front of him.

"Well, shall we go?" Lorraine said, offering her arm.

"Yeah, of course!" Henry jerked into motion and crooked his elbow. "Let's go." As they walked back to the car, Henry found himself saying, "So you're Lorraine."

Oops, did I say that out loud?

"Yes, of course, I'm Lorraine!" she laughed. "Wouldn't it be something if you picked up the wrong girl!"

Henry laughed too, and was grateful that the ice had been broken so easily. Nearing the car, Henry noticed Travis watching them, or more specifically, his date.

"And you must be Travis," Lorraine said as Henry opened the door for her. "What are you wearing?"

"Why, I'm a wicked pirate of the seven seas, me hearty. If you don't behave tonight, I'll have ye locked up in the brig!"

"I promise I'll be good—wouldn't want to walk the plank!" Lorraine quipped. "And Julean, that outfit just *kills*!"

Henry was glad that Lorraine was outgoing and kept the conversation lively. It meant he didn't have to try so hard to be witty, and potentially say something embarrassing instead.

"I can't wait to get to the dance and see what everyone else is dressed as," she said now. Turning back to Henry she added, "Julean says you're responsible for getting the school to agree to a Halloween dance, is that right?"

"Well, the student council did."

"Hank's just being modest," Julean said, "He's the president, and what he says usually goes—least that's the rumour around school."

"That's not *really* the case, Julean," Henry said, glad that the darkness of the vehicle covered his steadily growing blush. "What school do you girls go to?"

"Central Collegiate."

"Then how come you seem to know so much about what goes on at Balfour?"

"News gets around, Hank," Lorraine said, "and Travis talks about you all the time."

"Geez, thanks, man!"

"No sweat, buddy," Travis said, slowing down as they pulled up to the school. "Now where am I going to park?"

"There's the parking lot behind the school," Henry said, waving his hand. "We can go in the back door near the gym."

Travis cranked the wheel and the Fairlane turned into the parking lot. The four of them headed for the back door as Henry had suggested. Inside it looked like Mardi Gras; everyone was dressed up. Henry knew he'd never have the nerve to dress like some of the guys had. The centre guard of the football team wore a bonnet, dress and frilly apron like something out of Mother Goose. Tony, their star basketball player, was a Marilyn Monroe look-a-like—his balloon-enhanced "rack" barely held in check by a snug mohair sweater.

They reached the gym just as the hired band launched into "Dream Lover."

"Ooh, I love this song," Lorraine squealed. "Come on, let's dance." She grabbed Henry's hand and pulled him out into the middle of the gym.

As they danced, Lorraine laughed and joked about everyone and their costumes, Henry couldn't get over how much Lorraine's bubbliness and spontaneity reminded him of Jenny, though unlike Jenny, Lorraine didn't pay too much attention to him even while they were dancing. But, in all honesty, Henry wasn't paying much attention to her, either. He kept catching Julean's eye as she glanced at him over Travis' shoulder, kind of liking the way she lowered her gaze every time their eyes met.

After a few songs, Lorraine and Henry made their way to a table to catch their breath. Travis and Julean joined them.

"Would you like some punch, Lorraine? Julean?" Henry asked.

"Sure! That'd be great."

"Oh, I'd love a cup of punch! It's warm in here."

"Come on, Travis. You can help me."

"*Arrgh!* Aye, matey!" Travis replied.

Walking towards the canteen, Travis went on and on about

what a dish Lorraine was. "Do you mind if I dance with her, Hank?"

"Not at all." Actually, he'd been trying to think of a way to ask Travis if *he* could dance with Julean.

IT WAS A long drive from Jenny's house in the country to Springview High, and when they arrived the parking lot was almost full, the gym nearly bursting with people.

But all activity stopped when Jenny and James entered. The gym had been transformed into a ballroom and it was truly as if royalty had entered the room. If it hadn't been for the music the band was playing, there would have been dead silence as Prince Charming led his Cinderella to the dance floor. Jenny hoped the other students would quit staring and start to dance again. Gradually, they did, though they left a large circle of space around the royal couple.

Jenny didn't like being the focus of all that attention but James seemed to get a kick out of it. He was the envy of every guy there and he knew it.

WHEN HENRY AND Travis returned with the drinks, a couple of guys had swarmed Lorraine.

"All right, you yokels—scram," Travis said, only half joking, as he and Henry set the drinks down on the table in front of the girls.

"Just checking out the scene, Travis," one of them said.

"Well, check it out in the boiler room from now on."

"Yeah, yeah," the other guy said as they walked away.

At the first few notes of "Put Your Head On My Shoulder," Travis spoke up, "Wanna switch partners for this one, Hank?"

"Sure," Henry replied, "that is, if that's okay with you, Lorraine?" But Travis already had her hand and was leading her towards the dance floor.

As Lorraine moved into Travis' arms, Henry couldn't help but notice Eddy Zeigler and his well-endowed girlfriend. His head was buried in her bosom, and Henry imagined he was at that moment probably thanking God for his lack of height. Eddy opened dreamy eyes for a moment and caught Henry looking at him. He winked, then his eyes drifted shut once more. About halfway through the song, Henry gathered his nerve and asked Julean to dance.

Something about her touch, her hand in his, sent a slight tingle through him. Julean's hand was warm, soft and smooth. His hand locked easily into hers, and he pressed her a bit closer as they waltzed. He wanted to look at her, but every time their eyes met, each glanced the other way.

"It's a nice band," Julean said finally.

"Yeah, they are. We were lucky to get them. Lots of schools are having a dance tonight too, and they're a pretty popular group. One of the band members has a girlfriend who goes to our school, though, and she convinced them to play here."

As they talked, Henry studied Julean's eyes. Their dark depths held a sparkle he found intriguing. Her delicate nose, lush eyelashes and heart-shaped mouth Henry thought very attractive too. Personality-wise, she wasn't nearly as flamboyant as Lorraine, but Henry liked her gentle manner and sincerity. She wasn't drop-dead gorgeous like Lorraine, either, but he thought she was very pretty. Hers was a quiet beauty and Henry was disappointed when the music stopped. He wanted to keep holding her. They held hands as they walked back to the table. Neither of them made any move to do otherwise.

For a moment Henry forgot all about Jenny.

Just before they made it to their table, Eddy bumped him from behind. "Cute babe, Hank."

"Thanks, Eddy." Henry felt the heat of embarrassment on his cheeks and hoped Eddy would take the hint. Thankfully, he seemed to and went off in pursuit of his well-stacked girlfriend.

Henry escorted Julean to her chair and claimed the one beside her. "Thanks for the dance," he said. "I really enjoyed that." Inwardly, he cringed.

Eddy would've come up with something cool.

But Julean smiled at him. "So did I."

SEVERAL GUYS ASKED Jenny to dance, but each time she politely refused. Not only would James have been upset if she did, but she didn't think it was right for her to dance with anyone else.

"Some of these costumes are pretty hip," she said to him now. "Look at Mary Jo, she looks just like Little Red Riding Hood, with Jeff in that wolf mask. I wonder if he'll eat her up before the night is through?" she looked up at James through her lashes, flirting just a little. "And I can't believe our student council president dressed like Doris Day. What a scream."

"Looks like a fruitcake to me," sneered James.

"Oh, it's Halloween, James. It's all in fun."

"Maybe so, but you wouldn't catch me dead in women's clothes."

"I have to say, James," she said, laying a hand against his chest, "that you are certainly the most charming of all."

That was exactly what he wanted to hear. James' eyes brightened and his grip around her tightened.

JULEAN AND HENRY were still on the floor when the band broke into "One, two, three o'clock four o'clock, rock. Five, six, seven o'clock..." and within seconds there was hardly room to move.

As they twisted and turned to the music, he couldn't believe how easily he and Julean moved together. It was like they were made for each other.

"Wow!" he said when the song finished. "I sure hope they do that one again."

"So do I," said Julean, "that was fun."

LATER IN THE evening the band announced a dance in which couples were to exchange partners every time the band leader called out "bingo!" James was reluctant to let Jenny dance with someone else the first couple of times "bingo" was called, but soon several suitors were waiting in line to dance with her. As soon as James let her go, Jenny was whisked away into the crowded gym, and after it was over, it took another two dances for Jenny and James to finally reunite. James' body quivered with suppressed rage as he held Jenny to him. He didn't need to be so possessive and she tried to tell him so—she really wasn't interested in anyone but him—but though his jealousy unnerved her, she had to admit she kind of liked that he felt so strongly about her.

The hands of the clock said eleven-thirty as they finished the last slow, romantic waltz. "I guess we'd better go before the spell is broken and my Prince Charming sees nothing but a girl in rags," Jenny joked.

James grinned, glad to have an excuse to be alone with her for a bit. But as he escorted her back to his "pumpkin," she couldn't help but wish it was Henry who would come for her so they could live happily ever after.

Julean and Henry danced together for the rest of the evening, as did Travis and Lorraine. When it came time to go home, Julean didn't know if she should sit in the back with Henry or in the front with Travis. She caught Lorraine's eye; she had the same dilemma. In the end, they sat the way they had come. An uncomfortable silence fell over the car as they drove home.

After dropping off the girls, Travis steered the Fairlane towards Henry's place. "Oh, man, Hank—I'm sorry. I dunno what happened tonight. I didn't mean to dance with your girl so much. It just sort of happened."

"It's okay, Travis. Honestly, I didn't mind at all. I really enjoyed being with Julean."

"D'you mean that?"

"Sure. I really like her."

"That's great, Hank. Then…you won't mind if I ask Lorraine out next Saturday?"

"Not at all." Henry silently thanked his buddy for solving that problem. As Travis pulled up in front of Henry's house, Henry said, offhand, "I guess since you're gonna take Lorraine out, I'll ask Julean."

Travis looked up sharply. "Yeah, sure. That's okay."

"Could you give me her phone number?"

"You bet, Hank. I'll phone you with it tomorrow."

As Travis peeled away from the curb, Henry stared after him. He wasn't sure what Travis was mad about. Surely he didn't think he could have both girls, did he?

James parked down the lane just past the Sarsky home. A chill ran down Jenny's spine as he turned off the ignition, wrapped his arm around her and tugged her close. She'd known he'd try again, though she'd spent the last month or more telling him she just wasn't ready to make love and wouldn't be until she was married.

"Come on, Jenny. What's the difference? We're going to get married in a year or two anyway, so—"

"I just *can't*, James…" Jenny had tried many times to gather the courage to tell him about Camilla and her fear of bringing another child into the world without the security of a marriage and home. Having to give away another child would be more than she could bear. But she'd never been able to bring herself to tell him, worried he'd think so much less of her.

And something always told her to keep it a secret.

"What's wrong, Jenny? You're somewhere else again. And tell me, what's wrong with doing it? I love you and you love me, don't you?

"Yes, I do, James, but I just don't *want* to right now."

She slid out from under James' arm and glanced out her window. He no longer seemed like Prince Charming and she sure wasn't Cinderella. She so wanted to tell him about the rape, the adoption, tell him everything so he'd understand—and yet she couldn't. *What if he* doesn't *understand?* If they really loved each other she shouldn't be afraid to share these intimate thoughts and feelings, but something inside her told her that James would never accept it. She'd lose him. And she didn't think she could lose someone else she loved.

James tried to pull her across the seat to him again. "Come on, Jen, I love you and I want you so—"

"No!"

Jenny threw his arm off her, jumped out of the car and ran towards the house. She tripped on the paving stone driveway and wrenched one of her silver slippers off her foot, but kept on, walking now and limping a bit.

James started the car and caught up to her, rolling the window down. "Jenny! Aw, I'm sorry, Jen. Please get back in."

Jenny stopped walking and hung her head.

James parked, hopped out of the car and came over to her. "I really am sorry, Jenny."

She turned to him and fell into his arms. "Oh, James! I'm sorry, too. I'm just not ready to have sex. Can't you understand? I'm afraid…. Please be considerate of my feelings."

"Shhh, it's okay, Jenny," he said, rubbing her back and trying to make light of it. "Look at me." He tilted Jenny's chin so her eyes met his, tears tumbling down her cheeks. "I'll try my best not to let this happen until you tell me it's okay. It's just that you're so beautiful tonight, Jenny, and I want you so much."

Jenny was quiet, thinking of everything he didn't know. Everything she should be able to tell him. Yet she didn't.

"It's okay, James," she said instead.

She bent down and took off her other slipper then put her arm around his waist as they made their way to the front door. Frustration, hurt and confusion lingered in his eyes. Still, he put his lips to Jenny's and kissed her lightly on the mouth.

"Good night, Jenny. You know I love you very much."

"I love you, too, James." Jenny forced a smile, dashed a tear from her cheek and went inside. Before she closed the door, she peeked out once and threw James a kiss with a whispered, "G'night."

James stood on the steps for a long time after the door had closed, trying to understand. He didn't think this had anything to do with that Pederson guy. It seemed like maybe there was something else she was keeping from him, and though he didn't have a clue as to what it might be, he knew he didn't like it.

When Henry arrived home, his mother was reading a magazine in the living room. But Henry knew the magazine was just for show, a cover for her real intentions—to quiz him about how the evening had gone.

"Did you have a nice time?"

"Yeah, I did, actually. "It was fun. I'm glad I went."

"Good!" Before he could say good night, she added, "And how was your blind date?"

"She was a real doll, Mom, very attractive."

"So, you had a good time with her?"

"Well, sort of." Henry knew the moment the words were out that his mom would pounce on them.

"What do you mean, 'sort of'?"

No way was he getting out of this now. He resigned himself with good grace, took a seat on the chair beside her and told her the whole story.

"So, you and Travis aren't upset with each other for taking each other's date?"

"No, Mom—it's just one of these things that happens. It's funny how things turn out sometimes, isn't it? I mean, just when you think one thing about a situation, something happens that's completely different than what you expected."

"Are you going to see this Julean again?"

"Yeah, I think I am. In fact, I asked Travis for her phone number when he dropped me off."

"Well, I think that's great. It will be nice for you to have a girlfriend."

She glanced down at her magazine. After a long moment, she looked up, again, and studied him. "Do...do you still miss Jenny?"

Henry was surprised to feel relief that she'd spoken Jenny's name and was glad she'd asked; Jenny had been on his mind the whole night.

"Yeah, Mom," he said with a little sigh, "I still miss Jenny. I miss her a lot. I wonder all the time what happened to her and why she never sent even a single letter."

Mary's eyes reflected the disappointment and sorrow her

son felt so deeply. She nodded, saying as clearly as if she had spoken that she understood.

Henry thought again how like his mom was to Mr. Engelmann in that regard. Her empathy brought unwanted tears to his eyes. Henry looked down at the floor, hoping she wouldn't see them.

"Life is hard to understand at times," she said now. "I know how deeply you felt about Jenny, and still do. You might even feel that way for the rest of your life, and that's okay. But we must move on and not get stuck. I remember my cousin Drew. A year after he married Jeannie she was killed in that horrible car accident. Drew was devastated. But he found someone else, perhaps not the same, but his heart is now filled with Alice and their two wonderful children. Life does go on."

"Yeah, but at least Drew knew what happened to his wife. Sometimes I wonder if I'll ever know what happened to Jenny."

"Yes, not knowing is very difficult to accept."

"Yeah, that's what bothers me so much."

His mom nodded again. "It just might be something you have to learn to accept and live with, Henry."

Henry let his head fall, and a tear fell onto his pantleg. He rubbed away at it for the longest time as he reflected on his mother's words.

"Yeah, I guess so," he finally whispered.

Silence fell over them then, the mood in the room much different than when he'd first sat down, and yet it was healing somehow. The quiet between them carried understanding, caring—and love. He wasn't alone in his heartbreak. Someone else was helping him carry the load.

And so they sat for several minutes, not saying anything. Then Henry stood. "Think I'll head off to bed. Thanks for waiting up for me."

His mother looked at him and smiled.

He went over to her and kissed her cheek.

As he left the living room, Mary rose from her chair and followed. Henry turned to see her there, her arms open.

"Good night, son. I'm so glad you had a nice time."

"Thanks, Mom," Henry said softly as he stepped into her arms. Her hug carried with it the assurance that these difficulties would be made easier, that they too would pass.

"I'm so glad you like this Julean. She might just be the one who sweeps you off your feet again."

"Yeah, she just might be."

EDITH WAS STILL up when Jenny came in.

"You're home early," Edith called from the living room. "Come in and chat awhile."

Jenny blew her nose and dabbed her eyes with a tissue, then examined herself in the floor-length mirror in the foyer as the grandfather clock chimed twelve. Even though she still looked like a princess, she no longer felt like one. The magic was gone.

"Hi, Mom," she said as she came in and plopped herself on the sofa beside the dying fire.

Her mother set down the book she was reading and closed the cover. "Did you and James have a good time at the—have you been crying?"

Unbidden tears came quickly into Jenny's eyes once again.

Her mother moved beside her and took hold of her hands. "What's wrong, Jenny?"

"James and I are getting a little too close. I want to tell him about Camilla but I'm afraid to. I just don't know what he would think if I told him everything. You know, the rape and all...."

"I see. Jenny, you know why it has been a well-guarded family secret these past two years and why the only outsiders to know about it are the doctors and other professional care workers who were sworn to confidentiality. I know you shared it with Tammy and her parents, but that was because of the circumstances. Jenny, if you told James, he might not be able to handle it and he could tell others and it could affect your reputation at school.

"Perhaps, Jenny, it's best to keep it from James for now until you're married so you know he's committed to you. We all have skeletons in our closets that at times are best kept under lock and key."

"But didn't you tell Dad everything about yourself before you got married?"

"Well…yes," At her mother's hesitation, Jenny's head snapped up. "There are *some* things I kept from your dad—like some of the boys I went out with. There was no need to make him jealous and I'm sure he went out with other girls before we tied the knot."

"But this is different. I gave birth to a baby girl and she's part of my life even if she's adopted and I need to share that with the person I marry. James needs to know that and perhaps it would help him understand why I don't want to—" Jenny looked at her mom as her face flushed. She didn't want her mom to know every intimate detail.

"I understand, Jenny. Your father and I have tried to instill in you that sexual relations should wait until marriage. Perhaps that is what you are feeling, as well as your need to share with James what happened to you. Your instincts are telling you to hold off for now and maybe that's for the best. You're just starting twelfth grade and a lot can happen between now and the time you're ready for marriage. Until there's some serious commitment perhaps it's best to keep this between ourselves."

Her mother patted her hand then got up to stoke the struggling fire.

"Listen. Why don't you play hooky from school on Monday and you and I will take the train into the city and do some shopping? We could meet your father at the office later and then go out for dinner and maybe a movie. What do you say? A night out on the town would do us all some good," she added with a wink and a smile.

Jenny returned her mom's smile. "Yes, I'd like to do that, Mom. Dad looks so tired and overworked lately. Sometimes I wish he hadn't taken on that job as president and we had stayed in—"

Her mother shot her a sharp look.

"Oh, he'll have everything working fine in no time, Jenny. Being the president carries a lot of responsibility; it's such an important position. It takes time and hard work, but it will all be worth it in the end. Trust me, Jenny."

"Yes, I suppose so…it just seems like we were all happier before we came here."

"Now, Jenny, you're just saying that because you're upset. A good rest and a nice dinner at a fine café and a stop at the theatre after will fix everything up."

Jenny stood and kissed her mom's cheek. "I'm sure you're right, Mom."

HENRY LAY ON his bed in the darkness, unable to sleep. He watched the moon climb from branch to branch up the barren tree through his bedroom window as he relived the evening. He could feel the touch of Julean's hand as he remembered their first dance. The fact that he was attracted to her surprised him. She was the polar opposite of Jenny.

Jenny had blond hair; Julean's was a brunette. Jenny's eyes were blue; Julean's were brown. Both girls' eyes sparkled when they spoke, but Jenny definitely was more outgoing and expressive. Yet he had appreciated Julean's quiet manner and gentle genuineness. Henry wondered how he would feel the next time they went out, then wondered if she'd even want to go out with him.

Julean and Jenny swapped places in his mind for the longest time. Back and forth he went, and he began to dream. He was back on the farm riding a horse with two heads, one at the front and the other at the back. He tried to make it go, but it just stood there, unable to move either forward or backward. When he got off, he wasn't sure which head to pat. The more he looked at the horse, the more frustrated and torn he became. He was confused, not knowing which way to turn or go. He walked away and went into the dark barn, feeling his way into the pitch black and turning into a stall. He felt the hay beneath his feet and lay down on top of it. Instantly he fell into a very deep sleep.

JENNY TURNED ON the light then flicked it off again and walked over to the window. The moon was full, flooding the grounds with its bright light. Nature continued to be healing for her and yet as she gazed into the heavens melancholy washed over her.

She missed her baby. And more so than ever, she missed Henry. James was like him in so many ways. But if she were dating Henry, she would never have hesitated to tell him about her child and the circumstances surrounding Camilla's birth. She felt safe with Henry. She trusted and loved him. She felt that all so deeply now.

Oh, guardian angel, can you ever bring us back together again? Can we ever recapture what once was? Tears glistened like crystal beads as they caught the moonlight on Jenny's cheeks. Henry was just a memory. A memory that no longer had any life.

JULEAN TOSSED AND turned in her bed, knowing sleep would not come easily. Thoughts of her new friend would probably keep her awake for a long time. *What a wonderful evening,* she thought. *It was funny how it turned out, how we sort of switched partners. But I loved it. I secretly hoped it would happen as soon as I saw him in the car.* Julean smiled as she relived the feel of his hand in hers and how they had seemed to fit as they danced together and their attraction for each other.

Henry reminded her of her Uncle Emmanuel. Handsome and strong with character to match. *Henry has such a good reputation too.* His thick, dark brown hair and eyebrows framed his face. He was very good-looking.

Julean thought his eyes were green, but it had been too hard to tell in the dim light of the gym. She could tell from them though that he was sincere, trustworthy and dependable, *and that's so much more important than any colour.* So different from Travis, whose eyes roamed like a searchlight, always looking for greener pastures. She never knew where she was at with Travis. She could see right off how Lorraine drew his attention away from her.

Henry was more stable, secure, steady. She smiled again, parting her lips slightly. The dim light in the room caught her bright white teeth. She liked his shyness, his awkwardness, like he had not gone out with many girls. Then she remembered that Lorraine and some other girls told her that he never went out much.

She wondered if he'd had another girlfriend. There were moments when his mind seemed to be somewhere else, but then again if he did, he wouldn't have gone out with Lorraine and... *he did seem to be enjoying himself with me.* Julean felt hopeful. *On the colony that wouldn't be a concern, the men can choose several girls, several wives.* Yet that's what drove her parents away. *Mom would never accept Dad sharing his love with another. But maybe I could—if the man were right.*

I wonder what Henry believes and what he thinks about Mormons? Will I see him again? Oh, I hope I do...I think he likes me. I like him—a lot.

Julean tossed and turned again. Sleep was still a far way off. She replayed the same thoughts over again. This time she ended by whispering in the dark, "I hope and pray that he phones me."

CHAPTER TWENTY-TWO

A SOLEMN PROCESSION OF twelve board members passed through the reception area towards the elevator. Elaine counted them as they filed past her desk. Not one, not even Mr. Peakan, looked at or greeted her. Their collective demeanour was as though someone were gravely ill and on the verge of death. And perhaps that *was* the best way to describe the fortunes of the corporation. Elaine knew for some time the health of the company had been failing; the quarterly board meeting must not have been pleasant for Mackurcher's president either.

Ted Sarsky was the heart of the corporation and its beat under his leadership showed serious signs of a major attack. Like a foreboding ECG reading, the charts and graphs analyzing the pulse of the company indicated an alarming malady, a forecast of impending doom. The graph line, which for years had shown a steady increase in net profits with only minor bumps along the road, now showed decline even greater than when Ted had first taken over, the most serious of the company's history. The company was faltering, losing its competitive edge, and the warning bell was tolling.

Ted appeared at the boardroom's door at last, eyes downcast.

He didn't look up as he passed her and entered his office, closing the door behind him. Elaine had no doubts as to what he'd do next. She could imagine the splash of whiskey hitting the glass even now.

Well, it wasn't like he hadn't been warned. First Mr. Peakan and then several other board members had called at the end of each of the past few months, inquiring about sales and staff morale, and wanting to know what new incentives the president was implementing to improve the bottom line.

She knew that they had hurled those questions at him in person in the meeting they'd just come out of, and also knew from preparing the documentation that Ted couldn't provide any satisfactory justification for the serious loss of sales. He simply wasn't doing his job. He wasn't on top of things the way he should've been and Elaine knew that the board had delivered an ultimatum: restore their market share within the next six months or his resignation would be called for.

SIX MONTHS. His entire life and career had just been narrowed down to six months. If he didn't do something drastic he'd be out of a job. How had such a promising and fruitful career come to such a pitiful end?

In the beginning, Ted knew he'd done an excellent job. Profits had grown within a few short weeks of his becoming president. That is, until his personal life had insidiously crept into his corporate life and begun to erode the model image that had landed him the position in the first place.

Ted could no longer even begin to think of what he and Edith had done to their daughter. The lies, the deceit, the destruction of the letters between her and Henry; just the thought sent a flood of guilt, regret and remorse throughout his entire being.

Even time had failed to heal their daughter's broken heart. Jenny had long ago stopped asking if Henry had written a letter, but the evidence that she was still far from over the boy was there every time Ted gazed into his daughter's eyes. He'd seen it clearly just the other night when that Elvis fellow was singing "True Love," and it brought tears to Jenny's eyes. It was their favourite song, hers and Henry's. Ted recalled when Jenny had told him that, oh, ages ago, back when they still lived in Regina.

The song tugged at his heart as well, especially the part that hinted that angels had nothing to do but sit around heaven all day. Well, now those angels had gotten out of his safe and were flitting around on painted clouds and flying around his office all day!

At one time, he'd have had the fortitude to tackle and conquer these circumstances. To acknowledge the things he had done and resolve them. But not now.

And there was no one to turn to.

He couldn't go to his wife; Edith was adamant about staying the course and he no longer wished to suffer the ensuing arguments. He knew both the psychologist and family therapist in the personnel office and had confidence in them, but he'd never subject his personal problems to their scrutiny.

Not only was he too proud to ask for help, Ted felt he had to exude an image of perfection and strength. Solid as a rock, with no cracks or fissures. Being a president of a large corporation was like being a mountain climber. Each step had to be taken with caution, calculated and well-thought out. *Especially when you're at the top, one false move, one wrong decision, one sign of weakness and down you go.* There was always someone else waiting in the wings, ready to assume control.

Unfortunately, Ted hadn't yet realized how close he was to the edge of the cliff. Unless he got help soon and halted the company's downward spiral, he'd be thrust into the depths with a mighty and unforgiving crash.

Perhaps the one person he could go to was his secretary, Elaine. Ted knew how loyal she was and even suspected she knew of his excessive drinking. She was too professional to interfere, yet she was capable of running the company much better than him, especially now. He knew she'd gladly help but he could never allow himself to seek the help of a subordinate, not when he was the president of the whole company.

But help is what he needed. He needed a safe environment, someone he could trust. An atmosphere in which he was free, to let down all his defenses. A loving friend, a counsellor, a priest—anyone who would accept him in an atmosphere of unconditional love. He needed a Mr. Engelmann in his life. Someone who would take him as he was with no strings attached. A safe atmosphere where he could unload, be totally himself without fear so as to allow him to step back and see the error of his ways. Only in this way, receiving love and acceptance despite his shortcomings, could he begin to accept himself and begin to heal and correct the self-defeating thoughts and behaviour he was presently engaging in.

Unfortunately, Ted was so confined within himself he couldn't see the forest for the trees. He had shut himself into a protective prison and let no one into his inner world except his friend, booze. This illusory friend in whom he placed all his trust was now, however, beginning to betray him too. He needed more and more alcohol to suppress his ever-increasing guilt and shame and all the pressures surrounding him.

It was in those silent, alcohol-induced moments Ted saw the pewter angels float through the heavy steel door of his safe, though he knew, he *knew*, they were still sealed in the envelopes Henry and Jenny had sent to each other. They were out now all the time, flying across the sun-filled sky and perching on one of the clouds in the painting that concealed the safe.

Most of the time now he kept the painting covered up with the towel. It was the only way he could cope. He'd once looked forward to retreating to his office to escape Edith's manipulations at home, but the office had ceased to be a safe haven long ago, leaving him with nowhere else to go.

If only he'd put his family first. Sure, his work was important, but he should never have allowed it to take precedence over his wife and daughter. *Family is much more important.* And at the end of the day, if your home wasn't secure, if the heart from which you emerged every day to enter the work world wasn't intact, it immediately affected your abilities everywhere else.

Ted saw it clearly in the lives of his staff; how when there was a problem, it affected their work. He was in the same boat, only his was rapidly sinking. The heart within his home needed healing, needed attention, needed his love—and he needed his family's.

It was in rare moments like this that the obvious truth of what he should do stared him in the face. Yes, he finally had it together, he would drink to his insights. He got up and headed for the liquor cabinet again. He'd drink a toast to his determination to straighten everything out.

He poured himself a drink and then another. Yes, he'd overrule Edith's views and methods. After all, he was the father and surely he had *some* say in his daughter's upbringing and happiness. Father knew best, didn't he?

Ted took another drink to strengthen his resolve. Yes, he *could* disagree with Edith. He *could* exert his leadership of the family...

Soon, he forgot what he was drinking to. Was it destiny? Fate? Yes, it was fate. Yes, he was in fate's mercy; it would bring whatever it would bring.

CHAPTER TWENTY-THREE

WITH THE HALLOWEEN dance over and no future events planned, Henry could finally spend some time at the store. Since Christmas was just around the corner, there were lights and the Santa display to put up and, since it was the final year the store would be open, Henry wanted to do something special.

But Henry couldn't get Julean off his mind. He never would've thought that he'd enjoy being with any girl other than Jenny. He'd almost called Julean on Tuesday but was too nervous. He put it off on Wednesday and now Thursday was almost over. If he didn't do it soon, she might think he didn't like her or want to see her again. He couldn't wait any longer but still couldn't bring himself to pick up the phone.

After he'd glanced at the phone behind the counter for the umpteenth time, Mr. Engelmann commented, "You don't seem to be yourself today, Henry."

"I'm fine, just a little tired."

"Now, Henry. You know I know you better than that. You're not 'just a little tired.' I've always said you wear your heart on your sleeve, Henry."

Henry couldn't help but grin.

"So how was the Halloween dance?"

"It was fine."

"And the blind date?"

"That was fine too, but I ended up going with my friend's date instead."

"My goodness, how you young people can change things. You go with one girl and come home with another."

"Not exactly, Mr. Engelmann. It was just that by the end of the dance, the girl I was with seemed to like my buddy, and the girl *he* was with seemed to like me. Oh, I'm getting confused. Anyway, I really like this other girl and want to take her out."

"Well, have you asked her, Henry?"

"Not yet. That's what's been bothering me."

"Ah," said Mr. Engelmann, and smiled. "Are you worried that she might not want to go out with you or are you worried about what to say?"

"I think both."

"Well, worrying over how someone is going to react is more painful than if you saw their real reaction. Do you understand?"

Henry thought a minute. "Yeah, I think so. Being nervous and worried about something I really can't control or don't have the answer to is kind of crazy. It's better to just do it and then I'll know."

"There is one other thing," Mr. Engelmann said.

"And what's that?"

"Procrastination."

"What do you mean?"

"How long have you put off calling her because of your fear of how she will react?"

"Uh, five days now."

"Ah! And look how much you have suffered as a result," Mr. Engelmann nodded wisely.

"Yeah, I haven't been able to concentrate on a thing."

"See how it is affecting how you live in the present? It is important that you realize what you are doing so that you can correct it and do something about it. And I know I don't have to tell you what you should do."

"Yeah, phone her. Right away."

"Yes, yes, but I am also going to give you a little motivation."

"Motivation? What do you mean?"

"When I first met my Anna, I also wanted to take her out on a date. What I didn't know was that another man also liked her and had asked her before I did. Anna told the other man she would give him the answer in the morning because she was hoping I would talk with her before then. I called her that evening and asked her. After we were married, Anna told me that if I hadn't called on her that evening, she would have accepted the other suitor because she would have assumed I was not interested. So the moral of this story, Henry, is—"

"Yeah, I know, 'don't put off until tomorrow what you can do today' or else you could be very sorry."

Mr. Engelmann beamed. "Precisely! Do you have this girl's phone number?"

"Yes."

"And *still* you have not called her? My, my. Listen. I will go back into the storage room. I have much work to do, and if you wish, you can use the store phone. You have an important call to make, so it's all right. I will even keep you on the payroll during this time." Mr. Engelmann winked and disappeared into the back.

Henry reached into his back pocket and pulled out his wallet. He sorted through several bits of paper, wondering why he'd kept half of them, before he found it. He really didn't need the piece of paper. He'd memorized the number not long after Travis had given it to him and knew it frontward and backward.

Henry took a deep breath and dialled. His heart accelerated through the first ring and then the second until he thought he was going to hyperventilate.

"Hello?"

It sounded like Julean.

"Hello?"

"Yes, hello," Henry said. "Is Julean in?"

"This is Julean."

"Hi, Julean, it's Henry."

"Who?"

She doesn't remember me!

"Oh! Hank! The Lone Ranger. I thought that was you, but when you said Henry it confused me for a minute."

"Yeah, all my friends call me Hank, but at work and at home, my parents usually call me Henry."

And that's what Jenny called me too.

"Oh, okay. So what do you want *me* to call you?"

"Uh, Hank is fine."

"I really enjoyed myself at the dance the other night, Hank."

"Yeah, so did I." *Go for it!* "I was wondering, Julean…"

"Yes?"

"Would you like to go to a movie on Saturday night?"

"I'd love to go. Which movie did you have in mind? Not Lone Ranger and Tonto?"

"No," Henry laughed. "There's one called *Giant* they've brought back. It's about this rich Texan that owns all this land and oil. It stars Rock Hudson and James Dean—you know, the guy who died in that car accident."

"I love James Dean. That sounds great!"

"Was there another movie you wanted to see?"

"No, that one's fine. What time will you pick me up?"

"Well, I don't have a car so I'll ask my dad if he'll drive us, and maybe we can take a taxi home. Would that be okay?"

"Oh, that's way too expensive. Let's just take the trolley."

"All right," Henry said. They settled on a pick-up time then said good-bye.

Henry placed the receiver on the hook, not realizing until then how hot and flushed he was. His hands were sweaty and perspiration had formed circles under his armpits. And then it came—a rush of excitement he had not felt since Jenny said, "Quickly, hold my hand." He was on cloud nine. Mr. Engelmann had been right as usual.

In the blink of an eye, his emotions veered from nervousness and worry to elation and freedom. He'd allowed his lack of confidence and, and...*procrastination* to control him.

Well, not anymore!

Just then Mr. Engelmann moved the curtain aside and peeked through the doorway from the storage room.

"I see by the look on your face all is well?"

"It sure is. We're going to a movie on Saturday night."

"That is good, Henry. Oh, to be young and in love."

"Yeah," Henry answered absently.

"Now that it's over with, I guess I can expect to get some work out of you before you go home?"

Henry smiled. "Yeah, yeah."

He headed over to the shelves to find out what needed restocking, but by the time he reached the storage room he'd forgotten and had to turn around and look again. His conversation with Julean kept getting in the way.

After several attempts, Mr. Engelmann slid a piece of paper and a pencil to the end of the counter, shook his head from side to side and muttered, "Henry, Henry, Henry."

Before Henry left for the day, Mr. Engelmann asked if he could meet the girl who had turned his young assistant's world upside down.

Henry could see Mr. Engelmann was very happy he had found another girlfriend.

Chapter Twenty-Four

ICAN SEE YOUR mind is on your date tonight, Henry."

"It's that obvious, is it?"

Mr. Engelmann nodded. "When I dated Anna I was the same way. Pretty girls do it to a man every time." Mr. Engelmann winked, then asked, "Is your father going to drive you to the movie?"

"Actually my friend Travis can get his dad's car. When I told him I was taking Julean out he decided to ask Lorraine, the girl I went on the blind date with, and so the four of us are going to double date again only this—"

"My, my how quickly the right matches were made! You should be in for an interesting evening, no?"

Henry smiled, "Yeah, it'll be kinda awkward, but you know us men, we adjust very quickly when the right girl comes along."

"Well, you have a fine evening, Henry. Why don't you run along and get ready—I can handle the store. It's not so busy today. And besides, this is important—you want to make a good impression."

"Yeah, you're right as usual. Thanks, Mr. Engelmann; as you

already noticed, my mind just isn't on my work at the moment and I hate to be paid for—"

"Yes, yes, you go on now. Have fun, you are long overdue."

IT WAS AWKWARD for Henry to get out of the car to get Julean when just over a week ago it had been Travis knocking on her door. But as soon as Henry rang the doorbell, Julean answered.

"Hi Hank, come in. I want you to meet my mom and dad.

They were standing behind Julean, both wearing a pleasant smile as he came into the front entry. Henry didn't expect this and momentarily felt shy. Julean's dad must have just come home; he was still wearing a white smock and the label on his jacket read DR. CARTER.

"Henry, this is Vera and Jack Carter, my parents."

Henry extended his hand to Julean's mom and dad; their hands were already reaching out to him.

"Nice to meet you, Mr. Carter, and you, Mrs. Carter."

Henry heard them say something in response but was too nervous to listen. He was happy when Julean said, "We'd better get going or we'll be late for the movie."

When they got to the car, Henry could see Travis staring at them, like he was maybe expecting her to get in the front seat. Henry and Julean chuckled nervously as they climbed into the back and Travis sped off to Lorraine's place.

No sooner had Travis come to a stop, about to open the door to get Lorraine, when she burst out the front door of her house and ran to the car. Instead of getting in with Travis she opened the back door and climbed in beside Henry.

"Oh, I missed you so much, Hank, I couldn't wait to see you!"

"But what about *me*?" Travis protested, hastily turning around, "You're *my*—"

"My gosh, Travis! Am I supposed to be going out with *you* tonight?"

"Well, yeah…" A worried look grew on his face. He wasn't used to be being shunned like this.

Julean chuckled, "But I'm not leaving Hank's side! He's *my* date tonight, Lorraine."

"No, he's *mine!*" Lorraine grabbed Henry's arm and pulled him away from Julean with a wink of a sparkling eye.

Julean played along and tugged at Henry's other arm.

"Geez, what's going on here?" Travis blurted again, watching jealously in the rear-view mirror as his buddy got sandwiched between the two beautiful girls.

Seeing what Lorraine was up to, Henry teased, "Hey, I kinda like this, Travis. Just drive to the movies."

"No way! Lorraine please come sit up here with me. The car won't move unless you're beside me." Travis, for once, actually had a pleading look in his eyes.

Lorraine leaned forward and gave Travis a kiss on the cheek. "Does my new boyfriend really miss me?" And with that, she simply climbed right over the seat. "Well, at least now we all know who we're supposed to be going out with!"

Everybody laughed and at once felt at ease with the new arrangements. *That Lorraine sure knows how to make people laugh.*

"So what's it going to be, *Giant* or *Some Like it Hot*? I could easily take Marilyn Monroe for a couple of hours."

"Well, I think the girls might have James Dean and Rock Hudson in mind, Travis, and I don't think the Marilyn Monroe starts for another hour," Henry mused.

"I saw *Giant* with my parents when it came out just after James Dean died two years ago and I just fell in *love* with him then. He was such a good actor; I could easily see it again," Lorraine gushed as she turned and knelt on the front seat facing Julean. "Wait till you see him, Julean, is he ever cute! Kresge's Department Store had a poster of him with a cigarette dangling from his mouth. My God, I thought I'd die when I saw it!"

"Come on, Lorraine, wait till you see me with a smoke, it'll curl your hair." Travis' confidence seemed to have returned.

"Well, I'd like to see *Giant* and that's the one Henry originally picked," Julean said, squeezing Henry's hand for the briefest of seconds.

Lorraine turned around and sat back down. "That settles it, Travis, three to one. *Giant* it is."

"*Arrgh*," Travis snarled in his jokey pirate voice. "And I'll make ye walk the plank if I don't like it!"

Travis found a parking spot on Rose Street just off 11th Avenue. As the four walked the block to the Metropolitan Theatre, Henry couldn't get over the fact that he was actually taking another girl to a movie. It had been more than three years since he and Jenny had seen *High Society*.

"Look!" blurted Travis. There was a huge line-up at the Broadway theater across the street. "See? I'm not the only one who wants to see Marilyn."

"Oh, come on, Travis." Lorraine tugged his arm. "Be a gentleman and open the door for me."

Once seated, with popcorn and drinks, they watched a clip of Alfred Hitchcock's new movie, *North by Northwest*.

Henry leaned close to Julean and whispered, "My friend and I saw *Rear Window* a couple of years ago. It was sure a suspenseful flick."

Julean nodded. "I saw it twice. I got more out of it the second time. Hitchcock's movies always keep me on the edge of my seat."

Henry gazed into Julean's eyes as she spoke. He wished she had said more so he could've looked at her longer. He leaned ever-so-slightly closer, wondering if there would be a hint of lilac perfume. There wasn't—Julean didn't seem to wear perfume, though she smelled pleasantly of shampoo—and Henry was glad; it would only have reminded him of Jenny. He remembered so clearly the night they had gone to the movies and that big fat guy sitting between them. He'd wanted so much to put his arm around her and hold her hand, maybe even rub his cheek against hers. He now had that same wish and desire. Slowly he turned to look at Julean. She was watching the movie; the main feature had started and Henry hadn't even noticed.

They were sharing popcorn, and every now and then their fingers touched as they reached for another handful at the same time. Henry found himself trying to time when Julean would next reach in the bag. He remembered scheming like this when he was at first with Jenny, too.

Would she take his hand, as Jenny had?

Geez, Henry thought, *I've got to get into this movie.* Rock Hudson was buying some horse. *I wonder why? He's sure hitting it off with Liz Taylor. When does that James Dean come in? Or did I miss him?*

Julean had set the empty popcorn bag on the floor and put her hands in her lap. It would be awkward to reach over the armrest that separated them. How could he get close enough to hold her hand? *Maybe just put your arm around her.* That's what he'd wanted to do with Jenny and he'd been upset for days that he hadn't had the chance. *Go for it!*

Henry shifted in his chair, raised his left arm for what seemed like the longest moment ever and then let it slowly descend around Julean's shoulder. Ever so imperceptibly she responded, leaning as close to him as possible. Her hair touched the side of his chin and the fresh scent of her shampoo sent him into seventh heaven. He leaned a little closer still, lowering his head, hoping their cheeks would touch. They did.

Henry began to watch the show.

TRAVIS FIRED UP his dad's '56 Ford Fairlane and turned onto 11th Avenue, headed east.

"What do you say we go to Oscar's for a hamburger or something?"

"That's sounds great, Travis, I *am* a little hungry, even after all that popcorn. How about you, Julean?"

"Some fries would be nice, so long as I'm home by ten-thirty."

Geez, so that's *what her dad said,* Henry thought. *I was so nervous I completely missed it.* "Yeah, its only twenty after nine, we should be done by then," he said aloud, checking his watch.

Lorraine turned around on the front seat as she had before, kneeling towards them. "So what do you think of Jimmy Dean, Julean? Wasn't he adorable?"

"He was cute, but I think Rock Hudson is very handsome." Julean turned to Henry. "He sort of looks like you, Hank."

"Well, ya gotta like that, Pederson," Travis teased.

Henry just blushed. "I guess we might have the same kind of hair. His is more black, though."

"Your features are similar as well," Julean commented.

Lorraine squinted, looking Henry up and down over the back of the seat. "Yes, you *do* look a little like Rock, Hank," she agreed.

"All you need is a big ranch in Texas and you'll have it made, buddy."

"Yeah, yeah…" Henry replied, his voice trailing off.

"I don't know who you look like with that fire-red hair of yours, Travis, but it does set my heart ablaze," Lorraine quipped, and slid closer to him.

"Now *that's* my girl!" Travis said, freeing his right arm from the steering wheel and wrapping it around Lorraine's shoulders.

Henry wondered if he should do the same with Julean. Before he built up the nerve, Julean slid a hand off her lap into the space between them, almost touching Henry's hand which was already there. Henry could sense her warmth only microns away and he instinctively moved his hand onto hers. She turned her own slightly and curled her fingers around his.

The interior of the car was filled with a comfortable silence. Travis turned right on Winnipeg Street, then left at Victoria Avenue and headed east again. Oscar's was a drive-in restaurant just on the outskirts of town, a favourite hangout for high school students. As they approached Broder Street, Henry turned to Julean and said, "That's where I work on Saturdays and after school. Engelmann's Confectionery and Grocery."

"How do you find the time to work there with all you do at school?"

"Oh, I just do my best. I love working there. Mr. Engelmann is a very wise man; I've learned so much from him."

"Like how thick to cut the salami?" Travis snickered.

"Yeah, sure," Henry retorted, not wanting to get into it. He immediately tried to change the subject. "Maybe we can all go to that Hitchcock movie at the Met in a couple of weeks."

"There's another good one starting at the Broadway too," interjected Lorraine, "*Anatomy of a Murder*, with James Stewart."

"Geez, I like that guy," said Henry and began to imitate him. "Well, now, tha-that's right, Lorraine," Henry began, drawing out the words and lowering his voice a bit.

"My gosh, Hank, you sound just like him." Julean was so excited she pulled her hand from Henry's and clapped.

"You ain't seen nothing yet, kid."

Suddenly Henry was James Cagney and this time Lorraine recognized who he was trying to sound like.

Horns began honking as Travis turned into Oscar's. Travis honked back and waved his hand. It wasn't that busy tonight and Travis easily found a spot near the restaurant.

Hilda, Eddy's girlfriend, saw them and came over, adjusting her waitress uniform as she walked.

"And here comes Hilda. Look at those boobs just a-bouncin'. No *wonder* Zeigler's in love with her!"

Lorraine smacked Travis on the arm and Henry inwardly cringed at his friend's crude comment. Oblivious, Travis rolled down his window.

"Hey guys, what can I get you?" Hilda asked, leaning down to peer in the window, giving Travis a nice flash of her cleavage.

"I'll have your two milkshakes," Travis stuttered, transfixed.

But Hilda wasn't offended and merely asked what flavour.

"Whatever flavour they are, I'll take 'em."

This time Hilda saw where the conversation was going and so did Julean. She leaned forward and hit Travis' shoulder too. "You're just terrible, Travis! Apologize to her!"

Lorraine, arms crossed now, had slid away from him. She was clearly unimpressed.

"One more crack like that and you'll have a milkshake over your head," Hilda snapped.

"Okay already! A guy can't but help notice a girl so…gifted, can he? I was just joking. Okay, so what does everyone want?"

AFTER THAT THEY ordered, ate and talked about the movie and how James Dean had turned his little plot of land into a fortune by discovering oil.

Julean was the first to be dropped off.

Henry walked her to the door.

"I sure had a good time tonight, Hank."

"So did I, Julean. Maybe we can do it again next Friday?"

"That'd be great!"

"Oh, geez, I forgot! I have a basketball game next Friday. But maybe Saturday?"

"What if I came to watch you play? And we could go out on Saturday, too."

"That would be swell."

They fell quiet and stared at one another. Julean was so pretty. Her eyes glinted in the light from the porch as she stepped forward and kissed Henry on the cheek.

"Good night, Hank. Thanks again for a lovely evening."

Henry nodded. He wanted to kiss her but Julean turned and went inside.

Henry fully expected Travis to take Lorraine home first but was surprised when Travis drove to Henry's place instead.

"See ya Monday, Hank."

"See you, Hank," Lorraine echoed.

And Travis sped off, raising the dust on the empty street.

Henry turned into his walkway and sat on the front steps. He looked three doors down at Jenny's old place. It was now all only a memory, yet the ache for her lingered just below the surface. He turned back and thought of Julean and the evening. *She's a real nice girl, quiet but very sincere.* He liked that she'd got after Travis for kidding with Hilda; Henry hadn't liked it either.

The feel of her hand in his stayed with him. He wondered how he'd feel about her next weekend when they went out again. It seemed like a long time to wait.

Maybe I'll phone her tomorrow.

CHAPTER TWENTY-FIVE

MARY HAD NOTICED a distinct change in Henry since he'd met Julean. They had gone out every weekend for over month now, and he seemed so much happier, more alive. Inwardly, Mary breathed a sigh of relief—hopefully her son's heart had begun to heal.

It was Monday morning, and she was about to do the weekly wash before going in to work at the store when she noticed Henry had forgotten to bring down his clothes. She hurried upstairs to collect his laundry. As she passed his desk, she noticed the bottom drawer was partly open again. She thought of his plans to go to Ottawa after he graduated. Was he still planning to go now even though Julean was in his life?

Her motherly curiosity got the better of her. She set Henry's laundry on his bed then turned back to the desk. The drawer was open enough for her to see two envelopes, both bulging with money. He must have been saving for a long time.

"Oh, Henry," Mary whispered as her heart sank. She hoped he was doing the right thing. What if he went all that way and couldn't find Jenny? Or if he did, what if she had another boyfriend or simply wasn't interested in Henry any longer? All his savings would be for naught. Well, she supposed he needed to know what had happened to the girl he had loved so much. It would at least allow him to get on with his life. Perhaps it would be worth it for just that reason.

Mary sat down on the chair and opened the drawer further. Flipping through the envelopes, she counted considerably more money than had been there the first time she'd looked. She pulled out the plan from the first envelope and unfolded it. Two items had been crossed out, several other items had check marks beside them and three others had been added to the end:

- *Check the Ottawa phone book for a possible listing for Sarsky. (Number unlisted.)*
- *Ask Mr. Sarsky's secretary for a home address. (Cannot give out this information.)*
- *Phone all the high schools when you get to Ottawa. (Include the Catholic high schools.)*

Henry had written a telephone number across the bottom of the page below the list and "$378" below that. It was the number for TCA and the amount of his round-trip airfare. Mary marvelled at her son's determination. He must have been saving since Grade 9 and even though he hadn't heard from Jenny, he was still bent on finding her.

What a special love these two young people have...almost heaven made. She had heard it said before that first love could sometimes last forever.

She replaced Henry's plan in the envelope, put it back in the drawer and closed it, leaving it exactly as she'd found it, then collected Henry's clothes from the bed. On her way through the kitchen, she looked up at the crucifix hanging just above the door.

"Don't forget my boy. He needs Your help more than ever.

HENRY CAME HOME for lunch rather than eat in the cafeteria at Balfour. He knew his mom was helping Mr. Engelmann at the store today. He was determined to get Jenny's phone number. For the last three weeks he'd been phoning all the Catholic schools and only had five more public schools to phone. The Ottawa telephone directory he'd looked up at the library had listed private schools too, but he didn't think Jenny would opt to go to one of them. Anyway, there were five remaining public high schools left on his list. He'd learned to be direct and ask for Jenny to come to the phone. The initial approach he'd taken was to ask if a Jenny Sarsky went to that school and the usual answer was that they didn't give out that information. He had to wait a couple of weeks before phoning back and trying the more direct approach.

Henry looked at his list:

Elmwood High School
Fern Hill High School
March High School
Springview High School
Turnbull High School

Henry assumed that the Sarskys would probably be living in a ritzier part of the city but since he didn't know the different areas of Ottawa which might have helped him rule out this or that school, he'd decided to try them all.

Henry went to the fridge and took out some ham and cheese slices. He got bread out of the bread box and made a sandwich even though he wasn't very hungry. He hoped and prayed he'd find out where Jenny lived or at least what high school she attended today. He went to the fridge again and took out a bottle of milk, set it on the kitchen table, got a glass from the cupboard and sat down.

He just had to know where he was at with Jenny. Julean was becoming a bigger and bigger part of his life, and yet he'd been planning for all these years to find his first love. In only a few more months he'd have been able to realize a goal he had planned for over two years. Now uncertainty had set in. It would be so unfair to Julean to lead her on and then end the relationship. If only he knew what Jenny was doing. Did she have another boyfriend? Was she still interested in him?

Did she still love him like he did her?

Henry was so torn he didn't know which way to turn. He ate part of his sandwich and downed the glass of milk, got up and went to the phone on the kitchen wall. He turned back to the kitchen table, grabbed the list, then dialed the first number. He was glad he didn't have to go through an operator and could phone direct.

"Elmwood High School, how may I help you?"

"Hello, may I speak to Jenny Sarsky, please?"

"I'm sorry, we do not have a student by that name."

"Thank you, ma'am."

Henry dialed the second and third numbers and the responses were basically the same, except the last one added that if this was an emergency they could call the central office and locate the student for him.

Henry declined, though it was an emergency. His heart was breaking and he no longer knew for sure how to mend it.

He was getting weary; perhaps Jenny *had* gone to a private high school. It would be even more difficult to get her number.

Henry dialed the next number.

"Good afternoon, Springview High."

"May I speak to Jenny Sarsky, please.

"I'm sorry, she's in class. Who is calling, please?"

Henry didn't know what to say. He'd fully been expecting to hear the same negative reply. Should he say it was an emergency? That it was her dad calling? Surely they would know it wasn't.

"It's—it's a friend who's coming to town and wants to see her."

"You'll have to call their home, sir."

"May I please have their home number?"

"I'm sorry, we don't give out that information," the secretary said, asking again, "Who is calling please."

Henry thought for a second. Maybe he should leave his

name and Jenny could phone him. As he was about to respond, he heard the secretary talking to someone. "It's another call for Jenny Sarsky—the third one this week."

"Here, let me have it."

A male voice came to the phone. "This is Vice-Principal Broadman, who's calling, please?"

"Henry—Henry Pederson."

"Are you a student from another school?"

Henry didn't have time to think. "Yes, yes I am."

"What is the nature of your call, young man?"

"I want to speak to Jenny Sarsky or get her phone number," Henry answered again before he could think it through.

It was all happening so fast.

"Now see here, young man! We are not in the business of calling students out of class, relaying messages or providing a dating service. Do you understand?"

"But, all—"

"My advice to you is to do what any normal high school student would do. Call her at home. Don't phone here again."

Henry heard the phone click and then dial tone. He hung up, sweat rolling down his back and armpits.

"Wow! At least I know what school Jenny's at," he muttered under his breath.

But who else had been calling Jenny at school?

He took in a deep breath, trying to dissipate the lingering tension. If worst came to worst and he couldn't get Jenny's home number, he'd take a taxi and go directly to the school and wait as long as needed until he saw her. He knew he'd recognize her. He'd never, ever forget her.

But school will be out by then! Henry suddenly realized it would be summer holidays when he got there. His mind went into overdrive.

Geez, I've just got *to think of a way to get her number!*

CHAPTER TWENTY-SIX

Iт's so GOOD the principal decided to let you finish Grade 12, Tammy."

"I'm glad too. But, Jenny, everyone's gawking at me."

"Let them stare, Tammy. If it will make you feel any better, I'll wear my nightgown to school and strap a pillow around my waist underneath it."

Tammy laughed, "Jenny, sometimes you're just too much."

"Well, you're over halfway there. Soon we'll know what's hidden inside that tummy."

"I think it's a boy, I'm already so big and he's kicking all the time."

"Don't be too sure; Camilla kicked all the time too—and sooner than yours even."

"Well, it doesn't matter, as long it's healthy and...oh, I just wish Robbie would've accepted my decision. I know this all must be so awful for him. He still hasn't spoken to me after I told him I was going to keep the baby. I miss not seeing him and I miss his support. I was sure tempted to phone him last night."

Jenny took Tammy's hand. "I know how hard this is on you,

but I think you might just have to leave him alone and let him work this out for himself. If he's more concerned about what others think than accepting his responsibility and supporting you, perhaps it's best you know it now than find out down the road."

"Yeah, I know. But I really miss seeing him and having him around."

"I know what you mean. I'd have loved to have had Henry near me when I was pregnant too but…" Jenny's voice trailed off.

"So how are you and James doing?"

"Okay, I guess. Sometimes he does things that concern me. Guess it's a good thing I'm prepared to accept him and look for the good in things. Sometimes I have to look pretty hard in James' case," she chuckled ruefully.

"Why don't you go out with other boys, Jenny? I mean, I don't think there's a guy at Springview who wouldn't want to take you out."

"Really, Tammy, I think you're over-exaggerating."

"No, I'm not. It's obvious the way the boys ogle you."

"Well, for one thing, most of the boys who phone or talk to me seem immature compared to James and they just don't appeal to me…at least, not yet anyway."

"What is it that attracts you to James, Jen? He's handsome, for sure, and always looks like he's stepped right out of a magazine ad for Italian clothing."

"Yes, he certainly dresses well." Jenny was silent for a long moment before answering Tammy's question. "Initially, I guess, it was because he reminded me of someone…"

"I know, Henry Pederson, right?"

Jenny looked at her perceptive friend. "Yes, I loved the way James got so excited about his plans to improve his father's company. Henry was like that too. He wanted to improve the store he worked at." After a bit of thought Jenny added, "But it was different with Henry, somehow. His goals seemed different and more for the store owner he worked for and not himself."

Jenny opened the door for Tammy as they stepped out of the school.

"Speak of the devil, look who's here," Tammy said.

Jenny couldn't believe it, there was James leaning against a brand new shiny black BMW 507 holding a bouquet of flowers.

Jenny's soft, fair, luminous skin turned beet red. "I wish he wouldn't be so ostentatious."

"He's a pretty flashy guy, Jen."

A lot of students were already checking out James' car and now, as Jenny made her way down the steps with Tammy, attention turned to her as well.

As the girls drew near, he stepped forward and gave Jenny the flowers then kissed her on the cheek.

Jenny lowered her voice, "They're lovely, James, but I wish you would give me these in private."

"Well, I just want all the guys to know that you're my girl and they don't stand a chance."

"Really, James...!"

"Just kidding, Marj. I mean Jen."

James turned to Tammy and took in her rapidly expanding figure. "Hey Tammy, I see the addition is coming along nicely. So when's the due date again?"

"The doctor thinks the end of March to the first two weeks of April."

"So where's Robert?"

Tammy glanced at Jenny, then turned back to James.

"I haven't seen him in a while; I think he's thinking all this over."

"Well, bringing a kid into the world is a big responsibility—I can see how he would be scared about the whole thing."

Just as Jenny was going to compliment James on his insight, James added. "But then he's got to think about himself and his future, doesn't he? He was interested in getting a basketball scholarship, right? I can see why he might want to cut out."

"Well, he should've thought about that before..." Jenny

started, then faltered, "And what about Tammy and *her* future? Robert is just as much a part of this as—"

James could see Jenny was getting upset and he cut her off. "Yeah, I know, Jenny. Sheesh, I was just kidding, all right? So, can I give you a ride home?"

"I have my car, remember? Would you like to tow it behind yours?"

"Now don't get cute. I thought I'd drive you home and bring you back in the morning. You can drive your car home tomorrow."

Jenny didn't want to start a habit of having him pick her up every day. *Probably James just wants to let everybody know I belong to him. Oh that's too mean, Jenny, don't think that.*

"Thanks anyway, James, but I'll take my car. Besides, I have to drive Tammy home. Thank you again for the flowers; they're lovely."

James leaned forward and kissed her on the cheek again. "So I'll pick you up at six tomorrow. There's a new Italian restaurant I want to take you to. Take care, Tammy. I'm sure everything will turn out okay for you and Robert. Say, do you want me to talk to him?"

"Oh no, James, please don't. But thanks anyway."

James nodded to the girls, strode around to the driver's side door, jumped in and fired up the engine. He looked at Jenny once more then sped off, screeching the back tires, much to Jenny's chagrin.

CHAPTER TWENTY-SEVEN

B Y LATE NOVEMBER, the whiteness of sparkling snow had replaced the raw sienna colours of the grass and leaves of fall; blizzards and sharp, cold winds and sun dogs replaced the golden harvest moon, warm fall evenings and hot sunny days. The smell of harvest and the sight of combines and trucks on the outskirts of the city were but a memory. Short shirtsleeves, skirts and running shoes gave way to parkas, snow pants, felt boots, toques and heavy scarves. Winter had arrived full force and was firmly settled in.

Two weeks before Christmas, Mrs. Schmidt's son once again offered to help Henry put up the Christmas decorations and the huge Santa Claus display. After a few minor electrical repairs to several strings of Christmas lights, Mr. Engelmann's store was lit up, much to the joy and sadness of his customers. Everyone knew it was the last Christmas the store would be open and preferred not to talk about it. It would be a reality soon enough; better just to enjoy the moment.

"Thanks a lot for putting up the lights and Santa display again, Ron," Henry said. "We couldn't do it without you."

"No problem, Hank. I'll sure miss this store and that Santa

display. It was my dad's favourite decoration for years when he was alive. Oh well, life must go on."

"Merry Christmas, Ron, and thanks again."

"No problem, Hank." Ron hopped in his van and sped off.

As he watched Ron drive down the icy winter avenue, Henry shook his head and muttered, "Boy, what a great attitude that Ron has."

Mr. Engelmann had accumulated an incredible amount of inventory over the years and now was faced with the formidable task of somehow getting rid of it. Putting it on sale was one way, perhaps, but a thought occurred to Henry of another method that might be more exciting. After work one day before the end of November, Henry shared his idea with Mr. Engelmann.

"I think I've got a way to get rid of your inventory and also give a gift to our customers for their support and loyalty over the years. I think it'll be exciting and in keeping with the spirit of the Christmas and the holiday season."

"Yes, yes, what is it?"

"Over the last two years we've made a list of nearly 700 people who have come into our store. What would happen if we sent each of them a letter with this," and he handed Mr. Engelmann a sheet of paper, "written on the back of the envelope:

> *Have A Merry Christmas In January!*
> *This letter must be opened in front of Mr. Engelmann in his store any day during the month of January to receive the special gift indicated inside. Remember, no peeking! We want to see your smile when you receive your gift!*

"Go on, Henry."

"Inside the envelope there will be a letter explaining that you're closing the store at the end of next June, as well as a note of appreciation for their support over the years. On another slip of paper we'll list the prize or gift they've received.

One may be for a can of corn, say, and another for a pound of salami, a tube of toothpaste, a gift certificate for five dollars and so on. People are curious and will have fun bringing in their unopened envelopes, excited to see what they've received. January is usually a pretty slow month. This should bring a lot more people into the store."

"Yes, yes," said Mr. Engelmann, nodding.

"This will give us an opportunity to say goodbye, and I'm sure when they receive their gift most people will buy more items, both to make their trip worthwhile and to reciprocate for your generosity!"

"Uh-huh," said Mr. Engelmann, "but then are we not manipulating these people to buy more?"

"I knew you would think that. But let's look at it in the same way you always ask me to consider what you say at times." Henry smiled, and so did Mr. Engelmann, waiting to see what Henry would say next.

"Okay, fair enough, Henry, go on then."

"First, don't you think it's nice to give a gift to your customers?"

"Yes."

"Are you asking them to buy groceries, which they need anyway?"

"No, I suppose not."

"Well, then what's your concern?"

"My concern is that they are buying more because we gave them a gift. Isn't that manipulation?"

"How?" Henry countered. "It's their choice if they want to buy more or not. They will have to anyway, whether it's the day they come in or not, and what's wrong if they want to reciprocate to help you out? What's wrong with that?"

"Well, it's just the way we're giving away a gift with the intention that they will buy more."

"But *whose* intention? Certainly not yours, is it?"

"No."

"Well then, what's the problem?"

They looked at each other, trying to read each other's thoughts and think of something to justify or defend each viewpoint.

"Remember, the choice is theirs," Henry repeated. "They can receive the gift, say thank you and walk out without buying anything at all. And if it makes you feel better, you can stop them from buying other things, but I'm sure they will think you're kind of strange for doing so and that maybe you've gone bonkers since Anna died. Oops!" Henry brought a hand to his mouth, smirking, "did I say the wrong thing? I'm sorry...just teasing."

But Mr. Engelmann only smiled and waved his hand.

"But it's true, isn't it? People would think it very strange if you tell them not to buy groceries because you gave them a gift from the heart." After a short pause, Henry added, "And when you think about it, isn't a sale the same thing, in a way? We reduce the price of items to sell more, but at the same time to bring more customers into the store. Are we not trying to get customers to buy more then? Is that manipulation, too?"

Mr. Engelmann stared at Henry for the longest time. He arched his eyebrows as if he had not expected such a response.

"Henry, you are too smart for me. You young people know how to run a business much different from the way I know. It's time I got out and left it up to you. *Ach mein lieber Gott,*" Mr. Engelmann muttered, "a man no longer knows right from wrong."

After sifting through what Henry had said for a few silent moments, Mr. Engelmann finally responded, "I cannot find fault with what you propose to do. Go ahead, and if the Lord tells me different, I will let you know soon enough. But isn't this a lot of work, Henry?"

"You have a lot of stock to get rid of."

"Yes, yes, that is true. But this *is* a lot of work."

"Oh, a little, but not really. Mom, Mrs. Schmidt and I can write the names out in an evening, and we'll make up a farewell letter and perhaps twelve separate slips of paper with a different prize on each. Then it's just a matter of printing fifty or so of each, putting them in the envelopes and sending them off."

Mr. Engelmann stared, shaking his head. "*Mein lieber Gott!*" he said again. "Just like that, Henry! My, my, how your mind thinks. I wish Anna were here so I could tell her. She so enjoyed hearing your ideas."

Henry could tell the wheels were turning as Mr. Engelmann thought about it more thoroughly. To Mr. Engelmann, black was black and white was white; there was no sneaking into the grey area. If there was any question that something might be trespassed upon his beliefs, argument and reason were useless. His principles couldn't be compromised. There was no such thing as a white lie or venial sin. Everything to Mr. Engelmann was mortal. And in the end, whatever he did must serve both others and his Lord.

"Yes, yes," Mr. Engelmann suddenly returned, interrupting Henry's thoughts, "it could be fun, and January is usually slow. It would bring in more customers and it is a nice gesture, and it would help to reduce our inventory."

"That's right," Henry quickly agreed, feeling somewhat relieved that Mr. Engelmann was beginning to think more positively about the idea.

"Well, go ahead then, Henry. Let's see what happens."

"Great! Oh, and by the way, I've invited Julean to come to supper next Sunday. I'm anxious for you to meet her."

"That's wonderful, Henry, I've been looking forward to meeting her as well. From what you say, she seems like such a nice girl."

"She's looking forward to meeting you too, I talk so much about you, she says she knows you better than her own father."

Mr. Engelmann smiled. "Oh you will soon forget about me and have better things to talk about."

"Never, Mr. Engelmann, I'll never forget our talks and the time I spent working here. I can't wait for Christmas holidays so I can work full-time."

Mr. Engelmann approached Henry and clapped his shoulder. He smiled and shook his head. Although Mr. Engelmann didn't say anything, his love for his employee shone in his eyes.

"Well, tell me, everything is going fine at school?"

"Yeah, couldn't be better. If I could just sort this girlfriend thing out..." Henry trailed off. He knew his mentor understood what he meant.

Mr. Engelmann studied Henry for a thoughtful moment. "You still miss Jenny? And you're concerned over your growing fondness for Julean?"

"Yeah, you're right on both accounts, Mr. Engelmann. I really like Julean but I still ache for Jenny. I can't understand it after all these years."

"Yes, you have mentioned that to me several times. Perhaps it has something to do with lack of proper closure in your relationship? Not knowing what happened to her and not hearing from her. That can be very unsettling."

"That's part of it for sure. I really like Julean...but there's just something special about Jenny and I. I can't explain it. I still remember the morning we met here in the store. It was as if a spell came over me...my eyes seemed to burn in the most pleasurable way; it felt as though something like a, a sweet honey were caught in them. Oh, I don't even know if that makes sense."

"Well, Henry, I think it does. It is through the eyes that love and attraction first come to us when we meet another."

"That's right!" Henry blurted, "It was like seeing an angel when I first saw her. I am so attracted to Julean, too, Mr. Engelmann, but somehow it's not the same. I just can't explain it."

David looked at his protégé. He loved Henry deeply and when his adopted son hurt, he hurt. He wanted so much to help him. But he had to agree there was something special between Henry and Jenny.

He recalled that morning only too well himself. It had been incredible to see them locked into each other's vision and a sort of aura around them began to glow as they gazed into each other's eyes. Something out of the ordinary had happened that he couldn't explain. Electricity had filled the air. The hair on his arms had stood up. The customer he was serving at the time had felt it too. They had both turned and studied the young couple to see what was happening, and out of fear, curiosity or whatever, he had broken the spell. He remembered calling out to them....

I was relieved to see everything settle down, and here now my son is still feeling the effects of that morning.

Mr. Engelmann could see Henry was waiting for him to say something. Perhaps it was best to keep his observations of that time to himself. *Henry is confused enough and this would only add to his bewilderment.*

Just then a customer came into the store stamping his feet on the rubber mat, trying to remove the snow that clung to his shoes.

"'Morning, David."

"Good morning, John. Is the missus feeling better?" Mr. Engelmann asked as he returned to his usual place behind the counter.

"I'm afraid not, we had an ambulance take her to the hospital last night."

"I'll get back to work, Mr. Engelmann, thanks for listening." Henry said, heading for the storeroom so Mr. Engelmann could talk with the man.

David reached out for Henry's hand across the counter.

"We will talk some more later, in the meantime, let us pray for the good Lord's guidance and clarity."

CHAPTER TWENTY-EIGHT

"Henry, would you please bring up one of the folding chairs from the basement and set it at the table?"

"Sure, Mom."

"Is there anything I can help you with, Mrs. Pederson?" Julean asked.

"No, that's fine, thank you, dear. You can visit in the living room with Bill if you'd like. David Engelmann will be along any minute and I know how much he's looking forward to meeting you."

Just then the doorbell rang.

Henry came up from the basement, opened the chair and set it down. "That's Mr. Engelmann now!" he said excitedly, dashing to the door.

Julean stood in the living room doorway and watched as Henry and David hugged hello.

Henry turned to Julean and then back. "Mr. Engelmann this is Julean."

"Yes, yes, so I finally meet the angel who has flown into Henry's life!"

Julean smiled as she extended her hand. He ignored it and

stepped forward to hug her instead, taking Julean a bit by surprise.

"Henry, you said she was pretty but you are such a beautiful young woman. It is so good to finally meet you!"

Julean blushed. "I was looking forward to meeting you as well; Henry talks of you so often."

"Yes, yes, but that is because he doesn't know of anything better to talk about." Turning to Henry he added, "Henry, the Lord has surely blessed you. What a beautiful young woman he has brought into your life!"

"Well, I hate to rush, but dinner's ready. If you all don't mind, please come and sit for dinner."

"Mind? Never, Mary. It always tests my patience when I come over and have to wait a second longer for your meals. Even Bill, as good a conversationalist as he is, can't distract my roaring appetite."

"Well then," Now it was Mary's turn to blush, "please come in and sit yourselves down. Julean, you can sit beside Henry over there."

Everyone took a seat. Most of the food had already been set on the table.

"Could you please say grace, David?"

"Yes, of course. In the name of the Father, the Son and the Holy Ghost. Thank you, Father for bringing us together for this fine meal Mary has prepared. We thank you for this food and ask You to bless it and all seated at the table. We thank you for bringing a new guest to the Pederson home, Julean, and we ask You to bless this conversation."

Mary got up to get the vegetables and returned to the table.

"Well, it's a little crowded, but we'll all make do."

"It brings us all closer together, Mary; kitchens should be even smaller."

"That's a nice thought, actually, David," said Mary. "I never thought of it that way."

"Mr. Engelmann sees the good in everything," added Henry, for Julean's sake.

"That's a good way to be," Julean smiled at Henry.

"Have you had any response to all the 'don't peek' envelopes with prizes we mailed out two weeks ago?" Mary asked.

"Yes, yes. How that boy of yours keeps coming up with ideas for the business, I will never know. It's also giving such joy to many of the customers. 'David,' they ask, 'What kind of a game is this? What kind of a prize is inside?' They can hardly wait for January to come along! It's a secret, I tell them. I laughed at Mrs. Harold, she said her husband was so curious to know what was inside he tried to steam the envelope open to take a peek and see what the prize was. 'He's like a little kid, David!' she said. We both laughed."

Mr. Engelmann looked at Henry, "I'm glad you convinced me to do this Henry; it's a wonderful idea and I like what Mrs. Miller said yesterday, 'What an exciting way to warm up a cold January, Mr. Engelmann.'"

Henry smiled and nodded. He reached for some bread, trying to deflect the attention on him.

David understood. "Enough about me and the store. So, Julean, I understand you go to a different school than Henry?"

She nodded and waited until she'd finished chewing to answer. "Yes, I go to Central Collegiate. It's not too far from Balfour. Actually, Hank and I often meet halfway between the schools at lunchtime."

Mary and Bill looked up at the word *Hank*. His nickname was seldom used in the house. It was almost as if two different people were at the dinner table.

"Please pass the mashed potatoes, Mary. They are delicious with the roast beef gravy."

"I'll second that," said Bill. "Please pass them down, Henry, after David has helped himself."

"Henry mentioned that you have a sister?"

"Yes, Joyce is a year older than me. She's in her first year in the College of Education at the university in Saskatoon."

Mr. Engelmann turned to Henry, "That is what you were

going to do, Henry, but Mary tells me you have changed your mind?"

"Yeah, I decided to go into business administration. I like the store so much and you've always told me I'd be a successful businessman. But I must admit, teaching still tugs at me as well. I've learned so much from you over the years about human nature, life and values that I could pass on to students." Henry shrugged, "I'm still stewing about it."

"Well, the Lord will direct you to the right choice, I'm sure."

"And what about you, Julean, have you any plans after Grade 12?" asked Mary.

"Yes, I'm going into nursing, following my dad's footsteps in the medical field. Dad's a doctor. He has a general practice in the Medical and Dental building downtown. I'm planning on working in his office this summer after graduation."

"That's such a fine, caring profession," commented Mr. Engelmann.

"So, were you born and raised in Regina, Julean?" Mary continued, taking this opportunity to find out as much about the girl in Henry's life as possible.

"No. I was born on a farm community in southern Alberta. We moved to Regina when I was six."

"We come from the farm too, near a small town called Kendal. Actually, come to think of it, Henry was six as well when we moved to Regina."

"Yes, Mrs. Pederson, Hank told me that. Quite a coincidence."

"Yeah, it was destiny that we should meet," chimed in Henry.

"What's the name of the town you come from?" asked Bill.

"Well, actually the community we're from is a Mormon colony. Cardston is the name of the town."

Everyone stopped eating and looked at Julean. Henry hadn't told them Julean was Mormon. To be honest, he hadn't given it much thought until now. Jenny wasn't Catholic either; even though she and her parents had gone to church at St. Mary's, they'd attended mainly to get to know people in the neighbourhood. Perhaps his parents hadn't realized that. And Henry had just sort of assumed Jenny would naturally become a Catholic when they got married since her family wasn't committed to any one denomination.

But Julean not being Catholic, and Mormon to boot—how would that affect their relationship? Henry looked at Mr. Engelmann for an answer. Mr. Engelmann gave Henry a furtive glance and then turned to Julean.

"I don't recall any Mormon churches in Austria, but it seems to me there were some missionaries at the time. Regardless, tell me a little about your faith."

"Well, we're Christians. We believe in Jesus Christ, and pray daily. Family is very important, just as I see it is to you as well. And I'm hoping to go to midnight mass with Henry on Christmas Eve so then I'll be able to see more how our church compares with yours."

Bill interjected, "Aren't Mormons the ones where husbands have several wives?"

"Yes, that's what most people think of the Church of Jesus Christ of Latter Day Saints. That's unfortunate, as that practice is very strictly not allowed anymore."

"But it *was* permitted at one time," Bill continued to probe.

"Yes. When the founder first began the church as prophet, he did have many wives, but by 1890 it was strictly banned. There's a colony in British Columbia that still practises it. Actually, the reason my parents moved away from Cardston to the city was to get away from that perception. I must admit, my great-grandfather had three wives. My great-grandmother passed away two years ago."

"How do you feel about wives or women sharing their husband with each other?" asked Henry with sudden interest.

"Like I said, Hank, the church strictly forbids it today, however, I did have many conversations with Great-Grandma about it. She said in many ways it worked out fine; the women shared responsibilities, always had someone to talk to, helped each other raising the children, but she did say there were some pretty hectic squabbles at times, too, as you can imagine."

There was nervous laughter around the table at this.

"But how do *you* feel about it, Julean?" Henry asked again, looking straight into Julean's eyes.

An uncomfortable silence fell in the kitchen. Mary cleared her throat and said, "Well, we best let Julean eat her dinner. We've kept her talking so much she's barely had a chance to touch it."

"Everything's delicious, Mrs. Pederson," Julean complimented, trying to ease the tension.

Picking up on his wife's cue to change the subject, Bill turned to Mr. Engelmann, "So the sale of the store is now complete David?"

"Yes."

But Henry was no longer listening, his mind transfixed on the last question he'd asked Julean. What would it be like if he could be married to *both* Julean and Jenny?

"GOOD EVENING, MISS Sarsky, welcome to the Hamilton residence."

Jenny was surprised the butler knew her name.

"Hi…um, good evening to you too."

"Good evening, James. May I help you with your coat?"

"No, I'm fine, but Jennifer may require assistance."

Jenny already had her coat off and handed it to the butler.

"Mrs. Hamilton is waiting for you in the living room."

"Is Father home yet, Andrew?"

"I don't believe he is as of yet, James."

As Jenny and James walked through the huge foyer, James' mother appeared at the living room entrance. She was a very attractive, petite lady. Her hair was a silvery white, straight and short, and yet gave her a sophisticated appearance. Jenny loved her black dress. It looked formal at first glance, but the style and cut was casual. She smiled broadly as she approached Jenny.

"Why hello, Marjorie! It's so nice to finally meet you. James has spoken of you so often."

Jenny didn't know how to respond. Should she correct Mrs.

Hamilton about her name or not? James *knew* she preferred to be called Jenny. She wished he had relayed this to his mother so she wouldn't be in this awkward position. Extending her hand, Jenny decided to let it slide.

"Good evening, Mrs. Hamilton. It's nice to meet you, too."

Mrs. Hamilton took Jenny's hand in hers. "Come, let's sit in the living room. Jim isn't home yet. He had some business to complete but promised he would be home shortly."

Uh-oh, like father like son.

The elegant living room was very spacious, with two sofas and a large glass-topped coffee table in between, all of it set in front of a stone fireplace complete with roaring flames.

"Oh my, what a beautiful room," Jenny said, looking around. "And I love the fire, it's so cozy and warm."

Mrs. Hamilton led her to one of the sofas. James followed and sat next to Jenny. Mrs. Hamilton sat opposite.

"James tells me you're in Grade 12, Marjorie, and that you're involved in many activities and clubs, and even have time to be on the student council."

"I *am* a bit over-involved in extracurricular activities, if the truth be known. I'm thinking of dropping out of *Hamlet*, a school play I'm in, though I do enjoy acting very much."

The butler appeared in the living room.

"Shall I bring any refreshments, ma'am?"

"Yes, Andrew, that would be nice. What would you like Marjorie? The chef has prepared a delightful fruit punch, or would you rather have a soft dr—?"

"You can have wine," James interjected, "A sauvignon, perhaps?"

"Actually, the punch sounds lovely, James."

"And the usual port for you, James?"

"Yes, the Bordeaux will do."

"Very well, sir. And for you, ma'am?"

"The fruit punch is fine, Andrew."

Jenny was shocked that James was allowed to drink alcohol at home. In fact, quite uncharacteristically, she was at a loss as to what to say to James' mother. She was relieved when Mrs. Hamilton got up and excused herself to call James' father.

James and Jenny exchanged conversation about how big the house was and the deal his dad was closing. Apparently it was quite a coup. When Mrs. Hamilton finally returned, she explained that Mr. Hamilton would be detained longer than expected and that dinner was ready.

The dining room was adjacent to the living room. It was *huge*. Two chandeliers hung above a long table which could easily seat thirty people. The plates and cutlery were set at one end of it. Jenny stifled a giggle thinking about how loud she'd have to yell if their places had been set at opposite ends. It was all very fancy; crystal glassware and shiny silverware, framing gleaming white bone china plates. Two butlers stood stiffly at the far end of the table. As soon as Jenny was seated one of them stepped forward and placed the napkin on her lap. Another butler did the same for Mrs. Hamilton. James did his own.

"Would you care for some wine with your meal?"

Jenny didn't know quite how to respond. On occasion she drank wine at the dinner table with her parents. "Yes, that would be nice," she replied.

"Is there a preference between—"

James spoke, "Marjorie would prefer a sweeter wine, I'm sure. Check with André whether we have a sparkling wine— the Portugal Espumante or the Italian Franciacorta."

"Very good, sir."

Jenny recalled her mother's long-ago advice: *when the meal is more than one course, it's best to start with the cutlery furthest away from the plate and move in with each course served.*

"So, tell us about your family, Marjorie. Are you an only child?"

"I'm sure I told you she was, Mother."

"Oh, perhaps you have, dear. And what does your father do?"

"He's the president of a company called Mackurcher and Company. They're involved in—"

A butler set a bowl of traditional vegetable soup before Jenny.

"Thank you."

"Yes, we are quite familiar with the company; Jim has mentioned it several times. It's across Canada and now considering expansion abroad, I understand."

"Yes, it might be, I'm not cer—"

The butler took away the soup and replaced it with a green salad with a side dish of dressing.

"Thank you."

"It's not necessary to thank him," James said.

"What about your mother, Marjorie, is she employed?"

"No, she doesn't work. Well, not in the sense you mean. She looks after the estate since she doesn't want any domestic help, although we're entitled to have some. Oh my, that's a delicious salad dressing."

"I enjoy it too. I believe it's an egg mayonnaise dressing the chef makes up."

Jenny didn't know why she was suddenly caught up in this wealthy lifestyle. She felt very uncomfortable, yet enjoyed the pampering at the same time.

"Ah, here comes the main course. I asked the chef to make your favourite meal."

Jenny looked at the dish before her. Poached salmon fillet served with what looked like leeks and sautéed potatoes in a rich cream sauce.

"Oh, this looks scrumptious, James."

"So do you plan to work in your father's company?" continued Mrs. Hamilton relentlessly.

"Oh, no! I plan to be a school librarian. I just love books."

"Before I married Mr. Hamilton, I too got my degree in education. I was planning to teach English but once married, I never had the opportunity to teach in the classroom. Probably just as well—I don't know if I would have had the authoritative presence to maintain discipline with high school students."

"They can be a challenge," Jenny replied.

"I wish Father would come home, I'm anxious to learn how the negotiations went."

"Yes, it is getting late, isn't it? This is the third time this week Jim has worked overtime."

"Well, it does take a lot of planning and meetings, Mother."

"I suppose so. Marjorie, are you enjoying the meal so far?"

"Yes, it's delicious, but I'm afraid I don't think I can finish."

"Save some room for dessert: French apple and cinnamon pie with fresh cream. It's to die for."

"That does sound good. Perhaps just a small serving?"

After the meal, they retired to the living room for tea and Belgian chocolate wafers. By nine-thirty Mr. Hamilton still had not returned, and so James said he would take Jenny home. Perhaps she could meet his father on some other occasion.

As James was driving out of the estate a car approached.

"That's probably Father's limo."

As the cars passed one another they slowed and stopped.

Mr. Hamilton was in the back seat.

"Hello, James. Sorry I couldn't make it earlier."

"I understand, Dad. This is Marjorie, Jennifer Sarsky."

"Hello, young lady. I apologize for not sharing dinner with you. James speaks of you often and I was so looking forward to chatting with you. Perhaps we can have you over again in the near future?"

"Yes, I'd like that, Mr. Hamilton. Nice meeting you."

James rolled up the window and drove on.

"That's some deal Dad's putting together; it could net the company over $12 million in revenue in the next two years."

Jenny wasn't sure how to react or respond to a number like that. She was overwhelmed by the entire evening.

Butlers, even!

Later, when she shared the evening's events with her mother, Edith was thrilled.

"But they kept calling me Marjorie all night. James knows I prefer Jenny."

"Well, Marjorie does sound more sophisticated. Oh you'll get used to it, Jenny. James is such a fine young man; soon you'll be high society!"

CHAPTER TWENTY-NINE

CHRISTMAS CAME AND went. Even before Mr. Engelmann opened the store on January second at nine o'clock, two people were there waiting to open their envelopes, wanting to know what prize they could claim. It was a pleasure to see many of the seniors as excited as children opening birthday presents when they tore into the envelopes. And as Henry had expected, when people came in to claim their gift, they left with many other items.

By the end of the day, almost fifty people had come into the store. Mary, Mrs. Schmidt and Mr. Engelmann were run off their feet. It was the busiest day in January that Mr. Engelmann had ever had. There was only one other day, Mr. Engelmann recalled, that was almost as busy. It was in 1949 when a chinook passed through. The snow had melted and it was like a spring day. People ventured out to enjoy the weather and decided to shop.

This time, however, there was no chinook. People were coming out in 25-degrees-below-zero weather, motivated a little by the letter, but mostly because of their love for Mr. Engelmann. They wanted to show their appreciation for the service he had provided to the neighbourhood. By the end of the day, Mary and Mrs. Schmidt had restocked most of the shelves at least twice. Mr. Engelmann was concerned he would soon run out of stock.

"This idea of yours, Henry, will run me out of business!" he would joke in the days that followed.

By the end of January, over half of the 658 letters were returned and some of Mr. Engelmann's shelves were completely empty. It was looking more and more like a store soon to go out of business. It also looked like they wouldn't have to put much on sale. Mr. Engelmann was also encouraging his customers to get from Safeway what he couldn't supply anymore. When Safeway heard about that, the manager phoned Mr. Engelmann and thanked him for his professionalism.

MARY WAS RUSHING to get the household chores done; she had a busy day in store. She wanted to check in on Mr. Engelmann to see if his apartment needed tidying and then do some shopping at Eaton's before meeting Bill for dinner and then going off to a movie at the Broadway.

While she ironed Henry's shirts, her mind wandered over his plan to go to Ottawa. Had he changed his mind since his relationship with Julean had become more serious these past few months? Where was his heart now?

As she put Henry's clothes away, she glanced at the closed desk drawer. She didn't like snooping but she rationalized it was out of motherly concern. She hoped and prayed that the drawer would be empty as she pulled it open. And it was clear some significant activity *had* taken place. Over half the money was gone and sticking out from one of the envelopes were two TCA tickets.

He was going through with it after all.

Mary took the envelope out of the drawer. She examined the tickets. One ticket was stamped "July 2" and the return ticket was stamped "July 7." She took out the sheet of paper, unfolded it and studied his plan. He had added the names and telephone numbers of high schools in Ottawa and their addresses.

Presumably, if he couldn't get the information by phone, he planned to visit each school. But perhaps he didn't need to. All the schools were crossed out except for one, Springview High. It was circled and a note written beside it; *Jenny's high school* followed by several exclamation marks.

At the top of the page, Henry had written: Marriot Hotel reservation, July 2-6, confirmed, $56/night.

How had Henry kept it a secret from everyone all this time? He should know by now it was impossible to keep a secret from a mother. Mary smiled, feeling only a tiny twinge of guilt. *Well, he can't keep it a secret forever.* Sooner or later he was going to have to tell them. He couldn't vanish for a week and not tell anyone. Mary prayed it would work out for him. It had been in the works for so long that maybe not even the love he felt for Julean was strong enough to deter him from his mission.

As Mary was about to fold the letter, she noticed Henry had drawn the shape of a heart with an arrow through it near the bottom left of the page. Inside the heart he had printed: "H loves J." But who was the J? Was it Jenny or Julean…or both?

Mary tucked the folded page back into the envelope and carefully returned it to the drawer exactly how she'd found it. Once again, as Mary left Henry's room, she hesitated for just a moment, sending off a prayer to the crucifix above the bedroom door.

GEEZ, I HOPE I don't get caught. This is the third time I've played hooky from school to make these phone calls.

Henry knew his mom was off shopping today and later she and Dad were going to see *Anatomy of a Murder* at the Broadway. It was the perfect chance to carry out his plans. He would phone Springview High again and pretend to be an employee for a magazine company. He remembered that Jenny had subscribed to *Seventeen* magazine and often saw her reading it on the steps when he called on her. He'd say that a Jenny Sarsky had applied for a subscription but forgot to put her telephone number on the form.

If that failed, he would phone Mackurcher and Co. and ask to speak with Mr. Sarsky and ask him outright for Jenny's phone number. Henry was prepared to argue with Mr. Sarsky; that it was his right to speak to Jenny...*well, don't jump to conclusions, maybe you'll get the phone number right off.*

He felt prompted to call Mr. Sarsky first.

Henry dialed the number. His fingers trembled in the circular plastic holes. This would be a man-to-man talk. He *had* to show Mr. Sarsky he was determined to get Jenny's number one way or another. He was not going to take no for an answer and would threaten to come to Ottawa this very weekend if he didn't get the number...

"Mackurcher and Company, how may I help you?"

Henry lowered his voice and tried to speak as officiously as possible.

"Is Mr. Sarsky in, please?"

"I'm sorry, he's at a conference today. Is there anything I can do or a message I can leave for him?"

Henry's brain swirled; *perhaps there's another way.* He remembered Jenny telling him that she'd been born in Kelowna, British Columbia—and then his Uncle George who lived in Vancouver popped into his mind.

"Yes, it's George Snyder, here. We're relatives from Kelowna on our way to the East coast and wanted to speak to Ted or Edith before we left Ottawa. We can't find their phone number in the phone book..."

"No, their home number is unlisted."

"I wonder if I could trouble you for it? It would be nice to at least say hello to Edith before we head out of the city."

Elaine paused for a moment. She knew from Mr. Sarsky's records that they had resided in Kelowna. "Yes, I suppose I could do that. It's Mr. George Snyder, is that correct?"

"Right." Henry held his breath. He could barely hear the sound of Mr. Sarsky's secretary rifling through the index card holder over the pounding of his heart.

"Yes, here it is," and oh, thank God! she recited the number.

Henry was so nervous and anxious and excited he could barely write it down. He repeated each digit carefully and clearly making sure there was no mistake. He finally had a way to reach Jenny! He felt as though he'd received the code to a secret vault holding the greatest treasure on the Earth! *Finally! After three years...* A rush began to rise from the pit of his stomach. He made every effort to suppress it long enough to complete the call.

"Thank you for the number, miss."

"You're welcome, Mr. Snyder. Enjoy the rest of your trip."

His palm was so damp the receiver slid from his hand before he could hang it up. It dangled from the wall phone, stretching the cord as he let out a yell that surely must have been heard by neighbours three doors down. His heart thundered like it might burst through his ribs or explode outright.

He couldn't believe it! *After all these years!*

The rush returned; he thought he would soar like an eagle and surely would fly any moment. He picked up the sheet of paper, wanting to make certain it wasn't a dream. He actually held his first love's phone number and gazed at it long and hard until the number blurred with his tears.

Suddenly his legs gave way and he collapsed onto a kitchen chair, completely emotionally drained. He rested against the spindles of the chair and felt the cold wet of his shirt against his back. He took in a deep breath and let it out slowly. And then again. He needed to settle down, clear his mind and think what to do next.

Should he phone Jenny right away? He checked the kitchen clock: two-eighteen. It was later in the day in Ottawa. He didn't know if they were an hour ahead or two. She'd be in school now, perhaps on her way home. How long would that take?

How far does she live from the school? Maybe its best to wait until evening to make sure Jenny will be home. Yes, around suppertime would be best.

Henry went into the living room and picked up a magazine. He flipped through all 121 pages but didn't read a single word.

He went over the telephone conversation again and again, sometimes chuckling over his cleverness and at times bursting out laughing. Perhaps he'd go to his room and read the notes Jenny had written him. That could always occupy his mind for an hour.

He went to his room and got out the notes, but even they couldn't hold his attention for long. *I'm going to talk to her!*

He got up and paced the floor, looking at his watch hoping time would move faster. The minutes stretched into hours. He tried reading again but couldn't concentrate on anything but Jenny. The anticipation of finally talking to her overtook him. Henry couldn't wait any longer. It was four-thirty, it would be at least five-thirty, maybe six-thirty, there; he should've checked with the operator.

It didn't matter, anyway; it was time.

He had to know where he stood with Jenny once and for all. His feelings for Julean were getting stronger by the day. Thoughts of having both Jenny and Julean crossed his mind. What if he were one of those old-time Mormons and it was permitted to have more than one wife?

Geez, Henry, don't flip out.

Henry swallowed hard and slowly dialed the number. Perspiration rolled down his armpits once again. His heart raced as the call ran through the lines. How would she sound? It seemed like an eternity. Would she know him? Recognize him? Still like him? Still want him? It would be so strange to talk to her out of the blue like this.

His throat was drying up. He needed a glass of water, but it was too late.

The call connected, the phone rang once and then again …

"JENNY WE HAVE to get going or we're gonna be late."

"It's a long trip to the city and I have to go to the bathroom. I'll only be a minute."

The phone rang.

"Would you please get that, James?"

"Yes, just hurry *up.*"

The phone rang again and James hurried to answer it.

"Hello?"

"Hello, is this the Sarsky residence?"

"Yes."

"May I speak to Jenny, please?"

James' grip on the phone tightened. Instantly, strong feelings of anger and loathing swept through him. Just that afternoon he and Jenny had had an argument about all the boys who phoned her, all those guys who'd wanted to dance with her last Halloween. And ever since Jenny had told him about Henry Pederson, he'd just known someday the nerd would call. As soon as he heard the voice on the line his instincts told him who it might be. And his instincts rarely failed him...

"Who is this?" James asked sharply.

"Henry."

The name surged through him like a knife slicing his innards. Hate, jealousy and anger seethed from the inner incision.

"Is this Pederson? Henry Pederson?"

"Yeah...that's me." Henry said, surprised.

"Look, bud, I'm James Hamilton and Jennifer is mine. She's my girl and we intend to get married, so get lost creep and don't call here again!"

James slammed the receiver down, almost splitting it in two.

"Who was that?" Jenny asked, coming down the stairs. "You look so red and flushed. Are you angry?"

"No, no, it's no one. Just some drunk crank caller."

Jenny looked at him quizzically. Something was off.

"It was no one. Come on let's go or we'll be late for the movie."

HENRY HELD THE phone. He'd never hated a dial tone so much. He was stunned by what had just happened. Obviously, Jenny was engaged or planning to marry.

Geez, first it's her parents and now this James Hamilton comes between us. This can't be happening! It's not supposed to turn out this way! It's not the way I pictured it at all. I've just got to hear it from Jenny.

Henry dialed the number again. It began to ring.

JAMES HELD THE front door for Jenny as she walked out into the evening air. Just before he closed the door the phone rang.

"Maybe I should get it, James; it might be important."

"Jenny, it's probably that drunk calling again. If we don't leave now we'll miss the show."

James grabbed hold of Jenny's hand firmly and led her briskly to his shiny black BMW.

HENRY LISTENED TO the phone ring over and over until the dial tone kicked in again. He held the phone for a long, long time before he finally hung up.

Should he call again? *It just can't end like this.* And just as Henry reached for the phone again, it rang, startling him. It rang once more before Henry answered. He was almost scared to pick it up.

"Hello?"

"Hi Hank, its Julean. Are you okay?"

"Ye—yeah…why?"

"I had the strongest feeling you needed me. I just felt compelled to call and make sure you were okay. You're still coming over tonight, aren't you? I can't wait to see you."

"Yeah, I'll be there around seven-thirty…and thanks for calling."

And that was when Julean whispered, "I love you so much, Hank."

"I—I love you too, Julean."

Henry held onto the receiver with one hand and, with the other, disconnected the call.

Reaching forward as if to dial a number, he suddenly stopped in mid-air. He stared at the phone. In a trance, he finally, gently, replaced the receiver and walked away.

CHAPTER THIRTY

"Geez, Mr. Engelmann," Henry repeated for the third time, "I *finally* get Jenny's phone number only to run into another roadblock!"

"And this one is even harder to break through, Henry. If Jenny and this boy you mention, James, you say, are planning to get married, perhaps it is best to let go. After three years surely Jenny could have phoned or sent you a letter? It seems she has moved on, Henry, and besides you are now seeing Julean, such a lovely girl."

"I *do* love Julean but there was just something special with Jenny and me. I can't explain it. I keep going back to the morning we met in the store. It was as if a spell came over me..."

"Yes, yes, so you have said several times. But we can't keep living in the past, Henry. It was a special meeting, an attraction that was perhaps out of the ordinary—but this relationship with Julean can be too. Perhaps you're making more of your first meeting with Jenny than necessary, you were very young then. And as I've said on several occasions, the lack of closure makes it all the more difficult to let go."

"But that's why I *have* to talk to Jenny—to finalize it."

Mr. Engelmann took a deep breath and after some reflective thought said, "Okay, suppose Jenny had answered the other night; she would have been happy to hear from you but in the end she may very well have told you the same thing that boy said, 'I am going with him now, Henry, and we plan to marry.' It is reasonable to assume that she would come to the same conclusion as her boyfriend, isn't it? And it seems to me you've done everything you could to reach Jenny, and the doors have always remained closed despite your efforts and our prayers. Perhaps it is meant to be," Mr. Engelmann said, "for now anyway," he added, seeing the look on Henry's face. His tone was gentle. "Perhaps this is where the Lord wants you. What is that saying…'bloom where you are planted.'"

Henry stared at his mentor. He always made such perfect sense and yet Henry didn't want perfect sense—he wanted Jenny. Henry put his head down and almost in a whisper, said, "I know you're right, Mr. Engelmann, but I'm still confused about what to do. I love Julean but I love Jenny too; my feelings for her are still so strong. If only she'd sent just *one* letter I'd have pursued her immediately and nothing would have stopped me."

"Henry, in my heart I believe it is time for you to trust in Jesus. Move on. Trust that the Lord has brought this beautiful young woman into your life and much good will come out of it."

"I guess I'm just not as strong in my belief as you are, Mr. Engelmann. I find it hard to trust in something you cannot see, and God seems so distant at times."

Mr. Engelmann nodded, "Yes, but just because you cannot see the air it doesn't stop you from breathing, does it?"

Henry shrugged his shoulders and shook his head. "No."

"It's the same, Henry. Just because you cannot see God shouldn't stop you from believing either. It is a matter of knowing our Lord and how he works in our lives.

"Come, let us make some hot chocolate and sit in the back room; my legs are weary and I have lots to say. It's a cold day and all the shelves are stocked as best can be and I don't think too many customers will come in anymore this afternoon. Many are beginning to shop at Safeway at my request. The manager there is keeping his word to deliver groceries to customers on the list I gave them and he has even included others I've asked him to help out too. In any case, we will hear the bell on the door should anyone come in."

Henry followed his mentor to the storeroom. If it had been nicer outside, Henry would have loved to sit under the sun on the old grey crate; Mr. Engelmann's school of life. The times spent there with his teacher would never be forgotten, forever imprinted in his mind.

Mr. Engelmann set two boxes out in front of the condiment table. Henry had seen Mrs. Engelmann do this with many people in the neighbourhood when she talked to them and prayed for them. Perhaps that was what Mr. Engelmann wanted to do; pray for him and his indecision between Jenny and Julean.

Henry scooped heaping spoonfuls of cocoa and put it in the mugs while Mr. Engelmann filled the kettle with fresh water and turned on one of the burners on the small electric stove. Henry could sense Mr. Engelmann was preparing for one of his lessons.

The two men sat down on the boxes and looked at each other and smiled.

"You know me too well, Henry. I see it in your eyes you already know I have something important to share with you."

"Yup, I'm all ears, Mr. Engelmann. God knows I need some help and you've never failed me."

Mr. Engelmann tilted his head, accepting the responsibility of his role and then began speaking about something which seemed totally unrelated to the matter at hand.

But Henry had long ago learned to be patient. That was Mr. Engelmann's way. He was setting the stage, the background for a teaching that would cut deeply into his heart. Still, Henry wondered what else Mr. Engelmann could possibly say that he hadn't already that could help to deal with his tangled feelings.

Mr. Engelmann leaned forward and rested his elbows on his knees.

"Henry, some of what I am going to say may already be familiar to you, but there is much we have not discussed. However, I think now is the time to talk about the sovereignty of God and there are examples in your life that will clarify what I am about to tell you."

Henry mimicked his mentor by resting his elbows on his knees, leaning forward to make certain he didn't miss a word his teacher was about to say.

"I have spoken to you many times of how much God loves us. He even sent His Son into the world to teach us the way to Him and then Jesus died for our sins in order that we might have access to heaven. His purpose was for the salvation of the world; to bring everyone to Him in heaven. In his efforts to do this, to accomplish His purpose, He works in the lives of each of us daily, not by interfering with our free will but more indirectly, by softening our hearts, bringing people into our lives who say this or that which influences us, perhaps through the reading of a book or the promptings of our guardian angels or His Holy Spirit. It's a huge and immense concept to grasp, Henry. Theologians have called this the divine providence of God at work.

"Not too many people acknowledge this or are even aware of God's workings. Just as many take their guardian angels for granted and thus forfeit a thousand blessings that could have been bestowed upon them. But God's divine providence is perhaps the greatest daily miracle and it's going on every second of every day in the lives of all His children on Earth, preparing us for His kingdom."

Henry couldn't tell where this was going and how it related to his dilemma.

Mr. Engelmann knew he needed to clarify. But his protégé was ready for this lesson and he would soon understand. The kettle whistled just as Mr. Engelmann was about to continue.

"I'll get it, Mr. Engelmann."

Henry jumped up and used a tea towel to grab hold of the hot kettle handle and carefully filled the two mugs. After stirring them he handed one to Mr. Engelmann and held his as he returned to his seat. Both blew on the steaming hot chocolate and took a careful sip.

"*Ach mein lieber Gott, wo war ich?* Ah, yes, I was speaking of God's divine providence. It is hard to see the Lord's workings in our lives because they are usually so subtle and it takes time to deal with or solve problems. Sometimes it takes just days, but more often it takes months and even years; it's easier to see and understand this when we look back in our lives, especially if we have gone through a crisis of some sort.

"Do you recall the day you came to work and told me your father had left with another woman and your world had come to an end? You were in so much anguish, pain and suffering. The anger you held for your father for destroying the family you once knew was so great, you were certain your family would never be the same again."

Henry nodded; he remembered it all too well.

"But look now, its taken years, but see how much closer and stronger your family is and God is still working on it. Just the other day you commented how much closer you and your father have become. And during my visits, I too see how your father listens to you and treats you as an adult. This, Henry, is the working of our Lord, His divine providence.

"Remember at Anna's funeral when you and your father stayed behind because your father wanted to talk to you and ask for your forgiveness? You shared with me that he'd been prompted by the funeral, the talks, the speeches—even the writing on a tombstone—caused your father's heart to soften. You said he wanted to ask for forgiveness while he was alive because he didn't want to be like that fellow seeking forgiveness after he was dead."

Mr. Engelmann stopped and stared at Henry.

"This was God at work. The Holy Spirit and your father's guardian angel prompting him, guiding him and leading him through God's healing. These occurrences were no accident.

"And what about your father's new job? The Coca-Cola rep coming in to see me one morning to tell me that they were looking for a new man to service the equipment? I was immediately prompted by *my* guardian angel to think of your father."

Once again, Mr. Engelmann stopped and gazed hard into his student's eyes. "All these incidents, Henry, are examples of God's divine providence at work. Do you understand?"

Henry looked at his teacher and nodded. "I hadn't thought about it like that, Mr. Engelmann…so, then, did God cause my dad to run away in order to do all this?"

"No. God is not the cause of that. It was your father's personal choices that were the cause. God knew, however, that this trial would bring you and your parents closer together and happier than before."

"But why couldn't God just, I dunno, *zap* Dad and change him so he wouldn't have done that awful thing, and make him love Mom more and show more respect to me? Why go through all this suffering and pain? I know Mom is still hurting."

"Yes, that is a good question. Remember, Henry, God has given us free will to run our lives and make our own choices. We are not robots or dangling puppets on a string that He holds. Free will is a gift from God that we all want and appreciate, no?"

Henry nodded.

"So now you say, it's good to have our free will, but when things go awry then you want Him to come in and fix it. Perform an instant miracle and, as you say, zap your father. You can't have it both ways, Henry. We have to face the consequences of our decisions. But the good news is that God does not abandon us. He knows we are weak and are going to make mistakes and poor choices, and that is where His divine providence comes in. Indirectly He helps us along, as I have tried to show you—through the promptings of the Holy Spirit, our angels and by giving us the grace to straighten our lives out as we build up our character, pray to Him, believing in Him so we don't repeat what we did and are stronger to deal with life's challenges."

Henry was beginning to see the plausibility of what his teacher was saying. He was reading the Bible more and was being influenced by it. And it did seem there was a force or power working to make this all happen. And he definitely felt the promptings of his guardian angel. He had to admit that out of the terrible thing his dad did, a lot of good was happening.

He looked at his teacher. "It's a lot better at our house but it's still not perfect between Mom and Dad." Henry didn't want to bring up the bedroom arrangement, but it didn't seem to affect or limit Mr. Engelmann's response.

"Henry, as you say, it is much better than before. It may not be perfect, but God is still working on it. Someday you will look back and see all the good that the Lord has done. As I have said to you many times, God's time is not our time; His ways are not our ways, He has not abandoned us. The problem with humans is that we want our will done *right now*. We want our prayers answered *right now*. We want quick and immediate results because we are in pain and sorrow. And as I have already said, yes, the Lord could create a miracle in our lives and do what we pray or ask for immediately, but most often, Henry, He works slowly in our lives so we grow in trust, understanding, faith and in character. He is helping your parents to reconstruct a relationship that perhaps wasn't as strong as it could have been. But trust me, Henry, someday you will see that out of this sorrow much good will come, as indeed it already has. God is listening to our prayers—yours, mine and your parents'—who want their situation fully healed as well."

Mr. Engelmann took a sip of chocolate and then said, "Henry, God's ways are perfect. His timing is perfect. Trust Him."

Henry nodded. "You know, Mr. Engelmann, I think you're right. I sort of see God's hand in all this; I especially feel my guardian angel."

"It is very true what I say, Henry. I am a lot older than you and I have seen the good Lord's hand in so many ways and situations there is no room for doubt. I hope you can see this and believe it sooner than I did. It will save you much grief and aggravation in trying to fix things without turning it over to the Lord."

Henry simply nodded. He couldn't see any flaw in what his teacher was saying. It all seemed so real and true.

"Knowing what you know now, Henry, when this crisis occurred in your home, had you gone on your knees and said 'God, I trust you to heal this situation. Thank you for bringing our family back together and making it stronger than before,' and then gone about your business…?"

"Yeah, that would've saved me a lot of worry and heartache. But that takes a *lot* of trust in God."

"Yes, that is correct! And *that* is what God is doing with you now. He is building up your trust in Him through me, our discussions, through reading of the Bible, through your guardian angel. In all these ways and many more, He is building up a relationship between you and Jesus, just like you and I have built up a relationship over the years."

Mr. Engelmann looked deeply into Henry's eyes, "When you first started working for me, you did not know me and your trust in me was at a very low level. But you trust me more now than you did when we first met, no?"

"Yes, of course, Mr. Engelmann—I think we have a very close relationship…I trust you with my life!"

"And that is precisely what the Lord wants for you and Him! He wants you to grow close to Him too, to trust *Him* with your life!"

A look of awe grew on Henry's face.

"Let us look at our friend Eddy now, this will help you to further understand and believe in God's divine providence. Recall how angry and filled with revenge you were when he and his friends accosted you and Jenny? Even though you initially shunned my efforts to forgive Eddy, the seed was planted. God was using me to soften your heart. He loves you and wants what is best for you and for Eddy.

"Later that day when I shared your grief with Anna we both felt prompted to pray. We fell to our knees and prayed for you and Eddy and his friends so that you would forgive them, and for their healing as well. We prayed that the Lord would send you His grace to do so. And besides our discussions on the matter, I remember later in the school year your gym teacher made you captain of the basketball team on the condition you accept Eddy on the team and coach him."

Henry nodded.

"These things were no accident, Henry. *Alles hat seinen Zweck*—everything has a purpose. Do you see how your teacher's challenge further broke down your defenses? God was teaching you to love and forgive through the promptings of others who guided you in the right direction. In doing so, He was building your character and drawing you nearer to Him. Even though He influenced you both through others and your guardian angel, at no time did God take away your free will. You could have continued to be angry and vengeful, to forgive or not to forgive, correct?"

Again Henry nodded.

"But look at what has happened. Your heart was softened to be receptive to Eddy and now such a fine friendship is building. Look at the freedom you are experiencing instead of wasting precious moments of your life living in the past and thinking thoughts of revenge."

Henry was speechless. Mr. Engelmann's wisdom and instruction were always so profound that he could no longer keep his tears in check.

Mr. Engelmann gazed hard into Henry's blurry eyes and pointedly asked, "Henry think on this...how would you feel at this moment if God had not intervened in this way and if you hadn't forgiven?"

Henry knew the answer only too well. His memories of the hate and anger he'd felt still lingered in the recesses of his mind.

"And what about Eddy? Had you not come into his life, where would Eddy be right now? Just look at how you have helped him! He has gained recognition through sports and positive relationships. God wasn't just working with you, but with Eddy as well, Henry! This is how the Lord works with all his children in the entire world. Millions and millions of people every second of every day! Can you now see and understand the magnitude of His workings!?"

Mr. Engelmann was so excited he nearly fell off the box he was sitting on.

Henry, too, could barely sit still. His mind swirled, trying to grasp the teaching. He tried to express it in words, but there were none to define what he had just learned. Finally he blurted, "God is a genius!"

Mr. Engelmann could see the light going on in behind Henry's eyes. He himself had had many of those rare special moments as well. His heart was filled with joy to overflowing that his lesson had been learned at such a deep level.

"*Ach mein lieber Gott, danke, danke! Mien geliebter Sohn sieht das Licht!* He sees the light!"

Mr. Engelmann looked at Henry tenderly and shook his head in wonder. "Yes, He is a genius, but oh! so much *more*. There is no earthly term to define His sovereignty. Others have tried—He is omnipotent, omnipresent, omniscient, and so on, but a finite mind cannot even begin to describe an infinite one.

"God's divine providence is driven by the power of love because that is what God *is*. So in every situation the Lord orchestrates, He brings His love—and that is why everything, no matter how terrible or wrong, turns out for the good to those who believe! His purpose is to bring out the love that is at the core of our being, to love our God and neighbour and make the world better. By saying yes to Jesus, together we work towards the salvation of mankind!"

Henry's eyes lit up again. The scripture he had read in the Bible and heard Mr. Engelmann say so often had a new, richer, fuller meaning. He recited the passage: "God causes all things to work together for good to those who love God, to those who are called according to His purpose."

Henry was so stricken by the deeper meaning of this passage, by the fact that the Lord's words are really *alive* and *living*, it was as if the sun burst into the room and exploded on his face.

Once again Mr. Engelmann saw the look of insight in his student's eyes. "Now that you have a glimpse of His workings, who would you trust to run your affairs, you? Or God who knows everything, does everything perfectly and brings love into every situation."

Henry's answer came quickly. "In Him!"

"To be at peace in this world, Henry, we must continually turn over our will to Him and trust Him. That is why I start out the day in prayer, reading His Word and offering the day to him. He knows what is best.

"We must do this daily lest we slip back to that which is so easy to do. We feel He is not listening or hearing us, we become impatient and take control and just go around in circles, hitting our heads against a brick wall. Soon we mess everything up and come running back to Him pleading to straighten it all out!"

A soothing silence fell over the room. Henry so loved these times with his teacher. He learned so much from his wise mentor. Mr. Engelmann's head was bowed as if in prayer or deep thought. Henry was reluctant to break the peace of the moment yet another growing insight was flooding his mind and he had to share.

Henry spoke softly, gently piercing the silence. "It's *trust* isn't it? It's all about knowing and trusting in Jesus, isn't it?"

"That's a very wise thought, Henry. In a nutshell, that's it. The more we get to know of Jesus through reading the Bible, meditating on His Word, praying, going to church, receiving Him in Holy Communion and having discussions like this, the more he becomes part of our characters. We begin to trust Him just as you have learned to trust me, Henry. So much so that you are willing to put Him in the driver's seat, at the centre of your life and trust that He will direct it. In every situation we obey Him, His teachings and commandments, and He will give us the strength and grace to do so.

"Soon your thoughts, words and deeds become more and more like His. Your character will begin to reflect what is growing in your heart. You will find that you are more forgiving, kinder, more patient, more compassionate, more merciful to others, more at peace…" Mr. Engelmann's words trailed off.

Henry could feel the passion his mentor has for Jesus. What he just heard described perfectly both his teacher and Anna, when she was alive. Both were filled with the love of the Lord to overflowing, committed to bringing His love and healing into every situation, striving to work with their Master to make the world a better place and bring as many people into His kingdom as they could.

It reminded Henry of words Mrs. Engelmann had often spoken to him, those he had read at her funeral. "There is no hope without love. There is no forgiveness without love. We will never be able to serve the Lord or our neighbour without love. Love your Lord with all your strength, soul and heart. Love your neighbour as yourself. Live by this commandment, and you will be a King and inherit all the worthy treasures on earth and in heaven."

Henry was so overtaken by what Mr. Engelmann had shared and the insights he'd gained that he forgot how this discussion was related to his present dilemma with Jenny and Julean. But he was already getting an inkling of how his mentor was going to tie all of it together.

"I think I know why you told me about God's divine providence, Mr. Engelmann. You're going to suggest that I turn my feelings, this problem, over to Jesus and trust Him to handle the situation and turn it all into good. Right?"

"You are getting too wise for me, Henry. Soon there will be nothing left for me to teach you." Mr. Engelmann reached over and patted Henry's hands. "Yes, that is what I believe the Lord wants you to do. You can see how He has worked so faithfully and fruitfully in your life and those close to you. He will do the same in this present dilemma. Don't struggle with it any longer. Leave it up to Jesus and trust Him with all your heart."

"Yeah, that's the other scripture you keep quoting."

And as Henry began reciting the passage, Mr. Engelmann joined in. Together they said, "Trust in the Lord with all thine heart, and lean not unto thine own understanding. In all your ways acknowledge Him and He will make straight your paths."

They looked at each other with love and laughed.

Then Mr. Engelmann followed up on something he had said earlier. "It is my belief, Henry, that the Lord wants you to surrender your resistance and to love Julean fully and freely. You are holding back because of your uncertainty about Jenny and you're wanting to be faithful to her. Stop trying to control your future. It has not worked; we have seen how the doors keep closing for you. Let's try God's way now. Trust Him; you saw how He worked in the lives of your parents and Eddy. Now transfer this insight and belief to the situation at hand. I, too, don't know how to advise you or what is best. But this I *do* know: if you give it to the Lord and trust Him and bloom where you are planted with Julean, He will turn everything to the good. This is a wonderful opportunity to let go and develop your faith in the Lord. The path of your life will be paved with the Lord's love. He has a wonderful plan, a purpose that He will unfold in your life."

Mr. Engelmann leaned forward once more and patted Henry's hand, "You know, Henry, each relationship is special. We are all unique and what you and Jenny had together will always be special between you, and perhaps you will never forget her. But now you have Julean and *she* is special, too. Jenny has someone new and so have you. Perhaps someday you may meet under different circumstances…who knows what the Lord has in store."

Henry gazed at his mentor, tightened his lips, then nodded.

"Henry, I am going to do what Anna so often did. She always trusted the Lord so much and stepped out in faith in perfect expectancy that the Lord would act and answer her prayers. I would like to do that with you right now."

Mr. Engelmann slid off his box, setting his mug on the floor, and went to his knees. Henry instinctively followed. He lowered his head and waited for his teacher to pray.

"Dear Lord, I know you have a plan for our lives, that you care and love us and work constantly in our lives to bring us into Your fold. So many times we are like lost sheep and we need Your guidance to bring us back into the light. We know that when we walk in the shadows of life that You have not abandoned us but will bring great treasures if we but trust in You, dear Jesus.

"You have promised that where two or three are gathered together in Your name that You will be amongst us and hear our prayer. Besides Henry and me, I know my Anna is also here in spirit. Together we ask that You will provide a sign to Henry that will put his heart at peace in his relationship with Julean; that she is another angel of love in his life he desires to freely pursue and fly with. If this is Your will, we also ask that You grant Henry a peaceful, accepting closure to his relationship with Jenny and that she will always remain a special memory in his heart. We thank you for answering this prayer, dear Jesus."

And after a long while, Henry softly murmured, "Amen."

CHAPTER THIRTY-ONE

I N EARLY MARCH, Henry was summoned to the principal's office during English class to a chorus of *oooohs* and *"What'd ya do, Hank? You're in trouble now."*

He couldn't think of any reason he'd be called to the office. When he arrived, a secretary directed him to a seat. Behind Henry were a row of six or seven oak chairs. He chose the one nearest to the principal's office. He wondered what Mr. Mitchell wanted. Probably had to do with the student council and an upcoming event they wanted to plan. Perhaps graduation.

Mr. Mitchell appeared in his office door.

"Hello, Henry. Come on in."

Henry took the chair opposite Mr. Mitchell's desk. Mr. Mitchell seated himself in his leather-backed swivel chair and shuffled a few papers in front of him.

"At our last staff meeting, Henry, the topic of this year's graduation came up. The actual graduation ceremonies will be held on the Friday before the graduation dance. The staff has unanimously voted in favour of you being this year's valedictorian. We are all very proud of your grades, your leadership as president of the student council, and the outstandingly mature manner in which you have carried out your day-to-day affairs within the school. Students look up to you, Henry, and you have been an excellent example for them to emulate."

Henry blinked at Mr. Mitchell. "Th—thank you."

"Well, will you do it?"

Henry was so taken aback by the accolades he'd almost forgotten what the question was. After a moment, he replied, "Yes, I'd be honoured to give the valedictory speech."

The principal reached for a paper in front of him. "On this sheet, Henry, is a list of possible topics you may wish to speak about. If you have something else to say you feel is more pertinent, go ahead."

Henry nodded.

"There are two conditions, however, to which you must agree," Mr. Mitchell continued. "First, you must show me your speech one month before the date of our closing exercises, and second, I am allowed to edit your speech if I feel some things are not appropriate."

Henry looked over the topics listed on the paper Mr. Mitchell had handed him, though he already knew exactly what he wanted to talk about without even looking at it.

He looked up at Mr. Mitchell. "Yes, I agree to your conditions. I'll have the speech ready for your consideration the first week in May, Mr. Mitchell."

"Excellent! I look forward to reading it." Mr. Mitchell looked at Henry and smiled.

HENRY WAS SO excited that he'd been asked to be valedictorian he thought he would go to the store and share the news with Mr. Engelmann.

Halfway home, though, he felt prompted to call Julean instead. Mr. Engelmann's prayer for him to see a sign that he could love Julean freely and accept Jenny as a memory seemed to be working. He hadn't thought of her as much lately, and he and Julean were definitely growing closer with each passing day. Although he didn't think he'd ever forget his first love, he had to admit the memory of Jenny's charm, spontaneity and beauty that had held him in bondage for most of his high school years seemed to be dissipating.

Perhaps it was the fact that no reality accompanied the memories he held of her; each thought lacked physical support, a touch, a presence, a hug, a smile. While he still felt a strong connection to her, his memories of his first love were giving way to a reality with Julean, whose real embraces, smiles and tender kisses were beginning to take a stronger foothold in his life.

As Mr. Engelmann had often said, just as the night has to disappear to give way to a bright new day, so, too, his precious memories of Jenny had to disappear to give way to a bright new future with Julean.

CHAPTER THIRTY-TWO

J ENNY COULD HARDLY wait to see Tammy. She'd given birth to a seven-and-a-half-pound baby girl earlier that morning. The doctor had induced the delivery as the baby was already two weeks overdue, according to his best estimate. Jenny would have loved to have been there, but Tammy's mother wouldn't hear of it. She still blamed Jenny for changing Tammy's mind about having an abortion, and Jenny could feel the vibes loud and clear when in the presence of Tammy's mother.

As Jenny got dressed, she recalled the birth of her own little girl and that she hadn't been allowed to hold her, not even for a second. The memory of tiny Camilla being whisked away by an attending nurse to waiting adoptive parents in another room was still so strong and real. She couldn't wait to get to the hospital to see and hold Tammy's baby, to imagine what it might have been like to hold her own baby. If only it was little Camilla she was going to see and not Tammy's baby girl.

They would be almost three years apart, thought Jenny. *Well, not quite. Today is April 24, 1960, and Camilla was born May 24, 1957...* Jenny quickly calculated...*so they are three years less a month apart. My gosh how the time goes! Camilla is already three years old! Well, anyway,* reflected Jenny, *I'll now have two little girls to celebrate on the twenty-fourth of every month. They would've made such good friends. Three years' difference isn't very much; Camilla could have been a big sister to...I wonder what Tammy's going to name her little girl?*

Jenny slipped on yellow low-heeled shoes and went over to the floor-length mirror attached to her closet door. As she gazed at herself she wondered what Camilla might look like. Would she have her blond hair and blue eyes and oval face or would she look like...?

The thought unsettled her; she didn't want to think about the guy who had raped her and she didn't want that kind of stigma attached to her little girl. She was just a beautiful, innocent child, completely devoid of the intentions of her father. When she was pregnant with Camilla, Jenny had wiped the father out of her mind and replaced him with Henry. It helped her accept the pregnancy initially, but even the awful circumstances surrounding Camilla's conception couldn't keep Jenny from loving the baby growing inside her for very long.

Still, every now and then she allowed herself to think of that boy. Jenny wondered if he knew he had fathered a baby. *Does he ever think about that night and what happened?* How funny life could be with its twists and turns. Perhaps if she met him, he might turn out to be a really nice guy who just wasn't himself under the influence of alcohol. *I wonder if our paths will ever cross again?* A strange feeling swept through Jenny at the thought.

I can hardly wait to see that baby. Jenny ran down the stairs just as Edith was coming in the front door.

"Hi, Mom."

"Oh my, Jenny, you look so lovely in that yellow spring dress."

"Aw, thanks, Mom! How did the luncheon meeting with Isabel go?"

"Fine. So where are you off to?"

"Tammy had her baby this morning. She just called. It's a girl and over seven pounds, almost two pounds bigger than Camilla was. I'm just dying to hold her!"

Edith stared at Jenny, remembering only too well being in the delivery room when her daughter had given birth herself. She could still see the baby dangling from the doctor's hands, but even more remembered the look of longing in Jenny's eyes. Jenny had wanted to hold and kiss her baby so much. At the time Edith wouldn't have admitted it to anyone, but she, too, would have liked to have held her daughter's baby, her grandchild.

Ted had wanted to allow Jenny to keep the baby. He felt that it was their responsibility and actually had said he'd welcome the opportunity to raise another child, claiming it would give him the chance to be more of a father, to mark a new beginning, to be at home more and involved with the child's upbringing. That it would bring them all closer together.

But that was all talk. Ted just trying to deal with his guilt for not being home more with Jenny. No, it had been best, Jenny being the age she'd been, to give the baby up for adoption to a young couple—parents who could provide a loving, secure home. *But,* she thought, *it* would *be nice to hear the pitter-patter of little feet running through this sometimes altogether too huge house.* She looked at her lovely daughter and allowed herself to momentarily feel the loss of that decision. But Edith quickly pushed the thought out of her mind.

"Better take an umbrella, Jen, it's starting to rain. Here, take this yellow one; it matches your outfit. And give my love to Tammy. Tell her I can hardly wait to see her baby too."

JENNY PARKED THE car in the Ottawa General Hospital parking lot. She got out and opened the umbrella. It was a warm, gentle spring rain. She would have loved to have taken her shoes off and run over the lawn, the thought of which reminded her fondly of the day she and Henry had run home barefoot in the rain. The freshness in the air energized her now as it had that day, along with the many dazzling reflections of cars and people walking to and from the hospital. Unbeknownst to Jenny, however, was how the many people passing her stared a moment or two longer than normal. It was as if a ray of sun walked down the street, cutting through the rain. Jenny's yellow dress and umbrella reflected in the water on the street like gold. And once the passersby saw her features it was as if they were hypnotized by her beauty, unable to turn away.

A window cleaner caught the reflection of her approach in the entryway window he was cleaning. He quickly turned and held the door for Jenny, wanting to see for himself the bright yellow light that so distracted him.

"Thank you," said Jenny with a warm smile.

"You're welcome, miss." He smelled lilacs as she passed him.

A nurse tied a white smock at Jenny's back and gave her a mask to wear before seeing the newborn. When Jenny entered Tammy's room, her friend, so obviously a mother now, was nursing her baby. The sight sent spears of envy into Jenny's heart. She rushed to her friend's bedside and kissed Tammy's forehead through the white mask. She reached down and touched the baby's head.

"Oh, Tammy, she's so beautiful! Look at all her dark brown hair!" Tears slid down Jenny's cheek at the sight of the infant suckling at her mother's breast. So often Jenny had dreamed of holding Camilla to her breast, snuggling and loving her. Each day of pain as her milk dried up was a terribly vivid reminder of what nature had intended her to do. Jenny hoped and prayed that her daughter would forgive her for not being there for her; raised on formula and not the close, loving, nurturing touch of her real mother.

"Oh, Tammy, she's so beautiful," she said again. "Have you decided on a name yet?"

"I like Alicia and Ashley, but I was hoping Robbie would come and see the baby so I could get his input, but he hasn't been here yet."

Jenny's heart went out to her friend. She understood being

alone; how often she had wished that Henry were at her side when Camilla was born.

"Oh, he'll probably come, Tammy. Give him time."

The baby turned her head to look up at Jenny, releasing the nipple with a small *pop*. Tammy pulled her gown closed and held the baby over her shoulder to burp her.

Jenny marvelled at how quickly Tammy had known what to do.

"Would you like to hold her?"

"Oh, Tammy, could I please?"

Jenny bent down and gently took the baby from Tammy's arms and immediately brought the tiny creature close, nestled at her breast. *This is what it would have been like to hold Camilla.* Her sweet little girl in her arms, nursing. *This* was the memory her heart should hold, not her helpless baby dangling from a distant doctor's hand.

Jenny brought the newborn to her face, breathing in that unmistakable baby scent. She smiled at the infant and kissed her forehead through the mask. She wanted to remove the cloth and feel the baby's soft, soft skin on her lips. Longing flooded her mind. *This is what it's supposed to be like, my baby close in my arms,* she thought again. She wanted to hold the baby, skin to skin, to feel the closeness she had lost. Tears slid down Jenny's cheeks as one thought after another crossed her mind.

Oh to think that this beautiful infant was almost aborted. The thought sent a stab into Jenny's gut.

Jenny felt Tammy's eyes on her. She could probably guess what was going through her mind. She should give the baby girl back to her mother but Jenny wanted to hold her forever!

"Tammy, she is so darling, I could just hold her for always."

Just then Tammy's mother came into the room.

"Hi, Mrs. Anderson."

"Hello, Jenny," she replied coldly. She turned to her daughter. "I filled out some papers with the social worker. She'll be in to see you later this afternoon. I have to go now but I'll be back with your dad tonight. He wants to see what his granddaughter looks like."

"Give my love to Daddy and tell him I can't wait for him to see her."

Mrs. Anderson turned back to Jenny. "Please don't stay too long, hmm? Tammy needs her rest."

"Oh, for sure, Mrs. Anderson. I'll be leaving shortly as well."

As Tammy's mother left, an attending nurse walked in. She looked surprised not to see the baby in Tammy's arms. She quickly turned to see the infant tucked securely in Jenny's arms. "You had me worried for a moment there," she chuckled, "thought maybe we'd misplaced our new little addition to the world."

Jenny reluctantly handed the baby to the nurse.

"I'll be back with her in two hours for another feeding. Try to get some rest in the meantime."

When the nurse left, Jenny pushed a chair up to Tammy's bedside. No sooner had she sat down than tears began to flow from Tammy's eyes.

"I love Robbie *so* much and yet he doesn't seem to care about me or our baby. He thinks only of his future. I know I shouldn't have, but I called him two times last week. He seemed so cold and distant, Jen; I don't think he loves me anymore. Maybe he never did. I told the social worker I wanted three days to think it over, whether or not I want to give the baby up for adoption, I mean. What should I do, Jenny?"

Jenny knew exactly what she herself would do. She would keep the baby. She knew only too well the loss Tammy would suffer. Granted, given her age and the circumstances of her own pregnancy, Jenny realized that it was likely best to have given up Camilla, as painful as it had been, but Tammy was older and almost finished high school. It would be difficult at times, but Jenny believed the joy of raising her daughter would far outweigh the loss.

Jenny was about to speak when Tammy went on, "If I give up the baby, Robbie might come back to me and—and Mom wants me to give up the baby, too. She says I'm too young to be tied down like this and she wonders how it will affect my future choices about education and relationships with other men. She says that most men don't want to be bothered with someone else's child. She makes it all sound so *complicated*; that my future would be so burdensome."

"Oh, Tammy, I don't know if I should be saying this to you; it's your decision, after all. But I would keep her, don't give her away. I'll help you with your little girl, together we will raise her, and we're old enough. Tammy, she belongs with you, with her *mother*."

Just then Tammy's mother returned. "I just had to come back; I was concerned you might still be here. Please, Jennifer, Tammy needs her rest and she has a lot to think about without you adding to her troubles."

"Oh, Mom! Jenny's my best friend and I value her advice so much."

"Jenny, would you please just go? I wish to speak to my daughter alone."

Jenny got up, unsure what to say. "Of course, Mrs. Anderson." She turned to Tammy. "Should I come back tomorrow?"

"Oh, yes, Jenny, please do."

Mrs. Anderson shook her head and rolled her eyes as Jenny passed by her and left the room.

When she emerged from the hospital the sun was shining warm and bright. The walkways and streets were already drying up, except for a few puddles of rain caught in potholes and low-lying areas.

Although Jenny's face shone greater than the brightness of the sun, her heart was heavy. She felt so sorry for Tammy, under so much pressure to give up her baby. She knew Tammy's life was different than hers and that Tammy had her own guardian angel, and perhaps Tammy's little girl would be a gift of love to a couple yearning for a child of their own. She remembered thinking that about Camilla's adoption and had been comforted by the thought.

But, if Tammy could only understand the days, weeks and months of loss Jenny had felt anyway. If it hadn't been for the healing power of her guardian angel, nature and the wildflowers, she didn't know if she would ever have gotten through it.

And then from out of nowhere, perhaps from the flowers and budding bushes that lined the sidewalk, a beautiful monarch butterfly flew her way. She followed it with forlorn eyes as it flitted merrily about as if trying to lift her spirits.

It did distract her from her sorrow. She marvelled at its beauty, such a gorgeous orange and black butterfly. Perhaps it was as Carlos had said, a butterfly is a messenger of love from our guardian angels or a loved one, or even an angel in disguise. Could it be from Henry or Camilla? She knew monarchs travel great distances. Some go to California while others east of the Rocky Mountains migrate all the way to Mexico. They were coming back now. She wondered if one could possibly come from Regina, Saskatchewan.

As Jenny got into her car and closed the door, she noticed the butterfly still flitting about. She prayed a message of love to Tammy that her guardian angel would guide her with her decision. Jenny looked at the monarch just outside of her car window and whispered, "Go to Tammy's room with my love and cheer her up as you did me."

CHAPTER THIRTY-THREE

As SPRING SETTLED in, Mary helped Mr. Engelmann sort through the things in his living quarters. It took a few days for him to accept that Anna's possessions were only material memories and that someone else in need would make better use of them.

By the end of April, all that remained was a bed, end table, and lamp, a few changes of clothes in the bedroom, the fridge, stove, a table, a single chair in the kitchen, as well as the easy chair and end table next to the south window.

It was very busy at school, but Henry tried to help out at the store whenever he could. He noticed with each visit how much emptier the store looked. The store now lacked so many products that Mr. Engelmann felt guilty about being open and unable to supply his customers properly. Many of them had already switched to Safeway, however, some people understood and were just happy that he was still there and around to talk.

Most of the neighbourhood also knew by now that Mr. Engelmann was going into the priesthood and were very pleased and excited for him. It made them feel that they weren't going to lose him forever with the closing of the store, that they would be able to see him in some other capacity, perhaps in an even more intimate way.

A number of times, people brought along a camera to take pictures of the storefront in order to preserve some memory of the store. A lot of the time, they would ask Mr. Engelmann to stand in front and took a picture of him too. If Henry was at the store, they wanted him in the picture too. Mary got caught up in all the photography as well. She took lots of pictures of Mr. Engelmann and Henry, not only in front of the store, but inside as well. Some were of Mr. Engelmann behind the counter alone and then with Henry beside him, and then in the storage room sitting on boxes and chatting during break times.

The best photographs, though, were of the old grey crate out back which constituted Mr. Engelmann's classroom. It was here he imparted lessons in the school of life. There was one in particular Mary took at about ten-thirty in the morning one bright, sunny day that became Henry's favourite picture of Mr. Engelmann and himself. The shadows were strong on their faces as they sat together on the old grey box. The photo seemed to catch the intensity of their friendship. Henry was surprised by the quality of the image; his mom knew the special relationship he and Mr. Engelmann shared and tried to capture this bond and the love Mr. Engelmann and her son had for each other. All in all, Henry just loved the pictures she'd taken and would treasure them for the rest of his life.

Change was in the wind not only in their neighbourhood; the closing of Mr. Engelmann's store seemed to mark a slow transition in which the small corner store where people were considered family was becoming only a memory in many parts of the country. People everywhere were adjusting to huge shopping stores and chains springing up, slowly but surely taking over an old and cherished way of life.

At first, the bright store lights and rows of products appealed to the customers. But for those who had experienced it, what Mr. Engelmann lacked in products or flashy displays was more than made up by his personal interest and care for those he served. In the final days and weeks of the business, Henry often overheard customers say that it wasn't the groceries they missed at the larger supermarket, it was the camaraderie—the love, the talks, the daily interaction. Sure, they had a big, fancy new store full of things, but it had no heart.

AS PROMISED, BY the first week of May, Henry had finished writing his speech and presented it to Mr. Mitchell.

Mr. Mitchell's eyes widened at the number of pages Henry placed on his desk.

"This is quite a stack of papers, Henry."

"Yeah, I know it's a lot, but I really didn't know what to cut out of it. I was hoping you could help me with that. If you want, I can leave it with you and come back tomorrow or whenever you have time."

"No, that's okay. I'm sure it won't take me long to read, and I may have some questions to ask you as I go through it. Would you mind staying until I finish?"

"Not at all, Mr. Mitchell."

The principal shuffled through the papers again and inwardly rolled his eyes at the number of them, then tapped the bottom of the stack on his desk to align them. He sat back in his chair, tilted it as far as he could, then rotated his shoulders. He looked as if he were preparing to read a novel.

To occupy himself, Henry looked around the office at the framed degrees on the wall and the family pictures on a cabinet beside a tall bookshelf. He studied the titles of the books occupying the bookshelf. Most seemed to be about school administration and the role of the principal.

When Henry's gaze returned to Mr. Mitchell, he swivelled his chair to the side then turned it until his back was to Henry. As he did, Henry noticed what he thought were tears in Mr. Mitchell's eyes. The principal stayed in that position for nearly a half-hour. Henry was no longer interested in the objects in the room but rather in what Mr. Mitchell had read that triggered such an emotional response.

Finally, Mr. Mitchell rose from his chair, his back still to Henry. He walked to the windows overlooking the schoolyard, seeming to compose himself. He swiped a knuckle across his face, then turned and sat on the edge of his desk.

He held up the speech. "This is very good, Henry. It's a bit longer than we would want it, but I wouldn't edit any of it either. That's the finest valedictory speech I've ever read in my entire career. I'm certain you won't have any trouble holding everyone's attention. And the visual demonstration you included at the end really made me stop and think about my life and the way I live it. Very impressive!"

Henry gazed at Mr. Mitchell. Not exactly the reaction he had expected, but certainly the reaction he'd hoped for.

"That Mr. Engelmann has been quite an influential man in your life, hasn't he? All I can say is, you've been one fortunate young man to learn all this and at such a young age."

"But that's the whole point, Mr. Mitchell. We should *all* be learning these things while we're young so as we grow up, we'll know how to live successfully and be happy."

Mr. Mitchell just stared and shook his head. After a long pause he handed the speech back.

"Well done, Henry. I'm very proud of you. Well done."

HENRY WAS SO pleased that Mr. Mitchell liked his speech that he couldn't wait to tell his parents and Mr. Engelmann. But more than that he felt a strong urge to share it with Julean.

When he got home and received his mom's permission to borrow his dad's car to see her, he phoned her and said that he was on his way over. Julean said she'd wait for him outside since it was such a nice day even though the last of the snow still hid in corners here and there.

Henry could hardly wait to see Julean to share his news, yet he was feeling something else he couldn't explain…at least not until after he saw her. Then he understood.

When he arrived at Julean's place, she was sitting on the concrete steps at the front of her house, reading. Henry grabbed his speech from the front seat, got out of the car and made his way up the long walk. The sun was going down in the west but at that very angle it shone directly into Julean's face. It immediately reminded Henry of the first day he'd met Jenny. She too had been sitting on the front steps of her house, reading, and the brilliant sun had turned her blond hair into glistening gold.

An angel, Henry had thought then and an angel Henry saw before him now. The late afternoon sun had picked out the auburn highlights in Julean's dark brown hair and she glistened before him full of fire and warmth, igniting the simmering love Henry had held back in his heart. Instantly, his love for Julean was released and went out to her.

It was the sign that Mr. Engelmann had asked for in his prayer.

As he approached her, he shaded her from the sun's bright glare and she relaxed her gentle features. As he gazed into Julean's eyes, searching for that same sensation that had zinged through him when he met Jenny, something new touched him in a different way. *And it* should *be different,* he suddenly realized. Julean would never be another Jenny nor would he want her to be. Julean was special and so lovely; the attraction between them at that moment melted Henry's heart. A peace washed over him and he knew that Julean was meant for him.

An angel, he thought once more and then softly he whispered to himself, "Yes, my dear sweet Julean is as Mr. Engelmann prayed she would be…another angel of love."

CHAPTER THIRTY-FOUR

HENRY COULD HARDLY wait to pick Julean up on Saturday to celebrate their belated sixth-month anniversary. Although it should have been celebrated on the thirtieth of April, Henry had delayed it by two weeks for a few good reasons.

First, he was only able to get license plates for his new car two days ago. Secondly, he had decided to give Julean his class ring and had to wait over a week to have it sized to fit her finger. He had picked it up yesterday. And finally, the café he wanted to take his sweetheart to only had an open reservation for today.

Anyway, everything had come together perfectly and he was very excited to show Julean his 1946 Chevy as he pulled up in front of her house.

Julean dashed out of the house and rushed to meet him. "Hank, I love your new car! It looks in such excellent condition and I love the blue colour."

"Yeah, it belonged to an elderly couple and they had it sitting in the garage for the past two years hoping they could drive again."

Julean slid into the car as Henry hurried around and got into the driver's seat.

"Look at all the dials and it even has a radio!" Julean switched it on and Nat King Cole's voice filled the air. "Oh, Hank, this is perfect."

After a moment, she slid close to Henry and put her head on his shoulder as he drove downtown to their favourite restaurant.

L'Habitant was a small, quaint restaurant. You'd never know it was attached to the back of a Kentucky Fried Chicken outlet or that the owner used the same kitchen to service both places. The restaurant was only open during the evenings, sat only twenty-four people in total, and was run by a highly efficient French waiter who treated everyone as if they were a Rockefeller. The restaurant's ambience consisted of flickering candles and soft background music.

Henry had made the reservation over a month ago.

Now he reached across the table and held Julean's soft, warm hand, the candlelight sparkling in her eyes.

"I could hardly wait for tonight, Hank; I'm so happy to be with you."

"The day couldn't go fast enough for me, either. Our sixth anniversary—the time sure has gone quickly in that sense."

"Yes, happy anniversary, Hank." Julean gazed lovingly into Henry's eyes, sending him to cloud nine. Neither of them noticed the waiter standing at their table with the meal they had ordered until he cleared his throat.

"Oh my, that looks delicious."

"You can say that again," echoed Henry.

"I will be back momentarily to check that everything is to your satisfaction, monsieur, mademoiselle."

"I'm sure it will be, Claude."

As Julean cut into her steak she asked, "So are you all ready for your speech? The parts I read are so good. Your classmates are going to love it."

"Thanks, Julean. I must admit I'm little nervous about it all, especially the part that gets a little religious."

"Oh Hank, you'll do just fine! You're such a good speaker and besides, you believe so strongly in what you're going to say."

"Yeah, Mr. Engelmann sure instilled a lot of lessons in me that I know will be helpful to others too. And you remember my friend Gary I told you about that goes to Notre Dame?"

Julean looked up at him and nodded as she kept chewing.

"Even though Mr. Engelmann has been such a huge part of my life, I have to say it was Gary's boldness in talking about Jesus in his life that gave me the courage to include God's influence in my own in my speech."

"It's good to have friends like that, Hank. And I've seen too how God uses others as instruments to help us grow."

"Yeah, that's exactly it, Julean. Mr. Engelmann says that's God's divine providence at work."

"Oh, what does that mean?"

"I'll explain that to you later. I better start eating before it gets too cold."

"Well anyway, Hank, you'll do great. I have such confidence in you. And I'd like to meet your friend Gary someday."

Henry swallowed, then said, "He and his friend Jane are coming to Regina at the end of June for a week or so before they leave for Edmonton for missionary training. They're talking about going to India."

"Wow, that's unbelievable. Remember to let me know when they're here. They sound really interesting."

"Yeah, they're great people. Maybe we can go out for an evening when they come next month."

"That would be great."

They ate in silence for a few moments. Henry was pleasantly surprised by how easy it was to talk to Julean about stuff he normally would be embarrassed to mention.

"I'm going downtown on Monday to buy a new suit. I want to get all decked out for the occasion."

"You'll be so handsome! I wish I went to your school; I'd love to be there and hear you give your speech."

"Yeah, it would be great if you were there."

"Is this steak ever good," she commented after another mouthful.

"Pardon me, mademoiselle, is everything to your liking?" The waiter gazed at Julean.

"Oh, yes! I was just telling Hank how wonderful the steak is."

Turning to Henry, he simply raised an eyebrow, conveying without words the question he'd asked of Julean.

"Yeah, it's all great, just perfect."

Claude nodded again with a smile to each of them and left.

"Did you hear back from the university if you were accepted into nursing?" Henry asked as he resumed eating.

"Yes, I did and I am officially enrolled as of last Wednesday! My parents are very happy and Dad is looking forward to having me work at his office this summer."

"Yeah, I'm still not sure where I'm going to work. Mr. Mahoney, a man Mr. Engelmann and I know from the city, called and said he has a job waiting for me at City Hall. I'm not sure if I want to work inside during the summer, though. I'd sooner work outside. I applied for a job with the Department of National Defense. They have a lot of outside work like landscaping, painting wartime housing and that sort of thing."

"Sounds great. You'll probably get a dark tan while I'll be pale as a ghost."

"No, Julean—I love your skin, your eyes, in fact, everything about you!"

Julean smiled, the dim light only partly concealing the pink flush of her cheeks. "Thank you, Hank."

After the succulent filet mignon dinner, the waiter schmoozed them into a slice of cherry-topped cheesecake. When they told him they were celebrating their sixth-month anniversary, he made a fuss and insisted that the cheesecake was on the house. It was a treat just to watch him perform. He treated each patron as if they were the only ones in there and in return was rewarded with very generous tips.

After dinner, they drove to Wascana Park. As soon as they entered the grounds, the memory of that awful night with Jenny, when Eddy Zeigler's friends had grabbed her and brought her here, surfaced in his mind.

Henry struggled to suppress those anxious moments. *Please, guardian angel, remove that awful night from my heart.*

Julean turned to him as if sensing something troubled him.

He shifted in his seat and shook his head to clear his thoughts, gazing out at the placid lake through the trees.

Julean relaxed, though her eyes remained unsettled.

As he pulled into the parking area he was surprised at the number of spaces available. For some reason or other, there were at least five good spots facing the lake, the moon reflecting on its surface. Henry parked the car then snuggled Julean next to him. Slowly, his mind returned to his new love.

They sat there for the longest time, absorbed in their thoughts as they gazed out at the moonlit water. How Julean had stolen and healed his heart he would never know. For the first time in years, he felt happy and at peace. He knew without a doubt that Julean was his.

He reached into his jacket pocket and pulled out the ring.

"Would you go steady with me?" Henry whispered into her ear.

"Yes," she whispered back, thrilled, "I would love to."

Henry slipped his ring on her finger. Julean looked down at the half-inch red ruby mounted on a gold band. It was a little big for her delicate finger, but she beamed.

"Oh, Hank, this is so beautiful." She thrust her arms around his neck, bringing her face close to his, and looked him in the eyes for a long moment. And then with a voice soft as a feather, she whispered, "I love you so much."

"I love you too, Julean."

She closed her eyes as his warm lips touched hers.

Jenny was lying in bed reading a book when all of a sudden she felt a cold chill. Thoughts of Henry immediately came to her mind. Now that she thought of it, she'd been noticing a lessening of the spiritual connection she felt with Henry. She'd had difficulty summoning it when she gazed at the star of the east.

Jenny got up, turned off the lights and went to the window, guided by the light of the full moon shining through the pane. Thousands of stars adorned the sky, but her attention was for the brightest of them all, the east star. Jenny was so attuned to the love she felt from Henry held in the star's shimmering rays, she could tell its endearing warmth was waning. The love was still there, but she sensed a loss of his embrace; the feel of his arms around her seemed to have slipped away.

Although Jenny had been sure Henry had moved on and found another, she'd always held hope in her heart that she was still his only love…until now. Had their spiritual connection weakened somehow? Perhaps the angel guarding the star of the east was telling her Henry had not only found someone else but had opened his heart to her.

As tears slid down Jenny's cheeks, she thought of their anniversary poem, but this time there was a difference…

> *The star of the east we both can see,*
> *its warm rays so bright no more caressing me.*
> *If another love has come your way,*
> *please never forget our special day*
>
> *Perhaps in the future if it's meant to be*
> *your love will return and envelop me.*
> *I wish you happiness though from afar*
> *to fill your heart through this, our star.*

The moonlight caught a new sadness in Jenny's blurry eyes as she softly whispered, "Even though we may grow apart, you are forever in my heart."

ON THE FOLLOWING Monday after school, Henry met his parents downtown at Goldman's Clothing Store. Henry was excited to get his first suit. Mr. Goldman was chatting with Bill and Mary when Henry came in.

"Ah, and here's our clever young valedictorian now!" Mr. Goldman walked over and met Henry, hand extended. "Congratulations, it's quite an honour to have bestowed on you. Your parents are very proud."

"Thanks, Mr. Goldman."

"And a special occasion requires a special suit." Mr. Goldman studied Henry for a brief moment and then said. "A size 38 will fit you nicely at the shoulders—brown would look nice—but for this occasion and with your ruddy complexion, a dark navy is meant for you."

He walked over to a suit rack and thumbed through it, pushing suits aside. "Ah, here we are."

As Mr. Goldman walked back to Henry, he slipped the jacket off the hanger, tucked the trousers under his arm and held the jacket open for Henry to try on.

"I do like the colour, Mr. Goldman," Henry said as he looked at himself in the full-length mirror.

"The colour does suit you," Mary concurred. "It makes you look older and—"

"Like a lawyer... a millionaire!" Mr. Goldman interjected.

They all laughed. Henry welcomed the interruption. He was feeling self-conscious with everyone staring at him

"Here, take the trousers and go into the change booth and put them on. I'll make sure everything fits you just right."

Henry returned a few minutes later with the pant legs turned up. Mr. Goldman adjusted their length and marked them with white chalk. He also made a mark on each side of the jacket and on the sleeves.

After they decided on the suit, Mary and Henry picked out a white shirt and a navy tie with fine red stripes. And then the traditional bargaining began. A back and forth haggling in an attempt to get Mr. Goldman to come down on his price until everyone was satisfied.

Henry's dad started the dickering. "So, how much is the suit, Saul?"

Mr. Goldman checked the sales tag sewn to the left sleeve. "It's only $64.95, Bill and I'll only charge you three dollars for the alterations instead of the usual six."

"We don't have to pay for the alterations do we?"

"The suit is very well priced—it's 100% wool and—"

"Morton's Menswear down the street has a 25%-off sale right now and advertises free alterations," interjected Bill and quickly added as he looked at Mary, "Maybe we should have a look at Morton's suits before we decide."

"I see where your son gets his cleverness from. I'm sure Sarah can do the alterations for you. Okay, no charge for the alterations." Saul looked as though he had just given the store away.

"And will you match the sale Morton's is having—take at least ten dollars off?" Bill continued to bargain.

Mr. Goldman looked at Henry. "That suit was made for your son, look how good it makes him look…."

Bill backed up and turned, threatening to leave. "At least ten dollars, Saul."

Still looking at Henry, Saul raised an eyebrow. "My, my your father is shrewd." Turning back to Bill, he said, "Okay, Bill, I will give your son a graduation gift."

Saul took out his wallet. Henry's eyes grew wide at the bulge of money. Mr. Goldman took out a ten dollar bill and laid it on the counter. "There! I will pay the difference from my own pocket."

"Include a pair of navy socks and we have a deal."

"Oh, Bill, he's done enough," Mary covered her mouth, feeling a little embarrassed.

"We're good customers, Mary, and I bet Morton's would throw in a pair of socks."

Saul threw his hands into the air and in a voice filled with frustration he said, "All right, already!"

He walked over to Henry and took the jacket off. For a minute there, Henry thought Mr. Goldman had backed out of the deal. But then Saul said, "I will give the suit to Mrs. Goldman and she will have it altered perfectly for you by Wednesday afternoon."

Henry breathed a sigh of relief that the bargaining was over. He hoped the perspiration under his arms hadn't gotten on his new suit jacket.

After they left Mr. Goldman's place, they went to the Bata Shoe Store on Scarth Street and bought Henry a pair of cordovan-coloured oxfords. Henry could visualize how he was going to look and could hardly wait to try on the whole outfit.

On Wednesday, two days before closing exercises, Henry went to pick up his new suit at Goldman's Clothing Store. He couldn't get home fast enough to try it on and make certain the alterations were perfectly done. Within minutes he had stripped off his old clothes and was in his new outfit. He could hardly get over what a difference a suit made as he looked into the dresser mirror.

Mary was at the sink washing some knives when Henry inched into the kitchen behind her. He was about to make his announcement when she turned. Her mouth dropped as she saw her son and her eyes misted.

"Oh, Henry, you look so handsome!" she exclaimed. "That navy looks so good on you. Turn around. Let me see the back… Oh, it fits you so nice! Mrs. Goldman is such a good seamstress."

His father appeared at the doorway, holding the newspaper in his hands. He kind of shook his head and winked at Henry.

"Pretty dapper, son. You look great! Hmm, that tie knot needs a little more practice."

"Yeah. Thanks, Dad.

As Henry turned to go back to his room his mom called, "Oh, by the way, Henry, two letters came for you today; they're on the table by the front door."

Henry picked up the envelopes. One was from Gary, but the other didn't have a return address. *Could it be from Jenny?* It didn't look like Jenny's handwriting but that might have changed over the years. His heart pounded as he raced to his room, letters clutched in his hand.

He sat at his desk and quickly opened the mysterious letter. It was a short note from Julean:

> *Hi Hank,*
>
> *Although I can't be at the closing exercises I just want you to know that I'll be there in spirit. You'll do such an excellent job! I know your classmates will love it and get so much out of it.*
>
> *I love you so much.*
>
> *All my love, Julean*

That was really thoughtful of Julean.

He felt a twinge of guilt for getting so excited that it might be a letter from Jenny. He loved Julean so much yet feelings for Jenny were always just below the surface.

What if the letter had *been from Jenny?*

And what about his plan to find her when school was out?

CHAPTER THIRTY-FIVE

"I WISH TAMMY WOULD call," Jenny said out loud as she paced her bedroom floor. *It's been over a week and a half since I saw her at the hospital. What's happened to her...and to the baby?!*

Jenny had called her house several times and each time Tammy's mom told her Tammy wasn't at home and hung up. Tammy was no longer at the hospital either; Jenny had gone up there to see her four days ago and Tammy had checked out the week before. *Where is she?* Jenny wondered. Perhaps her mother wasn't being truthful. Jenny didn't want to cause any trouble by going over to their home. *Oh, Tammy, please call! I hope you and your baby girl are all right. I'm dying to know what you decided to do with the baby...*

Since she'd held Tammy's newborn, Jenny longed to go back and hold her some more. She'd loved those few moments of having the infant in her arms.

Jenny so missed her little three-year-old girl. Camilla would be walking and talking now, colouring pictures, asking a million and one questions, her bright eyes exuding curiosity. Oh, to hear her say "mommy" would be Jenny's greatest joy. *But she*

*is gone and so is Tammy. And now even the love I once felt from
Henry is waning too.*

Thoughts of her two lost loves flooded Jenny's mind like relentless waves of the sea upon the shore. A sea that was empty of
real life, only memories. Wave after wave of nostalgia and what-
might-have-been images washed up on this illusionary shore,
crashing into rocks, shattering all her dreams, all her hope.

Despondency flooded her. She rarely allowed this to happen,
but too many things were going on and her defenses and better judgment felt under continual attack. She went to her desk
and retrieved her address book and looked up a number she
hadn't called in a long time. She went to the phone in her room,
picked up the receiver and dialed the number.

"Social Services, how may I direct your call?"

"May I please speak with Erica Reinhardt."

"One moment, please."

"Hello, this is Erica."

"Hi, Erica, this is Jenny…Jenny Sarsky."

"Oh, Marjorie!"

"Yes, but please call me Jenny."

"How are you keeping, Jenny? I called your home about six
months ago and spoke with your mother. You were at school at
the time. She said you were doing fine. I told your mom to tell
you to call if you ever needed to talk."

"Oh, Mom didn't tell me you'd called."

"I guess she thought it best to leave well enough alone. Well,
anyway, how are things going?"

"Oh, I guess mostly it's fine. What I was calling about Erica
is that, well, for some time now and especially this past week or
so, I've been wondering if it will ever be possible for me to meet
and see my daughter? And I was wondering if—"

"Oh, Jenny. I know all this must be so difficult for you, but if
you recall, we went over this several times. Once you gave up
your baby for adoption, you lost your right to see her."

"But—forever? Isn't there some way around this? She *is* my
daughter. Have I no rights at all?"

"I'm sorry, Jenny, but, yes, that's the case. When your daughter is eighteen or older and if she is told that she was adopted and wants to know who her mother is, *then* it might be possible. In that case, we would notify you and let you know that your child is looking for you."

"What if Camilla is told *before* she's eighteen and requests to know who I am? Is it possible I could be contacted sooner?"

"Jenny, I've been here for ten years and I have not had a request like that. I'm not saying that it's impossible, just that it's highly unlikely—don't get your hopes up."

"I see."

"Are you going to be okay with that? Would you like to come in and see me? We could talk more or perhaps I could come out and visit with you?"

"No, I'll be fine. It's okay—I know where to find you."

"So, let me see, you would be in Grade 12 now, is that right?"

"Yes. I'm enjoying school and am quite involved in things."

"Oh, that's good. Have you met any boys yet that you like?"

"As a matter of fact, I have met a boy. His name is James. He reminds me a lot of someone I knew in Regina."

"Yes, I remember you telling me about him. Henry was his name, right?"

"You have a good memory. I still miss him though I'm quite fond of James."

"I'm happy you've found someone."

"Well, Erica, I don't want to keep you from your work, you must be busy with other people. Thank you for taking the time to talk to me."

"I'm so glad you called Marj—er—Jenny. Please don't hesitate to chat with me anytime. That's what I'm here for."

"Thanks again, Erica. 'Bye."

Jenny replaced the receiver, then tossed herself onto her bed and sobbed. Her heart felt so empty. If only she could just see her little girl, hold her—even for just a minute. A photo would be better than nothing. But there *was* nothing. Nothing but a memory of a tiny, squealing baby hanging upside down from a doctor's fist in the delivery room.

Would the people who adopted Camilla even tell her she was adopted? But even if they did, Camilla would have to be at least eighteen years old. Such a long time away.

Trying desperately to appease her aching heart, Jenny thought of holding Tammy's little girl.

But even Tammy has abandoned me.

The only consolation was that in a year or two she might be married and have another child. But would her guilt over giving Camilla away maybe prevent her from even being able to have more children?

Perhaps she should have accepted Erica's offer to meet. *It just seems so distant and cold.* And talking with her mother felt even colder and more distant. Her mother tended to just brush over her concerns as passing difficulties that soon would go away. She used to be able to talk to her dad, but he was so troubled lately, she couldn't bring herself to talk to him either.

Jenny punched the pillow in between sobs.

Broken-heartedness wore her down. She'd felt its sting before and knew she could never cope with it again. Out of desperation to escape it all, she got up and made her way to the bathroom. Jenny gazed into the mirror of the medicine cabinet. The hopelessness in her eyes stared back at her. Her world was rapidly closing in, blinding her to life's options. Heavy dark clouds descended upon her, shutting out all the light, leaving only one choice: complete darkness. Jenny opened the medicine chest and reached for the bottle of tranquilizers the doctor had prescribed for her after she'd given birth to Camilla. It had helped her sleep then, perhaps one or two would help now.

She opened the lid and tapped one out into the palm of her hand. Then another. And then the contents of the entire bottle. She looked at the pills. She wanted to sleep and never wake up. Everyone had deserted her or been taken from her; her father, her mother, her baby, Henry—and now Tammy and her baby too. And worst of all, in her hopeless state, Jenny finally realized that she was truly afraid of baring her soul to James, the one person she should have been able to confide in.

Tears fell and pooled onto the palm of her hand softening the white tablets. She raised the pills to her mouth and… stopped. Wisps of the dissolving tablets from her tears moved and swirled almost like wings, conjuring up the image of an angel in her mind. As she gazed at this incredible sight, a prayer popped into her mind. A prayer she'd always found comforting and had forgotten to say lately.

Tears streamed down her face as she whispered, "Oh Angel of God, my guardian dear to whom His love commits me here; ever this day be at my side to light and guard, to rule and guide my life, forever and ever. Oh guardian angel," Jenny pleaded, "Please help me."

No sooner had the words left her trembling lips than a warmth and peace ignited in the pit of her stomach and grew until it filled the emptiness inside. She looked at the pills through blurred vision and tossed them into the toilet. Her feelings of despair melted as she watched the pills dissolve and disappear, replaced by a feeling of hope that her guardian angel would make things work out.

Jenny knew she had lost sight of the reality of her life and that she must return her focus to the present moment, building upon each moment one at a time. She had discovered this truth once before and, just like the last time, her protector had helped her. Jenny had allowed the false perception of the loss of her loves and the bleakness of the future to overshadow the now of her life and obliterate the joy of living.

She was reminded once more, too, of the circumstances surrounding her rape and pregnancy. That her guardian angel had spared her the awful memory of that night and yet had permitted the pregnancy. And as she had concluded last time, a thought filled with assurance surfaced, confirming it all again: the birth of her dear, sweet little baby was not just an answer to the prayers of Camilla's adoptive parents, but there was another, special, design yet to unfold.

The thought sustained her now as it had back then and bolstered her spirits further. "Oh, thank you, my dear guardian angel! I will trust you to fulfill my heart's desires. If it is our Master's will, someday my loves and I will be together again."

The phone rang and Jenny rushed to answer.

It was Tammy!

"Tammy!" Jenny shouted, her heart soaring like an eagle. "Where *are* you? I've been phoning your home and your Mom says you're not there. I've been so *worried* about you. What did you decide about the baby?!"

"I'm sorry I haven't called sooner, Jenny...let me explain."

"Tammy, I'm on pins and needles, please hurry!"

"Well, remember when you came up to visit at the hospital and Mom came back and suggested that you go?"

"Yes, go on."

"Well, Mom did her best to convince me to give the baby up for adoption. But after she left I was distracted by what I saw out of the hospital room window. It was the most gorgeous, huge, black and orange monarch butterfly!"

"Oh, Tammy! I saw one that day too. Maybe it was the same one."

"Anyway, Jen, it reminded me of when I was little and I would play in the yard for hours on end chasing after the butterflies. I began to imagine my little girl doing that and then thought about all the other things I'd miss if I gave her up for adoption. It may sound crazy but it was just that little thought that made up my mind. I knew I had to keep her. I knew with your support I could do it."

"Oh, Tammy, that's wonderful! I'm so happy for you! And I'll help however I can."

"Let me tell you what happened then. When I told Mom what I'd decided, she was furious. She said I was throwing my life away, that Robbie would never want me. 'There goes your education, your future,' and on and on she went."

"Oh, Tammy—she was just trying to do what *she* thinks is best for you, but in the end it's *your* decision, *your* life."

"That's right and that's what I told her. Then Mom said that if I kept the baby I was no longer welcome at home. 'If you want to keep the baby then you look after it,' she said."

"What did you do then?" Jenny asked softly.

"I phoned Grandma and she said I could stay with her. Now Mom is so mad at *her* mother, but Grandma says she'll come around and that Mom's been mad at her before and that I shouldn't concern myself with it."

"That's so good that your grandma is being supportive."

"Yeah! So for now anyway I'm staying at Grandma's house. I have a doctor's appointment this afternoon; the baby isn't nursing very well. I think it's all the fuss lately and Chloe is sensing my nerves."

"You named her Chloe? That's so beautiful, Tammy."

"Since Robbie still hasn't shown up or even seen her I decided to name her myself."

"I love that name, Tammy, it has such a nice sound to it."

"Anyway, Jen, I'm home all day tomorrow and I'd love to see you and I know Chloe would like to see you too. Have you got a pencil and paper handy? I'll give you Grandma's phone number and address."

Jenny jotted down the information and then the girls exchanged goodbyes.

Jenny was ecstatic over Tammy's news. *She and her mother will make up soon and perhaps Robbie—if he's worth his salt—will come around too.*

Suddenly Jenny saw a flash of colour out of the corner of her eye. She turned to her bedroom window. Oh my God, it was the huge orange and black monarch butterfly! She rushed to the window and watched it fly away, but the sight of the gardens below filled her with awe and wonder.

Hundreds of monarch butterflies were flitting about, especially crowding around near her gazebo and wildflower garden. *They must be feeding on the nectar in the flowers.* And beside the fountain stood Carlos, his hands raised to the sky as if in praise to it all.

Jenny looked on in amazement. Her earlier feelings of sorrow, loss and abandonment had been completely replaced by exhilaration and hope. She was filled with thoughts of butterflies, of angels!

Jenny quickly changed into blue jeans and T-shirt and hurried downstairs and out into the garden.

"Miss Jenny," Carlos shouted as soon as he saw Jenny emerge from the kitchen patio doors. "It is a miracle! In a letter we received from my cousin in Mexico, he said the monarchs left late in March for their journey here. So knowing the great distance they must travel, Fernando predicted their arrival would be the middle of June. But somehow the butterflies have arrived almost a month earlier." Carlos looked at Jenny and then said, "There must be a reason."

Jenny thought she knew, said instead, "They're so beautiful, aren't they? And just look how many there are flitting about!"

"They are happy like angels! In Mexico when the monarchs migrate back there in the fall, the people celebrate for their return, *Bienvenidos Monarcas*. Each began life as a tiny egg. Think of the challenges they've overcome and the distance they've travelled."

"Perhaps we should celebrate their arrival too, Carlos."

"*Si*, I was already before you came out. I have never seen so many. They are attracted to the milkweed plant. That is where they lay their eggs and then must die. They give their lives so new life can begin and carry on the miracle of their migration. And all the while they give such joy to us as they do now."

"Do we have milkweed plants in the garden? I don't recall seeing any."

"Come let me show you. I planted several on the grounds late last summer so they would attract the butterflies this spring. Look there." Carlos pointed to several single stemmed, two-to-three-foot-high plants with orange flowers and elongated oval green leaves. Several monarch butterflies were eating nectar from the flowers.

"Oh! I didn't know those were milkweed plants, I've seen

those many times. The flowers become seed pods shaped like a tear drop."

"*Si*, Miss Jenny, that is correct and that is where the seeds come from."

"Why do they call them milkweed, Carlos, do you know?"

Carlos knelt down and cut into one of the green leaves with his fingernail and immediately a milky fluid was secreted.

Jenny nodded her understanding.

"We only have a few plants here and there, but I would like to plant more. I got these from the side of a country road near where we live."

"Yes, Carlos, please plant some in the wildflower patch and wherever you can. Let's make the grounds into a butterfly garden too! I just love seeing them all here, and their vibrant colour is so spectacular." Jenny reached out with her hand, enticing one to land on her fingertips. "It's amazing how they know when to leave for Mexico and come back and how they find their way, isn't it?"

"*Si*, they must return in the fall to escape our winter and in the spring they must leave Mexico as well in order to survive; it gets too hot, too dry and the days too long."

"I can't imagine how they find their way—it's almost a 3,000-mile journey!"

"Many say they are guided by the Earth's magnetic field, but I say it is the angels who show them the way."

Jenny looked at the insightful gardener and smiled, eyes twinkling and joy bursting in her heart.

"You know, Carlos, I couldn't agree with you more!"

Chapter Thirty-Six

A T QUARTER TO TEN, David locked the door and hung up a sign that read:

GONE TO HENRY'S GRADUATION
Sorry for any inconvenience

The store was so empty now, hardly any customers came anymore. Those who still did came out of habit and mainly to visit.

David had refused Father Connelly's offer to stay at the rectory until he left for the seminary. He wasn't ready to let go of the store and the memories it held, not just yet. As he ended each day, he walked through the store recalling the past, the customers they'd had and how they had become involved in each other's lives. He did the same as he climbed the stairs to his empty quarters, but this time the memories were of Anna. At times he could swear he still saw her sitting in her favourite chair near the south window, reading the Bible.

It was almost eleven when he finished his rounds of the store and arrived upstairs to prepare for Henry's graduation.

He wrenched his thoughts back to the present. By noon, he was ready and back downstairs, waiting for the Pedersons to arrive.

BY NOON, HENRY was dressed in his brand-new outfit. He looked good, even if he said so himself. His father had arrived home a few minutes earlier and was in the shower. His mother was in the bedroom getting dressed.

As he waited for his parents, Henry paced the kitchen floor, trying to work off the mounting nervousness of giving his speech. He had rehearsed it so many times in the past two weeks he knew every syllable and where each one happened on any given page.

At twelve-thirty, his father walked into the kitchen wearing a charcoal grey suit, white shirt and a grey tie with pink flecks here and there. When he met Henry's gaze, he grinned.

"Well, it's not every day you see your dad all spiffed up."

"Yeah," Henry replied, "you look great, Dad. Soon you'll be president of Coca-Cola and have to wear a suit *every* day."

"Hmph," his dad snorted. "That'll be the day."

His mother walked in then, and Bill let out a long, low whistle. "Wow, you look nice, Mom!"

Mary wore a new dress in a floral mix of lime greens and yellows, in a style that accented her trim figure. On her feet were white nylons and white high-heeled pumps. And, to top it all off, was a small chic white hat with a veil that came to mid-nose, and a pair of white gloves that ended midway to her elbow. Bright red lipstick outlined her smile and there was a subtle suggestion of rouge on her cheeks, even a hint of eyeliner.

Henry and his dad gaped at her.

"You look great, honey," his father said, kissing her cheek.

"Yeah, Mom, you'll be the main attraction there."

"Hardly, Henry. You're the one everyone's eyes will be on today. Are you ready for the speech?"

"As ready as I'll ever be."

Bill came over to Henry and patted his shoulder. "I'm sure you'll do very well, son. I'm very proud of you."

"Thanks, Dad."

"Well, we best get going," Bill said, checking the clock. "It's a little early, but we want to make sure we get a parking spot and we still have to pick up David along the way."

His dad pulled the car in front of the house, then got out and rounded it to open the door for his mom, who appeared very pleased by the courtly treatment.

"Why thank you, Bill."

"The pleasure is all mine, I assure you, ma'am."

"Oh, Bill!" She laughed.

Henry loved it when his mom and dad teased each other like that. It made him feel they loved each other and had something special going between them. *If only Mom…no…that was their affair.* Henry pushed the thought of the twin beds in their bedroom out of his mind.

CHAPTER THIRTY-SEVEN

I T WAS A beautiful late spring day. A few clouds floated across the vast dome of the prairie sky. The wind was—thankfully and unusually—light, and the weatherman on the radio announced an ideal seventy degrees.

No sooner had the Pedersons pulled up in front of the store than Mr. Engelmann came out. He was wearing his tan-coloured wedding suit, the one he'd worn for Anna's funeral. Once again, it reminded Henry of the bad dream he'd had on the day he'd met Jenny. The man in the dream was wearing that exact same suit, but wore a yellow flower in his lapel. Mr. Engelmann had looked so much like the man in Henry's dream on the day of Anna's funeral; he too had worn a yellow flower in his lapel. He wasn't today though.

Perhaps Mr. Engelmann isn't the man in my dream. Henry quickly suppressed emerging thoughts of the black-hooded figure that had turned the dream into a nightmare and made a valiant effort to let it all go for right now.

"Hi, Mr. Engelmann! You sure look spiffy today," he offered as Mr. Engelmann got into the back seat of the car with him.

"Well, today is your big day, Henry, we have to get dressed

up for the celebration. And just look at you! My, my, how hand-some!"

When they arrived at the high school, Henry suggested that his dad turn onto Ottawa Street where there were usually a lot of parking spaces during the afternoon since most of the residents were at work. Sure enough, there was lots of room.

Mr. Mitchell greeted them at the top of the front steps with a big smile, and opened the door.

"Good afternoon, Mr. and Mrs. Pederson. Hi, Henry. And is this the Mr. Engelmann you told me about?"

"Yes, it sure is, Mr. Mitchell."

"Well, I'm honoured to meet you, sir. You've had a tremendous influence on this young man's life."

Mr. Engelmann nodded. "Thank you."

"I see you beat the traffic somehow," Mr. Mitchell said to Henry's dad.

"Yes, Henry suggested a side street, and he was right," his father said. "We found a good parking spot."

Mr. Mitchell patted Henry's shoulder. "That's my boy," he said. "Are you all ready for the speech, today?"

"As ready as I'll ever be," Henry repeated as butterflies skittered through his stomach.

"I can hardly wait to hear it. I don't mind telling you Mr. and Mrs. Pederson, your son's is the finest speech I have read in all my years of teaching."

His mother and father looked at each other with wide eyes.

Mr. Mitchell then explained what was going to happen and when they should enter the auditorium after everyone was seated and assembled. He gave them each a program to peruse while they waited. According to the program, Mr. Mitchell would greet the assembly and acknowledge guests and members of the school board and deliver a speech about the past year and the vision he saw for Balfour. That would be followed by student awards, including two to be given to Henry: one for outstanding grades and a second for overall student of the year.

Students and parents streamed into the auditorium, and the main hallway emptied out.

Henry watched Mr. Mitchell talking to a group of ladies and gentlemen who were undoubtedly some of the dignitaries attending the exercises. They followed the last of the students trickling into the auditorium. He shuffled from one leg to the other, hoping to settle his nerves.

Mr. Engelmann walked over to him and put a hand on his shoulder. "Are you ready for your speech?"

"Yeah," Henry replied nervously.

"I hope you are a little nervous."

"Yeah, you can say that again."

"Ah, that's good, Henry. It means you are going to do an excellent job."

Henry looked at him questioningly.

"Remember, Henry, a little nervousness brings together all your resources to work at peak performance. If this didn't happen, you would be doomed to a mediocre job. Don't confuse the little butterflies you feel with some real danger, as if a car was coming towards you. These feelings are very similar, and as a result, they can confuse you into believing there is some real danger ahead and give you the urge to flee or avoid it. But what is it?"

Henry looked at him, dumbfounded, but said, "Well, there's no real danger."

"Exactly, Henry! So just be thankful that you feel this way, but don't let it fool you into thinking there is anything more. Simply acknowledge the nervousness for what it is, knowing its purpose, then forge ahead and do the job. Somehow the Lord forgot to put on the brakes when we are required to perform big tasks!"

Mr. Engelmann was right as usual. *What was there to be afraid of, really? They were just people like his family. Some were even his friends.* Henry's nerves settled as he brought everything into perspective.

"Are we ready?" Mr. Mitchell asked. At Henry's nod, the principal motioned Henry and his family into line behind the dignitaries. Mr. Mitchell gave final instructions for everyone to proceed and in what order then went to the front of the line and led the entourage into the packed auditorium.

As they proceeded onto the stage, a hush fell over the crowd. When they were seated, Mr. Mitchell stepped up to the podium and asked everyone to stand for the national anthem. When everyone was seated again, Mr. Mitchell returned to the podium to acknowledge the special guests and dignitaries, and speak about the school year and his vision for Balfour.

The director of education spoke after Mr. Mitchell's address and remained at the podium while he and Mr. Mitchell handed out the awards.

Henry was next.

Mr. Mitchell returned to the podium to introduce the valedictorian, and Henry had to coach himself to breathe. Perspiration soaked his armpits and tickled his forehead. He wished he was riding his bike into a 40-mile-an-hour prairie wind.

As Mr. Mitchell continued the introduction, Henry ran over the speech in his mind and panicked when he couldn't recall the first line. He vaguely registered Mr. Mitchell's account of his achievements. He looked down and straight ahead into the auditorium. With the lights off, Henry could barely make out the students. The only rows visible were the first two or three. His eyes rested on Mr. Engelmann and his mom and dad. They looked alternately at Henry and then at Mr. Mitchell. Their friendly, supportive faces instilled a much-needed calmness in him.

"And now, I proudly give you Henry Pederson, president of the student council and this year's valedictorian."

The students clapped, whistled and hollered as Henry approached the podium, reached into the breast pocket of his suit and retrieved his speech. He unfolded the sheets on the lectern, pressing them flat to ensure they would stay open in the same way he had seen Mr. Engelmann unfold Anna's letter at her celebration. A peaceful confidence swept over him, at the thought, and he focused his mind on the job at hand. He believed with all his heart that what he had written was what he needed to say.

Henry deliberately waited an extra moment after the applause subsided so that everyone would be ready to listen.

"Thank you, Mr. Mitchell, for that kind introduction. Fellow classmates, students, parents and honoured guests, I am honoured to have the opportunity of speaking to all of you today. When Mr. Mitchell asked if I would accept this role this year, I knew exactly what I wanted to say.

"For the last four years, I have had the privilege of working for an extraordinary man and his wife, who have imparted valuable lessons in life to me. I am extremely grateful to my parents as well for all their love, support and teachings. Sometimes, however, it is easier to talk to a friend or confidante about personal problems and life's challenges.

"I suppose I would have discussed these things with my parents, but somehow this man and his wife were there. I worked for them almost every day in an atmosphere conducive to sharing conversations from the heart. Almost every day I thank God for having allowed me to come into such an atmosphere in the most unexpected environment of an old grocery store. But it did happen. I sat on a weathered grey crate and drank root beer or Orange Crush and was taught by a very, very wise man. And I am very excited to share with you some of the lessons I have learned as a result of this experience.

"I will not be talking about future jobs and careers, or our past school year, or the pros and cons of attending a trade school or university. I will not explain how to get rich and own two cars, a boat and several houses. Mr. Engelmann taught me that while all of these things may seem important, they cannot bring you true happiness or measure your true success in life, regardless of how much you possess. I often kidded Mr. Engelmann that I would like to learn this for myself. And I did. Soon after getting something for my birthday or Christmas, I would find myself worrying again, or being upset about something or other. Material things really didn't keep me happy for very long.

"True happiness and success comes from within, and that is the subject I have chosen for my speech. What you believe in, the principles and values you adopt and live by every day, will ultimately determine the quality of life and the happiness you enjoy. The principles and values I'm talking about are honesty, truthfulness, kindness, fairness, patience, understanding, forgiveness, and so on. These are things taught by our parents, our teachers and all religions. The goal is to be a good person and to fulfill the commandment of God to love our neighbour as ourselves.

"When we choose to live this way, we develop a strong character. We become people of integrity. People trust us and like to be around us and like to be our friends. When we live by these values, decisions are easy. We know what to do when life's challenges come along, when we are tempted or tested. If we believe in honesty, we will then be honest; if we believe in fairness, then we will be fair.

"When we violate these values or principles, or if we are not firm in our belief and resolve to live this way, our problems begin and life becomes difficult. If we are honest or trusting today, but not tomorrow, we are no longer seen as people of integrity. But perhaps more importantly, we know in our hearts we are not being true to ourselves.

"People of integrity, people who choose to live by sound values and principles, also live more in the present, in the now of life. They are neither controlled by yesterday's wrong decisions nor worried about the future. People who do not live a life of integrity are only partially alive to the present because guilt, worry, shame or fear steals away precious moments from living in the present.

"So, we see that by living a life of integrity, we have a very rich life and are aware of the richness of life around us. We are then in a better position to serve the needs of others. And furthermore, by living in the present as people of integrity, we determine our past and shape our future. We are in control of our lives and destiny.

"What I am saying isn't really anything new. We all know what values and principles are. But perhaps what we *haven't* thought about is making a conscious choice to live by them. We must believe in our hearts and minds that this is the best way to live and then do it daily. Life's problems can sneak up on us and if we are not prepared, we can easily make wrong choices and decisions."

Henry then went on to talk about his struggle with wanting to reference God, the Bible and prayer in his speech because he didn't want to be perceived as a religious fanatic or someone incapable of running his own life. But he wanted to share it because it was what helped him the most in his life. Even people who said they didn't believe in God, and appeared so strong, were the first ones to turn to Him when trouble struck their lives. But what tipped the scale to including this in his speech was the influence of his friend Gary, who'd spoke so boldly about the effect God had made in his life and, of course, Mr. Engelmann's influence as well.

"Perhaps one of the most important things Mr. Engelmann has taught me is to meditate daily about the direction my life is going and how I am living it. What did I do yesterday that was not so good, and how can I do better today? At the start, when I failed to do this consistently, I quickly ran into trouble. Over the years, it has become a habit, and for me this has become as important as eating, if not more. If I make the wrong decision or choice, I have trouble eating and get indigestion.

"No, to live this way we must begin the day right and be in the right frame of mind. And, perhaps most importantly, we must realize that it cannot be done alone. There are too many temptations in life, and it is too easy to make wrong choices. We must pray and ask for God's help and strength. In fact, I read the Bible daily. All the values and principles for successful living are contained therein.

"Before Mr. Engelmann taught me to pray and meditate on my life, the thoughts I had were the same day-to-day. The thoughts I have today would simply be carried over to tomorrow. Nothing new entered my mind. I wasn't aware of my life and I wasn't growing as a person. I was stuck. I repeated self-defeating actions, the same behaviours and thoughts.

"Mr. Engelmann always told me that we are what we think. If we complain and think negatively, keeping the past alive by worrying about it, we get more and more of the same old negative thoughts. Mr. Engelmann taught me to be grateful and think positively, to write down everything I am thankful for and thank the Lord each day for all the blessings I've been given.

"It's funny, though. The more I'm thankful for, the more I seem to get. The list just keeps getting longer and longer. I have great parents and teachers. I'm grateful for my school and my role as president. I am also thankful for my friends, car, education, and on and on. And I ask God to help and to guide me in all my words, thoughts and actions.

"To live this way is more than a one-time decision. It's an ongoing process. Every day, we have to choose between right and wrong. We have to meet each new challenge head-on. As we form the habit of daily meditating, praying and living a life based on sound values, we will be richly rewarded. Since I have been doing this, I have never been happier or more at peace. I love life, have an abundance of energy and look forward to each new day.

"I must admit, however, that many a day I fail and still do. Fortunately, I have a good teacher. Mr. Engelmann never dwells on my shortcomings or setbacks, my failures. He always sees what I really am, a child of God, filled with beauty, talent and abilities. Mr. Engelmann always encourages me and says that each new moment in our lives is an opportunity to begin again, to start afresh and to decide to do what is good. Eventually we will grow and succeed. With each little victory we become stronger and better people.

"Mr. Engelmann likens growing in values to a child learning to walk. A child never sees himself as a failure or gets upset or discouraged when he falls. The child simply gets up again and again, living fully in the present moment, staying fully focused and determined until eventually—he walks. With each attempt the child reinforces his goal, feels more and more confident and is encouraged by his parents. He not only walks, but soon *runs* in free abandon. And so it is with us. Each time we choose to forgive or to be kind, just, honest, loving—and receive help and encouragement from God—we become who we are supposed to be: loving people of God, here to serve our fellow man."

Henry talked about how Mr. Engelmann's daily life had exemplified integrity. How he implemented honesty in his business. How he served his customers, not just by serving them their groceries but also serving their hearts. He loved unconditionally. If he had not seen Mr. Engelmann in action, living a life of integrity, he knew Mr. Engelmann's lessons on the old, grey crate wouldn't have impressed him as they had. But seeing it daily and consistently was what challenged and motivated him. He wanted to become like Mr. Engelmann.

"Seeing Mr. Engelmann live this way made me realize how important it is to be a role model. Walking the talk is very important. I don't think half of us know the tremendous influence we have over each other. Just like I mentioned earlier, my friend Gary has also been a strong influence on me. Our example may very well lead another person away from making the wrong choice. People who live in the present, the *now* of life, mainly because they have chosen to live by sound values and principles, stand out as a beacon, leading the path for all to see.

Mr. Engelmann stressed over and over to me that we need people of integrity, strength and example, but to be so, we must begin, and once we do, we feel so good inside it just keeps us motivated to go on. We are happiest when we are growing and doing good and serving others."

Henry talked about other people who lived lives of integrity and service to others. He talked about Ron Schmidt and how Ron had helped to decorate Mr. Engelmann's store at Christmastime and what a good attitude he had. They laughed when Henry told them that regardless of what he had asked Ron to do, his reply was always, "No problem, Hank."

Henry talked about Irvin Goronic and the story he had told at Mrs. Engelmann's funeral. How he had developed integrity as a result of Mrs. Engelmann's influence and become an executive at the age of twenty-four, the youngest man to be promoted to such a trustworthy position in his firm.

And finally, Henry talked about Mrs. Engelmann and how she had lived a life based on love. How she was the embodiment of everything he had said. How she was love in action. How she reached out to others. How she lived a life of service.

Henry explained how the Engelmanns' grocery store was not only there for making money, but for serving and helping their fellow man. How St. Mary's Church, perhaps the largest in the city, was packed for her funeral—a clear testimony to the number of lives she had affected.

"When people come to the end of their lives, they will be judged by who they were and how well they have lived. People won't be remembered and revered for their material success, but by the amount of love they have shown and given to others. 'Acts and words that touch the heart are never forgotten' was a phrase that both Mr. and Mrs. Engelmann often quoted.

"Before I conclude my talk to you this afternoon, there is one value or principle in life I would like to talk about because it is so important and seems to affect so many people's lives and relationships, and that is forgiveness." Henry paused for a moment, allowing everyone to refocus and be attentive.

"How many of us have not forgiven a friend, our mother or father, a brother or sister, or a teacher?" Henry paused. "Unforgiveness holds both the person who was hurt, as well as the person who caused the hurt, in bondage. On the day Anna Engelmann was buried, my father introduced me to a man whose tombstone asked for eternal forgiveness. This man was caught in the bondage of unforgiveness even into death. What a horrible existence he must have had; how he must have suffered.

"It is critical to have peace within a family." And here Henry used as an example, the issue of peace between his father and him. He didn't reveal the circumstances but rather described the joy of forgiving. Henry went on to explain how he had to learn to separate the undesirable behaviour or actions of others from the actual person.

"Everyone—parents, teachers, religious leaders—has weaknesses and frailties. We have to forgive, accept and move forward to be as fully alive as possible. If we don't, if we harbour unforgiveness, we feed the vicious cycle of hurt, resentment and vengeance, effectively cheating ourselves out of *life*. It's amazing how a forgiving attitude can melt away the hurt or anger—and in the blink of an eye, at times, those who have hurt us become our greatest friends. The bondage that chained both us and the one who hurt us is released, and the joy of forgiveness brings us happiness and peace. We can see and feel the difference in ourselves and those around us. We are free to live and to love."

As Henry paused for a moment, his eyes rested on his mother and for a brief instant their gazes locked. But in that split second, Henry knew she understood the message was as much for her as it was for his fellow students. A prayer that had been in Henry's heart for so long was sent and received.

"It may seem strange to hear these things coming from someone so young, but *is* it really that strange? These are things I have learned and put into practice in my life. Any one of you could, too, and perhaps many of you already have. Why does learning how to live for the better have to wait until we are old or ready to die? Isn't *now* the time to learn the best way to live? If we don't, we will stumble through life, learning the hard way, and perhaps being pretty miserable a lot of the time. Mr. Engelmann has always said to me that knowledge, a university degree, a big house and so on isn't really all that helpful if we don't know how to live right and are not happy."

Henry paused again. "To end my talk today, I want to remind you of what our English teacher, Mr. Derkatch, has always stressed. When you give a presentation, it's important to summarize what you said at the end. When I first wrote this speech, I listed all the points I felt I should go over again. However, when I looked up the definition of 'integrity' in the dictionary, I read: 'undivided in purpose.' It emphasized wholeness, being true, authentic, at one with yourself. The thought immediately came to me that a visual demonstration of a man or woman, being a person of integrity, living by sound values and principles, would be far more effective."

Henry held up a sheet of paper, white on one side and black on the other. "Suppose this represents you now as a whole person. And as you know, we are daily faced with making choices. For example, should I tell the truth in this instance or should I lie? Should I take something that doesn't belong to me or not? Should I hold a grudge or be forgiving? Well, each time we make a choice, we can either remain a whole person and undivided, or we can start to break down. For example, if we lie, it affects our character."

As Henry said this, he made a long tear down one edge of the paper, and as it fell forward, the black side was exposed, indicating a black mark against them.

Henry heard a murmur in the audience.

"If we steal, it further affects our character." Henry made another tear. "Unforgiving, mean, dishonest." Henry made another tear and then another.

Soon all that was left of the paper was a thin strip in the middle, showing all the black marks against them.

Henry then picked up another whole sheet of white paper and held them side by side.

After a brief moment Henry asked, "What kind of person do you want to be, a person of integrity or the other? Who do you think lives a better life? Who has fewer worries? Who is more free? Who lives more in the present? Who is more aware of life? In the end, who is more able to serve and fulfill the purpose for which we are here on earth?"

Once again Henry paused, allowing everyone to answer those questions themselves. It was so quiet in the auditorium that Henry was sure he could hear the proverbial pin drop, and he knew the demonstration had hit home. He knew his classmates understood what he was talking about. They could see it, and Henry sensed they now believed it. Somehow what he had said had made a significant change in at least some of the students in the same way Mr. Engelmann's words and teachings had changed him.

"I often remember a line we studied in English from Shakespeare's play, *Hamlet*. I think it is fitting here: 'To be, or not to be: that is the question.' And this is the thought I leave with you today. The choice is yours. Each day when you get up, you can choose to serve others or yourself, to build or destroy, to be happy or sad, kind or unkind, grateful or complaining, forgiving or unforgiving, to be truthful or untruthful, and on and on. Yes, to be or not to be...to be a person of integrity or not is the daily question we must ask ourselves without fail."

Henry concluded by wishing the students well and, turning to Mr. Engelmann in the front row, Henry publicly thanked him for the time he had spent with him and the lessons of life he imparted by his example and teachings.

When Henry finished speaking, an uneasy silence hung in the air. As he gathered his notes and turned to leave the podium, a few people clapped, then a few more and then, like dominoes falling in rapid succession, the clapping erupted into a thunderous applause. People stood, smiling, laughing, whistling.

Henry was shocked by the strength and length of the ovation. His eyes turned to his parents in the front row. They were beaming and clapping. He focused on Mr. Engelmann, still in his chair, not applauding but proudly watching his pupil. That day his protégé had demonstrated that he had gone beyond what he had been taught in Mr. Engelmann's school of life.

As their gazes connected, Mr. Engelmann said, "Well done, my son," and though Henry was too far away to hear with his ears, he heard it in his heart.

As Henry returned to his seat, the ovation grew even louder.

After five minutes, the principal rose, walked to the podium and raised his hands, signaling the audience to sit down. When the clapping finally subsided, he turned towards Henry.

"That's quite a demonstration, a very vivid example of the kind of person we should be. It leads me to remark on another point you made, Henry, that we must be a model to others, an example of how life can and should be lived. That's what you have done and that is why your fellow students and teachers have given you the award you received today."

Then he turned his attention back towards the audience and said, "Like Henry, I would ask all of you, today, to take up the challenge too, and follow this lead. You have certainly motivated me, Henry, and, I'm sure, all those present here today as well. Thank you very much."

Mr. Mitchell walked towards him, hand extended. Henry got up and met him halfway and as they shook hands, the people in the audience stood up and gave another sustained and enthusiastic ovation. Henry felt his face flush like he was going to burst any second. He didn't remember returning to his seat.

At the conclusion of the exercises, many students and teachers thanked Henry for his message, further reinforcing his thought that he should pursue a career in teaching instead of business administration. He knew it was where his heart was leading him. He was a people person and while he loved business, perhaps it was the people he dealt with and served in Mr. Engelmann's store that he loved more. It was then that Henry decided to change faculties and enter the College of Education.

As he looked around for his parents and Mr. Engelmann, Eddy Zeigler, having until now waited in the wings to talk to him, found a path through the crowd.

"Hey, Hank, that was pretty cool. You're all right, you know?"

As they shook hands, Eddy looked down at his feet, for a moment seeming to lose his air of self-confidence, then he slowly raised his head until his gaze locked firmly onto Henry's.

"You know, Hank, it's always sort of bothered me what some of the guys and I did to you and that blond chick back in Grade 9. I just want you to know…well, it was a stupid thing to do, you know?" Eddy shifted his weight from foot to foot, then back and forth on his heels. "The guys had a few beers. You know what it's like."

"I understand, Eddy."

"Well, Hank, I'm sorry for what we did…for what *I* did. I'm not very proud of it and, whether you know it or not, you've helped me in many ways these past three years. Thanks, buddy."

Joy and peace swept through Henry as he realized that his message had registered with Eddy too. Although he had forgiven Eddy back in Grade 9, what he'd said now went straight to Henry's heart, freeing him from bondage completely. Henry knew Eddy felt it, too. Eddy tightened his grasp on Henry's hand and tears formed in Eddy's eyes. Henry put his free hand on Eddy's shoulder and patted it.

"Thanks a lot, Eddy. That means a lot to me."

"Whatever happened to that blond chick, anyway, Hank? I remember you telling me she left out of the blue. Did you ever hear from her and find out if she was…well, you know?"

"Yeah, I know, Eddy. No, I never heard from her again."

"Tough break. You were pretty sweet on her."

"I liked her a lot. I wrote to her, but she never answered any of my letters."

Eddy squinted at Henry, studying him for a long moment and said. "Well, that brunette babe you've been hanging out with lately seems like quite the damsel. If I were you, I wouldn't hesitate to nab her while you can."

Henry grinned. "You're right, Eddy—and that's exactly what I'm gonna do."

Eddy started to say something else, but Mr. Dornan came from behind and swung Henry around.

"Mr. Pederson, that was some speech!"

"Thanks, Mr. Dornan. Excuse me for a second." Henry quickly turned back to Eddy, but he was walking away.

"See you, Eddy!" he called.

Eddy turned, gave him a thumbs up and kept on walking. Henry wanted to say more but turned back to Mr. Dornan. By now several other people had approached him too.

As Henry, his mother and father, and Mr. Engelmann headed out to the car, his father clapped his shoulder.

"That was *very* well done, son. I can't get over how much you've learned from Mr. Engelmann."

"Yes, I'm very impressed as well," his mother said. "Guess I'll have to start taking lessons out back on the old crate from you, too, Mr. Engelmann," she quipped.

Mr. Engelmann put his arm on Henry's shoulder and patted it as they walked back to the car. He didn't say anything. Didn't have to say anything for Henry to understand his feelings.

Finally, after they'd finished dinner and dessert back at the Pedersons, Mr. Engelmann spoke.

"I knew when I hired you, Henry, you were a special young man. The way you worked and took charge was a godsend. Anna and I were in trouble financially and physically. Anna was very sick. I was tired and couldn't look after the store and Anna both. Bills were piling up, and we were losing customers because we lacked product, didn't have the time to restock the shelves, and so on. When we hired you, all that changed.

"You were like a breath of fresh air. You worked and thought of ways to improve the store as if it were your own, and brought great joy and happiness to Anna and me. Six months after we hired you, we were out of debt, our customers had returned and the store was being fixed up." David glanced at Henry's dad and added, "Then you helped out, too, Bill."

Bill nodded and waved a hand, indicating it was nothing.

Mr. Engelmann turned back to Henry. "You have a natural talent to be a businessman. In fact, Henry, I believe no matter what you do, you will be good at it. You are multi-talented, and you put your heart and soul into everything you do."

He paused for a brief moment and then said, "I was happy to hear on the drive home that you have decided to teach. We need people who have big hearts and know how to live right. You are a fine young man, honest and upright, and will be a good example for all those young people who need someone to emulate and look up to. Although you would make a fine businessman, you will be a superb teacher."

Henry just sat there, taking that all in, trying to keep his head from swelling too much. Finally, he found his voice, "Thank you, Mr. Engelmann…I—"

Mr. Engelmann shook a finger at Henry. "No need to thank me. It is I who owe *you* the thanks." With that he reached into his breast suit pocket, exactly where he had reached for the letter Anna had written for her funeral.

Henry thought he might be pulling out her letter again. Instead, Mr. Engelmann pulled out an envelope and handed it to him. It was sealed, with Henry's name written on it. All eyes were now on Henry, waiting for him to open up the letter and see what was inside. Henry looked at his mom and dad and then at Mr. Engelmann.

"Go on, Henry, open it," Mr. Engelmann pressed, his tone one of excitement and pleasure.

Henry slipped a finger into the tiny opening at one end of the envelope and tore it open. He took out the letter inside, and as he unfolded it, a cheque fell out and fluttered onto the table face down. The letter was only a paragraph long:

Dear Henry,

Thank you, from the bottom of my heart and Anna's, too. You have made our store very successful, and if it weren't for you, I'm sure it would have failed. But more than the success you have brought to our business, you have brought great joy and happiness to our lives. Perhaps more than you will ever know. On behalf of Anna, who is with us now in spirit, thank you. As I'm sure you know, we love you very much, as if you were our own son. Enclosed is a small token of our thanks and love, to help you out with university. May the good Lord richly bless you always.

Love, David Engelmann

Unbidden tears came to Henry's eyes and a drop fell onto the back of the cheque lying on the table. He quickly wiped it away with his finger, picked up the cheque and turned it over. His eyes were so blurry he had trouble making it out. He wiped his eyes with the back of his hand, then looked up and, slightly embarrassed, laughed nervously.

Mr. Engelmann beamed at Henry. Henry dropped his gaze to the cheque. The cheque was made out to Henry Pederson, in the amount of $10,000.

Henry gasped, his jaw dropped and his eyes widened. He looked at Mr. Engelmann. "Are you sure?"

"Yes, yes, it is yours."

Henry looked at his parents, who were now on the edge of their seats, wanting to read the letter and know what the cheque was for.

"This is unbelievable," Henry said, looking at the cheque again.

"Well, what does it say, Henry?" urged his mother.

Henry handed her the letter and the cheque to his dad.

"My, my," his dad said, "that's awfully generous of you, David."

Mr. Engelmann raised his right hand and waved it off as if it were nothing, mimicking what Henry's father had done earlier.

Mary's eyes filled with tears as she read the letter. She got up and kissed Mr. Engelmann's cheek.

"Thank you, David, that's a real nice letter." Then she read the cheque and let out a high-pitched squeal, startling them all.

Henry pushed back his chair, almost toppling it, went over to Mr. Engelmann and hugged him. "Thank you so much, Mr. Engelmann, thank you! For everything."

"Well it's been a long day and I think I will go home early tonight."

"I can drive you, David," Bill offered.

"Oh no, it's such a pleasant evening, the walk will do me good."

After Mr. Engelmann thanked Mary for another wonderful meal and said good night to everyone, he stepped outside. Henry followed him down the landing and the two men stood at the fence gate.

"Thanks again, Mr. Engelmann, for coming today and for the money."

"It was my pleasure, Henry." He patted Henry's shoulder and repeated, "It was my pleasure and Anna's too."

"Can I share something with you before you go?"

Mr. Engelmann gazed at Henry tenderly, the streetlight putting sparkles in his eyes, "Yes, yes, of course, Henry. What is it?"

"You know, of all the great things that happened today, the one I'm most proud of is that my speech caused Eddy to come up to me after and apologize for what he and his friends did to Jenny and me back in the summer before Grade 9. But—but, more important is how at that moment I completely forgave him and wanted to hug him. All the lingering anger, hurts, revenge…everything *vanished*. It was like a heavy stone I've been carrying on my back for so long suddenly fell off. You have no idea how light and good inside it makes me feel."

"Yes, Henry," Mr. Engelmann nodded. "I *do* know how you feel. I have been there in my life as well. Today, Henry, you have completed the journey. For years you have forgiven Eddy from the head, but today it reached your heart. Today you loved like Jesus would want us to love. When we do that, we feel incredible peace in our heart."

Henry felt such joy he couldn't speak. He used all his strength trying to hold back the tears welling up inside of him. He just nodded.

Mr. Engelmann gave Henry a hug and another pat on the shoulder. "Well done, Henry. What greater evidence of God, His Son and His Holy Spirit do we need to prove their existence? Our spirits cry out to Him, to come to Him, to do His will, to love. This is who we really are, Henry. At the core of our being is love, there where our Creator resides, and when we touch it at moments like this, we know beyond a doubt we have come home."

Henry simply nodded still unable to speak.

"Can you now really see the truth and depth of His words and teachings? Can you now understand why it is so important to obey Jesus' commands not to judge, not to seek revenge no matter how justified you are? Rather than squander our precious moments endlessly feeding our minds reasons why we are right to be angry or to hate the other, inner peace should always be our goal; to forgive, to love in every situation. Only in this way do we promote healing and growth in ourselves and others, which in turn makes the world a better place."

The light of truth burned in Henry's consciousness so brightly he found himself squinting as he softly said, "I understand, Mr. Engelmann."

"Remember this moment; sear it into your heart so when others hurt you in your life's journey you will remember the freedom and joy of forgiveness and do so quickly."

Mr. Engelmann stepped back and added, a twinkle in his eye and the corners of his mouth turning up, "Today, Henry, you have put a huge smile on the Lord's face."

What Mr. Engelmann had said earlier about bringing and seeing love in every situation suddenly made such sense to Henry. *The more we see beauty in life and in others the more we see beauty in ourselves. We feel good and proud of who we are. If we dwell on resentment and anger and look for the bad in others, it simply is a reflection of ourselves. We see what we are filled with…we choose every moment to really live, or half live, and, all too often, live not at all.*

Henry's eyes brightened as he realized even more fully what he had said in his speech: *"to be or not to be," really* is *the question we must ask each and every moment of our lives.*

As MR. ENGELMANN walked off down the sidewalk under the night sky, Henry knew that the bright light glowing around his mentor was neither the streetlight that had just flickered on nor the moon.

"Yeah—David Engelmann," Henry whispered, "angel man…"

Chapter Thirty-Eight

HENRY NEVER FULLY realized how his speech affected his mom. She never talked to him about it. But later that same week, Henry arrived home to two trucks parked in front of their home. One was from Brown's Auction and the other, Sears. They pulled away just as Henry arrived at the gate. He knew what had happened and smiled, pure joy welling up in him.

Henry burst through the front door.

"Henry, is that you?" called his mom.

"Yeah, it's me."

"Home early?"

"Yeah, they let us out early today."

His mother emerged from the bedroom, and as she passed Henry, she kissed his cheek. When she'd disappeared into the kitchen, he looked down the hallway. She had purposefully left the door open. Henry heard the water running in the kitchen and felt it safe to have a quick look. He tiptoed to the bedroom and looked inside. In the space where the twin beds had been was one large single one!

Henry could hardly wait for his dad to come home so he could see his reaction. Henry settled at the kitchen table with a

National Geographic, completely aware of the number of times his mother checked the oven unnecessarily and how many times she glanced towards the front door. She suggested several times that he go into the living room, but Henry stubbornly stayed in the kitchen. He didn't want to miss his dad's reaction.

Finally, Bill arrived home. As usual, he came in, kissed Mary on the cheek, then headed into the bathroom for a shower. Although Henry had a magazine in front of him, it might as well have been a piece of cardboard for all he read of it. Henry had prayed for this so long he didn't want to miss anything. Five minutes later, towel wrapped around his waist, his father darted across the hall to the bedroom and closed the door.

Ten minutes later, a little longer than usual, he emerged from the bedroom, wearing a clean shirt and a pair of trousers. Henry glanced up quickly and then back down at the magazine.

Bill had a wide grin on his face.

"Hi, Henry," his father said as he entered the kitchen. He walked over to his mother, who as always had her hands in the sink. "Hi, honey," he said, touching her waist and kissing her cheek. "When's dinner ready?"

"Oh, in about ten or fifteen minutes. The casserole needs just a little longer. Enough time to start the paper. I'll call you."

What? Was that it? No passionate love scene or anything? What was going on here? Henry had fully expected his dad to swoop his mom off her feet and carry her into the bedroom and try out the new bed. Supper could wait! Henry couldn't believe his mom had told his dad to go read the paper, that she'd *call* him—as if tonight were no different from any other night! What was romantic about that? Why the small talk? Why not a conversation about the new bed? Or how exciting it would be to try it out? Henry guessed maybe they were a little embarrassed or felt awkward about it all with him sitting there. As far as Henry could guess, they hadn't slept together in several years, ever since his dad returned from Vancouver. Henry wondered if he should tease them a little about it but immediately thought better of it.

Supper was quiet. Too quiet. It just drew more attention to what his parents were trying to hide. His mom kept looking down at her plate rather than at either him or his dad, while his dad couldn't keep his eyes off her. Mary's face flushed and when she looked down, her long eyelashes veiled unsettled eyes.

Henry began to feel he was hampering them with his presence. He began to eat faster so that he could be excused.

Right after dinner, Henry decided to sort out his closet and drawers in preparation for leaving for university. Several shirts were missing buttons and he headed out to the kitchen to give them to his mom to mend. When he peeked into the kitchen, his dad was behind his mom with his hands wrapped around her, kissing her neck. Her hands rested on the edge of the sink, her fingers in the dish water.

The water was running, which explained why they hadn't heard Henry come down the hall. It was threatening to overflow, actually, and he thought about warning his mom about it, but he was so happy to see them like that he just couldn't bring himself to put it to a stop. It gave him such a wonderful feeling of security to see his parents show love to each other.

He turned and walked back to his room.

At nine-thirty, Henry decided to make some popcorn, but when he opened his bedroom door all the lights were out. His mom and dad had already gone to bed. That was a first. His mom always was up until at least ten-thirty. Henry smiled as he thought about it. They had a lot to make up for.

As he silently returned to his room, exhilaration flooded him. A warm gush of emotion in the pit of his stomach rose swiftly and spread throughout his being. Tears welled up in his eyes as he let out a sigh of utter relief and pure joy. The undercurrent of unforgiveness in his home, which had held all of them captive for so long, was gone, leaving in its wake freedom and peace.

Henry loved it. He re-entered his bedroom and quietly closed the door behind him, knowing that all was finally well once again in the Pederson household.

Chapter Thirty-Nine

THERE WERE ONLY two weeks left in June and Henry still hadn't mentioned his plan to go to Ottawa. He wouldn't be able to keep it a secret much longer. He was becoming very fond of Julean. He seemed to have that same dreamy-eyed look he'd had for Jenny.

Mary hoped that his relationship with Julean would change his mind about going to Ottawa. She hated to think what could be in store for him if he made it there. Would Mr. Sarsky even agree to talk to him? Was he even still with that company? Perhaps they had moved. Worse, Jenny might not be interested anymore. She knew Henry needed closure, but perhaps Julean was providing that.

She dried her hands on her apron, turned and looked up at the crucifix. "Oh, Lord, I know I shouldn't be snooping in my son's desk but I just have to. I promise this will be the last time. Please, forgive me."

When she entered Henry's room, she sat at his desk and stared down at the closed drawer.

"Oh, Lord," she whispered, "in a way I am just trying to help my son carry his burden. There is a spiritual sharing between us."

Although it was a weak excuse, it was strong enough to once again allow her to reach down and open the drawer.

The money, tickets and white folded letter were still there. All the pamphlets and what looked like the city map were stacked neatly and pushed into the corner of the drawer. Mary lifted out the envelope and set it on the desk. She wondered if he had added anything new to his plans or indicated what else he had accomplished.

Mary unfolded the letter, and her head snapped back so sharply that she almost tipped the chair backwards. The sheet of paper wasn't his plan. It was a letter addressed to her. She leaned forward and allowed her eyes to fall on the letter again.

Mary shook her head and exclaimed, "You rat, you!"

Dear Mom,

I have decided to abandon my plan. Ever since Grade 9, I have been planning this trip to Ottawa, but after the last several months of thinking about it, I am going to let it go. If Jenny had sent me at least one letter, I'd have followed through on this for sure. Some kind of closure to all this would have been nice, but since meeting Julean, I have come to love her just as much, and who knows, maybe more. In any case, I no longer need to know Jenny's whereabouts or what has happened to her as much anymore. I know I will always love Jenny, but it is time to move on.

How did I know that you've been following this? The first time you peeked in my drawer, you left your trademark. The teardrop stain on the bottom left hand corner of my plan never did fade away completely as you might have hoped. It was the same teardrop stain you left behind when you read my first love letter to Jenny back in Grade 9. I must say you managed to put the drawer back in the same position every time, and the envelope, too, but you had to be even more precise to make it appear untouched. You don't know all my secret little devices that let me know the goings-on in my room. Ha, ha.

Am I mad or upset with you? Of course not, how could I possibly be? What could I possibly ever hide from you? You have shared my sorrow and burden for so long. You have every right to know where I'm at in all this. I know how much you care and worry and want the best for me. All I can possibly feel is a deep gratitude for you. I may not have said it often enough, but you'll never know how much I appreciate your love and support.

And you have no idea how much I've enjoyed this secret little rendezvous with you. It was amusing to think that you thought you were doing this without my knowledge. How cautious you were and the guilty twinges you must have felt! It was all not necessary. You should've known that you couldn't possibly fool your bright young son!

Thanks for all your caring over the years, Mom, and for always being there for me. I thank God every night that He blessed me with a mom like you. I so regret having this come to an end. It gave me something to look forward to when I came home. The first thing I would do was to check to see if you'd had another peek. It was fun. I will treasure this always.

Love, Henry
June 17, 1960

Several more of her trademarks landed on the page, but it no longer mattered. Henry was no longer going to Ottawa. Mary smiled through her tears as elation filled her spirit. He wasn't mad at her. In fact, he'd known all along that she was snooping and was thankful that she had done it.

Mary read the letter over again, folded it, and put it into her apron pocket. She opened the second drawer in which Henry kept his writing paper, took out a sheet and wrote:

Dear Henry,

You loveable stinker, you. I should have known better than to think I could fool you. And the guilt I felt each time I snooped in your drawer, I confessed it three times to Father Connelly! My, my, what a shocking surprise. I almost fell over backwards when I saw your letter instead of your plan as usual. That was very clever of you!

Thank you for not being upset with me and for making this experience so special. You are a very understanding and insightful person. Your dad and I are so proud of you. You have been such a joy and blessing to us. You have turned into such a fine young man and we know you will succeed in whatever you do.

Thank you, too, for your words of wisdom in your valedictory speech. Who would have thought that your speech would make me aware of myself and finally bring me truly back home.

I love you very much, son. I wish you much hap-piness with Julean. She is such a lovely girl and I am happy you made the decision to abandon your plan.

Yes, now that it's out in the open, I can truly say
this was fun! I, too, shall treasure this experience
for always.

Love, Mom
June 19, 1960

As Mary folded the letter, several more trademarks landed
on the page, making the ink run. She placed the letter in the
envelope with the money, making it appear as if it were still the
one he'd written her and laid the envelope back in the drawer
as she had found it. How had Henry detected her presence? It
didn't matter anymore.

As she rose to leave Henry's room, she brought her fingertips up to her mouth and kissed them, then reached up to the
crucifix hanging above Henry's door, touching her fingertips
to Jesus' feet.

"Thank you, my Lord. Only You could have arranged something as beautiful and creative as this. What a wonderful way to
answer a mother's prayer."

Mary walked into her bedroom to the closet. She stood on
her tiptoes to reach her treasure chest of memories, which she
brought down and set on her dresser. She lifted the lid of a
small jewel box on her dresser and fished around for a small
key. With it, Mary opened the chest of the treasures of her heart.
She took out the letter from her apron pocket, read it one more
time, and placed it in the box.

HENRY AND BILL arrived home about the same time. As usual, both men appeared in the kitchen, kissed her cheek and
then went through their get-ready-for-dinner ritual. Bill had
a shower then settled in the living room with the paper, while
Henry spent time in his bedroom before washing and joining
his father in the living room.

She wondered if Henry had checked his desk drawer and
already knew.

"Okay, boys, dinner's on."

When they'd sat down to dinner and said the blessing, Henry looked at her and smiled. He had read her letter. They gazed at each other for a long moment, tears coming to their eyes. Occasionally, as they silently ate, Henry would smile and let out a little chuckle that he could no longer contain and then she would do the same.

Bill looked from Mary to Henry and back again.

"What? Is there something I should know?"

After a long pause while Mary regained her composure, she looked at Bill and said, "Over the past year, Henry and I have shared a rare experience that I only realized today." Tears in her eyes, she added, "Sometimes a shared experience of the heart is best left unspoken."

HENRY AND MARY were both in for another surprise when they all retired to the living room expecting to watch Perry Mason on TV. Bill usually fired up the RCA Victor and had the picture going on the screen by the time Mary came in, but not tonight. Henry looked at his mom and she returned his gaze. They both looked at Bill.

He remained uncomfortably quiet for a long time and Henry noticed his foot lightly tapping the rug and red blotches on his neck. Something was on his dad's mind that he was nervous about. Henry was certain his mom had noticed it before he did and so both of them were quiet, giving Bill time to say whatever was on his mind.

Bill cleared his throat and took a sip of tea Mary had brought in and then he spoke. "I think you both know how much I like listening to that Bishop Sheen fella. Every Sunday he keeps hammering on, saying that we should say the rosary. 'The family that prays together stays together' is nothing more than a slogan unless it's put into practice."

Bill stopped talking and cleared his throat, leaning down to pick up a bag beside his chair. He reached in and brought out three rosaries. "I stopped off at church on the way home yesterday and bought these. I know you have one, Mary, but

I thought I'd buy you another anyway. You may have one already too, Henry, that Mom's given you in the past, but again, I thought I'd get you one too just in case you can't find yours or it's gotten lost over the years."

Henry noticed the red blotches climb to the top of his dad's face. He was turning red as fire. He got up and handed Henry a rosary with brown wooden beads and a silver cross. Then he moved over to Mary and gave her one of clear crystal beads with a silver cross as well. He held his own black-beaded rosary in his other hand. He returned to the sofa, knelt down and in a hoarse, crackly voice said, "I hope the both of you will join me."

Mary was already at his side.

Henry was in awe. Never in a million years would he have expected his dad to do this. And then Mr. Engelmann's teaching filled his mind. *God's divine providence at work*. He would never again have to worry that his family would ever be separated.

His dad had already started the rosary when Henry finally knelt down beside his mom. Henry heard his dad say the first half of the Our Father but couldn't join with his mother as she said the remainder. He just followed silently along, his fingers sliding easily over the beads wet with tears. As Mr. Engelmann so often noticed, he wore his emotions on his shirtsleeves. He was too overwhelmed to speak. All he felt was the peace filling their home, that it really was a home of peace and safety.

A surge of security swept through Henry, and Mr. Engelmann's words, as they always did, came to his mind once more. *If you place Jesus at the centre of your life, you build your life, your home, on a rock that can weather any storm.*

Now, to his very core, Henry felt what his wise teacher meant.

The rosary was over half finished when Henry finally joined in, "Holy Mary, Mother of God, pray for us sinners, now and at the hour of our death. Amen."

Chapter Forty

"Thanks for putting the baby carriage in the trunk, Dad."

"You're welcome, sweetheart. Say hello to Tammy and tell her I can't wait to see her little girl sometime."

"Okay, I will, Dad. See you tonight."

Ted threw a kiss to Jenny and left for the office.

Just as Jenny was about to leave too, Edith entered the foyer.

"Is Tammy still at her grandma's place?"

"Yes, it's almost two months and neither her mother or father have spoken to her."

"And what about her boyfriend? Robert, isn't it?"

Jenny nodded. "He hasn't come around yet either, unless he phoned last night."

"Well, it's a good thing Tammy has you for a friend, you're there more than at home lately."

"Oh, Mom, you have no idea how much I love Chloe. Every time I go over there she's grown and becoming more alert. She's such a darling."

"Chloe, that's a cute name."

"Isn't it nice? So short and sweet. I just love it."

"You'll be home for supper?"

"Yes. We're going to the park to try out the new baby carriage. Tammy misses her backyard at home, but this will be okay. Her grandma lives in an apartment so it'll be nice for Tammy and the baby to get out and have some fresh air. Well, I better be off. It takes over an hour and a half to get there even when the traffic isn't too busy."

"Well, be careful, honey and say hello to Tammy. Tell her she's welcome to come for dinner on Sunday, your dad and I would both love to meet Chloe."

Jenny kissed her mom on the cheek, "Okay, Mom. See you around five or so."

Jenny buzzed up to Tammy's grandma's apartment.

"Oh hi, Tammy, I'm at the front door and have the baby carriage set up and ready. Do you want me to come up?"

"No. I'll be down in five minutes. I have the diaper bag and everything."

"I'll be waiting, I can hardly wait to see Chloe."

When Tammy came down with the baby she looked exhausted.

"Hey, Jen, I'm so glad you came. Chloe was up all night and I'm so tired. Would you mind taking her to the park? It's only two blocks down that way and the fresh air might relax her. I've just got to get some sleep. Do you mind, Jen?"

Jenny had been helping Tammy for the last month and though knew how to tend to Chloe, she felt a little uncomfortable going on her own. But it was clear Tammy needed to rest.

"Sure, Tammy. Just help me get her comfortable in the carriage and I'll take her for a nice long walk."

"Oh, Jen! Thank you *so* much! Grandma tries to help, but her arthritis is so bad she can't hold the baby."

Jenny took the baby from Tammy and cuddled her.

"Hi, Chloe! How's my little one? How's my little angel?"

Jenny put her in the carriage and covered her with the blanket Tammy had brought. She put the diaper bag at the foot of the carriage and then turned back to her friend.

"Okay, Tammy, I'm all set. Go get some sleep."

"If she fusses, I heated up some milk. It's in the diaper bag all wrapped up so it should stay warm for awhile. Thanks again!"

"Oh go lie down already—we'll be fine," Jenny said, trying to hide her nervousness.

Chloe started to cry, but as soon as Jenny began to walk forward and sort of shook the carriage at the same time, she settled right down.

Jenny wondered what was ailing Chloe, why she would be up all night. And from out of nowhere the thought came to her that maybe Tammy was so nervous about being on her own without the support of her mother and Robbie, she wasn't relaxed enough to release her milk like she should be.

Jenny was glad Tammy had sent along a bottle of formula. She was thankful as well that it was a beautiful day and the wind was calm. It helped relax her as she strolled down Silver Street towards Alexander Park.

So far so good. Chloe wasn't fussing, although she wasn't asleep either. Her round black eyes peeked over the covers.

Every now and then as she walked along, Jenny forgot herself and called the baby Camilla. Her own little girl was on her mind so much that Jenny couldn't help it at times. In a way, Jenny was living out what she'd missed with her own little girl. There was nothing wrong with that was there?

The park wasn't too crowded, but there was a lot of noise and shouting. She looked down at Chloe, still wide awake but thankfully content. Just as Jenny passed the swings to rest on a nearby bench one of the children threw a ball and it hit the side of the carriage, startling Chloe badly. She began to wail. Jenny quickly rocked the carriage and placed her hand on the baby's covers, trying to assure her someone was with her, but to no avail. Chloe was frightened and howled at the top of her lungs.

Jenny rushed over to the nearest bench, already occupied by a lady in her thirties. The woman could tell Jenny was flustered and offered her help.

"Yes, thank you. If you could rock the carriage for a minute while I get her bottle?"

Jenny opened the diaper bag and searched for the bottle but it wasn't there. Tammy must have forgotten to put it in the bag. But Tammy had also brought extra blankets. Jenny searched there and felt the bottle. "Thank God! Here it is."

Jenny squirted some formula on her wrist and it was still a little warm. The lady already had Chloe out of the carriage and now handed her to Jenny.

"Oh, thank you so much." Jenny was so flustered she couldn't think how to hold Chloe.

"Here let me help you." The lady took Chloe from her and repositioned her so she fit snugly into Jenny's left arm.

"Is this your first? I'm Alice, by the way."

Jenny gave Chloe the bottle and she immediately began eating, much to Jenny's relief.

"Thank you again, Alice. I'm Jenny, and yes, this is my first. Well, so to speak. I wish she were mine but Chloe here belongs to a friend of mine. She's at home resting and I thought I'd take the baby out for a walk."

"Chloe, that's a nice name. Looks like she was hungry besides being frightened by that ball."

"Yeah, that came out of nowhere, didn't it? I didn't expect it either. So which of these children is yours?" Jenny asked, scanning the children playing on the park amusements.

Alice didn't respond for a moment and then said, "None of them. I used to bring my daughter here all the time but..." her words trailed off.

Jenny studied her, not wanting to pry but sensing the woman needed to talk. "Is she okay?" Jenny chanced.

Alice stared straight ahead. "I'm afraid not. She passed away two months ago. She had cancer."

"Oh Alice! I'm so sorry! I don't know what to say. I can't even imagine what you must be going through. How old was she?"

"She'd just turned four," was all Alice could manage as tears filled her sad eyes. "I come here every now and then just to remember some of the times we had together. She loved to swing. That was her favourite one, second from the right." Alice pointed at a set of six swings.

"Oh dear, Chloe drank the whole bottle of milk!" *Now what am I going to do?* thought Jenny as the baby began to fuss again. Jenny rocked her but it didn't help.

"Come on now, Chloe," she shushed, "settle down."

"She needs to be burped, Jenny, she might have swallowed a lot of air."

"Oh for sure! Why didn't I think of that?"

Jenny turned the baby in her arms and brought Chloe up to her chest, the baby's head on her shoulder. She began patting her back.

Alice leaned over to place a clean diaper on Jenny's shoulder, but she was too late and Chloe threw up what seemed like half the bottle onto Jenny's sweater.

"Oh no! My gosh, Chloe!"

"Here let me take her, the public washroom is right over there. Why don't you go and get cleaned up. I think she'll be fine now."

Jenny looked at Chloe, who seemed to have settled down. *Maybe all she needed was to burp.*

"Okay, thanks, Alice, I'll just be a minute and then I'd better get her home in case she gets hungry again. Half her meal is on my sweater!"

Jenny rushed to the washroom, wet some paper towels and began sponging the formula from her sweater. She'd not been gone even five minutes when she returned. As she walked back to the bench, Jenny's heart sank. Alice and Chloe weren't there.

"Oh no!" Jenny became frantic. *Good heavens!* Surely Alice hadn't *taken* the little girl. Jenny thought she would explode... until she heard her name.

"We're over here, Jenny! The kids were starting to play ball too close to us and I thought it best to bring Chloe over here."

Jenny rushed over, relief washing over her.

Alice was changing Chloe's diaper on a bench.

"Oh, oh…thank you, again, Alice," Jenny said, trying to catch her breath.

"I see you got most of the formula off."

"Yes, it came out fairly easily, but I'll smell like a Jersey cow until I get home." The two of them chuckled.

"Well, she seems to have settled down some."

"That's good." Jenny picked up Chloe and put her back into the carriage. "I best be off in case she starts fussing again. I have no more milk for her. I suspect that's why she's been waking up so often at night. Not getting enough milk."

"That could be it. How old is she?"

"Almost two months."

"She does seem a little small. Better take her to the doctor as soon as you can and have her weighed. He'll advise you what to do pretty quick."

"Now that you mention it, Tammy was supposed to take her last week but was too sick. I think she goes tomorrow, though."

"That's good. Is your friend breastfeeding her baby?"

"Yes."

"She might want to supplement her feeding with the bottle more regularly too. I could tell Chloe was rather hungry."

Jenny nodded. "That's a good idea. Well, it was nice meeting you, Alice. Thank you for all your help—and I'm so sorry about your little girl. Perhaps well see each other here again."

"Yes, we just might. Good luck with the baby."

"Thanks, Alice. 'Bye."

Jenny pushed the carriage out of the park as quickly as she could and rushed back to the apartment. She began to appreciate the stress Tammy was under. Just taking Chloe out for a little walk to the park had proven to be almost more than Jenny would want to handle.

She buzzed up to the apartment and as soon as she heard a click she opened the door and managed to push the carriage into the foyer of the apartment building. As Jenny wheeled the carriage into the elevator and ascended to the ninth floor, she couldn't help but feel the conditions Tammy was living in were just too stressful and must only add to her troubles. The apartment was small, only a one-bedroom, and Tammy slept on the small couch with the cradle beside her. There was no privacy or anything. Jenny wished her mother would allow Tammy to come and stay with them, but Edith didn't want to interfere.

Both Tammy and her grandma looked very tired when Jenny entered the apartment. Jenny couldn't stand to leave her friend in this situation any longer.

"Tammy, why don't you stay at our place until things get settled at home? My parents said it's okay," Jenny lied. "There's the guest room and such a huge expanse of lawn we can stroll in with the baby. It's just a little too crowded here for you all, though it's so good of you, Mrs. Sullivan, to let Tammy and Chloe stay here with you."

"It's no trouble at all, Jenny. I like to have Tammy and the baby here."

"Well, maybe Tammy can come just for a few days and give you a little rest."

Mrs. Sullivan glanced at Tammy. "Well, that *would* be nice. But Tammy, you and the baby are welcome back anytime."

"Okay, Tammy," Jenny said, taking charge when she saw her friend was too weary to do anything other than agree, "let's gather your things together and get to my place. You might want to fix Chloe another bottle of milk, most of what I fed her she threw up on me. And she seemed really hungry. You may have to supplement your breastfeeding with a bottle. You've got a doctor's appointment tomorrow, don't you?"

"Yes, tomorrow at two-thirty. Will you be able to drive us?"

"For sure, Tammy."

Jenny didn't know how her mother would react to her showing up with Tammy and the baby, and she sure didn't want Tammy to feel any more stress than she already was. They got caught in a traffic jam and didn't get to the estate until almost seven-thirty. Her dad would probably be home already. Jenny drove up the circle drive to the front entry instead of the garage.

"Tammy, would you wait here for a second while I see if I can get my dad to come help carry some of the things in?" Jenny didn't wait for Tammy to answer, she quickly got out of the car and rushed inside.

Both her parents were in the living room. Edith heard Jenny come in and was just coming to greet her when Jenny entered the living room.

"Oh, Mom, I have Tammy in the car. It's so crowded at her grandma's apartment and her grandma doesn't look all that well and Tammy is under so much stress, can she please stay here?"

Edith sucked in a breath. "I told you before, Jenny, I don't want to interfere with the Andersons—they're already upset with us for sheltering Tammy before. You better tell her—"

"Now hold on just a minute, Edith, surely we can help Jenny's friend out. I think it's wrong for her parents to turn their back on their daughter like thi—"

Edith shot a look at her husband. "Ted. I *really* don't think we should get inv—"

"Edith, we are already involved; the girl's sitting in the driveway with her baby. She needs our help and we're going to give it and that's settled. I don't want to hear any more about it. I'll call Mr. Anderson later and explain things."

Ted pushed past Jenny and said, "Come on, let's help Tammy and her daughter inside and get them settled. Perhaps you could heat something up for the girls to eat, Edith."

Edith stood there in a huff, not knowing what to say or think.

Jenny came over and took her mother's hand, "Oh, Mom, it'll be all right. Please don't be upset."

Jenny turned and rushed to catch up to her father. He already had the carriage out of the trunk and was opening the passenger door for Tammy. Jenny was so happy to have her father's support. She'd never seen her dad so assertive with her mother, and she'd actually liked to see him take charge like that. She wished he'd do that more often. But she'd also noticed he too looked tired. And he was losing weight.

I wish he wouldn't drink so much.

But she loved what he did next.

As he held the door for Tammy and her baby, Ted said, "Welcome, Tammy! It's so good to have you stay with us. I can't wait to hold that precious little baby of yours."

Edith came to the entry as they reached the stairwell for the second floor. Her stern look softened into a pleasant smile, "Welcome, Tammy," she said.

"You know, Jenny I've been doing a lot of thinking these past two months about Robbie and me."

The two of them were sitting on her bed. It was a crazy kind of flashback to the sleepovers they used to have, only Chloe had joined the slumber party, and was, in fact, finally asleep in her bassinet. And Tammy looked more motherly, more mature somehow, even just in the last two months.

It's amazing how added responsibility can affect your appearance and how you carry yourself, Jenny thought.

"And?" she said aloud.

"The entire time I was at Nana's, Robbie never called or came over once."

Jenny reached over and patted her friend's hand, her eyes reflecting Tammy's hurt.

"In a way, though, I'm glad he didn't. It made me realize that we really didn't have a deep relationship. Well, not on Robbie's part, anyway. Maybe our relationship only lasted as long as it did because I gave in to his demands for sex."

Tammy shifted on the bed, pulling her knees up to her chest and wrapping her arms around them.

Jenny got more comfortable too, crossing her legs and settling her behind into the soft covers like a hen into a nest.

The girls smiled at each other.

"Anyway, Jen, I can see now how that was all so wrong. It made me think about Lynne in form 4C. She has such a reputation for being fast and letting guys get to first base with her all the time. Robbie told me all the time how the guys boast to see who can get her to bed the fastest."

"But surely Robbie doesn't think that of you, Tammy!" Jenny was shocked.

"Perhaps not, but *I* feel like I was used. At the time it makes you feel needed—loved in a way, but really Jenny, sex is nothing more than fulfilling our selfish desires. There's no commitment, no responsibility, and most important of all, no respect from the guys. There's is no self-discipline, either, especially on their part. All they want is to have their insatiable sexual appetite fed and gratified. It makes me wonder who Robbie's taking out now and trying to go to bed with!"

Jenny rested a hand on Tammy's knee, conveying support and some comfort for her emotionally suffering friend.

"Boys have to be reined in and learn to sacrifice and delay their sexual drives. I don't think most of them understand the big picture, and like you said, don't respect girls, or even themselves, for that matter. Look what happened to me—I was taken to the park as if I was nothing more than a sexual outlet."

"And what about me? Robbie led me to believe he loved me, but now I'm no longer certain of that at all. And to think that I almost aborted the little baby we created. I get so upset with myself for even thinking I could have considered doing that! And I'm very disappointed in my mother for encouraging me to do it!

"I now see so clearly that it's best to wait and get to know one another before you get physical. If I'd done that, maybe I would've understood Robbie better and realized that we really weren't really meant for each other in the first place."

Jenny nodded, thinking of Henry as she so often did. "You can have a lot of fun together without having sex, spending time to get to know one another, to become real friends who are there for each other through thick and thin."

"Next time I see Lynne, I'm going to tell her what she's really doing and how I got caught up in it too. Maybe because I'm the one who got pregnant, she'll listen to me. And if her reputation is true, I'm surprised she's not concerned about catching some disease, not to mention the guys who take her out.

"Oh, Jenny, it's awful to even talk about another person like this. It's all so sad when you stop to think about what a huge risk we take for a few minutes of gratification!"

Tammy reached out to grab Jenny's hand. Jenny squeezed back confirming her agreement about everything Tammy said.

"You know, Jen, the person I respect most of all in this entire mess is my dad. He's shown me the most support. He was against the abortion, and I know he did his best to convince Mom to help me. And I wish so much I had listened to him before all this. He's a man and understands men. He cautioned me so many times and always wanted to make sure I was home at a decent hour. He was usually asleep by the time I got home and Mom always lied to him for me that I'd gotten home earlier. I wish now he'd been more strict with me; and even Mom let me get away with far too much."

"Well, since we've both learned the hard way what's best, why don't we make a pact to never engage in premarital sex? Let's try to be an example for other girls. Somehow we have to get this message out there to others. We're all in this together and sharing things like this is so important."

"I know, we're all afraid to talk about sex and yet we all need direction and guidance, a chance to think about what we're doing and the consequences of our actions and decisions, but more than that, to talk about them."

Jenny's eyes brightened. "We have one more student council meeting next Monday. I'm going to bring it up as a recommended project for our next student representative council. The new president will be there and so will Mr. Morgan, our advisor. He's young, he's married, and very understanding. I'm sure he'll support the idea. Maybe he can get a speaker to come in and talk to the entire student assembly." Jenny was getting more excited about the idea by the minute.

"That sounds great, Jen. But I'll tell you one thing for sure, whether Robbie and I get back together or not, or if ever I go out with another guy, there are going to be some serious parameters in our relationship!"

Jenny smiled at her friend, her eyes again conveying perfect agreement. Jenny put out her hand and Tammy echoed the gesture, holding Jenny's hand firmly in her own.

"Here's to our agreement to remain chaste until we give ourselves freely and completely to the man of our dreams."

And so a covenant between them was made.

Chloe began to stir in her crib.

"It's just about time for her feeding. Maybe we should carry the bassinet down to the guest room now. She's been waking up around three in the morning for her feeding, so I'm glad I won't be disturbing your sleep. I sure hope your parents won't hear her, either."

"Oh no, I'm sure they won't. And, Tammy, if you're ever too tired to feed her just wake me and I'll get a bottle for her. I'd love to feed her anytime." Jenny's eyes sparkled at the thought of holding baby Chloe close, just the two of them in the soft, dark hours of the night.

But Tammy knew beneath the sparkle of her dear friend's eyes, Jenny yearned for her own little girl.

Chapter Forty-One

JUNE 30 ARRIVED faster than anyone expected. According to the purchase agreement, David Engelmann had to be moved out before midnight.

Memories had haunted him all throughout the previous night. Memories of how the wood and concrete structure around him had served as his home.

He had spent that last night in what had been his and Anna's bed. She had been so excited when she had seen it in the antique shop. It had a royal look about it. After so many years as their marriage bed, the Salvation Army would be taking it away, along with the kitchen table, chair, fridge and stove.

The chair next to the south window he could not part with. As the sun rounded that side of the building, its rays would warm the chair and whoever was sitting in it at the time. It had been Anna's favourite place to read her Bible.

When the weather was right, she would open the window an inch or two and let the warm summer breeze flutter the pages as she sat talking with the Lord. Many times David would come upstairs to find her asleep, Bible on her lap and head resting on the high-cushioned chair back. Often the sun was peeking through the venetian blinds, casting light and dark shadows across her, the chair and the floor. She looked so peaceful as she slept, and yet the stripes reminded David of prison bars, holding Anna captive in the disease she had fought for so many years. He had prayed so fervently that the Lord would heal her in this life, but it was not to be.

Yet, in the midst of her sickness, she had been so strong, so uncomplaining, so giving and so full of love. David believed her illness had brought her closer to Christ, closer to His suffering. And through her suffering, she understood the pain and sorrow of others.

The armrests of the chair were worn and tattered. Anna had made no attempt to mend them. "It shows character, David; the chair is growing old, just like us," Anna would say.

He remembered the day she had put doilies on the armrests; she'd taken them off the next, saying that it didn't look the same.

"Let it show its journey with us," she had said.

The rattle of the front door stirred him from his reflections. He descended the stairs, and opened the front door to let in the men from the Salvation Army. After exchanging pleasantries, he led them upstairs then got out of their way.

He looked around the empty shelves and bare counters downstairs, seeing the store filled with customers. Mrs. Goronic by the meat counter, waiting for him to cut some salami. Mr. Tearhorst at the cash register, asking for another package of Vogue tobacco and cigarette paper. He recalled the times they'd talked about the old country and their desire to go back for a visit. It could happen now, he had the money and the time, but it wouldn't be the same without Anna...

David's thoughts were interrupted by the moving men carrying the kitchen stove out to the truck. A few minutes later, the men returned, one of them carrying a tool box.

"I hope you're not in a hurry, Mr. Engelmann. It's gonna take some time to get that beautiful bed apart. Some family will sure be lucky to get it."

"That's what I was hoping. And, no, I am in no hurry. Take all the time you need."

The men disappeared up the stairs again as David walked behind the counter as he had done thousands of times. He took out a soft white cloth from the shelf below the register and out of habit wiped the top of the marble counter. Like the chair upstairs, the counter had heard many stories, problems and concerns over the years.

He turned towards the old cash register and struck the "No Sale" button. The drawer sprang open with the bright sound of a bell; he never tired of hearing it—the more times it rang, the more he could contribute to their meagre living. He'd tried selling the till, but no one was interested in an antique cash register so he had decided to leave it behind. The meat cooler had stopped working the previous week and it made no sense to repair it. It too he would leave.

As the moving men walked the various parts of the bed and frame out to the van, Mr. Engelmann tried to visualize where each belonged, trying to see it again as a whole and not in pieces. In the end, he looked away. It bothered him too much to have his memories dismantled and disappear before his eyes.

By noon, the upstairs was empty except for the chair by the window. The men asked about it and offered to find someone to re-upholster it. But David decided it would be better to let it retire along with the store.

He walked the men to the door and watched them drive away with the last of his possessions, locking the door behind them. He turned and, one final time, walked through his store, his home. Henry and Bill would arrive shortly to drive him to the rectory where he would stay for the next week and a half before going off to the seminary in Gravelbourg.

He slowly climbed the stairs and inspected each empty room. The entire apartment was bereft of emotion now, as it had been when he and Anna first moved in. It had been a shell then and it was a shell now. He and Anna had made it a home, but that was all gone and soon he would be too.

Emerging from the bedroom he blinked back tears. The sun shone through the venetian blinds, casting that familiar light-and-dark pattern across the chair, outlining the window on the hardwood floor. He went over to the window and raised the blinds, erasing the prison bars.

"There," he muttered, "you are free, Anna. Free of all pain and suffering."

His Bible still sat on the window ledge. He picked it up as he sat in the chair. When he opened it, the scriptures he had read a thousand times before greeted him. He searched for something that might bring him solace, his spirit heavy-laden with so many memories. All the things that had made up his life—Anna, the store, his customers, his home—were gone. Loneliness, regret and sadness washed over him. He wiped away the tears with the back of his hand, but they kept coming. He closed the Bible and sobbed as the entirety of his loss hit him.

But perhaps the Lord was asking him to break all ties to the past so he could begin the important work He had for him to do before he and his Anna were reunited.

The sun's travels west shifted the light through the window, sending a ray of sunlight down the stairs almost as if it were pointing the way to his future. He had never seen it happen before. *"Trust in the Lord with all your heart and do not lean on your own understanding. Acknowledge Him in all your ways and He will light and guide your path."* And just as he was about to close the Bible on his lap, Psalm 119:105 came to him: *Thy Word is a lamp unto my feet and a light unto my path.*

"Okay, Lord. It is time." He pushed himself out of the chair, his hands registering the familiar worn armrests one last time. He patted it with his hand and nodded, as if to say, "Thank you, you have served us well."

At the top of the stairs, he looked back, then turned and followed the light cast by the sun.

Downstairs, as he had thousands of times before, he checked the back door to make sure it was locked, though there was no longer any reason to do so. He emerged from the storage room to tapping on the front door.

Henry was peeking through the glass with both hands cupped around his eyes.

"Coming!"

"Hi, Mr. Engelmann," Henry said when he opened the door.

"Hello, Henry."

"Is there anything I can help you with?"

"No, I have my Bible and there are just a few things in my suitcase there, behind the counter."

"That's all? No pictures or anything?"

"Oh, I have just two, packed in the suitcase. One is of Anna and me. Most of our family photographs were left behind when we escaped from Austria, and we don't have any others." They'd never had a camera. Now he wished they'd invested in one.

"Well, Henry, I am ready to go. Is Bill in the car?"

"No, he had a service call to make."

Mr. Engelmann put a hand on Henry's shoulder. They stood there for a moment, looking around the empty store.

"We sure did a lot here together," Henry finally said.

"That we did, Henry, that we did," Mr. Engelmann replied, patting Henry's shoulder. Mr. Engelmann bowed his head and prayed, "Dear Lord, thank you for this store, and the living it provided for Anna and me and Henry. It has been good to us. It has allowed us to serve You."

Mr. Engelmann clapped Henry's shoulder again as they moved towards the front door. But neither could leave. Not yet.

Henry turned to his beloved teacher. "Could we go out back one more time and sit on the old grey crate?"

"I guess great minds think alike, Henry, the very same thought entered my mind as well. Come, let us sit and warm our faces and spirits under the sun."

Henry only nodded, already struggling to hold back his emotions.

CHAPTER FORTY-TWO

IT COULDN'T HAVE been a more beautiful day. The sun shone as it hadn't in a long time as the two men stepped out back and headed for their favourite chair. A warm summer breeze cooled their faces. Henry recalled the first time he took a Dr. Pepper from the cooler and came out and sat on this very same crate. He'd loved it back then and he loved it even more now.

Mr. Engelmann lowered himself onto the grey crate next to him and patted Henry's knee, turning his face towards the sun, though really it was heavenward, Henry thought.

He knew he was right when Mr. Engelmann spoke.

"We've had a lot of good talks out here, Henry. My Anna loved to see us come out back and have our discussions. She knew how much I loved to sit and chat with you under the warm prairie sun."

"I've learned so *much* from you, Mr. Engelmann; I'll never forget what you've taught me in this classroom. I hope the sun has burned all those lessons in my mind. And I've always appreciated you taking me as I am, accepting me and making it feel safe to tell you almost anything."

Mr. Engelmann turned to him. "And I have learned much

from you, as well, Henry; we made a good partnership. And, yes, in relationships it is very important to accept one another —through love and caring both people grow. So many relationships fail because one tries to control the other, to change the other to suit themselves, being judgmental or fault-finding. This immediately closes the door to fruitful communication."

"Yeah, I see it all so clearly; Gary once told me he and his dad were always at odds with one another, and when he decided to just step back and accept his dad, their home was more peaceful. Each of them was able to begin looking at himself rather than defending their own point of view."

"Yes, Gary has learned a lot from the college he is attending."

"As have I in our classroom," Henry added.

Mr. Engelmann patted Henry's knee again. "It was good for the Lord to bring the both of you into each other's lives. Together, you are for the better as a result."

"Yeah, for sure."

Henry looked at his mentor and thought this might be a good time to ask him something he hoped Mr. Engelmann would not be offended by.

"Mr. Engelmann, you know at the end of the summer Gary and his friend Jane are going to Edmonton and then Toronto to prepare for an eventual trip to India, right?"

"Yes, he shared with me that he wants to do mission work for a year or two before going into the priesthood."

"Well, you know how close Gary and Mrs. Engelmann were...?"

"Yes, they had a special bond as you did with my Anna too."

"I hope you won't be disappointed that I'm suggesting this but I was wondering if I could give Mrs. Engelmann's Bible to Gary, to take with him as a reminder of her love and care for him—well, *our* love and care for him, too—it really is such a special gift to me, but somehow I feel called to give it to him."

Mr. Engelmann looked at Henry and put an arm around his shoulder. "Henry, Henry, Henry, it is the Lord, and perhaps Anna too, who is touching your heart. To give something up that we love and treasure for another is a blessing. It's a sign of the true friendship between you and Gary. Yes, you have my blessing to give Anna's Bible to him. I know how much he will appreciate it. He loved Anna very much too."

"Yeah, I know he did. Thank you, Mr. Engelmann, for understanding."

"Well," Mr. Engelmann said, "let me share something with you. Anna was torn as to who she should give the Bible to, you or Gary. She always considered you our son, though, and wanted you to have something to remember us by when you left the store after Grade 12. So giving it to Gary will not go against her wishes either. And since I am going into seminary, I would like to give you *my* Bible."

"Geez, are you sure, Mr. Engelmann? That would be great! But what will *you* read? You need it, don't you?"

"I will receive a new one from the church. It will soon be marked up like my old one and serve as a reminder of my new life in service to the Lord."

"Well, thanks a lot, Mr. Engelmann! I know how much you treasure it."

"And now you know how much I treasure you." Mr. Engelmann patted Henry's hand, resting on the crate next to him.

They were silent for a few moments and then Henry spoke. "I'll always remember the day you told me the meaning of your family name. 'Angel man' is so true and fitting; you've always been a guardian angel to me."

Mr. Engelmann patted Henry's hand again, "Thank you Henry."

"And you've always walked in a manner that glorifies God. You've been such a big influence on me."

"And you have been both Anna's and my greatest joy. We were so blessed the day you came into our lives."

This time Henry reached over and patted his teacher's knee, thanking him. The mutual gesture of love and respect brought a smile and a soft chuckle, despite their teary eyes.

Henry wiped his cheek with the back of his hand and went

on to say, "You know, Mr. Engelmann, about angels? A thought came to me this morning when I was reading Matthew 18:10."

"Ah yes, 'See that you despise not one of these little ones; for I say to you, that their angels in heaven always see the face of my Father who is in heaven.'"

"Yeah, that's it exactly, Mr. Engelmann! As I thought about that scripture saying that angels always see the face of God, I prayed especially hard that I do His will and walk with integrity like you. I wouldn't want my guardian angel to have an unhappy or disappointed face that God sees because of something I'm doing wrong. This may sound childish, but I want Jesus to always see my guardian angel with a happy face."

"You are developing a closer relationship with Jesus and your protector, Henry. The deeper meaning of scripture is coming into your awareness. That is a good sign you are communicating with the Lord. You have grown much, Henry; there is little else for me teach you."

"You were right about my mom and dad too, that God's divine providence would work things out in their lives. I've never seen them happier and I'm so grateful! They hug and kiss a lot more, Dad shares his feelings with Mom and me, they walk down the street holding hands and Dad isn't ten feet in front of Mom like he used to be, and Dad even has us saying the rosary together each night! And, most important of all, Mr. Engelmann, I don't see the hurt in my mom's eyes anymore, she's completely forgiven Dad and he seems so at peace too."

"Praise the Lord!" Mr. Engelmann responded. "He turns everything into such good. It is good that you have seen this and understand the Lord's workings, His divine providence."

"Yeah, when it first happened I thought for sure that was it for our family. That was all she wrote. I was so afraid and unsure."

"You saw only one piece of the puzzle, Henry, while God saw the whole puzzle. He saw that out of this trial your father's heart would change and that he would grow to be much stronger. He saw your mother growing in forgiveness and their relationship becoming stronger."

"It took years to happen and I wouldn't even have noticed it as God's divine providence if you hadn't pointed it out to me."

"All God's purposes are fulfilled in due time."

Henry nodded.

"That is how the Lord works," Mr. Engelmann continued. "It takes time for us to grow in character, faith, strength and trust. It does not happen overnight. And, as you say, we don't even see it happen until one day, like now, we are back in the light, through the trial and amazed to see what the Lord has done!"

"Well, this has all sure helped increase my trust in Jesus."

"That is good, Henry! This helps to increase your faith and gives you something to draw on when other difficulties arise. And there will be future trials in your life, Henry. God is in the business of building character, creating strong people who can withstand the storms of life, warriors who work with Him for the salvation of all mankind.

"Always remember that God never abandons you. Remember this experience when you walk in the shadows or darkness of life and God seems distant or taking forever to solve your problem or heal your crisis. He is there working, bringing good out of whatever dilemma you face. Never forget the beautiful treasures He brought into your family when all seemed so dark.

"I've said this before, Henry, but it is worth repeating. Welcome trials into your life and trust Jesus—you will remain at peace and you will come out stronger each time. When times are good and the sun is shining, we think we have no need of God. It is the wise man who trusts and loves and prays to God regardless of the season, the time of day or how good his life is at the time. When we do this we are always prepared and ready to do the work of the Lord and accept His will in our lives because He loves us, wants what is best for us and wants us to become a warrior for Him."

"Anna was a warrior...I mean, Mrs. Engelmann always worked for Jesus?"

"Yes! She was such an influence on others, Henry, especially me. I would not be the man you see today if not for her example and love. She taught me much in developing a close relationship with Jesus. Anna was so close to the Lord, Henry, she wore Him on her skin."

Wow, a relationship can't get any closer than that.

Henry couldn't help but feel lucky to have been part of the Engelmanns', to have learned so much and felt such love and acceptance. And Mr. Engelmann's teaching on divine providence, Henry still couldn't get over that.

"God's divine providence is such an amazing thing, Mr. Engelmann, how can He be everywhere like that at the same time, helping people all over the world?"

"I have thought about that as well, Henry. It is a mystery, and as I said before, a miracle of the first order. But I finally wondered if God's Holy Spirit wasn't a bit like electricity."

"What do you mean?"

"Well, let's use the city of Regina for example, close to a hundred and ten thousand people. Now, electricity is a mystery to me as well and yet man has figured out how to harness it and make it available to all the homes in the city at the same time. And continuously, too. It provides heat and power for each person. They can, at any time, plug in a toaster, a radio, a fan and everyone in the entire city can do the same and at the same time too. Anyone can turn on a light or shut it off at the flick of a switch. The power or electricity is available to the whole city at any time, even though we cannot see it or understand it.

"Now think of God and His Holy Spirit as a source that provides power. Not only to our city but to everyone in the entire world. He is there in every residence too, but the real home He occupies is the mind and heart and soul of every person. At any time His love, His 'electricity' is available to anyone. They can turn it off and remain in the darkness or, with the flick of a switch in their mind or heart or soul, enter the light. He is always available to hear our prayers or intercessory petitions or to work His divine providence. It is a wise person who always stays connected and remains in His light!" Mr. Engelmann raised his eyebrows and winked, then quickly added, "And do not forget there is another spirit assigned by the Lord to us—one we spoke of earlier: our guardian angel. He protects our soul and body in both ordinary and miraculous ways every moment of our lives. In this way too the Lord sees and watches us, as you said before; angels always have their eyes on their Lord at the same time as they watch over us. In any case, Henry, that is the best explanation I can offer."

"Wow! That's pretty good, Mr. Engelmann—excellent way to describe it! I guess you've figured out just about everything there is to know!"

But Mr. Engelmann was quick to correct him.

"No Henry, only the Lord knows all things. But I do pray for wisdom each and every day to know the will of God so I may serve Him completely."

That triggered another question.

"Can angels see into the future, Mr. Engelmann? Do they know what is going to happen in my life and…?" Henry paused.

And…what? Mr. Engelmann wondered what Henry had stopped short of asking. He had an idea but thought it best to wait for Henry to express his heart and simply answer the first part of his question in the meantime.

"No, Henry, I do not believe that angels can see into the future—only God can, unless He chooses to reveal it to them. However, angels, like humans, can predict the future on the basis of cause. For example, if you mail a letter, I can predict it will be delivered in the future. Or if you say you are going to lie out in the hot sun for the afternoon, I can predict that you will come in either very tanned or very burned.

"Angels have a much greater intellect than humans, though. They can grasp a complicated concept and understand it at once, whereas humans have to study it and slowly learn about it in stages as they develop, grasping a little bit at a time. Having said that, I would expect that angels have far greater predictive powers about the future than we do. Why do you ask?"

"Well, Mr. Engelmann, while I am at peace in my relationship with Julean, Jenny and I had such a strong spiritual connection I just can't seem to shake this feeling of being tied to her, even though we've been apart for so long. Will it ever go away? If angels can see into the future, maybe I could pray they'll give me a sign of what will happen or whether I'll always have this feeling..." Henry's words trailed off.

Mr. Engelmann reflected carefully on Henry's lingering concern. If he himself had not been there that morning in the store and felt the energy between them or seen the aura that had surrounded those two, the way their gazes locked into one another, he would brush it aside as a figment of Henry's imagination. *Something* had happened, but what?

Mr. Engelmann shrugged. "All I can say is that God has a reason and only time will reveal what it is. Maybe for now Henry, your prayer to your guardian angel should be that he help you to accept this feeling as part of your life, and perhaps help to lessen it too. That is all I can suggest. I will pray for you too."

"Well, I guess I *have* sort of accepted it and I've definitely moved on with Julean, but maybe Jenny will always be a strong part of me. You know, my first love and all."

For the first time, Mr. Engelmann wasn't sure how to counsel his student any further. He had never witnessed anything like it. *The power of human attraction,* he thought, *or was it something more than human love?*

Henry interrupted Mr. Engelmann's thoughts. "How do angels work in our lives, anyway? Has anyone ever seen one?"

Mr. Engelmann answered the second question first. "Yes, Henry, the Blessed Virgin saw the Angel Gabriel when he appeared to her to announce that she would be the mother of Jesus."

"Oh yeah, I forgot about that."

"And an angel appeared to St. Paul when he was in prison and freed him of his chains. Angels have appeared to many prophets in the Old Testament and many saints have written of encounters with their celestial protectors. Too many to name.

"And regarding your first question, as you already know, they guide us, protect us, prompt us, inspire us, pray for us and go to the Lord on our behalf to ask forgiveness of our transgressions …the list is endless Henry. The more we acknowledge them and become aware of them, the closer to them we become. They are our best friends and allies, our unseen link to God.

"And as you said earlier, since they constantly see the face of God, they are filled with adoration, love and radiance, all the while attending to us. They are examples of what we might become, and with the insight you shared earlier, it seems to me that perhaps your angel is beginning to rub off on you!

"You also said that you thought it was childish to want your angel to reflect a happy face to God on your behalf. And you are on exactly the right track. The Lord *wants* us to become like little children—childlike, rather than childish—adopting their character, for theirs is the kingdom of heaven. And what are the traits of children? They are honest, kind, quick to forgive, trusting, with no false pride or pretended humility and so on. *That* is what the Lord wants us to become."

Mr. Engelmann studied Henry and asked, "These questions about angels, have they got to do only with Jenny and Julean?"

"Oh, not really, but if you're concerned about Julean and me, don't be. I love her very much and feel closer to her with each passing day. We're going steady now, and every now and then there are hints that marriage may even be in our future."

"Yes, I see it in your eyes like you see the renewed happiness in your mother's. The Lord is working His healing in your life as well. Julean is such a lovely girl, Henry, inside and out, and she comes often to church with you."

"Yeah, she really likes the ritual of the mass and seems to be drawn to the communion part of it. You know, when the bread and wine turn into the body and blood of Jesus. She finds that so intimate and wonders what it would feel like to receive the Host herself."

Mr. Engelmann nodded. "Transubstantiation is a miracle that occurs at the consecration of every mass. And, yes, I agree, there is a special closeness in receiving the Lord at communion. Anyway, it is good she is showing an interest in the faith, especially if you two are contemplating marriage."

"Yeah, she believes in a strong family and that there should be no divisions in the marriage or in the parenting of children."

"She is very wise, Henry."

The sun had travelled further to the west and was beginning to hide behind Mr. Falhman's large elm tree. The growing coolness brought with it a sadness that pricked Henry's skin. The time to go was drawing near, but Henry sensed that neither of them wanted to leave.

Henry looked at his teacher. Silent tears were streaming from his closed eyes; the sun glistening off the wet trails on his cheeks. How many times in the past had the sun dried the tears from their faces?

He is such a wise and holy man, so close to Jesus. What he said about Anna applies to him, too, he also wears Jesus on his skin. 'Angel man' is so fitting; he has the very same traits of the angels he describes.

His beloved mentor must be feeling so much, Henry thought. Leaving the store, his home; thoughts of Anna and the many talks he and Henry had shared now slipping into the past and becoming mere memory. *Clearing out of the rest of his stuff this morning must have been hard on him.*

Mr. Engelmann put his hands on either side of himself as if readying to push himself up. And as Henry thought of all the talks and laughter and good times and sorrowful times they had had together out here in the classroom of life, he lowered his own and place one on top of Mr. Engelmann's. A surge of love passed through them and Henry lifted his head to the sky, closed his eyes and wept along with his teacher.

The last sliver of light from the sun slipped down, completely hidden now behind the neighbour's elm tree.

Darkness had suddenly fallen. Both men opened their eyes with a start, looked at one another and smiled.

"I was just contemplating, Henry, how the Lord in His infinite wisdom made us so we grow into loving people and know our ultimate goal, where true happiness lies. Without sorrow, we would never appreciate or understand joy. If we never had problems and trials, we would never grow in character. If we never walked in darkness we would never taste the happiness of the light. If we never experienced hatred, we would not fully understand forgiveness and love. And even the most beautiful times in the world—times like this that come close to what heaven must be like—even these times, too, must come to an end so as to motivate us all the more to want to be with Him, to have everlasting joy."

Mr. Engelmann slipped his hand from under Henry's, then patted Henry's hand and squeezed it. "*Ich liebe dich.* I love you as my own son, Henry."

"And you'll always be a second father to me. I love you, Mr. Engelmann." Henry's voice cracked on the words.

Mr. Engelmann pushed himself up off the crate. Henry did the same and was surprised Mr. Engelmann didn't complain about aches and pains from sitting so long. Ever since he announced he was entering the priesthood, he had become more youthful, energized by the new life he would lead serving the Master.

Henry hugged his mentor. A moment or two later, Mr. Engelmann broke from the warm embrace and, arm still around Henry's shoulders, walked with him to the back door.

"We shall have more such talks, Henry. This is not the end. You will come to me in confession and visit me in the rectory and we shall continue our friendship. I suspect you will become *my* mentor someday soon!"

"I don't think that'll ever happen, Mr. Engelmann."

"In any case, I am happy that you are closer to your father and talking more with him. I encourage you to do a lot of that. There is so much joy in a father and son sharing as we have done."

With one last look at the old weathered grey crate, their "classroom," they stepped inside. Henry picked up Mr. Engelmann's suitcase from behind the counter. It was light, as if there was nothing in it. Henry smiled. His teacher needed no moving van to carry his worldly possessions. Most everything of value he had accumulated over the years he held in his heart.

Henry opened the front door. Mr. Engelmann followed, at the last moment turning back to flip the sign on the door over. CLOSED, it said.

Henry set Mr. Engelmann's suitcase on the passenger side of the back seat then opened the front door for Mr. Engelmann.

"Thank you, Henry," he said, getting in.

Henry drove a block down Victoria Avenue then made a u-turn and headed back the way they'd come. As they passed, their eyes were drawn to the store on the corner.

ENGELMANN'S GROCERY STORE & CONFECTIONERY

To a passerby it might look like any other corner store. Yet those who knew it knew what a service of love and friendship the store had provided to the people of the neighbourhood. Gary was right when he'd said the store was more like a church. Mr. Engelmann and Henry waved goodbye as they sped by.

Five minutes later, Henry pulled up in front of St. Mary's Rectory. They stared at the entrance to Mr. Engelmann's new, temporary home. The lawn was well manicured. The concrete walkway led up to a dark oak door. The façade of the rectory was brown brick and blended well with the main part of the church. Such a dichotomy in residences—a grocery store to a church. And yet, would it really be such a difference?

Henry stepped out of the car and walked around to Mr. Engelmann's side, intending to open the door for him. But before he reached the passenger side, Mr. Engelmann opened the door and got out. Mr. Engelmann didn't want to be served anymore. He was there to serve.

"Well, Henry," he said, looking towards the rectory, "if I have to move, what better place to have as a new home than the Lord's house?"

"What a great thought, Mr. Engelmann."

At that moment, Father Connelly opened the door to the rectory and came out. He waved. "Welcome, David."

Mr. Engelmann smiled. "Hello, Father."

Father Connelly came to the car, shook hands with Mr. Engelmann, then turned to Henry. "Hello, Henry. Come. Bring David's suitcase. Is there anything else?"

"Nope, this is it," Henry replied.

"Good. Come in, then. We will have a feast tonight, David. I asked our cook, Millie, to make the best German dish she knows."

"Ah, thank you, Father."

Father Connelly turned to Henry, "And you too, Henry."

"Oh, no thank you, Father. I'm meeting my girlfriend. We're going to a movie later, and we're off to Saskatoon in the morning to look for a place to stay. I still have to get ready."

"Well, please come and visit. This is a home just like yours, Henry. We're ordinary people just like your family, so please feel free to come, anytime."

"Thank you, Father." Henry turned to Mr. Engelmann. "Well. I'll see you, Mr. Engelmann."

"Goodbye, Henry."

Henry made his way halfway down the walk and turned.

Silhouetted in the doorway, Mr. Engelmann raised a hand in farewell.

Memories of his first day of school came to Henry's mind. He'd been so frightened and had not wanted to leave his mother's side and the safe world he had known until then. He wondered if Mr. Engelmann was feeling the same way now.

As he opened the driver's door, Henry looked up to see Father Connelly close the rectory door, severing the last tie Mr. Engelmann had to his old world and marking the start of his new journey.

CHAPTER FORTY-THREE

"PLEASE SEND AN ambulance to Montgomery Plaza, corner of Lyon and Sparks! Eighteenth floor. I just found my employer on the floor of his office. He may have had a heart attack. Please hurry!"

Elaine acknowledged the operator's promise to contact the hospital immediately then hung up the phone and ran back into Mr. Sarsky's office.

When Ted hadn't answered her knock, she'd entered the office to find him lying on the floor next to the liquor cabinet, the odour of liquor assaulting her as she'd bent to check his pulse. She'd picked the glass up off the floor and set it on the corner of his desk, then ran to the phone to call for help.

With the assurance that an ambulance would soon be on its way, Elaine rolled Ted on his back and loosened his tie. After a few moments, he began to moan and stir. She stood and going to the liquor cabinet, she screwed the cap back on the bottle of whiskey on the counter, then pushed it to the back of the cabinet and closed both doors. She thought about giving him some gum or a candy to mitigate the smell of alcohol on his breath, but thought he might choke and decided to leave it.

He moaned some more and Elaine knelt beside him again.

He blinked. "W-what happened?" Ted asked, looking up at her, confused, holding a hand to his head.

"You passed out, Mr. Sarsky. I thought you might have had a heart attack. I've called for an ambulance. They should be here any minute."

"Oh, Elaine, you di'n't really, didja?"

Elaine stared at him. He was actually going to be *upset* with her now? She couldn't find her voice so she nodded instead.

"Call 'em back ri' away and cancel it! I'm *fine*. Jus' overworked. I'll take a few days off."

Elaine had just put her hand on the phone when it rang.

"Mackurcher and Company, Elaine speaking. How may I help you? Oh, yes, just a moment, please." She covered the mouthpiece with her hand. "It's the front desk, Mr. Sarsky. The ambulance attendants are in the lobby and the commissionaire wants to know if it's okay to send them up?"

"No, no, tell 'em it was a false alarm or somethin'. Just cancel the whole thing. *Please.*"

"Hello? Yes, I've checked and everything seems to be fine here. Apparently, there's been some mistake. Everything is fine. Please extend our apologies to the attendants ... Yes, everything's fine, thank you."

Elaine hung up then turned back to Mr. Sarsky. Ted stared back at her. His pallor frightened her. It was like all the life had drained out of him. She watched him make a huge effort to regain his composure.

"Thank you, Elaine. I appreciate your concern," he finally said, propping himself up on his elbows, then rising to his feet. His diction had improved. "I, uh, I think I *will* take that time off and get some rest. I've been under a lot of pressure lately."

Elaine stared at him, not knowing what to say. He was an alcoholic and needed help, but it wasn't her place to suggest anything to him or even dare talk to him about it unless he brought it up, according to the brochure on alcoholism she'd picked up at the doctor's office last year.

She'd just been rereading it the other day after she'd come across it in the drawer where she kept new typewriter ribbons. It was amazing that Mr. Sarsky had held out all these months. No, years. He'd been showing symptoms of the advanced stages of the disease for so long now. Ted needed help desperately, but until he finally admitted he had a serious problem and was ready to do something about it, she could only be supportive.

"That will be all, Elaine," he said as she stood there, frozen.

"Yes, o-of course, Mr. Sarsky. If there's anything you need…?"

"No, I'm fine, really, thank you again for your concern."

It was only as she closed the office door behind her that she realized her blouse was soaking wet. It took her a full ten minutes to regain her own composure and refocus on the report she was preparing for the next board meeting.

Mr. Sarsky *really* needed help. Should she call one of the board members? One of the other executives? She was split in two; her loyalty at war between her president and the company, her employer. Everyone was depending on Mr. Sarsky to pull the business out of the proverbial muck, and if business did not improve soon, everyone's job would be in jeopardy.

Indecision weighing heavily upon her, she began to type, hitting letters that formed no words. She was so flustered she typed for at least a minute before realizing nothing made any sense—not on the paper in front of her and certainly not in the whole bizarre situation she found herself in. Here she was on the eighteenth floor of a huge corporation, occupying the office that was the heart and core of the company, but lacking any leadership or guidance. Suddenly Elaine realized just how easy it might be to start drinking to relax, to get away from it all.

It's a good thing I have an addiction to the Lord instead.

TED STOOD IN front of the open liquor cabinet searching for the bottle of whiskey he'd started. He finally found it hidden at the back of the cabinet. As he set the bottle before him, the world spun around and he grabbed the side of the cabinet until the black spots before him settled. Then he took the cap off the bottle and poured himself a tall premium whisky, which he drank in one gulp. He relaxed the moment the alcohol hit his bloodstream. He put the glass and the bottle back into the cabinet and closed the door. *Good thing it was just Elaine.*

Straightening his suit jacket, he walked over to the window that overlooked the park below. He'd always loved to watch the arrival of spring and then summer. The view of the canal and park were beautiful. So much new life, the trees so green and the flowers in full bloom. All signs of new beginnings and yet inside it felt as if he were dying. He was no longer the man he'd been. The Ted Sarsky who stood for honesty, reliability, high standards and impeccable character was dead.

He had let the board, his colleagues and the hundreds of employees who relied on his leadership, down, but most of all he'd let his daughter down. She had trusted him implicitly with her heart and soul and he'd reneged on that trust. He was miserable. An indescribable self-disappointment was lodged in the core of his being and ached unmercifully.

How had he allowed this to happen?

The scenic view before him offered little relief. It did make him think, however, of his estate and how beautiful the grounds there were too, and yet he never took the time to enjoy the place like Jenny did. He was glad they had given refuge to Tammy and her baby. He guessed he could take *some* credit for that.

It reminded him of the early years of his marriage when Jenny was born and he'd spent more time with her, as a father should with his daughter. Then he got busy at work. Too busy. But Tammy's baby took Ted back to those early days of raising Jenny. If only he'd realized then the importance of his role as a father. But it was too late now, all in the past.

And what about Jenny's baby, Camilla? If Jenny had kept her, he would be a grandpa. With Chloe in the house, Ted sometimes imagined her as Jenny's little girl, thinking of what it would have been like to come home to another little member of the family.

But that chance to give his whole family a new start had

passed them by, the opportunity whisked away with one poor decision after another.

Ted no longer dared even look at the landscape painting hanging on his office wall. He had pulled off the towel he'd hidden it under previously; it hadn't kept the angels locked away in their letters where they should be, hadn't kept them confined to the wall safe behind the painting at all. For months now, the angels were always out, streaking across the sky or sitting on the clouds in the painting, reminding him of his wrongdoings. He thought of getting another painting, but then the angels would probably just come out on that one, too. Ted kept most of the company's important papers in his desk drawer now rather than in the safe; he was afraid to go near it. He couldn't help but feel he was being submitted to some sort of torture.

The punishment was unbearable. Oh, if only he had confessed it all before things had gotten so out of hand. How many times had he gone over the scene in his mind? He'd take Jenny by the hand and they would stroll to her beloved gazebo on the estate and have a heart-to-heart, bringing everything out into the open. He had rehearsed it over and over so many times, he had his speech completely memorized.

He wondered if he should go home early today. He still felt woozy from the fainting spell. It was a beautiful day and Jenny and her friend and the baby would probably be out enjoying the sun and flowers. Yes, perhaps this just might be the day he and Jenny would take a stroll to the gazebo and have a little talk.

WHEN TED CAME home, Edith was outside on the patio drinking a glass of lemonade.

"Oh, Ted! You startled me. What are you doing home so early?"

"I wasn't feeling well and thought I'd come home and enjoy the afternoon with my family. Where's Jen?"

"James wanted her to go downtown to do some shopping. She shouldn't be too much longer; they left first thing this morning."

"Are Tammy and the baby up?"

"The baby is sleeping. However, Mrs. Anderson is over; she and Tammy are having a talk on the west side of the grounds. I think they might be working things out and Tammy will be going home."

Ted looked across the expanse of lawn and saw Tammy and her mother sitting on a bench near the new wildflower garden.

"Well, I think I'll change into something more casual and come out and join you. I'd like to spend some time with the girls today."

Edith gazed at her husband, not sure what to think. He looked so tired. She was glad he'd come home; he certainly could use some rest.

Nightmares often kept him awake half the night.

"So, which suit looks best on me, the charcoal grey or the navy blue?"

"They both look good on you, James. You're such a handsome devil." Jenny winked and then decided. "I think the grey gives you more of that executive look and it goes so well with your black hair...yes, definitely the grey one."

Turning to the salesman, James asked, "How long has this suit been on the rack?"

"Oh, a week or so. I'm not sure."

"Have many people have tried it on?"

"Perhaps a few, sir."

"Do you have any of this size in storage?"

"No, all of our stock is out. Is there a concern?"

"I don't like things that have been handled by others. I prefer them brand new; do you know what I mean?"

"I assure you, we take the greatest care in keeping our clothes perfectly clean."

"Well, let me try the trousers on and see how they fit."

James took the pants from the salesman and went to the change room. When he came out Jenny and the salesman were having a friendly chat about what college he was going to.

They were enjoying themselves too much, in his opinion.

"Hey, bud," James called the salesman over.

The salesman, however, was so engrossed with Jenny he didn't hear him, much to James' displeasure.

So James got louder. "Hey, you! Whatever your name is! Come here."

This time the young man heard him and rushed over. James took him into the change room and reprimanded him for getting too friendly with his girl.

Jenny could see in the reflection of the floor-length mirror that James was giving the salesman heck about something. She hoped it wasn't about her.

The salesman came out of the back and rushed passed her.

"What were you talking to Don about?" Jenny asked, coming over to where James was flicking imaginary lint off the new trousers.

"Oh? Is it 'Don' already?"

"Oh, James, what's wrong?"

"I simply told him to tell the manager that if they'd dry clean the suit I'd take it."

"James, really! People try jackets on for only a few minutes. I'm sure it's perfectly fine. Its just like the TV you got for your room this morning. The floor model was fine, but you made the salesman get one that was unopened from the warehouse. Aren't you going a little overboard with this cleanliness thing?"

"It's just that I like to have things brand-spanking new, Jenny," James tried to make it a joke, but he was dead serious. "I don't want it if it's been touched by someone else. That TV had fingerprints all over it."

"Oh, James, don't be so silly!"

But the more Jenny thought about it, the more she realized it was beyond silly. It was as if he had smacked her across the face. What would he think if he knew she had been raped? Something about James had always kept her from being comfortable enough to share her past with him. Perhaps this was what her instincts had been warning her about.

WHEN JENNY GOT home, her parents were sitting outside at the patio table.

"Hi, Mom, Dad—what are you doing home so early?"

"I wasn't feeling well and decided to take the afternoon off to spend some time with my two favourite people."

"Well, that's great. Where's Tammy?"

"Her mom was over earlier and they had a good talk. I think Tammy and the baby might be going home this weekend. Apparently Tammy is the youngest of five children. Mrs. Anderson is working now and doesn't want to be tied down raising more children but their social worker thinks the government can help out a bit with the expenses and providing funds for Tammy to get a part-time babysitter."

"And I'll always be there to help out, too. Oh, I'm going to *miss* her if she goes home. She's been like a sister. We have so many good talks at night when Chloe goes to sleep."

"Well, it's a good thing summer holidays are here. Tammy will have time to prepare for the fall. She still plans on going to college, right? It will be hard, but others have done it before her."

"You can tell Tammy we'll be here for her anytime, Jenny," offered Ted.

"So, how was your outing with James?"

"Oh, Mom, he drives me crazy sometimes! He's got such a fetish about things being clean. Everything has to be spotless."

"Frankly, Jen, I like his impeccable appearance. His shirts are always crisp and freshly laundered, his shoes always shined; to me it's a sign that he cares about his personal appearance."

"There's more to it than that, Mom—there can't even be a fingerprint on anything and he wants everything to be new and untouched."

"Well, cleanliness is next to godliness, they say. I think he's a fine young man, a very good catch, and if you end up marrying him you'll just have to be a super housecleaner," Edith joked.

Jenny wasn't so sure it was something to laugh about. Perhaps she was being unfair, judgmental and too critical—but then again...

"What do you think of James, Dad?"

Her father had drifted away. When he didn't respond, she shook his arm. "Dad, did you hear me? What do you think of James? We're thinking about getting married and—"

"Hm? Sorry, Jenny. James? Well, he's a fine, handsome young man, but you're still too young to be getting serious. He's really the only boy you've been out with except for that boy…back in Regina," Ted said hesitantly, avoiding Edith's eyes, and quickly adding, "What about all the boys who keep phoning here? Have you ever considered going out with any of them?"

"Oh, sure. It's just that they all seem so immature compared to James and I do love his interest in business. He's at the top of his class in university and he keeps telling me how his dad and the board members are amazed by his understanding of the business and his instincts in decision-making that have resulted in incredible profits for the company. His father is very proud of him, and can't wait for him to complete college and take over."

"He *is* good at business, I'll grant him that. It's just that he seems a little overly ambitious. If you think *our* family life is stifled by my work, you may find life with James even lonelier."

"He tells me when we get married he'll structure his time more efficiently and not take his job home at the end of the day."

"I've said that myself many times, Jenny. Once you're married it's hard to change a habit—even harder if it's ingrained into your character. My advice to you is to go out with other boys. It's going to take you three years to get your arts and science degree, four if you enter education, so there's no hurry, sweetheart."

"And if you want my opinion," Edith chimed in, "I think James is a fine young man. He comes from a fine home and I'm sure you'll never lack for a thing."

"I know that, Mom. He promises me the world; a beautiful home, clothes, my own car, anything my heart desires. But really, all I want is to be happy, to really love someone and *be* loved…" Jenny's words trailed off.

Edith and Ted gazed at their daughter, each knowing full well who Jenny was thinking about.

"I've never seen so many butterflies," Ted commented, shielding the sun from his eyes and changing the subject. "Reminds me of when you were young, Jenny; swarms of them used to follow you around."

"All of them angels singing to me. Carlos thinks they send messages of love too." Jenny stopped and looked at her parents, not sure if she should go there. Her mother tried so hard to discourage these kinds of thoughts. Instead Jenny said, "Most of them are monarchs that migrated here from Mexico. Carlos planted some milkweed plants on the grounds last year and that's what's attracting so many here this spring. The females lay their eggs on the leaves of the milkweed plant and you can see the tiny eggs. Lots have grown into caterpillars already and are getting ready to turn into butterflies. I've been fascinated watching them day to day."

"Well, I'd like you to point them out to me, Jenny. In fact, I thought we could take a little stroll together through the grounds. Did Carlos show you the new wildflowers I asked him to plant?"

"Yes, I saw them—they're beautiful, Dad; especially the Baby Blue Eyes. I'd love to take a walk with you. We haven't done that for such a long time. In fact, I can't remember when we last did."

The phone rang.

"I'll get that," said Ted. He picked up his glass, took it into the kitchen and picked up the phone.

Jenny knew the glass her dad held wasn't filled with the lemonade her mom was drinking. Both she and her mom listened to Ted as his voice rose and became more defensive.

"No, Mr. Peakan, I'm fine, just taking today off … Yes, I have Jason and Ken, my best two negotiators on that contract … Yes, I'll be assisting them—I know how important the contracts are, I'm certain we'll get them signed … I see. Yes I understand …No, I won't need anymore time off, I'm fine. Talk to you tomorrow."

They heard Ted hang up the phone then the familiar sound

of a cupboard opening followed by the clink of a bottle against a glass.

Edith shook her head, "Don't keep your hopes up for that walk, honey."

Jenny gazed at her mother, sadness growing in her eyes.

"I see Daddy trying so hard lately to be more involved with us. I just wish things were the way they used to be before we moved here, Mom. Daddy worked hard then, too, but it didn't seem to be so hard on him. Lately, I have this feeling that there's something deep that's really bothering him. What do you suppose it could be, Mom?"

Edith gazed at her daughter, a lump growing hard in her throat and making it impossible to speak.

It was just as well; whatever she said would be far from the truth that she knew.

CHAPTER FORTY-FOUR

"DO YOU HAVE any wrapping paper, Mom?"

"I think there's some in the cupboard. Wrapping a gift for Julean?"

"No, for Gary. I'm going to give him Mrs. Engelmann's Bible."

Mary looked at her son, "Are you sure? That's such a beautiful gift she gave you. It was her most prized possession."

"Yeah, I know. But she loved Gary, too, and with him going away to do missionary work, I thought it would be a reminder of home and well, you know. And I already asked Mr. Engelmann if I could and he said that it was okay. He said someday he was going to give me his Bible."

Mary handed a roll of patterned bluish-coloured wrapping paper to Henry. "Well, that's awfully nice of you, Henry. I'm sure Gary will be thrilled to receive it. When's he leaving and where's he going again?"

"He's leaving tomorrow night by plane. The archbishop is sending Gary and his friend Jane to Edmonton until Christmas to work with the poor, like they did here last summer. But more importantly, they're going to take a course to prepare them for missionary work in poor countries. After Christmas they're going to Toronto to continue working in the poorer areas of the city until spring. The bishop thought they should maybe go to a place like Peru first before going to India. It might be too big a change for them to work in the slums of Calcutta right away."

"My gosh, that's really something for Gary to be doing. It's hard to believe your little friend from down the block grew up to be so committed to Jesus."

"Yeah, that's what I keep thinking. And the way he talks, that he wants to be with the poor, to love them and serve them and become their friend, to pray with them…" Henry's words trailed off in awe that he was talking that way about his *friend*.

Mary shook her head, "Yes, it is really something."

"Well, thanks for the wrapping paper, Mom."

Henry went to his room and sat at his desk. He picked up the Bible. He felt Mrs. Engelmann's warmth as he read what she had written to him: *To Henry, whom David and I, in our hearts, adopted as a son.*

A rush of love swept over him as it had when he had first read it. To be included as a member of their family was such an honour. He almost hesitated in signing the Bible to Gary. He and his friend were the fourth generation to receive it.

Henry picked up his pen and wrote a short note just beneath Mrs. Engelmann's words:

> *Gary,*
>
> *I want you to have this. Mrs. Engelmann loved you as much as she did me and considered you her son, too. May this Bible be a reminder of that love for you and know her spirit and guidance and protection will constantly be with you in your work for God. You're my very best friend, Gary, and I love you. I'm so proud to be your friend and brother in Christ.*
>
> Henry
June 29, 1960

Henry sat back and took a deep breath. The Bible had been such a meaningful gift for him and he knew Gary would appreciate it just as much.

Henry opened it to the plastic bookmark and read the passage Mrs. Engelmann had underlined, Isaiah 26:3. "Thou wilt keep him in perfect peace, whose mind is stayed on Thee."

That's a good one for Gary, Henry thought, but he didn't want to leave the marker there. He'd decided to keep it as a reminder of the Bible Mrs. Engelmann had given to him. And besides, it had the guardian angel prayer written on it; the one he had said almost every night since he'd met Jenny. He was still amazed that Mrs. Engelmann had said that prayer as well.

When Henry gazed at the image of the angel hovering over a boy and girl in harm's way, flashes of being with Jenny flooded his mind. The many days that summer they too had held hands like the children in the picture.

Henry reached for the letter near the back of the Bible trying to distract his thoughts. He opened it and read it through again. There were so many beautiful memories of his time spent with Mrs. Engelmann, reading to her, her presence in the store, her love.

Well, I'd better get this wrapped before I change my mind. Henry placed the Bible in the centre of a section of wrapping paper and began folding it around his precious gift. After it was wrapped he suddenly realized that the gift wrap, rather than enhancing the gift inside, somehow detracted from the message it held. The message he had gotten when he received it. Henry unwrapped the Bible and picked up the brown paper bag, still on the floor at the edge of his desk. He placed the Bible inside as Mr. Engelmann had when he'd given it to Henry.

"Yeah," he muttered, "No, pretension, no showiness, just humbly here to serve the poorest of the poor."

"THANKS FOR DRIVING me to the airport, Hank."

"No problem, Gary. I'd never have missed seeing you off."

Henry held the door to the Regina airport open for Gary. He

could see Jane and her parents waiting near the ticket counter. Henry still couldn't get over how normal Jane was. He still half expected her to be different somehow. Quieter, more reserved, holier-than-thou, but yet she there she was, a very attractive, outgoing girl just like other girls he knew. The only difference was she wore no makeup of any kind and her dress was always very modest.

"Hi, Jane," said Henry, wearing a broad smile.

"Hi Hank. I'd like you to meet my mom and dad, Tony and Edna Regier."

Henry shook their hands. "It's nice to meet you, Mrs. Regier, Mr. Regier. Jane told me you have a farm?"

"Yup, just outside of Kipling, a mile or so," replied Tony.

"I guess you're going to miss Jane, Mrs. Regier."

"Oh yes, we do already." Mrs. Regier squeezed Jane's hand.

Turning to Gary, Henry said, "Well ol' buddy, I'm sure gonna miss you too. Here, I have something for you."

Henry handed Gary the brown paper bag.

"I was wondering what you were carrying that for, Hank. Is it lunch for the trip?"

"No," Henry chuckled, "It's food all right, but not the kind you're thinking. You can open it up on the plane and let me know what you think when you write me."

"You sure have me curious now; I can't wait to open it."

"Well, I've got a date with Julean, so I'll leave you to say goodbye to your family."

Henry gave Gary a quick, hard hug. They pounded each other affectionately on the back and separated to stare at each other through blurry eyes.

"I'm sure gonna miss you, man."

"Me too, Hank. I'll keep you in my prayers."

Henry nodded, and waved at Jane and her parents, "See ya Jane, nice meeting you Mr. and Mrs. Regier."

Henry didn't really hear their reply. He strode away and then stopped, turning back to see his buddy quickly wave at him again. Henry returned the wave with all the love he could send.

"OH TAMMY, I hate to see you go. It was so nice having you stay with us. And I'll miss Chloe so much, too. Having you both here gave me a chance to see what life would have been like if I hadn't given Camilla away."

"Jenny," Tammy looked at her friend with compassion. "You would've been such a wonderful mother to Camilla, but you were too young to take on such a big responsibility. You can see how difficult it is for me."

Jenny sighed. "Yes, I know—it was the right thing for me to do. And I hope you don't mind the odd time I slipped and called Chloe Camilla by mistake."

"Of course not, Jenny. I completely understand. But I hope you're still willing to help me. I couldn't have done this without you and I am *very* thankful you helped me to decide to keep Chloe. I love her so much. Oh, and how much I would've re-gretted giving her up for adop— Oh Jenny! I'm sorry, I didn't mean..." Tammy gave up in embarrassment.

"Oh, Tammy, of *course* I understand what you mean and you don't ever have to worry about what you say to me. Just whatever's in your heart. I do with you all the time."

"Being here with you, talking and walking in the gardens has changed the way I think about nature and the soul and God. I didn't know you believed so strongly in angels."

"I'm glad I convinced you, Tammy. The more you acknowledge them, the more you'll be aware of them in your life. My guardian angel has helped me through so many difficulties."

"And I love the guardian angel prayer you taught me. I say it every night for Chloe, for her guardian angel to watch over her and forever be by her side. And you know, I've started to pray to Jesus again too."

"That's great, Tammy."

The girls smiled at each other with the wonder of it all.

The moment was broken by the toot of a car horn.

"I think Dad has everything packed and ready to drive you home. Are you sure you don't want me to come with you?"

"No, I think it's best I go back by myself with Chloe. I think

Mom will be more comfortable with just me and the baby to deal with."

"Your mom will love Chloe in no time, she's so adorable."

"I know she will too. I just wish Robbie would've come to see her already. The thought that he doesn't love or care for Chloe or…me—"

"Oh, Tammy, I know how hard that is on you. Perhaps it's for the best. But time will tell…" Jenny's words trailed off.

Tammy gave Jenny a huge, warm hug. "You're such a good friend. I love you dearly."

"I love you too, Tammy. Please call me tonight and let me know how things are going. If it's okay, I'll come over this weekend."

"I'm sure it'll be fine."

Jenny walked Tammy and the baby out to the car.

Edith was out on the front steps, giving Ted a list of items to pick up on the way home.

"Thank you again, Mrs. Sarsky."

Edith smiled and gave Tammy a hug. "We'll miss you both. I never realized how much I'd enjoy having a little one around again." She looked at Jenny and then quickly away.

Tammy got into the car and waved as she and Ted drove off.

Jenny and her mother went in to the quiet stillness of the living room. They didn't speak and their sudden awareness of the silence in the huge house amplified loud and clear what they had missed.

CHAPTER FORTY-FIVE

T HE PHONE RANG, jarring Henry from a deep sleep.
His mother knocked on his bedroom door. There was
panic in her voice and the rapidity of her knock.

"Henry? Henry, wake up!"

"What's is it, Mom? Come in."

She opened the door enough to poke her head in.

"Henry, Mrs. Kartusch just called. She says a big machine is
on the lot beside Engelmann's Grocery Store and they told her
that they were getting ready to tear it down."

*Why couldn't they have waited another week when Mr. Engel-
mann would be in Gravelbourg.*

"Phone Mr. Engelmann and let him know. He might want
to see it."

"Do you really think so?"

"Yeah, for sure, Mom. We should at least let him know and
then he can decide for himself."

While Henry quickly got dressed he strained to hear his
mother's conversation with the rectory.

"Good morning, Father. Is David up yet? ... Oh, he did? ...
When? ... Oh, Mrs. Kartusch phoned him already, too ... Yes,

she just let us know ... Okay ... Well, we're going, too. We'll see him there. 'Bye, Father."

Henry landed in the kitchen as she replaced the receiver.

"David's already there."

"Well, let's go, Mom. I want to see it, too, before it goes down. Is Dad coming?"

"No, he's on a service call. He left an hour ago."

"I better call Julean and tell her I'll probably be late."

The grinding of the Caterpillar's chains greeted them when they arrived at the store. Mr. Engelmann and several other neighbours were watching the demolition from the other side of the street.

"They sure didn't waste much time getting rid of it, did they, Mom?"

"No, they certainly didn't."

They waited for the light to turn green and hurried across the street. Henry studied Mr. Engelmann as he approached. His mentor stared at the store and the huge mechanical monster about to destroy what had been his livelihood and home for almost twenty years. Henry thought he was stunned.

What was going through his mind?

"'Morning, Mr. Engelmann."

"Good morning, Henry. Mary. Come to watch, too?"

"Yes, David, we had to take one last look. I see we're not the only ones."

More and more people had gathered. At least two of the spectators were snapping pictures. Henry made a mental note of who they were so he could get copies for his scrapbook.

The Caterpillar inched its way towards the store, raising its bucket as it approached, looking for the right spot to attack. The operator's strategy appeared to be to knock down the second storey first, then work his way lower. However, as the Cat pushed, the main floor began to buckle and part of the second storey threatened to fall out towards the machine, almost as if to ward it off from going any further.

The operator backed off and studied the structure for a moment, then manoeuvred the Cat around the back and disappeared around the south end towards Mr. Engelmann's school of life. Henry had a sudden impulse to get the old grey crate and save it as it held so many memories for him.

Neither he nor Mr. Engelmann made any attempt to cross the street so they could see what the machine was up to behind the building, like some of the other spectators had done. Neither of them could bear to see their classroom go.

The sound of the Caterpillar motor grew louder as the engine revved. They held their breath, anticipating the store would suddenly fall in. They saw the building shift, but still it didn't collapse, almost as if it didn't want to fall. The Cat inched its way over to the north side of the building, prodding it, looking for just the right vulnerable spot that would cause it to cave in on itself. The Cat eventually appeared on the south side again as it worked its way back. The building showed more signs of weakening towards imminent collapse.

Barricades blocked off traffic and pedestrians from the east side of the street, and the operator patiently and methodically worked on the north and west sides, keeping away from the spectators.

The operator raised the bucket towards the second floor again and prodded at the store like a cat toying with a mouse. Then, almost in slow motion, the store gave way, collapsing inward, exposing the interior walls, Mr. Engelmann's bedroom, then the kitchen. Mr. Engelmann flinched and shifted his weight from foot to foot. Part of him, too, was being destroyed.

Finally, the first floor could no longer support the weight of the upper storey and buckled. A huge cloud of dust rose as the second floor dropped into the first, gushing out its breath.

The Cat operator backed off and waited for the dust to settle. Some of the spectators took out their handkerchiefs and held them over mouths and noses as the dust rolled towards them. When it had cleared, they could see part of the second floor was still intact, though hovering dangerously, held together and propped up by one or two 2 x 4's on the main floor.

The Cat pushed the rubble into a large heap. More of the dust settled, eerily, like mist burning off in the advancing morning sun. Incredibly, the chair that had sat by the south window was perched on the very top of the pile of twisted and broken boards and rubble.

Then a 2 x 4 stud splintered, letting go of the portion of the second floor wall that was still standing, and fell down across the top of the chair. Attached to the 2 x 4 by an electrical cable was another broken 2 x 4, which javelined forward in a sudden thrust, flying through the air like an arrow, its sharp splintered end piercing the back of the chair and coming through on the other side. From the angle from which Henry and Mr. Engelmann watched on the sidewalk, the two boards formed a cross over the chair.

There was a gasp amongst the spectators. Even Mr. Engelmann grabbed Henry's arm in reaction. It was so symbolic of the cross the Engelmanns had picked up every day and carried. The very chair they had used in their spiritual talks with the Lord was now holding up the cross. It was a reminder of Christ's suffering, and Anna's own pain. And just as Jesus had shed His blood, pierced by a spear when hanging on the cross on Calvary, so, too, did the chair spill its inner heart and soul in the only way it could. Cotton, felt and spring parts protruded from the chair as its worn, fragile fabric tore open.

The chair with its cross sat high on the rubble as the Caterpillar worked all around it, almost defying destruction. Those watching silently cheered it on, praying for some kind of miracle. Mrs. Kartusch, next to Henry, made the sign of the cross. Mr. Engelmann stepped forward as if to get ready to go over there and ask the Cat operator to salvage the chair.

The operator, completely unaware of the dramatics, lowered the Cat's bucket to ground level and scooped up debris which had fallen onto the fringe of the site and pushed it towards the central heap. As it did so, the chair toppled from its perch and the cross fell off to the side, both in front of the Caterpillar. The operator, oblivious to what had happened, drove forward. The metal studded chains of the Cat crushed both chair and cross instantly.

Within ten minutes, the store was nothing more than a pile of rubble. A huge truck at the end of the lot fired up, belching black smoke out of its vertical exhaust pipe. The truck ground into gear and rumbled towards what remained of Engelmann's Grocery Store to park beside the Cat. The operator scooped up the debris and dumped it into the truck.

Henry turned to see how Mr. Engelmann was holding up, but he was no longer there.

"Where's Mr. Engelmann?" Henry asked his mom.

"He left right after his favourite chair was destroyed. I guess he could no longer bear to stand here and see all those memories demolished right before his eyes."

"If only they'd waited another few days until Mr. Engelmann was at the seminary, he wouldn't have had to witness all this."

Concerned about his mentor, Henry walked to the edge of the crowd. He saw Mr. Engelmann about a half block down Broder Street, plodding north rather than south towards their place. He debated running after him but knew it wasn't what Mr. Engelmann needed. He needed to be alone to sort through what had just happened. When Mr. Engelmann reached the end of the next block he turned left and disappeared.

Henry worked his way back through the crowd and stood beside his mother. Her eyes were moist as she stood there, absorbed in her own thoughts.

The truck was filled and piled high. The Caterpillar had crushed the rubble so much that the truck held almost the entire remains of the store. As the truck, like a hearse, lumbered off the lot on its way to the burial grounds, Henry thought, '*Dust thou art and to dust thou shall return.*'

A few minutes later, another truck carrying a load of dirt pulled into the lot. The driver backed towards the open hole of the store's basement. The back end of the truck tilted up and dirt slid out of the tailgate into the basement. The Cat returned as soon as the empty truck pulled away to push the dirt into the basement. More dirt and gravel would be needed to completely level it off.

Henry felt sad and nostalgic, and as he thought about it, his eyes filled with tears. His mother, too, was wiping her eyes with the back of her hand.

"Let's go, Mom."

They took one last look, trying to visualize the store, but all they saw was emptiness.

The Cat idled nearby, quietly licking its chains.

CHAPTER FORTY-SIX

IT WAS ALMOST nine-thirty by the time Henry pulled up in front of Julean's house, two hours later than they'd planned. Julean already knew where she was staying; her parents knew people in Saskatoon and had made arrangements with them for her to stay there. Julean wanted to meet them and also see the room she would be sharing with her friend. Henry was hoping to find a place he could share with Travis. Of the places on the list of boarding houses the registrar had sent him, Henry had underlined the ones he wanted to check out.

"G'morning, Julean," Henry said as she ducked into the car.

She slid up beside him and kissed his cheek.

"Good morning to you, too! Well, do you think your new car will make it okay?"

"I certainly do."

"So I heard they tore down Mr. Engelmann's store?"

"Yeah, it's all gone. I'll tell you about it on the way."

As Henry let out the clutch and sped off, Julean said, "Well, you seem to have *that* down pat."

"Yeah, I'm getting used to it. I feel like a race car driver."

"Just remember the speed limit."

It was a beautiful summer day. Henry rolled his window down and let in the warm, fresh morning air. There wasn't a cloud in the sky. It made him think "blue skies, smiling at me, nothing but blue skies do I see," and he started to hum. He loved Louis Armstrong's version. Henry lowered his voice, trying to make it sound as gravelly as possible, and began to sing like Satchmo.

"Gosh, Hank, I forgot about the impersonations you do! Boy, do you ever sound like him. Sing it again."

After his Louis Armstrong encore, Henry impersonated James Stewart, Jimmy Cagney and several other famous movie stars. Julean laughed and gushed at his talents.

Julean studied the map as they exited Regina. Lumsden, the first town, was in the valley. The highway went right through town. The streets were deserted except for a gas jockey filling a half-ton truck at the corner service station. They had to slow down a bit for a dog loitering on the street in front of them. They passed through town in about two minutes, then started up a steep hill that would take them back to the flat prairie. Fourteen thousand years before, during the last ice age, glaciers had cut through the flat prairie and gouged out that beautiful valley. Henry vowed that someday he would own a slice of it.

The town of Davidson marked the halfway point between Regina and Saskatoon so they decided to stop and fill up the gas tank and have a Coke and a muffin. The café was packed, mainly with farmers and local residents. The locals followed their progress through the café as a waitress showed them to a booth.

When they arrived in Saskatoon, an hour and a half later, Henry recognized some of the street names he had memorized from the registrar's list the night before. Within fifteen minutes they had found the campus of the University of Saskatchewan.

It was old and beautiful. All the buildings had been built with greystone and had a rich heritage look about them. As they drove in and out and around the various buildings, they located the College of Education Building and the Nursing

Building. Beside the University Hospital on the edge of campus was the dean's residence. It was a regal-looking home, a three-storey mansion overlooking the Saskatchewan River.

A beautiful view met them when they stopped at a stoplight at the top of the hill leading down to a bridge. The South Saskatchewan River divided the city in half, spanned by several bridges. Downtown Saskatoon began on the other side.

As they made their way over the bridge, Henry drew Julean's attention to the city's famous Bessborough Hotel, one of the last big hotels built by the Canadian National Railway, and imagined walking with Julean among the tall, well-established trees on the edge of the river beside it.

"Very picturesque," Henry commented to Julean, who nodded.

Except for the campus and beautiful river, Saskatoon was pretty similar to Regina, and Henry found that a comfort. It had the main department stores: Simpsons-Sears, Eaton's and The Bay. Like Regina, it had some really nice restaurants and neat shops. Julean and Henry decided to have lunch at Golf's Chocolate Shop and Diner on 2nd Avenue. Julean said anyplace with the word "chocolate" in the name had to be good. And she was right.

After lunch they set off to look at the homes Henry had marked off on his list. He decided to put a deposit on one on Munroe Avenue, only two blocks from the campus. The lady seemed nice and very friendly. The room Henry rented was clean, with two small cots and two desks. A makeshift bookshelf spanned the space between the desks.

They were way ahead of schedule. It was only three-thirty. The next stop was Julean's room in a home around the corner on Temperance Street.

"There it is!" shrieked Julean as the house came into view. "It's that white bungalow with the picket fence. Oh, I can hardly wait to see what it's like, Hank."

Henry parked the car at the curb, then he and Julean stepped out. Henry opened the gate and they walked into the yard.

A middle-aged woman greeted them at the door a minute after they pushed the doorbell. She was short, and her weight testified to her enjoyment of food. Her hair was mousey white and her round-rimmed glasses complimented her chubby face.

"Hi," Julean greeted her, "I'm Julean Carter. I think my parents called to say I'd be coming today to look at the room I'll be sharing with my friend Louise."

The woman stared at Julean and then at Henry for a long moment. "Hello, Julean. I'm Mrs. Saunders. Yes, your parents called to tell me to expect you," she finally said, and then looked at Henry again.

"Oh! Pardon me. This is Hank Pederson. He's boarding at a place a little closer to campus."

"I see," said Mrs. Saunders. She stepped back and gestured for them to come in. "Please take your shoes off. I'll show you to the room where you'll be staying."

She introduced them to Mr. Saunders when they passed the living room and their daughter, Martha, when they passed her bedroom.

Julean's room was surprisingly spacious. It was set up the same as the one Henry had rented: two single beds, two desks and a high bookcase on the far wall. The room, however, was nicely decorated with frilly curtains and bedspreads. Julean opened the closet to see how big it was, then did the same with the drawers in the dresser and small chest.

"Oh, this is very nice," Julean finally said, breaking the uneasy silence.

"I'm glad you like it," replied Mrs. Saunders. "We don't allow boys in the room and no alcohol, either," she added, surprising them with her frankness.

Julean and Henry looked at each other.

"Oh no, Mrs. Saunders—you don't have to be worried about that," Julean said.

"That's good," Mrs. Saunders said, leading them back to the kitchen. "Breakfast is at seven-thirty every morning. Lunch will be prepared for you to take to university,and dinner will always be at five-thirty sharp."

Julean nodded.

"Do you have any questions?"

Julean thought for a moment. "I can't think of anything right now, Mrs. Saunders, but if I do, I'll call you. Well, Hank, I suppose we should be going. We have a long drive back to Regina."

"Yeah," Henry said, "we'd better get going. Nice meeting you, Mrs. Saunders."

"It was nice meeting you, too, Hank." For the first time, her stern look melted into a pleasant smile, instantly lifting the cold chill in the room.

When they got into the car, Julean said, "I'm sure glad she smiled before we left. I was beginning to think I had made a mistake."

"Yeah," Henry said. "Mr. and Mrs. Temperance, for sure. I'm certain they named the street after them."

Julean laughed and hit him on the knee. "Oh, Hank, you're cruel."

IT WAS JULY 6th. *My anniversary with Jenny.* It was the first thought that entered his mind as soon as he awoke. His love for Jenny was tucked deep into a corner of his heart and perhaps always would be. As much as he loved Julean, Henry's memories of his first love just would not leave him. He had to admit that his feelings had subsided somewhat, the ache and the longing were more tolerable, but that special connection when he'd first looked into Jenny's eyes Henry knew would forever be a part of his life.

He was sad that Mr. Engelmann was leaving for seminary today and yet at the same time glad that he had this major distraction to keep him from slipping into the past. Henry quickly got dressed and made his way out to the kitchen.

"'Morning, Mom. Dad already gone?"

"Yes, he just left a few minutes ago. He said for you to say goodbye to David and wish him well. You can say the same for me too."

"Yeah sure, Mom. It'll sure be different without him around."

"Yes, life is changing all the time. Soon you'll be gone to university and then married someday. That's life."

Henry could sense his mother's anxiety over his departure and how quiet the house would be, especially with his absence at suppertime. But his mom and dad were getting along so well now, their renewed love for each other clearly evident to him. And he loved that they were still saying the rosary every night together after supper. He was so proud of his dad for showing leadership and starting that practice. It just seemed to wrap the house in a powerful safety blanket, uniting the family under the warmth and cover of the Creator of the universe.

After Henry finished his breakfast, he got up and kissed his mom on the cheek. She hadn't said much and was quiet as she slowly washed dishes she and his dad had used earlier.

"Give David a big hug for me, I'll surely miss not having him over for supper on Sunday."

"Yeah, I know—it'll take some getting used to for all of us. Have a nice day, Mom. Perhaps you'll work a bit in the garden?"

"Yes, that's what I thought I'd do."

"Boy, I'm sure going to miss you, Mr. Engelmann," Henry said, as they stood in front of the church rectory. Father Connelly was behind the wheel of the Buick at the curb.

"I will miss you, too, Henry. Well, we should all be back home for Christmas, the good Lord willing. You're getting all set to go to university in a few weeks?"

"Yes."

"Well, they will soon know that a Pederson is there."

"Yeah, I'm anxious to get started. The summer will go fast, I'm sure. I'll be working for the city next week until the end of August."

"It was kind of Mr. Mahoney to get you to work in his office."

"There's a lot of clerical work he wants done so it should be okay for a few weeks…" Henry's words trailed off.

They stood there somewhat awkwardly, not knowing what to say, but a feeling of love surrounded them like an electrifying cloud, conveying much more than words ever could, making this parting bittersweet.

Mr. Engelmann opened his arms and Henry walked into them for a warm, lengthy hug. Mr. Engelmann patted his back.

"You're a good boy, Henry. You will do very well. You have all the tools. And speaking of tools, Henry, there is one more I would like to give you."

Mr. Engelmann opened the passenger door of Father Connelly's car and grabbed something lying on the seat. He turned back to Henry, a brown paper bag in his hands.

Henry knew what it was; Mr. Engelmann's Bible.

He wasn't sure his teacher would be able to part with it. He wasn't sure he should take it if Mr. Engelmann could.

"Here, Henry," Mr. Engelmann said, handing him the bag. "The most important tool for living your life."

Unbidden tears came to Henry's eyes. He couldn't speak. If there was any material thing Mr. Engelmann loved, it was his Bible. For Mr. Engelmann to give away that Bible was like the richest man in the world giving away everything he owned.

"Are you sure?" Henry managed.

Mr. Engelmann gazed tenderly into his adopted son's eyes. "Yes, I am sure, Henry. Even though this is God's Word, our love for Jesus should be greater than our most valued treasure. The more we can let go of them, the freer we become to love like Him. People fear poverty, giving up or losing their possessions, and so we play into the evil one's hands. When we realize we really have nothing, that it all belongs to God and that the only thing of value is Jesus in our lives, it is then we become the richest people in the universe."

Henry thought he understood. People need to be free of all attachments to really know Jesus and make Him Master of their lives. It touched Henry's heart profoundly.

"One thing's for sure," he said now, "you'll be the best priest that the seminary will ever produce."

Mr. Engelmann only smiled. "I'm not one for writing letters, Henry, but if you have the time, send me one. I will do my best to write back. Perhaps that will ease the pain of withdrawal from our usual chats at the store. I have missed them already."

Henry hugged his teacher again and whispered, "Thank you, Mr. Engelmann, for your Bible. I will treasure this gift more than anything."

Mr. Engelmann clapped Henry's shoulder and slid into the passenger seat of Father Connelly's black Buick.

They stared at one another, unwilling to say goodbye. Henry reached out and rested a hand on the door ledge of the open window. Mr. Engelmann put his on top of Henry's.

Their gazes locked as the love between them flowed freely into each other's hearts.

Father Connelly broke the silent farewell. "Well, Henry, I'll see you at church on Sunday morning,"

Henry nodded as Father Connelly slowly drove away; Mr. Engelmann's hand sliding away beneath his. But Henry knew that no one could ever separate the spiritual bond between them.

Exhaust fumes lingered in the air as the car rolled down the street, reminding Henry of another sad departure.

It had been nearly four years since Jenny left.

He waved until the car disappeared into the distance, a void growing rapidly in his heart. He felt alone and insecure. Mr. Engelmann had always been there, ready to help, comfort and guide him. Proverbs 17:17 slipped into his mind, soothing his spirit. "A friend loves at all times."

Mr. Engelmann was his truest friend and because of his lessons and example, Henry knew he had it in him to be a good teacher himself. He was full of ideas and anxious to impart what he had learned and make the world a better place. And yet as he stood there in the middle of the street, his heart and mind so full of idealism, feelings of insecurity besieged him.

At that moment, a young barn swallow zoomed down and

perched itself on the branch directly in front of him. Its tail flicked, its head pivoted in all directions, then it looked right at him, its gaze carrying a message of wisdom. As Henry stared at the tiny bird, he thought of how a mother bird would encourage and finally push her young out of the nest to fly and fend for themselves. Wasn't that what life was all about? Growing up with the support of family and friends, but finally leaving to face the challenges of life?

Mr. Engelmann's parting words said it all: "You will do very well, Henry. You have all the tools."

Of course. He had everything he needed and now he needed to test his wings, be pushed out of the nest and learn to fend for himself on his own. To put into practice what he had learned.

Henry opened the bag and pulled out Mr. Engelmann's Bible. He could scarcely believe the treasure he was holding. His mentor's warmth surged through him with a mighty power. He was not alone. He would never be alone. He held the wisdom and love of the greatest Teacher and Comforter in his hand. This was the most important lesson that Mr. Engelmann had taught and instilled in him. This was what his teacher was reminding him of through this beautiful gift.

"It's all there, Henry," he had so often said. "It's very important to read the Bible every day, so you stay focused on what is really important in life. All the psychologists, philosophers and psychiatrists in the world have not really discovered anything new. They are simply relating what has already been taught from the beginning when our good Lord walked the earth and showed us the way, the truth and the light."

His teacher's words stung his heart as he stood in the empty street. Henry took a deep breath of the warm summer air. There was already a tinge of fall in it. Some of the leaves had begun to change colour. The swallow took off and flitted away into the sky without a single doubt of its ability to fly. Confidence surged through Henry's body as he realized that he, too, was ready. He had all the tools and more. He squeezed the greatest and most important one of all in his hand.

His teacher would be forever at his side.

As he headed back to his Chevy, he felt light and sure-footed. He felt as if he could fly like the swallow or a hawk, soaring on the updrafts of the vast prairie sky. He closed the door with a louder *thunk* than usual. His key was right on target as it entered the ignition. The engine roared to life, echoing the fire he felt inside. He hit the gas and let out the clutch, but instead of zipping away like a barn swallow, the car jerked forward and conked out. He had let the clutch out too fast.

Embarrassment flooded his cheeks and he hoped nobody had witnessed his mistake. He pressed the starter and pumped the gas pedal, hoping to recover quickly. The engine turned over and over; it would not start. The odour of gas told him that he'd flooded it. He sank low into his seat and stared straight ahead.

In the blink of an eye, he had gone from a soaring hawk to a deflated balloon.

"Life always has its ups and downs," Mr. Engelmann would say. Henry pictured himself sitting there, the wind gone from his sails, dead in the water. Then he remembered another very important piece of advice Mr. Engelmann had tried to instill in him: "Don't take yourself too seriously."

It started with a little chuckle and grew. Before he knew it, he was laughing at himself.

Mr. Engelmann would be proud of him.

After settling down and putting things into their proper perspective, Henry tried the starter again and the engine sprang to life. He pushed in the clutch and then shifted into low, let out the clutch and slowly pressed the gas. The car rolled smoothly ahead. He still felt ready to conquer the world—but with a somewhat more humble attitude.

CHAPTER FORTY-SEVEN

A WEEK AFTER MR. Engelmann left, Henry was driving to work at City Hall when he noticed Eddy waiting for the trolley. Henry pulled over to the curb and Eddy hopped in.

"Where you headed, Eddy?"

"Downtown. I got a job at Richardson Greenshields, it's a brokerage firm downtown."

"Hop in, I'll give you a ride. So how'd you land that job and what do you do?" Henry asked in quick succession.

"My uncle's one of the brokers there and Pop asked him if he could get me on. I went back for a second interview a week and a half ago and they gave me a job. I started the next day."

"That's cool, Eddy. so what do you do?"

"Not too much yet—run errands, do some filing, get coffee for their breaks and I'm always watching how they trade. It's interesting."

"So is this just a summer job? Are you going to university in the fall?"

"Naw, folks can't afford that and I'm not really interested in going. I kinda like what I'm doing now. There's a lot of turnover of cash. People making money and others losing. It's quite the game. I like the action, I guess. I'm getting a handle on it. The boss can see I'm pretty good with numbers. He says they might send me on a course in the fall."

"That would be great, Eddy! Maybe when I make my millions as a teacher I'll come to you to make investments for me."

"For sure, Hank, just look me up. You can let me off at the corner here, I can walk the rest of the way; I wanna have a smoke before I get to work."

Henry pulled over to the curb and Eddy got out. Just before he closed the door, he asked, "Wanna shoot some pool at the Royal sometime?"

"Geez, I haven't shot a game in months, Eddy. But, yeah, maybe tomorrow night. I've got a date with Julean."

"Sounds cool, Hank. Gimme a call if you can make it."

Henry watched Eddy walk away. No more then five steps and he pulled out his weeds and lit one up. There was a cool confidence about Eddy as he walked along, like he owned the world. He wore a white shirt but the top two buttons were open and his tie was loose. Eddy was comfortable with himself in the total sense. Didn't pay too much attention to what others thought and played pretty much by his own rules. Henry liked that about Eddy and wished he had more of this indescribable quality. It had to do with not seeking others' approval or being overly concerned by what they thought. It had been abundantly evident even in high school.

Henry watched his friend until he disappeared around the corner. *I've got a feeling Eddy's gonna make it big.*

WHEN TAMMY AND her baby went home she was surprised to find that her father had fixed up a beautiful suite for her in the basement. It was completely self-contained with a washroom, kitchenette and living room. There was a large bedroom for her and a smaller one for the baby. The upstairs door had a lock on Tammy's side. She was free to lock it or to come up anytime to visit with her parents. She could be as private as she wanted to be but was always welcome upstairs.

Tammy was thrilled and thanked her parents profusely. Once settled in her new little apartment, Tammy called her best friend to tell her all about it.

"That's great, Tammy! I'm looking forward to seeing it. We've sure missed you and Chloe since you went home."

"We miss you too. But wait, it gets better; guess who phoned?" But it was Tammy who couldn't wait. "Robbie!" she burst out. "He phoned over a week ago and asked to come over to see Chloe!"

"So *that's* why I haven't heard from you! See, your wish on the shooting star is already starting to come true."

"Maybe so far. But marriage is an entirely different matter."

"Well, you never know what the heavens can do."

"Anyway, Jen, the first time he came over it was very awkward—I was still furious with him for not being there for me and Chloe and acting like he didn't care.

"He said he was ashamed to come visit and that he had a lot of thinking to do. He promised me that he hasn't been out with other girls and that he still cares for me. He wanted to kiss me before he left but I would have nothing to do with it."

"Has he come back since?"

"Yes, every night. Oh, Jen, he says he's falling in love with Chloe and is glad she has my brown eyes and hair instead of his hazel eyes and red hair."

"Chloe would be adorable either way."

"Well, I was phoning to see if you would like to go with me to a movie tomorrow night? *The Apartment* is starting and I hear it's supposed to be good. It's got Shirley McLean and Jack Lemmon and I can't remember who else."

"That sounds great, but what about Chloe? Is your mom watching her?"

"Actually, I asked Robbie to babysit. He knows how to hold her, change her and feed her if he needs to. But she'll be in bed and asleep by the time we leave. I'm sure he'll be fine. So come for supper and we'll leave right after."

"Sounds great, I can't wait to see Chloe. I'll be there shortly after four."

"Tammy, I can hardly wait to see Chloe, where is she?"

"What about me, Jen? I'm the mom who created that little bundle, don't I count for something?"

"Yeah, it's good to see you too, Tammy." Jenny walked over and gave her friend a hug.

"Chloe's in her room, I heard her a few minutes ago. Why don't you get her and bring her out."

Jenny tip-toed into the baby's room and saw two dark little eyes staring up at a plastic white angel dangling from a string.

"Who's a baby angel? Are you ready to fly? Hi, sweetie, it's Auntie Jenny." Jenny uncovered Chloe and began tickling her tummy. "How's my precious little angel, huh? Come on, give Auntie a big smile, come on…that's it…oh I *love* you. Let's see if you need to be changed…"

Jenny checked Chloe's diaper and after changing it, carried her out to the kitchen. "Look who's here, Mommy!"

"Is that my little darling?" Tammy poked Chloe's tummy, making the baby giggle. "Are you getting hungry? Should Mommy fix you something? And we better have dinner ourselves too; Robbie will be along in twenty minutes or so."

"This is a real nice place your dad fixed up for you."

"Yeah, it's good, isn't it? We're separate from the rest of the house when we want to be, yet we can still be connected when we want to be. Anyway, it gives them and us some privacy."

"For sure—great idea."

"We're just going to have cheesy macaroni casserole and Caesar salad. Sound okay, Jen?"

"Yes, wonderful."

"Why don't you put Chloe in the high chair and prop her up a bit with her blanket. I've just heated some pablum. You can start to feed her if you want."

"Sure."

Jenny put Chloe in the chair and tied a bib around her neck.

"Okay let's see what we've got," Jenny mixed a peas and meat mixture and took a little taste. "Mmmm, just right! Here it comes." Jenny took a little spoon full and waved it front of Chloe, then swooped it into her mouth.

Looking on from the stove where she was scooping out mounds of casserole, Tammy asked, "So, how are things going with you and James?"

Jenny didn't answer right away. "Oh fine, I guess. When I do see him we usually go out to dinner and a movie. But that seems to be happening less and less. The company demands so much of his time."

"I still think you should go out with other guys, you could have the pick of the litter."

"I know it's going to be a rocky road with James, and yet I still feel drawn to him, Tammy. I can't explain it."

"If you weren't so accepting of others, Jenny, I'd advise you against it. Your life could be a very lonely one."

"I know Mom's was, but she said she got used to it. I'm hoping I can convince James to be more of a family man."

"Well, what was it you told me? It's best to know beforehand how the dog is going to behave before you buy him?"

Jenny laughed, "Well, I sure hope he doesn't turn out to be a pit bull!"

Tammy rolled her eyes, "Good heavens, I should hope not!"

"So did you finish writing all your exams?"

"Yes, I wrote math last week and that was the last one. It was easy and I didn't have to study too much for it."

"It's a good thing your grades were so good before you had little Chloe here."

"That helped for sure, but your studying with me and helping me to catch up this summer while I stayed at your place was a godsend, Jen. I know I couldn't have done it without you. And Mr. Thompson is such an understanding principal, always ready to give me extra time if I need it. Actually, all the teachers have been great—I think they all just want me to have a chance."

Jenny nodded. "I like Mr. Thompson too. Every now and

then he attended one of our student council meetings and was always so supportive."

Just then Chloe let out a loud screech and waved her hand, hitting the spoon out of Jenny's fingers.

"See, I was talking and not paying attention to our little angel, here." Jenny put on an exaggerated frown and mimicked what Cloe might be thinking if she could speak. "'Give me more food and quit gabbing already,' that's what you're telling us, isn't it, love bug?"

Jenny got so close to Chloe her nose rubbed into the green pea mixture that had spread all over the baby's face. Jenny scraped some off her little cheeks with the spoon and popped it into Chloe's mouth.

"In any case," continued Tammy, "it suddenly seems to be all working out and I'll be ready to start nursing in September."

"I admire you so much, Tammy, how you've handled all this! All the pressures and responsibility of being a single mom. I'm so proud of you!"

"Thanks, Jen, but like I said, I couldn't have gotten this far without you and all your friendship and help."

Jenny just smiled; it had blessed her too. "Have you got a babysitter for the fall?'

"You'll never believe it! Mom asked Tillie, our next-door neighbour and she said she'd love to watch Chloe, that it would fill in her time now that all her own kids are gone. Her husband passed away last year and she feels lonely. And can you believe she only wants $25 a week for doing it!"

"That's wonderful, Tammy. See, how your guardian angel is looking after you!"

"*That's* for sure, and—"

The doorbell rang.

"Oh, that must be Robbie. I'll get it."

A moment later Robbie walked in, ducking his head to make it through the doorway.

"Hi, Jen, how you doin'?"

"Just fine, Robbie. My gosh I think you've grown another six inches since I last saw you."

"Yeah, I hit 6′3″ a couple of months back but haven't grown a fraction since then."

"We'll be sitting down to dinner in a few minutes. Are you going to join us, Robbie? There's enough here."

"Yeah, I would like that, if it's okay?"

"Sure. Maybe give Jen a damp cloth to clean Chloe and then after dinner you can give her bottle and then off to bed."

"Sure, Tammy," Robbie said nervously. He laid the cloth on the table in front of Jenny. "Hi, Chloe, how's Daddy's girl?"

Chloe smiled, the green pea mixture coating her mouth and cheeks.

Jenny washed Chloe's face and gave her a spoon to play with and then turned to the table, ready to have dinner herself.

As they sat down to their meal, Tammy surprised her guests by requesting that someone say grace.

"How about you Robbie?"

Robbie's already ruddy complexion turned even redder. "I don't know any prayers, Tammy." For a big, strong, virile-looking man he seemed shy and unsure of himself.

"Just say anything to thank God for the food we are about to eat. Actually there, I said it!"

The table fell silent until Chloe started to babble.

"See there, Chloe's saying a little prayer. Actually, I can't wait to teach her that guardian angel prayer you taught me, Jen."

"Yes, I love it; I say it all the time."

"Funny thing. Since I started saying it, I think I told you I've started to pray for the first time in a long time. I don't feel so alone on the inside somehow…" she said, then added, "I guess another good thing coming out of all this is that I'm thinking about going to church again. In fact, I even called the Anglican church a few blocks away to see if they have Sunday School. He said they do, but Chloe's a little too young."

Jenny and Robbie chuckled.

"Maybe in a couple of years, Tammy," Jenny smiled.

"The pastor did, however, praise me for wanting to give my child an early start. He also invited me to come to church this Sunday. Where do you go to church, Jen? We didn't go when I stayed at your place."

"Well, actually, I go occasionally to a United church that's a couple of miles from our place. When I was in Regina, I was surprised when Dad took us to a neighbourhood Catholic church. He wanted to meet some of the people in the area and of course I was glad because that's where my friend Henry went. It was a big church and very crowded. The ritual of the mass seemed so holy. But since we've moved to Ottawa, I'm the only one who goes—if I'm up early enough. Dad's been saying lately that he wants to join me at church but he hasn't yet."

"I remember we all went while my brother and I were growing up, but when Mom started to work when I was young, we gradually stopped. I missed it for the longest time. It was a family thing we did together, just, I don't know, being part of the community and sharing our worship of God."

"It's the same with us, Tammy. When we lived in Kelowna—the city I was born in—we used to go all the time, too. I just loved getting dressed up in my Sunday best and it seemed we were more of a family then and shared a common belief. Going to church reminded me of Jesus and that I wanted to be a better person for Him. If it weren't for those times my parents took me to church, I probably wouldn't even be going the occasional time now—or even thinking about God."

Finally Robbie butted in. "What's with all the church stuff, Tammy? Are you getting religious on me?"

Tammy stopped eating and looked at him. "Well, maybe I am. Now that I'm a mom, I want to make sure my children learn good values and are brought up right. If parents don't show or lead by example, how are children going to develop in faith and learn what's right and wrong? In our family, none of us seem to think about God; we don't pray to Him or say grace at meals, there's nothing—just work and going out the odd time. It just seems like something very important is missing. You know, what's the purpose of it all?"

Jenny looked at Tammy and then Robbie, not sure how to answer that question. Instead, she filled the growing silence with something she was more certain of.

"I have to agree with her, Robbie. Where else will children learn about Jesus and God and right and wrong? Well, most of that parents are supposed to teach, but what about the schools and churches?"

Tammy jumped back in. "I want to make sure Chloe goes to a Christian school. She'll get good training from me," and turning to Robbie, she continued, "and from my husband if I get married, but I know I want to start now by going to church. It's too important a part of our lives to ignore and yet we treat it as if it were nothing."

Then Tammy took a risk. "Would you like to come to church with Chloe and me this Sunday, Robbie?"

Robbie looked at Jen and back at Tammy. He shrugged, confused, then absently scratched his arm, thinking about it.

"Yeah, sure, if it makes you happy, Tammy. At least until I leave for university." Robbie turned red again and picked up his fork.

"So what college *are* you going to, Robbie?" Jenny wanted to know.

"I was offered two basketball scholarships—one in Florida and the other in Texas. I've signed up for the Florida team. I leave the last week of August." Now it was Robbie's turn to take a risk. "They have dorms for single players and also for players with families." Robbie looked at Tammy, suddenly shy. "I'm hoping Tammy and Chloe will come with me."

Tammy glanced at him but didn't respond. She stayed quiet, then rather abruptly began clearing plates from the table.

"We'd better go, Jenny. The show starts in three-quarters of an hour and it will take us at least twenty or thirty minutes to get there."

Placing the dirty dishes on the countertop next to the sink,

Tammy picked up Chloe, who had been contentedly cooing and playing with the spoon while they'd eaten.

"My gosh, you've been a good little girl, Chloe, listening to all this grown-up talk," Tammy gushed as she handed the baby to Jenny. "Would you check her diaper again, Jen, and I'll get the bottle heated for Robbie."

"Sure, Tammy," Jenny replied, jiggling the baby girl in her arms, aware of the awkward tension that hung in the air.

Doesn't Tammy want *to go with him?*

Tammy picked Chloe up off the couch after Jenny had changed her diaper and buried her nose in the baby's neck. "I love you, little lamb. Be a good girl for Daddy, now."

She handed the baby to Robbie.

"You'll do just fine, Robbie, don't look so nervous—and don't forget to burp her. Mom said she'd come down and check on things a little later."

Just as the girls were about to close the door behind them, Chloe began to cry. Tammy motioned to Jen and whispered, "Let's go, they'll be fine."

"ROBBIE SEEMS TO really want to be part of things now."

"Yes, he really loves Chloe. The other night he apologized to me for wanting me to have an abortion. Now that he sees the beautiful little girl we would have destroyed, he's very sorry. He was sincere, Jenny; I've never seen Robbie cry before."

"So," she had to ask, "are you going with him to Florida?"

Tammy was quiet for a long while. "No, I don't think so. Maybe we'll write and he can come home and see Chloe. I just think he needs more time, time to grow up a little more and make certain he wants to commit himself and take on the responsibility of a family."

"Do you still love him, Tammy?"

"Oh, Jenny, I really *do*—I never stopped! But I don't dare show it. Robbie's going to have to go a long way to earn my affection. And if we do decide to marry, there will be no sex until our wedding night. My mind is very clear on that matter. I'm determined to make sure Robbie and I know each other and that we become good friends, first and foremost. I must say, I think he respects me more since I've restricted our relationship to talking and looking after Chloe. He appreciates me more."

Jenny nodded, reaching her hand out to her friend. "I'm so proud of you, Tammy, for taking this responsibility on. I think you're doing a great job with the baby; you've really grown into yourself since Chloe was born. I love you and I admire you, and I absolutely *adore* that precious little girl of yours. She's growing so fast and catches onto things in the blink of an eye. I can hardly wait to have a little one I can raise and shower with love."

Tammy squeezed Jenny's hand. "You'll be a great mom, Jen."

CHAPTER FORTY-EIGHT

SEPTEMBER 1, 1960. Henry's Chevy was loaded to the hilt. After an emotional farewell with his mom and dad, Henry pulled up in front of Julean's place where two suitcases and three boxes waited outside her front door. Just as he finished packing her luggage in the trunk, she and her mother came out.

"Hi, Hank," Julean called out from the doorway.

Mrs. Carter waved. "That's quite a load you have."

"Yeah, it sure is," Henry replied, "and I still have to pick up Travis and his things, too."

"Well, it'll be some juggling act," Mrs. Carter laughed.

"Julean, are you ready?" Henry asked, even though he already knew the answer.

"Yes." She turned to her mother and they embraced briefly. Julean had a tear in her eye and looked like she might cry, but somehow she held it in. "'Bye, Mom, I'll write right away."

"I will too, Julean."

Minutes later they arrived at Travis' house. He bounded down his front steps carrying a single suitcase as soon as they drove up. He tossed the suitcase in the back seat then ran back into the house and emerged moments later carrying two boxes, one of which Henry stowed in the trunk and the other in the back seat.

In Saskatoon, Henry dropped Julean off first, then went directly to the place he had rented for Travis and himself. Travis seemed to like it. He thought it was a little small, he said, but the price and proximity to the university made up for it. They soon learned, however, that the meals the landlady made for them left much to be desired. Besides her own family of six, another eleven boarders were crammed into the three-storey home. Every day they compared their lunches with those of other students and their meal never measured up.

One evening during a pillow fight, the landlady appeared in the door in the midst of a cloud of feathers like a fire truck in a blizzard, her fuming red face contrasting sharply with all the white in the room. Within minutes they were given an eviction notice and had two weeks to find another place.

The four boys—Travis, Henry and the two others who had shared another room in the house—decided to rent the upstairs of a three-bedroom home on the west side of Saskatoon, on the fringe of the downtown area.

Their new landlord lived in the basement. He was a conductor for the Canadian National Railway and so was gone most of the week. It only took them a short while, however, to realize why the rent was so cheap. They were in a very seedy part of Saskatoon, and the landlord was both an alcoholic and a bootlegger. People came to the door at all hours of the night to buy booze. The landlord always apologized for disturbing them and even lowered their already cheap rent by twenty-five dollars because of the inconvenience and aggravation.

They also were in the red light district. Every time they went to the nearby café they were propositioned by several girls. Raids for drug possession in different homes on the block were common. The boys only had to look out the front living room window to see which house the police had raided the night before.

After much discussion they decided to stay anyway. The rent

was good, and things were sure interesting. They did, however, agree to always walk in pairs or take a cab otherwise.

Henry never was quite sure whose meals were worse, their old landlady's or the ones they were now making themselves. Somehow, however, they managed and didn't starve, and most of the time had fun.

ONCE THEY SETTLED into university life, time passed quickly. Before they knew it, Christmas holidays loomed. It had snowed a lot over the two weeks prior to when they'd planned to leave Saskatoon, and Henry's and Julean's parents were concerned about the driving conditions.

The day before Henry and Julean were set to go home for the holidays, the temperature rose above freezing, melting the snow. However, it plunged again that night, turning the highways into sheets of ice. They drove very slowly all the way back to Regina, passing numerous cars that had landed in the ditch. It took them six-and-a-half hours to get home instead of the usual two-and-a-half.

"Oh, I'm so glad you're home safe and sound!" Mary said, grabbing Henry in a hug, "All day they were saying on the radio that the roads were terrible." She looked at her son, her eyes filling with tears. "It's so good to see you, Henry!"

Henry hugged her again, and then his dad.

"Yeah, it sure is good to be home. I can hardly wait for a home-cooked meal."

"You men, all you think about is your stomachs!"

"Well, you can't blame the boy, Mary. You're just too darn good of a cook. I can hardly wait to come home every day myself."

"Right, Mom—so what's for supper?" Henry put an arm around Mary and led her into the kitchen, the smell of roast beef already wafting towards him.

As they sat around the kitchen table, Henry told them story after story about university and the place they had rented. Mary was very worried about the neighbourhood, but Henry assured her that the four of them stuck together and looked out for one another, and that they actually enjoyed many of the people in the neighborhood.

"So," he said at last, turning to his father, "Mom wrote me that you got promoted, Dad?"

"Yeah, I guess they recognize a good man when they see one," Bill winked. "Yup, I'm no longer fixing Coke machines or compressors, I'm selling them now."

"You should see him, Henry, he looks so handsome all dressed in a suit every day and he's such a good salesman. Two Pepsi customers already switched over to carrying Coca-Cola in their store because of him." Mary reached over and placed her hand on her husband's.

It made Henry's heart glad to see that. It just made him feel good when his parents complimented each other or joked around.

"Well, it does mean a lot of traveling, but it's mostly nearby towns. Moose Jaw is the biggest area to cover and I'm usually home every evening, which I like." And then turning to Mary, he teased, "Mainly because of your mom's cooking, of course."

Mary rolled her eyes and Bill took the cue, "Honestly, honey, it's really because I can't stand being away from you. Not even for a night."

"Now that's better!" Mary got up and checked the oven to see how dinner was coming along.

"So Julean likes university too?"

"She loves it—and she's doing so well. Straight A's."

"That's great. Oh, by the way, David called last night and said he'd be back in Regina on Friday and that he can hardly wait to see you. Of course, he also said that *he* can't wait for one of my meals, either…I just can't get away from it, can I?"

"Nope, you're doomed to being a professional home-grown chef, Mom—the best in the world."

"Well, your dad's gotten to be a pretty good cook too, you know. On the days I work at Simpsons, he sometimes has dinner ready for me when I get home, and I must say they're very tasty."

"It's because you're a good teacher, Mary. And, in all honesty, you have most of the meal prepared already. But I do a heck of a job in getting it into the oven and turning on the stove!"

"Oh Bill, you do more than that!" Mary slapped him on the shoulder.

"Well, Mom and Dad, I think I'll get cleaned up. I may go over to Julean's place for awhile tonight but I should be home early. It sure will be good to see Mr. Engelmann on Friday. It's only two days away, so not too long a wait."

When Mr. Engelmann walked into their home late Friday afternoon, Henry couldn't believe his eyes. In fact, his parents couldn't believe their eyes either. For a minute Henry thought Mr. Engelmann had a younger brother. He looked years younger and had lost a good fifteen pounds. Perhaps it was no longer having all the stress of working long hours at the store and tending to Anna, or maybe he'd just grown closer to the Lord, if that were possible.

"My gosh, Mr. Engelmann—or Father, should I say," Henry corrected in jest, "man, do you ever look good. I hardly recognize you!"

"I'll second that," echoed Bill. "What's the secret, David? Been to heaven and back?"

Mr. Engelmann beamed. "All this studying is a lot of hard work for someone who has been out of school for all the years I have. But I am up before the sun and retire when it goes down and I feel very rested. I *love* what I am doing: training to be a shepherd for the Lord."

"You already were that, Mr. Engelmann," Henry said.

"Maybe so, Henry, but soon I will be an officially ordained one."

"Well, come in, David, come in. Let me take your coat. It's so good to have you here for supper and a visit. We've all missed you so much."

"And I've missed you all, too." Mr. Engelmann handed his

coat and hat to Mary and then gave each a hug in turn, keeping an arm around Henry as he asked about university and Julean.

Dinner lasted almost two hours before everyone seemed to be talked out. It was so good to have everyone back together, like old times. Henry loved the family get-together and the fun, laughter and good will. It offered such a respite from study and work. Mr. Engelmann came over twice more for dinner, on Christmas Day and New Year's, much to everyone's delight.

It was sad to see the holidays come to an end. If it hadn't been for the fact that Julean was going back with him, Henry would've found it downright agonizing to return to school. The day they left, Mr. Engelmann came to see them off before heading back to Gravelbourg himself. After hugs and goodbyes, they were off.

Henry and Julean returned home to Regina at the end of February and again at Easter. Before they knew it, their first year of university was under their belts and they felt like pros. Both of them had done very well in their studies.

Travis, though, had failed two of the five subjects he'd taken in the College of Engineering and would need to repeat them. Too many late nights with the girls, they teased. Henry couldn't get over the number of times Travis hadn't come home at night and the wild parties he attended. Travis' one-night stands caught up with him, though, when he contracted a venereal disease. Rather than stop, he vowed to be more careful and use a contraceptive. Henry and Julean found it difficult to understand how guys and girls gave of their bodies so freely without commitment or concern about the consequences. It was an eye-opener for them both.

Back in Regina, Henry got a job over the summer working for the Department of Defense as one of the maintenance crew. Mr. Mahoney again offered him a job at the city taxation department, but Henry wanted to be outdoors and so took the government job instead. He looked after the building's grounds, keeping the lawns and flowers watered. He worked with two other students and a horticulturist. The horticulturist was older and knew everything there was to know about plants and their care. The job required Henry to get up at five a.m. and be at the job, ready to start, by six. Henry soon eagerly anticipated watching the sun come up, basking in the peace that surrounded that part of the day. He actually often got up earlier and used the time before five-thirty to read the Bible and meditate.

During the last week of August before they headed back to university, Mr. Engelmann made a special trip to Regina to visit with the Pedersons and especially Henry. After another great dinner and visit with his parents, Henry drove Mr. Engelmann back to the rectory. When Henry parked the car, the conversation shifted to his deepening relationship with Julean.

"So, Henry, if you and Julean are talking about marriage already, this is becoming quite serious."

"Yeah, in more ways than one. Not only can we hardly wait to get married, but we also really want to make love to each other. Do you recall the discussion we once had out back of the store about sex and waiting until you're married?"

Mr. Engelmann nodded. "I take it that you are struggling with that again?"

"It's all I think about, especially when we're alone together."

"Yes, it is very difficult to abstain before marriage. It is such a strong desire, especially when two people love each other so much. Anna and I struggled with it, too, as I'm sure most young couples do."

"I just don't know if I can wait any longer."

"I understand. The good Lord put this great desire in us and then He expects us to behave and control it."

"Yeah!" Henry turned to Mr. Engelmann. "Just what does He expect from us?"

"Obedience, self-discipline, intelligence. Remember what I told you back then? We are not animals. We are not Pavlovian dogs conditioned to react to our base instincts. We are children of God, to whom He has given a beautiful body along with intelligence, a moral code and free will. And He expects us to use

441

it wisely and diligently, and not recklessly. Our bodies are a rare gift to be treasured and honoured and respected."

Henry looked at Mr. Engelmann, suddenly angry. A moment ago Henry thought Mr. Engelmann had been agreeing with him, supporting his feelings, justifying them. Then Mr. Engelmann had said the Lord expected him to be some kind of high-and-mighty super-creature, rising above the instincts that the Lord had Himself given him! It was infuriating!

"I can see you are confused and frustrated, Henry. Yes, the Lord has instilled in us the desire to procreate. But he wants us to do this when we are married, in an atmosphere of commitment and respect so that children can come into the world in a home in which there is love and security. This is a special gift that only humans possess. And with this gift comes responsibility to do the right thing."

"You know, the guys I share the house with in Saskatoon go out all the time, party and have sex. One of the them even got a disease for doing it too much."

"That's a perfect example of what we are talking about. Your friends lack moral responsibility and self-discipline. They are just using their female friends for self-gratification. We seek one pleasure after the other with no thought to the consequences of how a few minutes of pleasure can turn into so much pain and hurt. How many girls may already have become pregnant or received the disease your friend has? He has no intention of marrying any of these girls, does he? It is easy to see what the right thing to do is, Henry."

"But see, that's why it's different with Julean and me; we *are* going to get married."

"Now our discussion is going around in circles and getting nowhere. You either believe in your heart that it's best to wait like the Lord wants you to or you don't. You either make the sacrifice of waiting and giving yourselves to each other completely and purely or you don't. Look at what your friends are doing now and the consequences of their actions. But more importantly, what are they going to bring to their wedding night when they *do* get married? What are they going to offer their spouse, their lifelong partner? A sinful past? Or a past that was chaste and showed restraint and moral conduct? It seems to me just over a year ago I listened to a fine speech a young man gave to his fellow students about being people of integrity," Mr. Engelmann smiled, but his words were serious.

"That insightful young man talked about choice; that every moment of our lives we choose to be a person of integrity or not. To live out the values we believe in or not. 'To be or not to be' was the way the young man put it. I will never forget that phrase. It's short and filled with so much power...to be a man of truth, of integrity, of honour—or not to be, that *is* the question, isn't it, Henry?"

"Geez, Mr. Engelmann," Henry sighed. "You do it every time, your teachings cut like a knife into my mind, always carving out the stupid stuff."

"It seems to me, Henry, you know full well what you should do but you're allowing yourself to be distracted by all these thoughts of making love to Julean. As we've talked about before, the thoughts we entertain lead to feelings of arousal or hunger or whatever, and eventually our feelings, driven by our thoughts, lead us to act—either like an intelligent person in control and guided by his beliefs or like an animal driven by instinct." Mr. Engelmann gazed into Henry eyes, "Is that not correct?"

"Yeah, it's more than correct."

"Well? What is the solution, Henry?"

"Not to allow myself to think those thoughts. But I've tried to get rid of them, to push them out of my mind and the harder I try the worse it seems to get!"

"Ah yes, that is true, but what if you don't resist? What if you just let the thought come but chose not to get engaged with it? You cannot deny your thoughts and feelings, they are a part of you. The first and most important step is to *accept* those thoughts. Acknowledge them and then gently replace them with other thoughts and insights which are more wholesome.

The imagination is a powerful tool that can be used either for us or against us. 'Yes,' you might say when a temptation comes into your mind, 'I *do* desire Julean and would like to make love to her more than anything, but I choose to delay that pleasure until we are married. I can see I am mainly seeking sexual gratification. She is not an object of my desire but the love of my life and I am willing to make this sacrifice for that special night when we can offer each other ourselves fully and freely, and completely without shame, guilt or regret."

"Geez, Mr. Engelmann, it's amazing how you can turn things around."

"You must use your thoughts and imagination to your advantage. The mind reacts to your thoughts and…"

"Yeah, I know, the thoughts you think lead to feelings of arousal and then you act, and maybe do something stupid."

Mr. Engelmann chuckled. "I couldn't have said it any better myself. But remember too, Henry, to continually pray for wisdom, strength and guidance from the Lord. Temptation can be very powerful and we need the Lord's strength to keep us on the straight and narrow. Keep filling your mind with good thoughts. Remember, no two thoughts can occupy the mind at the same time, so dwell on the beauty of God and His creation. Fill your consciousness with the wholesome things of life and think thoughts continually that do not lead you into temptation. Why torture yourself needlessly?"

Henry nodded, unable to think of anything that would be a reasonable rebuttal of Mr. Engelmann's wisdom and understanding. *He's going to make such a good priest.*

"The problem with humans, Henry, is that we are selfish; all too often we seek one pleasure after the other and want it instantly. The Lord gave us a most beautiful and powerful antidote for this. Willpower. Many people act as it they don't even realize they possess this gift or rarely exercise and develop it. Begin to deny yourself; maybe when you want a soft drink, say no. Refuse a second helping at meal time. I know how much you love popcorn, deny it to yourself every now and then.

"That is part of the purpose of Lent; we give something up for the Lord. It's also to remind us of this gift of the will He gave us and helps us to keep disciplined when we encounter temptation. The more we do this, the more conscious we become and our willpower grows. It creates self-discipline within. We begin to feel that we *do* have control over our thoughts and desires.

"You see, Henry, God gave us the whole ball of wax. He gave us all the equipment and more. The Lord made us perfect, not helpless like a leaf in the prairie wind. It all comes back to choice again, Henry, doesn't it? And our choices are based upon our values, what we believe in. See how everything is so beautifully tied together? If we believe in the sanctity of marriage then we will abstain from premarital sex. You see, Henry? To make the sacrifice now and give to each other yourselves completely on your wedding night is very possible indeed."

"Yeah, that's what Julean keeps telling me."

"She is a wise girl. Her parents must have guided her well."

"Yeah, she says her parents, especially her dad, drilled into her the importance of waiting. She understands the importance of honouring herself like that and she wants to honour her parents, too."

"My, my, that is good to hear. Such a sensible, responsible young lady. You are a fortunate young man indeed to have a level-headed, self-respecting girl such as Julean."

Henry nodded in agreement and hung his head.

"It is no longer a matter of just choice, Henry, it is a matter of honour, and respecting the wishes of your loved one and her parents. I will pray for you, Henry. I understand how difficult this all is," Mr. Engelmann said as he opened the door. "I am going back to the seminary in the morning. If at any time you wish to call and talk, please do."

"Thanks, Mr. Engelmann."

Before getting out of the car, he patted Henry's hand. "'Come unto me all you that labour and are heavy laden, and I will give you rest.'"

Henry nodded.

Mr. Engelmann nodded back and smiled, then stepped out onto the sidewalk. Henry stooped over so he could see Mr. Engelmann and waved as his mentor walked towards the front door of the rectory and went inside.

FROM THE WINDOW of the rectory Mr. Engelmann watched Henry in his car. He knew his son was mulling over their conversation. He reached in his pocket and began praying for him and Julean, his fingers and thumb fumbling fervently from one bead to another on the rosary. *Please instill wisdom and purity of mind in our children, oh Lord, and give them Your strength.*

HENRY REVIEWED HIS conversation with Mr. Engelmann, overwhelmed by his teacher's wisdom and understanding, so clear and persuasive…and yet the desire was so strong.

"Lord," he said, looking up. "You put this desire in me for a reason, and I know it's best to fulfill it when I am married, but unless You help me, unless You give me the strength, I don't think I can carry this out. It is truly my heart's desire to do what is right. Please, Jesus, please help me."

A warm peace soothed Henry, as if he were lying in a tub full of hot water and feeling its warmth as he sank into it. His worries and anxiety fled like a flock of birds taking flight. He felt at ease and in control. He thanked the Lord.

After a long while, he turned the key, filling the silence with the sound of the Chevy's motor. He put the car into gear, let out the clutch and drove slowly away.

THE SECOND YEAR of university flew by just as quickly, if not faster, than the first. Henry, Travis and the other two boys rented the same rooms, which were waiting for them. It seemed no one else was foolish enough to want to rent in that part of town. Travis didn't return to university with them after Christmas break, though, since his grades hadn't improved any. He was just too interested in girls to study.

By mid-term break in February 1962, he and Julean were

talking more often about their favourite topic: getting married. The main reason, of course, was because of their growing desire not just to be with each other more, but also to be with each other more intimately. So far, Henry had been able to honour Julean's wish to give the man she married her purity; it would be her gift to her husband. In doing so, they were also respecting the rules and guidelines of their parents, especially Julean's father.

Henry had shared some of the teachings Mr. Engelmann discussed with him, and he and Julean implemented those suggestions as well. What further helped them to curb their desires and limit their time together in teasing, tempting and inflaming their passions was Julean's landlady's strict rule that she had to be in by ten on weekends with no outings during the week. They both began to suspect after awhile, however, that perhaps Julean's dad had had something to do with Mrs. Saunder's strict curfew and house rules.

But more and more lately, their desire for one another, to be together all the time, was increasing and they both saw no way forward but marriage.

"I don't know what my parents will think. Girls on the colony did marry early, many when they were fourteen or fifteen. But both Mom and Dad disagreed with that and strongly felt that was way too early."

"Well, you're twenty, Julean, and I'm twenty-one. We're not teenagers anymore. I think those are reasonable ages for us to tie the knot. And what about your older sister, Joyce, aren't she and that intern from the University Hospital considering getting married?"

"Yes, Dad seems to be agreeing to that. So maybe that will give us some support. But he's always stressed that he wants us girls to be finished university before we get married."

"Well honestly, honey, I know I can't wait another two years. I love you so much I just want to be with you all the time. "

"And I feel the same, Hank. I have a lot of money saved up."

"And so do I. I still have all of the money Mr. Engelmann

gave me and last summer I managed to add another $450 to my savings account. I'm sure we can make it until we graduate and get jobs—then we'll be rolling in the dough."

"Well, besides the financial considerations, there's the faith issue too. I know my parents don't like it that I'm going to church with you all the time. I did tell them that I'm drawn to the Catholic faith and that if I marry you I'd want to submit to your leadership of the family. We are very strict about that in our family and church: the man is the head of the household. But I have to admit, Hank, I'm growing to love your church more and more all the time and can't wait to have Holy Communion. The thought of receiving the body and blood of Jesus in the form of the Host just ignites my heart with such passion. I can't think of having a greater intimacy with Christ."

"I'm sure glad you feel that way, Julean, because my faith is very important to me too."

"It's so important for a husband and wife to be of one faith in a marriage."

A comfortable silence fell between them.

"I'm getting so excited just thinking and talking about this Hank," Julean said, "let's break the news to our parents this weekend that we're planning to get married!"

Henry took his right hand off the steering wheel and drew Julean in, pressing her close to him. He loved her so much.

But fear of facing Julean's dad put a damper on the joy and excitement he should be feeling as well.

A WEEK LATER as Henry and Julean drove back to Saskatoon, they reviewed the many discussions they'd had with both sets of parents. Neither of their parents really liked the idea of them getting married, but for different reasons. While both maintained that it would be better for them to finish university first, Henry had begun to feel that on Julean's side it had more to do with his family's religious faith and social status.

While both Henry's parents and Julean's came from a farming background, it seemed to Henry that Julean's father, in particular, strived very hard to make it in the medical community and establish the status associated with his chosen career. Dr. Carter, Henry felt, wanted a greater social standing for his family. And then there was the religious thing. Both Mr. and Mrs. Carter were opposed to Julean's growing interest in the Catholic faith.

"I really think it's got to do more with our religious differences rather than my dad being a doctor and all, Hank," Julean said, the frustration they both felt clear in her voice.

"But the reason I think that it *does* is because they've given your sister their blessing to marry Brandon, and he's interning to be a doctor."

"But don't forget, Brandon's also decided to join the Church of Jesus Christ of Latter Day Saints."

"Well, that's just the feeling I get, Julean"

"Well, in any case it's settled. We're going to get married with or without their blessing. I told Mom and Dad that I really want them to be happy about our decision and that I was so sorry for not obeying them," and turning to Henry, she said with tears in her eyes, "I just love you so much, Hank, and want to be with you forever."

Henry's heart burst with the same feelings for her. He reached out for her hand and the engine of his 1946 Chevy roared a little louder as they sped down the highway.

Chapter Forty-Nine

THE MONITOR ABOVE Ted Sarsky's bed blipped rhythmically along with the weakening beat of his heart. A second heart attack in detox had landed him in ICU with the prognosis that he would likely not live through the night.

Jenny and Edith sat at his bedside, staring at his face, then at the monitor, then back to his face, wondering how much longer they had together before his life ended.

TWO MONTHS AFTER Elaine had found him on the floor of his office, Ted began experiencing recurring, unpredictable blackouts. One of them had happened as he stopped for a red light on his way home after work. When the light turned green and his car didn't move, traffic backed up almost four blocks before a police officer arrived to control the angry motorists.

The doctors discovered that his blood-alcohol level was unbelievably high. So high that they wondered how Ted had been able to drive his car at all.

He had no longer been able to hide his alcoholism from the board of directors at Mackurcher and Co., and they delivered an ultimatum: either enter a rehabilitation centre immediately or hand in his resignation.

Ted had agreed. He'd chosen a place near Chicago, far away enough, he'd hoped, to protect his family's privacy.

His health had improved immensely over the two months of treatment. He gained weight and looked rested. He met with the board of directors and assured them that he was back in control and that the personal problems which had caused his drinking were resolved. The board agreed to extend his role as president for a further six-month trial period.

When Ted returned to his office, the liquor cabinet was gone. All that remained was a drinking glass and a crystal glass pitcher of water. He didn't have a problem with that.

It was the painting on the wall he couldn't cope with.

As Ted gazed at the landscape, the two angels he had seen before sat atop the clouds as if they'd never left, not even for a minute. Ted swung his chair abruptly away. A few moments later, feeling a bit more settled and confident, he twisted the chair back and glanced at the painting. *They're still there!*

He stormed over to the painting, intending to take it down to the furnace room and burn it, but when he reached the wall, the angels had disappeared.

He stood there, dazed. Then he swung the painting aside, exposing the wall safe. He entered the combination, but the safe would not open. He had misdialed. He tried again and heard a click after entering the last number. Inside sat the two letters he'd placed there, oh, years ago now.

He hesitated, then took a deep breath as he reached in and pulled out the envelopes.

They were still bound together by two elastics, the second still holding despite being frayed. He grunted in mild bemusement; even a frayed, tenuous elastic was holding onto this union like a steel chain. He felt the envelopes and the metal objects inside them. Ted relaxed. The pewter angels were still secure within each envelope. He must have been mistaken. There was nothing perched on the clouds in the painting.

He felt the objects again through the paper envelopes, no-ticing a strange warmth emanating through the paper as if the pewter had life. Ted quickly shoved the envelopes back into the safe, way at the back, then closed the door and spun the dial. A whiff of Jenny's lilac-scented perfume lingered in the air. What should have been a pleasant aroma only reminded him of his deceit. Ted stepped back and swung the painting until it was flat against the wall again, and the movement fanned away the accusation of his daughter's perfume. He hoped the landscape would hide his treachery.

Somewhat relieved, Ted returned to his desk and tried to set his mind to the report in front of him, except the angels beckoned him. The more he resisted looking at the painting, the stronger the desire to look became. Beads of perspiration sprang up on his brow. He was no longer conscious of what he was reading, his mind was once again on the painting...and the angels.

But the angels are locked in the safe and can't possibly get out!

Despite his rationalizations, he could no longer fight the growing compulsion to look. He *had* to know, one way or the other. Slowly, he turned his head as sweat poured over his body, soaking the back of his shirt to his skin. He tried to focus only on the frame and avoid looking at the actual painting, but he couldn't. And there on the clouds were the two angels, star-ing directly at him. All the old repressed feelings of guilt and shame swarmed him like demons.

Throughout his eight-week treatment, Ted had never re-vealed or discussed what had driven him to the bottle. He was too ashamed to let anyone know what he had done to his daughter; how he had lied to her.

He knew he was losing control. He needed help, and he needed it now. He launched himself from the chair and sped past the painting to the bookshelf. Books flew left and right until Ted's hands landed on the thirteen ounce bottle of vodka he'd hidden there in case of an emergency.

He gazed at his friend for a moment then whispered, "Thank

you. Thank you." Opening it, he pressed the mouth of the bottle to dry, trembling lips and drank non-stop until half its contents were drained.

Within minutes Ted relaxed, the liquor washing away the guilt that had surfaced only moments earlier. In control once more, he returned to his desk to read the report.

But this one lapse turned into another and then another, until within a month Ted's drinking was out of control once more. This time, he couldn't hide it from the board and, with further declining sales and his colleagues' loss of confidence in him, he was forced to resign.

In the month that followed, Ted landed back in the rehabilitation centre, filled with so much shame over the loss of his job, his position as president, and guilt over how he'd lied to his daughter—and so stressed over the strain of detoxification—that he'd suffered a massive heart attack.

ELAINE ENTERED MR. Sarsky's hospital room just after Jenny and Edith stepped out for dinner and some fresh air. She sat beside his bed and looked at the sorrowful figure lying before her. He had been such an outstanding man in the beginning. She'd so respected and admired him, and had wanted to help him.

Elaine waited for a half-hour or so, watching and praying for Mr. Sarsky. How could someone who had appeared to have everything end up this way? He'd had it all: money, power, the presidency of one of the largest corporations in Canada, an estate, a family and a beautiful daughter. Why did human beings make such destructive choices day in and day out that eventually cost them all they had? How could such an intelligent man be so utterly stu— Elaine, out of respect, could hardly bring herself to think it, but she could think of no other word to describe what Mr. Sarsky had done to himself. It *was* stupid.

Mr. Sarsky moaned, then opened his eyes. Elaine moved to the edge of her chair.

"Mr. Sarsky?" she said softly, not wanting to startle him. "Ted?"

He turned his head to look at her. She knew he saw the tears in her eyes. He lifted his hand, and she instantly reached out for it and held it tenderly.

"Elaine?"

"Yes," she nodded. Uncertain whether he'd recognized her, she said again, "Yes, it's Elaine."

Ted smiled, but even that simple act seemed to drain him of his remaining energy. She knew this might be the last time she ever saw him alive.

"Mr. Sarsky, the new president is coming in next week. He'll need documents that I believe are in the wall safe of your office."

No response.

Did he even have the cognitive abilities to understand what she was asking or to recall the combination?

"Mr. Sarsky? I need to know the combination to the safe."

Ted stared at her.

"I understand," he said finally. He closed his eyes as if he were about to drift off again. "Begin at zero and then four..."

Elaine scrabbled in her purse for the small notebook she always carried and jotted down the number as he spoke.

"And then turn left to...twenty-nine...and right..." his voice grew faint and his speech more slurred as he drifted away and then back. "Eighteen...and back to...forty...nine."

When Elaine looked up from her notebook, Mr. Sarsky was asleep. At that moment, a nurse walked in, clearly surprised to see her there.

"I'm afraid you have to go now, miss," the nurse said. "You're not family and Mr. Sarsky needs a lot of rest."

"Yes, of course," Elaine replied as she brushed past the nurse with one last look back as she slipped into the hallway.

WHEN JENNY AND Edith returned to the hospital after a hurried dinner, Ted was tossing back and forth, muttering about angels and letters under his breath.

Jenny rushed over and laid her hand over his.

"The letters."

"What letters?" Jenny looked at her mother, who simply stared back.

"Angels. Deliver the letters."

"What's he talking about, Mom?"

Her mother shook her head. "I don't know."

Ted cried out again, "Please deliver them…the letters….the angelic letters…deliver them…" Ted took a deep breath, "Jenny, I have something to…"

"What is it, Dad?" Jenny gripped his hand.

Edith leaned forward, her eyes widening, her mouth open in anticipation of a long-feared, dreaded confession.

"Jenny, I…I'm so sor…"

Edith drew yet nearer to her dying husband, praying he wouldn't…

Ted moaned, and opened his mouth to speak…but whatever he had been about to say only God would know.

He let out his last breath on a long, slow sigh that lasted an eternity, as if he were finally letting go of all the turmoil he had buried so deep inside him. The anxious expression on his face eased. His heart stopped beating, the jagged up-and-down on the monitor replaced by a single line. Ted was finally at peace.

When Elaine left Mr. Sarsky's hospital room, she headed right back to work. It was after six so no one would be there, but she had to know if she had the right combination. If not, visiting hours or no visiting hours, she'd have to return to the hospital and ask Mr. Sarsky again.

The elevator opened at the eighteenth floor, the hall lit only by a few overhead lights. There was something eerie about an office building at night. For the first time she noticed the sound of her footsteps as they tapped across the tile floor to the office door and the loud hum of the florescent fixture above her.

She fumbled in her purse for the keys, then tried to steady her trembling hand as she inserted it into the deadbolt. Uneasiness swept over her. She began to wish she had waited until morning to try and open the safe, but she knew she'd never be able to rest until she knew whether or not she'd written the numbers down correctly.

But if she were brutally honest with herself, she would have to admit that mostly she wanted to see what was in the safe. Her instincts told her that it held more than business documents. She couldn't shake the feeling that she was about to enter the secret inner world of Ted's mind. A vague memory surfaced in her thoughts to the time when, oh, three or four years ago, she'd entered the office and seen Mr. Sarsky at the safe, holding some envelopes and, it appeared, talking to them. He was so engrossed with the letters he hadn't even noticed her standing there. But perhaps those were merely business letters and surely they would be gone by now anyway. Still...

She closed the main doors behind her then walked to what once had been Ted's office and opened the door. It was dark and silent and cold. She flipped on the light, her eyes on the painting as she went right to it. She swung it open to the left, as she had seen other presidents do over the years.

Exhilaration and anxiety commingled as they flowed through her. She was about to get a glimpse into a mystery that had always troubled her, and yet she was nervous, because to solve the mystery she'd had to venture where she had never before been allowed. She glanced at the notepad in her hand, then with trembling fingers, turned the dial.

The handle did not yield.

Was it forty and then nine or was it forty-nine? she asked herself. She tried again, but the safe still would not open.

Perhaps in the rush to find her notepad she had misheard the first digit. She struggled to recall what Ted had said. His words began to ring out in her mind as if he were standing next to her. *Maybe it wasn't four, but fourteen.* A peace washed over her as she re-entered the numbers: 14...29...18...49.

Click.

Elaine stood there, her mouth open and her eyes wide, trying to see into the dim interior. It was an old safe, unusually deep. It used to have an interior light that turned on automatically as soon as the door opened, but the bulb had burnt out years ago, and neither Mr. Sarsky nor previous presidents had replaced it.

Normally, Elaine would feel wildly uncomfortable to be standing there staring into the safe that only presidents were allowed to access. But she was surprised by how at ease she was. It was as if she was meant to be there, a part of some overall plan that had begun long ago.

She brought out a generous handful of documents, then set them on Mr. Sarsky's desk to sort through. Nothing but the company papers she needed. They smelled faintly of lilacs, though. It triggered a memory, of…what? It had been so long ago, she couldn't recall what that scent was associated with.

She stood on her tiptoes and looked inside the safe again.

Seeing nothing else, Elaine began to close the safe's door, let down. She'd fully expected to find evidence of some dark, hidden secret. Just before the heavy steel door once again sealed the fate of the letters within, a loud *snap* echoed in the interior of the vault. She opened the door wide once more and peered inside. She moved her head to the side, allowing more light into the dim interior and there, way at the back, was something. Excitement and fear surged through her body. Her heart raced as she reached inside, the safe almost swallowing the full length of her arm. Her fingertips touched paper and she pulled out what she thought was one envelope, but was, in fact, two, held together by an elastic. No, two elastics, the broken one caught beneath the one still intact.

Elaine gasped. If it hadn't been for that snap, she wouldn't have been drawn to look deeper inside. How strange that one of the elastics had chosen to break at that precise moment.

A shiver tiptoed up and down her spine. Something very weird was going on. Her gaze locked onto the envelopes in her hand. There was something strangely familiar about them, especially the pink-coloured one. *Lilacs.*

"So, *that's* where it's coming from," she said aloud.

Elaine turned the package over, but only the backs of the envelopes were visible. They'd been put together address side in.

Elaine walked over to Ted's desk again, completely absorbed. She pried off the remaining elastic and flipped the first letter over. She sucked in a sharp breath as she read the names on the envelopes. The one from Henry Pederson showed a postmark of December 1956. Jenny's letter wasn't stamped; it had never been mailed. Presumably, Ted had held it back. The two letters had somehow crossed paths in this office.

Elaine suddenly recalled the day Mr. Sarsky had asked her to take an envelope down to the furnace room to burn. She'd watched him put two letters in the envelope, one of them a pink one addressed to Henry Pederson. *Ah yes, that lilac fragrance stayed with me as I took the envelope all the way to the elevator.*

But Ted had called her back just as she had reached the end of the hall. Meeting her halfway, he'd taken the letters from her, having decided to deal with them himself. She'd often wondered what had happened to them, and why Mr. Sarsky had changed his mind at the last moment. She had thought he'd sent them on, but it was obvious now he hadn't. But *why* hadn't he?

Was *this* what had caused Mr. Sarsky's excessive drinking? These letters and the ones in the box he'd asked her to destroy? Yes, these were probably the letters Mr. Sarsky was talking to that day. It seemed to her that the one he'd been holding was pink. It was all coming together so amazingly.

In her palm, the envelopes seemed to grow warm. She felt an inexplicable sense of comfort, and her anxiety faded into peace and calm. Something heavy shifted inside each envelope as she tipped them back and forth. The corner of one had been resealed with Scotch tape. She resisted the temptation to open it. She didn't want to suffer whatever hell Mr. Sarsky had.

In all the years she'd worked for the company, she'd never once sat in the president's chair. Countless times she had discreetly assisted various presidents to make sound decisions, but always from her secretarial role. She sank deep into the leather cushion and reclined, revelling for a moment in the power emanating from the chair. *So this is what it feels like to sit here and make important decisions.*

And she did have a very important decision to make.

What to do with those letters? It all made such sense to her now: Ted Sarsky had taken a dramatic turn for the worse after the business with these letters. Something about them had obviously caused him terrible grief and anguish.

Mail them.

Yes, that was it. Mr. Sarsky's downfall had started right around the same time he'd asked her to take that box of letters down to be burned in the incinerator. For the longest time she'd regretted not keeping one.

But there was no need to see or read their contents. It was none of her concern. All it would reveal was correspondence between two teenagers. What should have been done right from the start was to mail the letters to their proper recipients. Not doing so had likely cost Mr. Sarsky his life.

Elaine leaned forward, bringing the huge chair upright. She gathered the business documents and the broken elastic. Normally, she would have tossed the broken elastic into the garbage but couldn't, for some reason, bring herself to do that now.

"Dear Lord, You have a divine plan for everything and everyone...even to the last, most minute detail."

She put the broken elastic in her jacket pocket.

Elaine returned to the wall safe, set the bundle back inside, closed the safe door and spun the dial. *First thing in the morning.* She stepped back feeling quite important and swung the painting flat against the wall.

She studied the beautiful landscape. Oh, how this painting must have given such moments of peace to her president whenever he had the time to gaze upon it. Perhaps he should have taken its serenity more to heart and mind.

Elaine walked to the door and flicked off the light. Her work for the day was done. She glanced at her own desk and chair in the reception area as she made her way to the main office door.

They seemed meagre and unimportant in comparison to those she'd just left. She closed the office door behind her.

Downstairs, the commissionaire looked up as she stepped off the elevator.

"Good night, John."

"Oh, good night, Elaine. You're working late tonight."

"Yes," she agreed. *A president's work is never done.*

She opened the front door and stepped out into the humid evening air. It had rained while she was inside. Silvery clouds scurried past, revealing a full, round moon suspended in the centre of the heavens, twinkling stars all around.

She took in a deep breath of fresh air washed clean of the day's dust and exhaled slowly.

The streets were wet and empty and glistened in the city lights. She heard traffic in the distance but couldn't actually see any. Her gaze followed a shimmering path of light on the pavement leading to Joe's Diner just across and down the street. It was still open. A single customer, a man, was seated at the counter, slouched over a plate. Elaine was momentarily intrigued by his reflection in the large puddle at the side of the curb. She thought about going in for a coffee and sandwich, but decided to go home instead. A cup of herbal tea would be just fine.

As she walked to her car, Elaine visualized Ted Sarsky in the hospital, on the doorstep of death. Sorrow and compassion weighed her heart as a scripture passage came to mind: "The wages of sin is death." Mr. Sarsky had lied, for years, and he had paid the price with his health. The lies, deceit, the terrible feeling of unforgiveness and guilt for his misdeeds, had stolen his peace. Now she knew what she'd seen in his eyes every day. If only Ted Sarsky had done with the letters what she now planned to do, he would have been spared so much.

Yes, she congratulated herself as her eyes brightened in the strong moonlight, *I made a sound decision tonight...I would have made a damn good president.*

CHAPTER FIFTY

J ULEAN AND HENRY couldn't pack their stuff fast enough on the last day of classes to head back home. They both had summer jobs waiting for them, Julean working for her dad in his office, while Henry returned to his job with the Defense Department. He hoped to work with one of the tradesmen that summer.

All the way home, Julean and Henry had talked about getting married and all the plans they had to make.

"Oh, Hank, the summer is going to *fly* by, there's so much to do. Our premarital classes with Father Connelly start next Tuesday and then there's all the planning for the wedding itself; the invitations have to be sent out before the end of July, there's the guest list and I still have to get my gown. I'm getting so nervous about it all."

"It'll all work out, Julean. We've both been reading the books Father Connelly gave us last time we were home. We'll have to zoom through the course because you'll need as much time as you can to study so you're ready to turn Catholic before the end of August. You'll need to be baptized and confirmed and…"

"And then I can finally receive Holy Communion. I don't know why, but I just can't wait for that moment."

"It *is* special, Julean. I'm afraid I've taken it for granted. You're excitement has renewed my faith when it should be the other way around!"

"Have you heard from Mr. Engelmann yet about performing the ceremony?"

"In his last letter he said he had to speak with the archbishop about it since he won't be officially ordained by that time. But he hasn't gotten back to me yet."

"I sure hope he can do it."

"So do I. Mom said I got a letter from Gary. I asked her to open it and let me know if he said he could make it home to be my best man, but she said he wouldn't be able to—Jane's contracted some virus and he wants to stay with her. Apparently she's pretty sick. I might ask Travis. After all, if it wasn't for him, we might not have met."

"Oh, I think Jesus would have figured out some other way to get us together."

"Yeah, probably, but I'm also wondering about another guy I know—you haven't met him—his name is Eddy Zeigler. We've become very good friends since high school and I think it would mean a lot to him, and me, if he were my best man, too."

"Well, why not have both Travis and Eddy, just like I'm having two bridesmaids?"

"That's a good idea," he said, grinning at her. Then he sobered. "I sure hope your mom and dad give us their blessing."

"I do too, Hank. I'm sure they'll come around. It's a lot for them to take in; both their daughters getting married and leaving home. We'll just have to pray about it, Henry."

"Yeah, that's what Mr. Engelmann would say. I'll start praying to my guardian angel as well. I used to do that all the time, but this last year or so I've sort of forgotten to say the prayer I used to say every night."

"Oh?" Julean was curious. "How does it go?"

Henry thought about Jenny; it was the prayer they shared

and together so believed in. Henry struggled to pull his thoughts away and answer Julean's question.

"Well, it goes like this: Angel of God, my guardian dear, to whom His love commits me here; ever this day be at my side —and Julean's," he added, smiling at her, "to light and guard, to rule and guide. Amen."

"That's beautiful, Henry. Say it again, I want to memorize it and say it each day, too."

"Are you sure?"

"Very sure," she nodded. "So how did it go? 'Angel of God,' and then what?"

"My guardian dear, to whom…"

When they got back to Regina, Henry unloaded Julean's suitcases and boxes at her place and then hurried home. He was just in time for supper and could hardly wait to open the door and smell his mother's cooking. He was right: fried potatoes with onions, slow-cooked breaded pork chops and creamed corn met his senses.

Earlier that spring Bill had been promoted to the head of sales, so his father spent most of the meal telling Henry about some of the promotions they were carrying out, including putting Coke machines in all the high schools and donating some of the profits to the student councils of each school.

Later that evening as Henry prepared for bed, he sat down at his old desk. He was excited about his impending marriage to Julean, yet it bothered him immensely that her parents hadn't given their spoken consent or any hint of blessing.

He recalled the evening he'd asked for Julean's hand. Julean's mother remained silent while her father said they should wait not only until university was over, but also a few years after that until they were established in their careers. He'd seemed firm in his decision and refused to discuss the matter further.

Henry would never forget what Julean had finally said. "Dad and Mom, I love you both very much and I have always obeyed you. But I love Hank very much too and we want to be married.

We're praying for your approval and it would make me the happiest girl in the world to receive your blessing. But…" and tears had come to his beloved's eyes as she said what must have been so difficult for her. "Dad, you've always taught me to stand up for what I believe in and so," and here she'd taken a deep breath, "with or without your consent I am going to marry Hank. I pray with all my heart that you and Mom will give us your blessing."

Henry shook his head as he recalled it. He'd been certain the Carters would welcome him into their home, but they'd just remained silent.

As Henry thought about it all, he felt again the rejection he'd received from Jenny's parents too. Neither family seemed to approve of him. The lack of acceptance of these very significant figures in his life stirred a feeling of insecurity that began to seep into his inner being. It was perhaps this sense of not being good enough that set him on a course of seeking the approval of others rather than the approval of God, which Mr. Engelmann had so ardently tried to instill in his student.

Absently, Henry opened the middle drawer of the desk. Jenny's notes were still inside, along with a copy of the last letter he'd sent to her. He was tempted to read them all again—it had been years since he had—but decided against it. He didn't want to stir up old feelings over a relationship that had simply vanished. And he loved Julean. Loved her deeply. And this time he would allow nothing to come between him and his beloved.

Henry gazed at the letter and notes for a long moment, trying to decide if he should tear them up or not. He decided not to decide, for the moment anyway. He closed the drawer to his desk, then knelt down beside his bed and crossed himself.

"Dear Lord, thank you for all my blessings, for my mom and dad, for Mr. Engelmann, for bringing Julean into my life. Please give me the strength to continue to respect Julean and her wishes to remain chaste. It's so difficult to control my longing for her. Please help me, dear Jesus."

He prayed that the future would be filled with much love and happiness. He prayed that Julean's mom and dad would like him and accept him as their son. And he prayed, too, that God would bless Jenny. He hoped she had found someone and that she, too, was filled with much love and happiness.

"Oh, guardian angel, guardian dear, watch over all of us, continue to protect us..."

Henry crossed himself again and climbed into bed.

It was at times like this when he was overly tired and his defenses were down that thoughts of Jenny surfaced. Although he deeply loved Julean, deep down he still wasn't over Jenny.

Henry tossed and turned for over half an hour until finally he drifted off to sleep. The last thought he had was to wonder again why Jenny hadn't answered any of his letters.

If only he had received just one...

Perhaps it was this last thought that caused Henry to dream of letters, thousands of them, like a thick, heavy snowfall, flying everywhere. White wings stuck out on either side of the envelopes, fluttering gently as they moved about. They were angelic letters, some filled with words of love, some with hope, others of sadness and still others with answers to prayers...destined for someone.

And of the hundreds of thousands of letters, two of them, their envelopes pink and white, separated from the flock and fluttered away, each to its own destination, soaring up into the heavens above and beyond the rest until they seemed to become one and disappear into the starlit sky.

CHAPTER FIFTY-ONE

THE FOLLOWING NIGHT Henry phoned Eddy but was surprised to learn he had moved out three months ago. Mrs. Ziegler gave Henry her son's new phone number.

"Hello?"

"Hi, Eddy?"

"That's me. Hey, I recognize that voice! How you doin', Hank, ol' buddy?"

"Great! Your mom told me you'd moved out."

"Yep, I came into some extra cash and thought I'd move into a place closer to the brokerage firm where I work. And I figured it was about time I got out on my own anyway."

"Do you have time to meet for a few minutes? I'd like to talk to you about something—it won't take very long."

"Sure. I'm at the Balfour Apartments on Smith and Vic, but I'm just headed out."

"The Balfour Apartments? Geez, Eddy that's pretty swanky!"

"Yeah, like I said, I came into some extra dough and thought I should be comfortable. I tried to get the folks to move but they like the old place."

"Well, since you're going out, is there a better time to talk?"

"Actually, Hank, I'm just going to shoot a couple of games of pool at the Royal on 11th with a few of the guys from work. I can meet you there in fifteen minutes."

"How about I pick you up and take you there? Dad and I were going to go out to a show soon anyway."

"Thanks, man, but I've got my own set of wheels now. I'll see you at the hall in a bit."

Henry went to the living room where Bill was reading the paper. "I'm going downtown to meet Eddy for about fifteen minutes. What time does the movie start?"

Bill flipped through several pages of the paper and came to the movie section. "Let's see, I'm sure the second feature starts shortly after eight…yeah, here it is, eight-twenty. We should leave here by quarter to eight for sure, son."

Henry checked his wristwatch. "It's only six-fifteen. That should be plenty of time."

As Henry drove down 11th looking for a parking space, he saw Eddy getting out of his car.

Unbelievable! Is that pink Caddy convertible Eddy's car?! Henry honked the horn and drew Eddy's attention.

Eddy saw him and waved.

Henry pulled up beside his old friend and motioned him in.

"Hey, Hank, ol' buddy! How ya doing?" Eddy stuck out his hand and Henry was quick to receive it.

"Geez, Eddy, is *that* your car?"

"Yeah, got it a month or so ago. I saw a magazine where Elvis was driving one like that so I thought I'd join the club. It's a cool car, Hank. Hard on gas, but what the hell, eh? If you can afford the buggy, you should be able to afford to feed the horse."

Henry chuckled. "So did you rob a bank or something?"

"Nah. I just learned how to play the stock market. The guys at Richardson Greenshields can't believe how lucky I am. But it's not really luck, timing's the key."

"You *must* have good timing—looks like you've got it made

in the shade! But where did you get the money to play the stock market?"

"I made a deal with one of the boys that if he gave me a loan I'd show him how to make a lot of money. He gave me a small amount at the start and when the time was right, the day before Texaco announced their offshore drilling results, as a matter of fact, I bought options on the stock. Sure enough, next day the stock shot up like a rocket. I took the profits the same day before the stock fell back and that's how I got some start-up cash."

"You've always been good with numbers, Eddy. I remember in math you even showed up the teacher a few times."

Eddy chuckled, remembering. "Yep, I like numbers and the firm recognized it pretty quick, too. They sent me off on a course to train as a broker over a year ago. As soon as I turned twenty-one and was allowed to play the market, I did. I've lost a couple of times when I got greedy and hung on too long, but now I know better. A bird in the hand is worth two in the bush."

Henry shook his head. "Well, if I ever have some extra cash, I'll know who to come to!"

They heard honking. Henry checked the rear-view mirror. "Geez, I was so wrapped up in your car and your stocks, I'm still double-parked." Henry stepped on the gas and found a parking spot halfway down the street.

"So what's up, Hank? What did you want to see me about? Want a job at the firm?"

They both chuckled. Eddy reached in his shirt pocket and pulled out a pack of Black Cat.

"Mind if I smoke?"

"Still the same brand, I see. Yeah, sure, go ahead."

Henry shifted in his seat so he faced his friend.

"I think I told you last Christmas that Julean and I were getting serious and a wedding might be in the wind?"

"Yeah, I remember you telling me. That's great, Hank. Julean's a real good-lookin' chick…great legs; you got the whole package."

Henry laughed. "I see you noticed."

Eddy took a deep drag, squinted his left eye while his right, filled with curiosity, studied his friend.

"You know, Eddy—" Henry coughed at the growing smoke in the car.

"Geez, sorry, Hank." Eddy cranked down his window. "So you were saying?"

"Well, all through high school we kind of hung out and still do whenever we can, right?"

Eddy kept his gaze on Henry and waited, taking another drag and trying to direct it out of the side of his mouth.

"Well, Eddy, I consider you one of my best friends, and I was hoping you'd agree to be one of my best men at our wedding."

Eddy still didn't say anything. He stared at Henry for the longest time.

Henry would've loved to have known what was going through Eddy's mind. They hadn't always been the best of friends; *in fact, we were like enemies to begin with.*

"You know, man, that's the *coolest* thing anyone's ever asked me. Hank, I'd be honoured to be your best man."

"Thanks, Eddy; it means a lot to me," Henry shot his hand out towards Eddy and Eddy pumped it, hard. "Me, too, buddy."

"It was great taking in a movie with you, Dad."

"I enjoyed that too, son. It's hard to beat a good western. I'm sure it'll become a classic. It's great when they bring movies like that back to the theatres so we can watch them again."

"Yeah, I think *High Noon* won quite a few Oscars, didn't it?"

"I recall reading something about that. Wouldn't surprise me if that Cooper fella won for best actor when it first came out."

"He sort of reminds me of you, Dad. You're like him in a way, sort of on the quiet side and a straight-shooter, if you know what I mean."

Bill chuckled. "So how did things go with Eddy?"

"Real good. He felt great about being one of my best men. I'm sure glad I asked him."

"I only met him once, back when you were in Grade 12,

seemed like a nice boy. It's too bad Gary couldn't make it. Your friendship with Gary goes back a long way."

Henry nodded. "Yeah, it is too bad. But I guess Jane is quite sick. Gary sounds very worried about her in his letter. And maybe it's more important for me to have asked Eddy."

"Maybe so, son. There's a purpose to everything."

A silence fell over the car as the Oldsmobile sped down 11th Avenue. Henry and his dad had grown a lot closer over the last couple of years since Mr. Engelmann had encouraged him to talk to his dad about more personal matters.

But the thing he really wanted to talk to his dad about was the overwhelming sexual desire he felt for Julean. Each time he saw his wife-to-be it was increasingly more difficult to control his overactive hormones.

He was about to speak then chickened out at the last minute.

"Was there something you wanted to say, son?"

"Yeah…geez, Eddy sure hit it big on the stock market."

"How so?"

"Well, I think I told you his parents couldn't afford to send him to university and so after Grade 12 he got a job at Richardson Greenshields. Well, about six months ago he played what you call options or something like that, and I guess he made a bundle. Bought himself a new Cadillac convertible, lives downtown in a ritzy apartment."

"Well, good for Eddy. But he better watch himself. Easy come, easy go."

Once again it was quiet in the car and Henry tried to muster up his courage again. *Geez, why should I be afraid to talk to my dad about our human urges? He understands these things just as well as Mr. Engelmann, maybe even more, and besides it would be good to share this with him.*

"You know, Dad, what I really wanted to say was, well…"

"What is it, son?"

Henry tried to remind himself of the efforts his dad had been making to be more affectionate and show leadership in the family. Well, maybe he should make some effort, too. Even if his dad couldn't help him much, he still wanted to be closer to him, so...*here goes.*

"You know, Dad, I can hardly wait to get married to Julean."

"Yeah, Mom and I can see you two getting excited about it."

"Well, what I'm having trouble with is that I can hardly wait to...to make love to her."

Suddenly the interior of the car *really* fell silent. Even the drone of the engine seemed to retreat. Bill started to turn and look at his son to see if he was serious, but then he stopped and looked straight ahead through the windshield.

Henry could just visualize the red blotches on his dad's neck. *He doesn't know what to say.* But encouraged by the words of his mentor that sprang into his mind just then, Henry pressed on, forcing some sort of communication.

"Did you and Mom have sex before you were married? You don't have to tell me if you don't want to. I was just wondering because I sure want to with Julean and I don't know if I can wait anymore, even though the wedding is so close."

Bill cleared his throat but instead of speaking, he nodded in the affirmative much as Gary Cooper had from time to time in the movie they'd just seen. And then he said, "Yes we did, son. But it was my doing. I pressured her into it."

Now Henry was at a loss for words, and the car was quiet again. And just as Henry was about to speak, Bill started again.

"I knew she did it for me and she was worried about it. You know, if she was pregnant or not. She often said that she would surely die if she got pregnant and had to tell her parents...so if you haven't done it yet, maybe it's best to wait."

"Yeah, I suppose it's better too, but I'm sure having trouble with it."

"Mom thought it was a special night...I guess us fellas don't see it the same way, but I know what she means."

"Yeah, Julean feels the same. Boy, the Lord sure made it hard to control these drives, didn't He?

"Yup...He sure did."

Henry could see beads of sweat on his father's forehead

as his dad turned the car onto Broder Street. Light from the streetlights they passed flashed into the car, illuminating them in spurts. Henry could feel perspiration roll down his back and armpits as well. They were only a block away from home and Henry was glad he'd asked his dad. It was the toughest conversation he'd ever had with his father, but it was the most special one too, one he wouldn't soon forget, as brief as it was.

Rather than pull into the garage, Bill parked in front of the house. Just before he got out he reached over and touched Henry's shoulder, and said something Mr. Engelmann might have.

"It's the right thing to do, son, to wait—I know you'll do the right thing."

"Thanks, Dad. Thanks for going to the movie, too. I sure enjoyed that."

"Me too, that Cooper is sure something. I like his acting."

"Yeah, I do too."

When they got into the house, Mary was already in bed.

"Well, son, I think we'd better hit the hay."

Bill looked at Henry and for the second time since that moment at the cemetery, he put his arms around his son. It was awkward and sort of clumsy for the both of them, yet it was warm, real and gently beautiful.

Henry felt the dampness of his dad's shirt. His dad could probably feel his sweaty T-shirt as well.

"Good night, son, I enjoyed the evening…all of it."

Bill stepped back, quickly turning to make his way down the hall not ready yet to show his tears of care and love.

Yes, Henry thought, as words spoken by Mr. Engelmann sprang to mind as they often did, *God's divine providence is always at work through His helpers, the Holy Spirit and His fleet of angels.* Henry could see the results, not just in himself, but in his dad's heart, too.

He turned off the kitchen light, and as he made his way to his room in the dark he softly whispered, "Thank you, Jesus."

CHAPTER FIFTY-TWO

THE SMELL OF fresh-cut vegetables and simmering borscht consumed Mary's kitchen. She had been in her garden most of the morning, reaping the fruits of her summer labour: beets, turnips, tomatoes, carrots, and of course, dill. Everything was washed and neatly laid side by side on the kitchen counter.

When the doorbell rang, Mary wiped her hands on her apron and went to see who it was.

A uniformed man carrying a satchel waited on the other side of the screen door. When she opened the door, the postman, holding an envelope, greeted her.

"Good morning, ma'am. Is Henry Pederson in?"

"No, he's at work," Mary replied.

"I have a special delivery letter for him. Could you sign on his behalf?"

"Yes, I'm his mother."

The postman handed Mary a clipboard and pen. Mary signed her name and the date, August 27, 1962, on the form.

"Thank you, ma'am," he said, then added, "Borscht?"

"Yes, I'm making it for dinner."

"Smells just like my grandmother makes. Have a nice day."

473

"You, too."

Mary absently closed the front door as she read the return address.

"Jenny Sarsky," she whispered in shock. "After all these years..."

She sat down in the kitchen and, resting her elbows on the table, stared at the letter between her hands. How many days had Henry rushed home, hoping a letter from Jenny had arrived? How many days had Henry's heart broken a little more when he was told, no, there had been no letter? Many a day she'd thought of pretending to be Jenny and writing him a letter herself to help alleviate his crushed feelings.

And now, suddenly, out of the blue, a letter had flown to their door by special delivery six years later.

"But it's too late!" Mary put a hand to her forehead and shook her head. Henry was getting married in just over a week!

"Dear Lord, what should I do?"

Suddenly the weight of the object inside the letter shifted, rotating the letter downward between the fingertips of her right hand. She shook it from side to side and the weighted object slid easily as if it were flying inside. She grasped the object between her fingers trying to discern what it might be. It felt strangely warm.

Should she give the letter to Henry when he came home from work? He had such a beautiful dark tan from working outside and looked so healthy and happy, it would be so unsettling for him and might very well renew his heartache all over again.

Henry and Julean were getting married. They were happy together. This letter could jeopardize their relationship and ruin everything. A chill trickled up and down her spine.

Henry hadn't mentioned Jenny's name in years, and Mary felt certain it was over between them. And what about Julean? It wouldn't be fair to her, either. She and Henry had been dating for four years. Besides, what had attracted Henry and Jenny to each other might very well have changed. After all these years, would they still find each other the same? There might still be a glow for one another in the recesses of their hearts, but if they were suddenly to see each other, would the fire that once flared between them still be there?

The odour of boiled-down borscht reached her from the stove. She had forgotten about it, and most of the water had steamed away, reducing and strengthening the broth until the pot was only a third full. She poured some water from the tea kettle into the pot so it was almost half full, where she wanted it. She cut up the rest of the vegetables lying on the counter and tossed them into the pot to simmer. She put a lid on the pot then returned to the table.

As she sat back down in front of the letter, she decided it was best to just leave things be and not even tell Henry about it. If the letter had come a year ago—even six months ago—perhaps, but now, just days before he and that pretty young girl were to be married? Mary shook her head...*no, no, it's all too late!* The impending turmoil, the ensuing unhappiness and grief would all be too much now.

Before anything further changed her decision, Mary rose and headed to her bedroom, bringing down her treasure chest from the top shelf. She retrieved the key from the jewelry box on the dresser and unlocked it. There on top was the letter Henry had written her two years ago when he had been planning to go to Ottawa after Grade 12. One of the reasons he had aborted that plan was because he had never once received a letter from Jenny. Would Henry go now if she gave him the letter?

"No! I've made a decision, and I believe in my heart it's the right one."

Mary looked into the chest that had once belonged to her mother. It contained her mother's death certificate, but she'd long forgotten the rest of the contents. Mary reached into the box and lifted out other letters and objects with one hand, and put both Henry's letter and Jenny's on the bottom, burying them beneath everything else. She closed the lid to the treasure chest as if closing the lid of a coffin, bidding farewell to a relationship between her son and Jenny that she considered dead and gone. She pulled out the key and returned it to the small jewelry box, stirring the contents slightly with her forefinger so the tiny key would work its way to the bottom, out of view.

With the chest in her hands she stared into the mirror in front of her. Eyes were the mirror to the soul, and try as she might to rationalize her present actions, hers belied a twinge of doubt about this decision to keep the letter from Henry, the letter he'd yearned for, for so long.

As she stood there, vacillating, weighing the pros and cons once again, she decided that, ultimately, the play was over for Henry and Jenny. The final scene was finished, the curtain had come down and a new play was about to begin. Her son had found a new love. He was about to begin a teaching career, to settle down and perhaps raise a family. *Life must move forward, not backward.* Like watching an old movie, it was never the same. It had lost its depth. And she was sure that whatever Jenny and Henry had once had, it had lost its depth as well.

Mary forced a smile into the mirror, but only sadness reflected back in her eyes. She couldn't quite bury the memory of the anguish and despair her son had suffered. She'd always suspected Mr. and Mrs. Sarsky had prevented Jenny's letters from reaching Henry. She had prayed over and over that she could forgive them, that the Lord would touch their hearts and allow their daughter to send her letters. Now she had become another villain in the play, keeping this letter from her son and doing the very thing she'd accused the Sarskys of. But the present circumstances warranted such a decision, didn't they?

It was best for everyone involved.

Mary nodded with a sense of conviction into the mirror, trying desperately to change the expression of her reflected image to one of approval. With that, she picked up the chest and walked back to the closet, giving it an extra push to the back of the shelf, hiding it from view, not wanting to see it again. Mary walked out to the kitchen, hoping the room she so loved would give her comfort. She resumed preparing the borscht, sprinkling in a little dill weed, and then a little more. She hoped the savoury aroma would act as a drug, clouding the deed she had just done.

TWO DAYS AFTER Ted's funeral the front door bell rang.

"Would you please get that, Jenny?"

No answer. The doorbell rang again.

Mrs. Sarsky emerged from the laundry room.

The doorbell rang again.

"Oh, where is that Jenny? Why isn't she getting the door?" Edith muttered under her breath as she padded down the hall. She wasn't at all dressed for greeting guests.

When Edith opened the door, she found a postman on the landing, holding a letter and a clipboard.

"Good morning."

"Good morning," Edith replied, looking puzzled.

"I have a special delivery letter for a...," he glanced at his clipboard, "Jenny Sarsky."

"That's my daughter. She's not here right now, but I can sign for that."

The postman handed Edith the clipboard and she signed on the dotted line.

"And here's the letter, ma'am. You have a nice day."

"Thank you," Edith said, though only out of habit as she registered what she held in her hand. She looked at the original post date, December '56, and then at the stamped date just below, August '62.

Where on earth had it come from?

Upstairs, the shower turned off. Jenny would be down in a few moments. What should she do? Should she give Jenny the letter after all these years? The funeral had been so hard on her. But she was seeing James and they were planning to be married.

"Oh, what should I do?"

Edith stood frozen in the foyer. Above her, the bathroom door opened—or was it the bedroom door? It was the bedroom door! Edith heard Jenny walk down the hallway towards the stairs, then down them. Quickly she shoved the letter under her arm and ducked into the kitchen as Jenny came down the last few steps. Edith opened a cupboard, tossed the letter behind some dishes, and slammed it shut just as Jenny burst into the kitchen.

"Boy," said Jenny, "did that shower ever feel good. It was just what I needed. I've been feeling so sad and sluggish lately and it just revived me."

Jenny's hair was still wet and the amber-blond colour was a shade darker than usual. It would glow and grow lighter as her hair dried. Still, Jenny looked radiant as she stood in the bright sunlit kitchen, the tip of her nose was shiny and her blue eyes sparkled in the light.

Then Jenny's gaze met her mother's.

"Is something wrong? You look so flushed."

"Oh, I'm fine, Jenny. Just a little tired still from the funeral."

Jenny nodded. She wasn't herself either. "Is there anything I can do? Do you need help with the laundry?"

"No, I just put the last load in, and Maggie is in tomorrow to do the cleaning. I'll ask her to do the ironing, too."

"Well, I guess I'll have some breakfast. Care for some, Mom?"

Edith's heart stopped as Jenny opened the cupboard and reached for a bowl.

"Oh, Jenny!" Edith said, trying to distract her.

Jenny grabbed the bowl and turned towards her mother at the same time. "Yes, what is it?"

"Oh…oh, I—" Momentarily lost for words, Edith struggled to continue. "I may be going downtown later. Care to go too?"

Jenny thought a bit. "No, I'm reading a good book. Think I'll hang out at home and read awhile. I'm also still a little tired myself from all the commotion of the funeral."

Jenny set the bowl on the table then turned to another cupboard for a box of Kellogg's Cornflakes. On her way back to the table, she got out a bottle of milk from the refrigerator.

Just as Edith thought it was safe to breathe, Jenny glanced up at her. "What letters was Dad referring to the night he died?"

Edith's blood ran cold and rushed to her head. She felt faint.

"You *sure* you're feeling all right? You look feverish now."

Edith was at a loss for words. Her hands trembled so much coffee sloshed from her mug onto the countertop. She was cornered and guilty. Ted's last words had been a plea for her to deliver those letters, and moments ago she'd had in her hand the one that should have been delivered to her daughter, and now she didn't know what to do. How complicated matters could get when things weren't done as they should have been right from the start. But it was much too late for all that. She needed time to think it all through.

Trying desperately to avoid further discussion, Edith quickly said, "You know, I do feel somewhat flushed, Jenny. I think I'll lie down for a bit in the living room."

Jenny helped Edith to the couch, retrieved the blanket draped over the armchair and pulled it over her mother.

"Thank you, Jenny. Why don't you go on out to the patio and read your book? It's such a beautiful morning."

"Yes, that sounds like a good idea. I'll prop the kitchen door open—if you need anything, just call.

"Thanks again, Jenny." Edith closed her eyes as Jenny stood over her, hoping that would send a signal to her daughter to leave, and end any further conversation.

Edith's mind churned as she lay on the couch. What should she do with the letter? There must have been another letter, too. Ted had said *letters*. With an S. He'd also talked about angels. That made absolutely no sense. She wondered what that boy, Henry, was doing now. He could be dead or married for all they knew. Why should she give a letter to Jenny and start that mess all over again?

Jenny was going out with James and seemed content enough. And yet, at times, she sensed that Jenny still thought of that darn boy from Regina. Perhaps she should call that grocery store. Engelmann's, wasn't it?

Perhaps the owner could tell me what happened to Henry. Maybe that would help me to decide what to do.

Feeling somewhat better for having made a decision of sorts, Edith relaxed. All the cares of the morning dissolved into a dreamlike reverie. But she couldn't shut out Ted's last words: *Please deliver them...the letters...the angelic letters...deliver them....* The words were indelibly imprinted on her heart and mind. She had an obligation to fulfill the wish of a dying man, and yet it would go against all she'd believed in over the years.

At first it was a comet streaking across the sky in her dream. As the bright object neared, she saw that it was an angel, its wings spread wide, slowing his speed and finally settling down in front of a young girl. *Jenny.* The angel held a white, glowing envelope and reached out to give it to the young girl.

"Mom, mom!" Jenny's voice broke through her dream. Edith blinked and looked up at her daughter's face etched with worry. "You sure were tired. You slept all morning and most of the afternoon. It's almost three o'clock."

"Oh my," Edith said. She tossed the blanket off her and lowered her feet to the carpet. She shook her head slightly to shake off the drowsiness. "What have you been up to?"

"I've been reading all day."

"What would you like for supper?"

"Oh, just soup and a sandwich will be fine, Mom. Don't bother making a big meal tonight. I'm going out with James to a movie later, and we usually stop at a café afterwards. I'll get something there if I'm still hungry."

"All right, that sounds fine."

"Well, I think it's my turn for a nap now." Jenny went over to her mother, smiled, and kissed her cheek.

As her daughter disappeared upstairs, Edith sat on the couch, sifting through the images from her dream. It had been so vivid and real. An angel delivering a letter to Jenny. Could it be the letter she'd received that morning? Was the dream trying to tell her something? She felt a chill as contradicting thoughts of what to do about the letter flooded her mind.

Oh yes, she was going to call that grocery store to see if she could find out what had happened to Henry. Once she knew, maybe she would know what to do with the letter too. Edith went into the kitchen, picked up the phone and dialed 0.

When the operator answered, Edith asked for Engelmann's Grocery Store in Regina. The operator connected her with an operator in Saskatchewan and Edith repeated the request. When the operator told her the number no longer existed, she asked for the number for Pederson on Broder Street. Moments later the operator recited the number and Edith jotted it down, repeating it back to the operator to make sure she had all the digits correct, then hung up.

As she looked at the phone number, heat suffused her body again. She retrieved the letter from the cupboard and stared at it for a long time. She took a brown bag from a drawer and put the letter inside. She set the bag on the kitchen table then made a fresh pot of coffee.

As the water warmed, Edith returned to the phone.

"Operator. How may I help you?"

"Yes, operator, could you please connect me with the Pederson residence in Regina, Saskatchewan."

"And what is the number, ma'am?"

Edith read the number she'd written down.

"Please hold while I get a Saskatchewan operator to dial that number."

"Thank you." Edith wiped her sweaty palms on her slacks so she wouldn't drop the receiver, but there was nothing she could do about the rivulet trickling between her breasts. *What if Henry answers? I hope he's not there. Oh my, what have I done? I should have thought this through more carefully...*

"Hello?" came a female voice.

"Hello," Edith said, her voice trembling. "Is this Mrs. Pederson?"

"Yes, it is. May I ask who's calling?"

"You may not remember me, Mrs. Pederson. My name is Edith Sarsky. We used to live just three doors down from you. My daughter and your son were good friends."

"Oh, you're Jenny's mom!"

"Yes, that's right. I'm Jenny's mother." There was a long pause. "Is Henry at home?"

"No," replied Mary, "he's at work."

"Good. May I ask you a personal question, Mrs. Pederson?"

"Well, it depends—I…of course."

"It has to do with a letter that Henry sent Jenny."

"Yes…?" Mary said after another rather lengthy pause.

"Well, I was wondering, Mrs. Pederson, if Henry has received a letter from Jenny?"

There was complete silence as if the phone had suddenly gone dead.

"Hello? Are you still on the line, Mrs. Pederson?"

"Yes, yes, I am…" There was another long pause. "As a matter of fact, I received a letter from your daughter just this morning."

"Has Henry seen it yet?"

"Why do you ask?"

"Well, we also received a letter from your son today, and I'm wondering if I should give it to Jenny."

"Mrs. Sarsky," the woman on the other end of the phone took a deep breath, "my son is getting married in less than two weeks. Jenny had more than enough time to write to Henry. I…I've decided not to give it to him under the present circumstances."

"I see," Edith said, looking down. "Jenny is seeing someone else as well, and they are also contemplating marriage. I also thought it best not to stir things up again."

"Perhaps, then, it's best to simply leave things as they are? It's too late to start things over and it sounds like it would just cause a lot of trouble and heartache for all concerned—"

Edith interrupted. "Yes, I understand. Can we agree then to discard the letters and not concern our children with them?"

There was a long silence. "Yes, I—I agree with that, Mrs. Sarsky. Both our children seem to be happy with their new partners. Why create unnecessary turmoil?"

"Yes, Mrs. Pederson, I understand your point of view completely. I'm very happy that I called. You've helped me make a very difficult decision."

"Well, then perhaps we can just leave it at that?"

"Certainly, Mrs. Pederson. You won't be hearing from me

again, but you can rest assured that Jenny will not get this letter while I am alive."

"Fine," Henry's mom replied, "Nor will Henry."

After another long pause, Jenny's mom said, "It's been a pleasure talking with you. I'm certain you have many things to do. I appreciate your understanding."

"As I appreciate yours, Mrs. Sarsky. Goodbye."

Edith held the receiver against her ear long after Mrs. Pederson had hung up. She was still holding the receiver when Jenny came through the kitchen door a moment later.

Edith finally replaced the receiver on its hook.

"Who was that?"

"Oh, no one. I was just going to call a friend to see if she wanted to go downtown but I changed my mind."

Jenny went to the fridge and took out some orange juice.

"Looks like your coffee's ready, Mom."

"Yes, of course," Edith said. She rushed over to stove, thinking about how long the coffee had been percolating.

After adding cream to her cup, Edith joined Jenny at the table.

"You look better, Mom. Not so feverish."

"Yes, I do feel more rested. It's been a very trying time."

Then Edith noticed the brown bag on the table. She couldn't believe she'd forgotten about it. Much to her horror, Jenny followed her gaze, then picked the bag up.

"What's this, Mom?" she asked, ready to open it.

Edith snatched it out of her hand. "Oh, it's nothing, Jenny— none of your business. Something your father forgot to deal with." Edith jumped up from her seat, still holding the bag.

Jenny looked at her mother with a hurt, puzzled expression. "Are you sure you're okay, Mom? I'm really not trying to pry."

"Oh, will you quit worrying about me! Of course, I'm fine. I just need more rest." She stormed out of the kitchen.

Jenny sipped her orange juice and wondered what had gotten into her mother. The funeral had been tough, but she'd been acting strangely all day. And that bag, it sure felt warm. What on earth was in it that she wasn't supposed to see?

Jenny downed the rest of her juice in a single gulp then rose from the table to set her glass in the sink.

As Jenny walked past the phone, she noticed a telephone number on the pad beside it. Jenny studied the number. It wasn't an Ottawa number and yet she knew she'd seen it before. Who on earth had her mother called?

"MOM ARE YOU up?"

Edith pushed herself out of her chair and opened the door. Jenny stared at her, trying to decide if her mother was all right.

"Are you okay, Mom?"

"I told you to stop worrying about me."

"I don't have to go to the movie with James. Would you rather I stay home with you?"

"No, no, Jenny, that's fine. Please run along and have a good time. It's been such a hard week; I just need some rest."

"Well, if you're sure…"

"I am. Positive. Just go. Say hello to James for me?"

Reluctantly, Jenny turned and walked down the hallway. At the head of the stairs, Jenny looked back. Her mom was at the bedroom door.

"Just go," repeated Edith as she shooed Jenny with her hands "Have a good time. I'll be just fine. I need some time alone."

Finally, something that made sense.

Of course Mom needs some time alone.

"All right, Mom, I won't be too late. See you in a couple of hours. Oh, by the way? This is driving me crazy—the number by the phone looks so familiar, but I can't remember whose it is. Who were you calling?"

Edith thought she might faint on the spot. How much more of this could she possibly take?

"I…I don't know. I was just doodling numbers as I talked to Doreen. Now go on. Have a good time."

Jenny studied her mom. "Really? Because I—"

"Yes! Go!"

As soon as Jenny left with James, Edith emerged from her room with the brown paper bag and headed downstairs to the kitchen.

"How could I be so careless?" She ripped off the top page of the pad with the Pederson's phone number on it, glanced at it and walked into the living room. She put several logs into the fireplace and lit the fire. Crumpling the paper, she tossed the page into the flames and watched as the evidence of her phone call to Mrs. Pederson burned away.

Whew, that was close.

Edith pulled the letter out of the bag and set it on the coffee table, then crumpled the paper bag and tossed it too into the fire. Edith watched as it unravelled, bursting into flames. Her face brightened momentarily as the bag flared then turned to ash.

Edith picked up the letter next and took it too to the fireplace. Before she placed it over the flames, she remembered Ted doing the same thing almost six years ago when they had decided to destroy Henry's and Jenny's letters. She recalled how awful Ted had looked and felt after he'd tossed Jenny's letter into the fire. She remembered, too, Ted's dying plea that she deliver the letters. *His final wish.*

Twinges of guilt tugged at her conscience. For a brief moment Edith questioned her objectives but instantly recovered. Ted had been delirious. Had he been in his right mind, he'd never have made such a request. And furthermore, Mrs. Pederson too had decided not to show her child the letter Jenny had sent. No, she was doing the best thing for everyone concerned.

Edith frowned into the fire, deep in thought. About to drop the letter into the leaping flames, she felt the heavy object inside the envelope slide down its length, jarring her hand when it struck the end. It felt warm in her palm and sent a strange, ominous vibration through her. She withdrew the envelope from the threatening flames. A mixture of guilt and foreboding swept over her. Perhaps that was what Ted had been feeling all those years: sorrow, remorse—and fear.

"I certainly don't want to end up like he did."

Edith backed away from the fire and glared at the menacing flames. The pervasive sense of foreboding within her strengthened. All the memories surrounding the letters flooded her mind, weighing her down.

As if guided by an unseen presence, Edith turned away from the fire and went upstairs to her bedroom. She opened the closet door and gazed up at the top shelf. Standing on her toes, she reached up with both hands and pulled down a wooden chest, a keepsake box with beautiful ornate carvings, passed down from her mother. She had received it when her mother had died. Edith loved that box; it held both special memories of her mother and all the things Edith herself had treasured over the years. She pulled a silver key from under the paper liner in the top drawer of her dresser.

With a twist of the key, she opened the lid and removed the contents one by one: her first communion certificate, some report cards, photos of old boyfriends and girlfriends, and love letters—the first and the last she had received from Ted before they were married. When the box was empty, she placed Henry's letter to Jenny in the bottom of the chest, then buried it under all the items she'd taken out. After closing the lid and pressing the latch to lock it, she returned the keepsake chest to its spot in the closet. Almost instantly a restful calm soothed her, letting her know that, at least in part, she had done the right thing by not destroying the letter.

Edith changed into her nightgown, robe and slippers, and went downstairs to make herself a cup of chamomile tea and sit out on the patio under the bright full moon. She thought about the pact she and Henry's mother had made. How similarly they felt. Under the guise of a mother's love and concern for the welfare of their children, together they had sealed Jenny and Henry's fate. She sipped her tea. Both the soft light of the moon and the warmth of the herb soothed her. She stared into the night, allowing her mind to drift aimlessly. She was too tired to direct or control her thoughts any longer.

CHAPTER FIFTY-THREE

I T WAS A torturously hot day. Ninety-two degrees in the shade with virtually no wind. The only saving grace was the dry, humidity-free prairie air. It would be a perfect day to be at the beach or swimming pool. It wasn't a day for working outside, especially painting houses.

Henry's painting partners, Sid and Harvey, were two elderly men the government had hired over twenty years ago. Together they maintained all the government offices and the over one hundred and fifty wartime homes in the west end of Regina where military families mostly lived. Henry's summer assignment was to paint the exterior of as many of those homes as possible. The interiors would be done during the winter.

On very hot days like today, when even the wind seemed to lack the energy to blow, their strategy was to stay ahead of the sun. The paint stayed workable longer and they avoided sunburn. Another thing that helped was daily naptime. Without fail, around two o'clock every day, Sid and Harvey set their brushes down, covered them with a moist rag to prevent the paint from drying out, and had at least a half-hour siesta. At first, Henry feared that a superior would catch them sleeping on the job, but it didn't seem to bother Sid or his partner the least bit. It didn't seem to bother the foreman either; he'd just wave as he drove by.

This particular workday was almost over.

"Start cleaning up your brushes," Sid called out from around the corner of the house. Because they were working with oil-based paint, they had to use paint thinner. Sid liked using fuel oil rather than commercial paint thinner. Fuel oil was slippery and much friendlier to the hands, almost like soap.

Henry finished cleaning his brushes in record time. He was going to visit Mr. Engelmann, who had made a special trip down from the seminary to meet with the archbishop at the rectory right after work. A few weeks ago, the archbishop had rejected the idea of Mr. Engelmann marrying Henry and Julean. However, due to Mr. Engelmann's age and some studies in theology and philosophy Mr. Engelmann had acquired before the war, the archbishop had later decided that he might be able to make a special dispensation. This additional meeting was to see if there was any possibility of relaxing the requirements.

Henry pulled up in front of the rectory shortly after five.

Mr. Engelmann answered the door after the first ring.

"Hello, Henry! My gosh, you are so brown. You will soon have the colour of an African!" he laughed.

Henry smiled, his white teeth glowing against the dark tan of his face.

"Hi, Mr. Engelmann," Henry replied as they hugged.

"Whew, Henry, what is that odour? A special perfume or cologne?"

"Yeah—eau d'fuel oil," Henry replied with a chuckle. "I tried to wash most of it off, but it's hard to get it out of your skin. Julean teases me about it all the time. She threatens to sit in the back seat when we're driving, but it's funny, in no time flat there she is right next to me, cuddled up under my arm."

They both laughed.

"Well, come in."

Henry followed him to the huge study. Two black leather

chairs sat in front of a fireplace. Two leather couches sat behind the chairs, separated by a rectangular coffee table strewn with a few magazines. The entire west wall was a floor-to-ceiling bookshelf hosting hundreds of books. Henry had never seen such a display except in a public library. On the north wall, several banks of windows opened on a view of an inner courtyard laden with flowers. There was a fountain in the middle of it all.

"Have a seat, Henry." Mr. Engelmann motioned for him to sit in one of the armchairs in front of the fireplace. The rectory was air-conditioned so the leather felt cool as Henry sat, a welcome sensation from the blazing heat he'd felt all day.

"Well, you missed Julean by a half-hour. She returned some of the books Father Connelly lent her. I understand her first communion went over very well last Sunday. I am so sorry I could not attend to share in your joy."

"You should have seen her, Mr. Engelmann, she was all dressed in white and had a matching ribbon in her hair. She looked like an elementary school girl. So excited and radiant. She could hardly contain herself."

"Father Connelly says he has never seen a more devoted student and convert to the church. I spoke to her briefly when she left; such a lovely girl. She asked if I would be doing the ceremony at your wedding."

"So what happened? Are you allowed to do it?"

"Well, Henry, as I already told her, I do not have completely good news. The archbishop said it would be impossible for me to be ordained before your wedding and he couldn't allow any dispensation for me to perform the wedding service without being ordained first. They have to follow a very strict procedure. If they start making exceptions, it could lead to serious problems down the line and lower the high standards of the Church."

Mr. Engelmann read Henry's disappointment. "But, Henry, I will be right there beside Father Connelly, assisting him with the ceremony. It will be almost as if I am the priest saying, 'I now pronounce you man and wife.' In fact, I will whisper it along with Father Connelly."

Feeling a little better, Henry finally said, "Yeah, okay. But it would've been so perfect for you to actually marry Julean and me."

Mr. Engelmann nodded. "It was something I would have liked to have done very much, Henry. So the date is set for September 9?"

"Yes," Henry replied, "in less than two weeks I'll be a married man! Julean and I seem to have everything under control. She and her friends have been making flowers out of tissue for over two weeks now and stringing them together to decorate all the cars. The flowers are alternating white and blue, and it's all going to look so great! We only pray that it doesn't rain." Then Henry added, "Julean's girlfriends had a shower for her last Saturday and the boys are having a stag party for me this weekend."

"I see you both are very busy."

"Yeah, you can say that again! I've got a new black suit, new shoes, socks, shirt and tie. I'll look pretty spiffy."

"I hope I recognize you at the altar," Mr. Engelmann joked.

"Mom said she was making borscht for supper. Want to come over for some?"

"No, Millie already made dinner for Father Connelly and me. She loves to cook, too, and would be disappointed if I suddenly went out after she prepared a larger dinner for us."

"Okay. Thank you, again, Mr. Engelmann."

He nodded. "I think you'll be pleasantly surprised and pleased with the way Father Connelly and I have planned the service. You go on now and enjoy your borscht," Mr. Engelmann said, leading Henry back to the front door. "I am leaving first thing in the morning to go back to the seminary, but I will be back next Wednesday, though, so Father Connelly and I have time to prepare for the big celebration on Saturday."

"Yeah," Henry said loudly, feeling a surge of excitement. He brought his hand up to his mouth, in mute apology for not maintaining silence in the rectory.

Mr. Engelmann waved it off with his hand. "Not to worry. You should hear Father Connelly crank up the stereo when he plays some of his Irish music. Loud enough to wake up the whole neighbourhood, including the dead in the cemetery beside us!"

Henry laughed, feeling completely absolved as one should when leaving the church.

Henry turned and hugged Mr. Engelmann, and his teacher patted his back as he always did. "Have a good time with Julean. And put on some different cologne," he said, wrinkling his nose.

"Hi, mom, I'm home!"

His mother turned as he entered her sanctuary.

He kissed her cheek. "Boy, does that ever smell good!"

"Yes, it boiled a little longer than usual so the broth's a little stronger today." She added with a coy smile, "It does taste very good, if I say so myself."

Mary walked to the fridge, opened it and then closed it. She walked to the stove and opened the oven door, but nothing was baking. Henry sensed his mother was nervous or maybe distracted.

"Everything okay, Mom?"

"Oh, everything's fine, just the heat and being in a hot kitchen all day. Why don't I make us a nice glass of iced tea and we can sit on the front steps and wait for Dad?"

"Sounds great. Let me go have a quick shower first to try to get some more of this fuel oil off me."

"Oh? Funny, I didn't notice it."

"That's because of your soup, the fresh dill is wonderful." Henry said with a chuckle.

Freshened by his shower, Henry joined his mother on the front step. They had just about finished their glasses of iced tea when his dad pulled up. He stepped out of the car and slung his jacket over his shoulder. His tie hung loose and his shirt had circles under the armpits.

"Hi, Mary. Hi, Henry." His dad bent to plant a kiss on his mother's cheek.

"Hi, honey," his mom replied. "Long day?"

"Yeah. Think I'll take a quick shower."

"Well, supper's ready as soon as you are. I'll have a glass of iced tea ready for you, too."

"Thank you, dear." He stepped between Mary and Henry and opened the screen door. "Boy, does it ever smell good in here."

Henry's mother smiled.

"So, how was your day, Mom?"

Her head snapped up, her eyes wide for a moment.

"Oh, nothing eventful. I was out in the garden all morning, gathering vegetables for the soup. Then I made the broth, cut up the vegetables, cleaned a bit and before I knew it, it was dinner time." That part was the truth. "And how was your day? It must have been difficult to work in this heat."

"Yeah, it sure was hot out there today. I could hardly wait for the day to be over. I went to see Mr. Engelmann right after work about his visit with the archbishop."

"Oh, yes?" Mary sat straighter on the step. "And?"

"The archbishop told Mr. Engelmann that it was impossible for him to be ordained after only two years in the seminary and only an ordained priest could marry people. There was no way he could make any special dispensation."

"Oh, that's too bad."

"But Mr. Engelmann will still be assisting and promised that it would almost seem like he was performing the ceremony."

Mary's eyes lit up. "Oh, that sounds so nice. I'm sure everything will go over just fine."

Mary studied her son for a moment longer, hoping her stare would not arouse any suspicions over what she'd done earlier. He seemed so happy and excited about the wedding. *To have given that letter to him would have caused so much turmoil. I made the right decision.* She slapped both hands on her knees and stood.

"Well, Dad will be down in a few minutes and you know how he likes to have dinner right away."

"Yeah," Henry said, "I can hardly wait to eat. I don't know what you did today, Mom, but that soup smells better than ever."

If you only knew, son. If you only knew.

Chapter Fifty-Four

Henry stopped in front of Julean's house shortly after seven and honked the horn. Since he never felt comfortable in her parents' presence, he often tapped the horn when he drove up so he wouldn't have to go in.

Julean bounded down the walkway as Henry stepped out and rounded the car to open the door for her.

"Thank you, kind sir."

On the way to the movie, a slapstick comedy starring Bud Abbott and Lou Costello, Henry told Julean what Mr. Engelmann had said. She had heard about most of it earlier when she was at the rectory herself. She expressed a little disappointment but perked up when he told her of Mr. Engelmann's idea.

After the movie they went for ice cream at the Milky Way, which was extremely busy. They squeezed into a spot at the curb and Henry stood in line at the window.

"So, what do you fellows have planned for the stag party?" Julean asked, when he returned with the cones.

"I think two belly dancers are coming in."

Julean just rolled her eyes. "Well, if you guys do have strippers, then the girls and I want to be there."

They laughed and Henry said, "Oh, I don't think you have to worry; we'll probably end up playing poker and drinking beer and then going out for Chinese food like we usually do."

They arrived in front of Julean's house about quarter to eleven. Even though she was soon going to be married, Julean still had a curfew. She and Henry were glad it had been extended to eleven. Henry had to admire Mr. Carter's commitment to protecting his daughter right up until the end, and Henry himself had long since decided to impose similar strict rules for any children they might have as well. He just wished his relationship with the Carters was better; he'd have to work on that. It wasn't good for a marriage to have problems with either set of parents.

Henry turned off the ignition; they had at least another fifteen minutes together. Last summer they used to go to the park and neck, like most of their friends did. They soon realized, though, that they were just asking for trouble and torturing themselves. So now Henry parked in front of the house and when they were inside Julean's home, they had started to keep the door to the rumpus room open as well.

As Mr. Engelmann had said to Henry on many occasions, *if there is an area of temptation in your life or you want to overcome a habit that isn't in your best interests, you must have a plan, a method of attack, waiting in the wings. If you don't, then as soon as that desire or temptation arises, your resolve will be washed away like a house built on sand.*

Henry and Julean often talked about friends of theirs who had chosen differently and the anguish some of them had gone through. The breakups and the heartaches; the unplanned pregnancies and the abortion one of Julean's friends had had.

The more they talked and practised what they preached to each other, the more they were able to rise to the occasion. However, with their impending marriage, Henry found it increasingly difficult to honour their commitment.

As he sat in the front seat, embraced in Julean's arms, his entire body ached with desire. For months he had been too embarrassed to walk her to the door after necking for a short while.

"It's just another ten days," Julean said, and he knew she understood full well what was in his mind and heart.

"I talked to my dad about sex before marriage after the movie we went to a week ago. Man, that was hard for us to talk about. But we did it."

Julean laughed. "That's because you've never discussed it before in your family. In our family, we talk about it openly all the time. Just last night Dad said again that it's his job to make certain his girls are chaste, right up to the day before they get married. And he fully expects us to honour his wishes. And he and Mom have explained the reasons so many times before, as well."

"Yeah, I don't know why my parents never did, but I'm sure glad Mr. Engelmann talked to me about it. It really helped me see the big picture about sex and the importance of only validating it in marriage. But right now all the reasoning in the world doesn't seem to help."

Henry growled, not entirely playfully and lunged for his bride-to-be. He pulled Julean close to him and kissed her long and hard. Julean broke from Henry's strong grasp and backed away ever so slightly, startling him.

"I think I'd better go now."

"Oh, just a little while longer," Henry pleaded. There was urgency in his tone.

"I feel the same way you do," acknowledged Julean, "but we've come this far, and I so want to save everything for our wedding night. I promise I'll give myself completely to you and never again withhold my affection."

Her words had a calming effect and he sighed, running a hand through his hair.

"Yeah, you're right, honey. It's just that I want you so much—"

"Just think," Julean interrupted him, "only ten more days, and we will be able to make love whenever we want."

"I can hardly wait!"

Julean reached over, trying to keep a safe distance from him and kissed Henry on the cheek.

"Good night, Hank," she said tenderly. "I love you—so much."

Henry sighed again as he got out of the car and jogged to catch up with her. He was surprised by how quickly his manhood responded to certain words and thoughts. When they arrived at her door, Henry wrapped an arm around Julean's waist and drew her hard against his body.

Julean quickly resisted him. "Good night, Hank."

She stepped back and opened the screen door.

Henry managed a crooked smile and thought how ridiculous he must look. Julean chuckled and, for the first time in the three years they'd gone together, she said, "Ooooh, Henry."

"G'night, Julean," he finally said, seeing as how he wasn't going to get any further. "I'll call you tomorrow."

"Yes, please do," she said, "And remember I've got a gown fitting tomorrow night, so I won't be seeing you."

"Oh, yeah, I forgot. I'll call you after that. G'night, honey."

She waved and smiled. With half her body hidden behind the front door, she raised her skirt a few inches and thrust her leg out like a seasoned showgirl, then slowly pulled it in and closed the door.

Henry groaned and headed stiffly back to his car.

ON SUNDAY, JULEAN and Henry went to the twelve o'clock mass, holding hands as they walked down the aisle together. In Julean's free hand, she held a white pouch containing a pearl beaded rosary and a white leather-covered Sunday missal. Henry had given it to her for her first communion. He was very grateful that Julean had accepted his faith so willingly and lovingly.

They genuflected and entered the pew, then knelt again and silently prayed. Henry was the first to rise and sit down in the pew, waiting for mass to start. Julean continued to kneel in deep prayer. She had taken her rosary from its case and was slowly moving it through her delicate fingers. At the sight of Julean's sincere devotion, Henry wondered if he lacked faith.

Henry couldn't stifle a yawn as he waited for Father Connelly to start the mass. The guys at his stag party had kept him up until two-thirty the night before.

Finally, Father Connelly entered from the sacristy and they all stood. Julean jabbed him in the ribs numerous times with her elbow, trying to keep him awake during the sermon. By communion time Henry found himself wide awake. At their turn, Julean and Henry stepped into the aisle and into line to receive communion.

Since Henry had gone to confession the previous Saturday, he felt he was free from sin and prepared to receive communion. However, as Julean walked in front of him, his eyes wandered down and took in her shapely figure and long slender legs. Her hips swayed from side to side, and he knew he was in trouble.

Henry looked to the side, trying desperately to find some distraction, his gaze finally resting upon the statue of the Blessed Virgin Mary, portrayed with a blue mantle draped loosely from her shoulders, her hands together in front of her chest in prayerful repose. It suddenly occurred to Henry that she, too, was a woman. Sure, she gave birth to Jesus, and even though Joseph had been a chaste spouse, Henry thought for sure he must have had the odd temptation. It was amazing how quickly he was able to justify, defend and rationalize his sinfulness to himself.

Henry began to see the statue of Mary from a whole new perspective. Behind that cloak was a woman's body. Henry nearly gasped out loud as he looked away. *What am I thinking?* He quickly looked back at Julean, trying to wipe out the multitude of sins he was committing. Better that he had such thoughts of Julean rather than of the Holy Mother!

He looked up, glancing from side to side, hoping no one was watching. He so desired Julean. He just couldn't seem to shake the image he held so firmly in his mind. Other impure thoughts he'd entertained in the past came flooding out of nowhere too. He felt he was sinning and didn't know if he was worthy to receive communion.

Julean stepped forward and knelt at the communion rail. Henry hesitated and then knelt beside her, his elbow touching hers. The moment of truth had arrived. Should he kneel and receive Holy Communion, guilty of all the sexual thoughts floating around unharnessed in his mind or should he walk away?

He decided to stay.

Look, Lord, You made me this way. I've tried to be good, but I don't have the strength anymore. I desire my Julean so much I just can't think of anything else. If I am guilty of a sin, please forgive me.

Out of the corner of his eye he saw Father Connelly and an altar boy making their way down the rail. As he waited for the priest to reach him, beads of perspiration formed on his brow.

"The body of Christ," Father said as he gave communion to Julean. "Amen," whispered Julean.

The altar boy moved to Henry and held a tray below his chin to catch any Host that might fall. When Father Connelly came and stood in front of him, Henry closed his eyes and opened his mouth.

Father Connelly paused.

He knows. He knows my thoughts and won't give me communion. Henry opened one eye a tiny bit, squinting at the priest through a maze of eyelashes, and then dared open the other as well. His tongue was drying up.

Father Connelly was smiling at him.

Oh, God, does he know?

Father Connelly then reached into the gold chalice, took out a round white Host and said, "This is the body of Christ, Henry." As the priest's hand brought the Host towards his mouth, Henry squeezed his eyes together, expecting something awful to happen. He was sure that when the Host touched his tongue, it would erupt into a lashing of fiery hellfire.

But instead, as Father Connelly placed the Host on his tongue, a surge of peace swept over him, and all the passion and desirous thoughts went away. As he stood, he felt completely absolved and at one with the Lord. Henry thanked Him for coming to his rescue and allowing him to receive Him in such a beautiful and unabashed manner.

CHAPTER FIFTY-FIVE

EDITH COULDN'T GET the conversation with Mrs. Pederson out of her mind, particularly what she'd said about Henry getting married in less than two weeks. She knew how much her daughter had loved him and deep down suspected Jenny still did.

And then there were the dreams—so real, invading her mind nearly every night. In them Ted urged her to confess all to Jenny. *It's like he's come back from the dead.* A shiver ran up and down her spine just thinking about it.

There's still time, Edith said to herself as she thought of the letter from Henry in her keepsake box. She could pretend the mailman had just delivered it and let Jenny handle it from there. My God, how utterly complicated things could get. She had never really thought about it all like Ted had. Perhaps in the end it might be best to simply step out of fate's way.

Jenny and James had announced their plans to marry after James' university convocation in another year. James had promised Jenny the best wedding money could buy and Jenny had smiled at his extravagance. But Edith knew her daughter still longed for a relationship filled with love, and that in the recesses of Jenny's heart, she longed for Henry—or at least someone of his character. Someone who would put their relationship before financial concerns.

Edith liked James. He was smart, very handsome and would one day likely be very wealthy. His family had status; they moved in jet-set circles. But lately, she questioned whether those assets really held any importance. Jenny seemed happy but was she really? Edith thought she was beginning to understand the desires of her daughter's heart. Since Ted's death, Edith had let her guard down and had begun to see what Ted had seen and understand what Ted had known all along. The special sparkle in Jenny's eyes, even when she was around James, just wasn't there.

Edith felt guilty. Perhaps the stand she'd taken all those years hadn't been the right one, after all. Maybe the real reason she hadn't burned the letter from Henry the other night was because down deep she'd known it was wrong. Perhaps she should relent and tell Jenny everything, come hell or high water.

And yet she'd made a pact with Henry's mother.

With each passing day, the struggle of indecision overwhelmed her. Henry would be married in two days. After that it definitely *would* be too late. But even if she told Jenny, there was simply no time for Jenny to really do anything about it. She couldn't call Henry and say, "It's me, Henry, I still love you. Stop the wedding, I'm coming back to you," could she? Or, perhaps it was that simple. But how terrible for Henry's fiancée! No, she'd promised that she wouldn't show the letter to Jenny while she was alive—she couldn't break her word. If she did, it would put Mrs. Pederson in a predicament, too.

Edith rose from the patio chair, no longer able to sit still. Not even the beauty and serenity of the estate's gardens could offer her solace. More than anything, Edith wanted her daughter to be happy. Perhaps she could allow Jenny a five-minute conversation. That's all it would take to let Jenny know the truth. That's what Ted would want her to do. But the potential hell those few minutes might cause kept Edith from giving in.

Jenny met her just as she stepped into the kitchen from the

patio. "Hi, Mom. I was just coming out to join you. It's such a beautiful day, I want to enjoy it fully. Soon classes will start again and I won't be able to sit out here."

"I can't believe that you're in your third year already. Where does the time go? Have you decided on your second major?"

Jenny nodded. "Uh-huh. I'm thinking history in addition to English. That'll be best for when I'm a high school librarian helping students to look up information for their social studies classes."

"And this is James' final year in business administration too, isn't it?"

"*If* he finishes—he threatens to quit all the time. He never studies and gets straight A's all the time. I heard from one of the others in his class that he knows more about business than most of his professors and often argues vehemently with them. What concerns me is the time he spends at work. When he's not at school or with me, he's at the office with his father planning the next merger."

"Well, honey, running a big corporation is very time consuming. You'd better get used to it."

"That's just the thing, Mom—I don't know if I ever will. It bothered me so much when Daddy was so involved at work all the time. I think family should come first."

Edith was silent for a minute. It had bothered her as well, the amount of time Ted had spent at work. But after awhile she'd gotten used to it and accepted it as part of their life. But maybe she shouldn't have...*maybe Ted would still be alive if*...

"I hate to remind you, Jenny, but we have to leave this house soon to make way for the new president. You'd better enjoy it all while you can."

"Oh, Mom, so soon? I thought for sure they'd let us stay here for a few more months."

"Mr. Peakan called two days ago, saying he wanted to meet with me next week. Perhaps I can negotiate a bit of an extension. We'll see."

"I'm really going to miss the gardens, the flowers and all the greenery. And in the next week or so all the monarch butter-flies will be heading off to Mexico. It all reminds me so much of Cami—" Jenny stopped short of saying her daughter's name.

Edith looked away.

"I hope we can find some place like it," Jenny said. "I told James just the other day that when we get married I want an estate just like this one. I told him I wouldn't leave home unless he promised me a paradise. I was joking, of course, but now I'm really thinking about it—I'll miss this place so much."

"Oh, Jenny, an estate isn't everything. As long as you're in love and happy, that's the main thing."

Jenny stared at her mom but said nothing further. As mother and daughter studied each other, Edith was reminded again of the spark missing from her daughter's eyes. Something of Jenny's internal fire was gone, buried deep in the recesses of her heart. Since leaving Regina, that special brightness which had so characterized Jenny's younger years had grown dimmer and dimmer. Ted had mentioned it often before he died, and Edith had chastised him for seeing pain where she'd been blind to it. But now she saw it too.

Yes, Jenny had James, but neither he nor all the things he promised could fill Jenny's longing for her first love.

God help me. I've lost my sense of direction. I don't know what to do anymore. Edith turned from Jenny's perceptive gaze and walked briskly through the kitchen towards the laundry room, hoping that something in the act of cleansing would wash away the cumulative stains of her wrongdoing.

"HI TAMMY, I'M leaving in about fifteen minutes so I should be there about four. The traffic shouldn't be too heavy by then."

"That's great. Chloe's been asking for you all day. 'When's Auntie Jen coming? Where's Auntie Jen?' If I hear her say it one more time, I'll scream. Sometimes I think she's forgotten that *I'm* her mother."

"Oh, Tammy," Jen laughed. "I bought the cutest little outfit for her at Fannie's in the mall. It's a blue denim jumper with a white t-shirt. And guess what it has written on the front?"

"Probably 'I Have the World's Greatest Auntie.'"

"Tammy! How did you know? Have you seen it already?"

"Nope, but I'm a good guesser."

The girls laughed.

"So, where are you and Robbie going tonight?"

"He wanted to go to Al's, his usual steak place, but I suggested La Roma's, I think it will be more intimate."

"It is, James took me there last month. It's a *very* romantic setting, candles and all, and the Italian food is to die for."

"Well, Robbie said, 'La Roma's it is,' without any argument. He's been so nervous all week; I think he might be proposing to me tonight."

"That's wonderful, Tammy! It looks like your wish is coming true."

"Yes, it just might. See? I told you if you make a wish upon a shooting star at the very instant you see it, its dust settles in your heart and your wish comes true."

Jenny chuckled. "I'll keep watching, Tammy. But getting back to Robbie, I just love how he plays with Chloe, and much as she likes me, she can't wait to see him—he's becoming such a good father."

"Yes, I know. He keeps asking me to go with him when he leaves again next week. I'm almost tempted to, for Chloe's sake, but I want to wait until he finishes college next spring. He's doing so well in his studies and is captain of the basketball team. The college has even granted him another scholarship, did I tell you? Besides, my final year of nursing will be done in January, so it might all just work out for the best."

"I love the way he looks at you, Tammy;, I can tell he really loves you a lot."

"The best thing I ever did was to derail that whole sex thing, even though many times, especially lately, I really want to make love to him, too. But he respects me so much and he's become more mature and responsible and considerate."

"I'm so glad for you, Tammy. I remember how worried you were about being without him."

"I'm telling you, Jen, someday I'm going to write a book and tell all the girls never to sell themselves short. Put parameters around your relationship, respect your body and see it as the beautiful gift from God that it is. And for God's sake, if I may put it so bluntly, Jen, don't screw around!"

Jen laughed, "They should have *you* as a guest speaker at Springview. Seriously, the student council followed up on our suggestion and they've been having speakers in for the last two years. Next time I run into Mr. Morgan, I'm going to suggest your name."

Tammy's voice came down the phone line loud and clear. "When I think of all the hurt and pain girls and couples go through—what you went through, and me too—well, it's just terrible, Jen. It's been such an eye-opener for me.

"And you know, another thing I've learned—partly from you too—has to do with the way girls dress. You always look so lovely, yet you dress modestly. When I was first dating Robbie, I know my cleavage probably showed too much and I wore such tight sweaters, I don't think much was left to the imagination. What I wore said the wrong thing about me. No *wonder* he was on me all the time. It was just asking for trouble.

"But speaking of what to wear, I'd better go get ready for tonight. Is there an outfit that says, 'I'd like to be your wife'? See you in a bit!"

CHAPTER FIFTY-SIX

HENRY WOKE UP early Friday morning in a panic. There was so much to do. He had already picked up his suit from Goldman's yesterday. His mother, Aunt Darlene and Mrs. Fix had spent the entire day making cabbage rolls and stuffing turkeys, and volunteers had started the decorating of the hall. Today, he planned to help the volunteers finish decorating. The band leader would be delivering all the instruments and setting up and testing the sound system, and all the wedding party cars needed to be washed and decorated. Then the rehearsal.

Henry was tired just thinking about it all.

And by nightfall, he *was* exhausted. He arrived home just before nine o'clock, as his mother and several other ladies were putting the finishing touches on the salads. Once the final bowl was finished and the last lady had left, his mother dropped onto the sofa next to him with a long, drawn out sigh.

His father was reading the paper.

"Well, Mr. Pederson," his mother said to him, "are you all ready?"

Henry smiled. "You bet."

"Are you nervous about it at all?" she asked.

"A little," Henry replied, "but everything's ready and so am I."

"Not getting cold feet are you, son?" joked his father.

"Wouldn't you two be surprised if you came to my room in the morning and saw I had flown the coop!"

"Wouldn't that be something," Mary repeated, her tone indicating the scariness of the prospect. Quickly she changed the subject. "This will be your last night at home."

"Yeah."

"Well, it's not like you're going far away and won't visit for years on end," interjected his father.

"Well, no," Mary countered, "but it won't be the same anymore, either. It's going to be so hard getting used to Henry not coming through the door at suppertime."

"Well, at least I won't have to worry anymore that all the food will be gone by the time I get home," his father quipped.

"Oh, Bill, quit teasing. This is serious. I'm really going to miss our boy."

"I'll miss you, too, Mom. I'm going to miss trying to guess what you've made for supper just by the aroma in the air."

"Is food all you think about?"

"Oh no," Henry said. "You know what I mean. I look forward to seeing you and Dad, but mealtime is a special part of it all."

"I know what you mean, son," Mary said. "We were just teasing."

"Yeah, I know."

"So, are you nervous?" Mary repeated, nervous herself.

"A little," Henry said again, "but it's going to be good."

They sat in silence, each with their own thoughts. This would be the last time they would sit there together as a family without the addition of Julean. Henry looked at his mom and dad. They had each gone through this before themselves, like their parents had before them. It was all part of God's plan. A man and woman fall in love and leave their families to raise one of their own. Soon his parents would be grandparents, and then…they would be gone. Just like his grandparents. And Mrs. Engelmann.

Henry didn't want to think such thoughts right now. He just wanted to be in his parents' presence, savouring this last evening together as a family, just them, prolonging it as long as possible. After tonight, he'd be starting a new life with his bride and things would never be quite the same. They all knew it.

"It will be good to see the out-of-town relatives again," Henry said, finally breaking the silence.

"Yes, that it will," replied Mary. "Quiet a few dropped in already today. I can't get over how so many have changed and gotten older. Uncle Frank from Kendal seems to have aged so much. His hair has turned from almost black to snow white since we last saw him."

When his father began to snore, Henry and his mother looked at each other and smiled.

"Well, I guess that's my cue to get going," Henry said. He pushed himself off the sofa, went over to his mom and kissed her cheek. "I love you, Mom. Thanks for all your help and for everything you've done for me."

Tears came to both their eyes.

She could barely get the words out but managed to say, "I love you, too, Henry."

Henry tried to hold it in, but a tear fell freely upon his mother's shoulder as he straightened up.

His father stirred in time to catch the last part of their exchange.

"Going already?"

"Yeah," Henry said, "it's time to hit the hay. Big day tomorrow, you know?"

Henry walked over to his dad and instead of shaking hands like they usually did, Bill quickly stood and they hugged one another, his dad patting his back just like Mr. Engelmann did.

"Good night, son—I wish you all the best."

"Thanks, Dad, and thanks for everything too."

Before going to his bedroom, Henry looked at his mom and dad one more time. Redness rimmed his dad's eyes and tears rolled down his mom's cheeks. Henry raised his hand and sort of waved to them. He was too choked up to speak any further.

MARY WATCHED HER son walk to his bedroom through her tears, trying to etch his image in her mind. She had watched her son go to bed hundreds of times over the years, but there was a finality to it this time. She would miss him deeply.

He was marrying Julean tomorrow. But she knew he could very well have been marrying Jenny. If she hadn't withheld Jenny's letter, if she'd given it to him, the future might have been completely different for everyone.

Mary felt deeply the power of what she had done. Her decision had literally determined Henry's fate. It was a markedly uncomfortable feeling, playing God.

Mary prayed that Henry would be as happy with Julean as he might have been with Jenny. Julean was such a nice girl and Mary knew Henry loved her deeply, even though he had never seemed to have gained her parents' approval.

Still, they will be very happy together.

No matter how hard Mary tried to justify hiding Jenny's letter, she couldn't rid herself of the guilt. Deep down she knew it was wrong, that she had no right to control her son's destiny, let alone that of another person. And, at the end of the day, for better or for worse, Henry should be making the final choice.

Mary wished she had shared what she had done with Bill or Mr. Engelmann, but now it was too late. Her son would wed tomorrow and the burden of her decision would be hers and hers alone.

Her unresolved feelings were compounded with apprehension about going into her bedroom that night. She hoped the closet door would be closed. Ever since she'd hidden the letter in her treasure chest and stored it in the closet, the once dark closet seemed brighter somehow. In a way she welcomed the additional light, but it was very unsettling.

These anxious thoughts raced through her mind, disturbing her immensely. Feeling suffocated, she could no longer stand still. She needed to go to her sanctuary, her kitchen. She needed to find some peace. Even though she was tired and it was late, she had to bake something, anything. Sleep wouldn't come easily for her that night, she knew. Perhaps the aroma of an apple pie baking in the oven would sooth her raw nerves.

HENRY CAME OUT of the washroom and got to the door of his bedroom, turning to look down the hallway. His mom was watching him from the entrance to the kitchen, her eyes filled with tears. What she was thinking? Neither said anything, neither one wanted to make the first move to break what was becoming an uncomfortable silence. Finally his mom gave him a watery smile and he responded with a little wave before she disappeared into the kitchen.

In his room, Henry went to the window and looked out into the evening sky ablaze with millions of stars, the moon hanging low, partially hidden by Mrs. Goronic's elm tree. Henry turned to the east, looking for the first star in the evening sky, but it was impossible to tell which of the thousands it was. Still, it made him think of Jenny and the wish he had sent to her so long ago that the star of the east reflect his love for her. He knew they could both see the star at the same time; it was what connected them. And before he'd made that wish all those years ago, he'd prayed to his guardian angel to bring back a letter from Jenny to him. And it had never happened...

Maybe, though, maybe the angels knew that no answer *was* the answer. He'd met Julean, after all. Julean, his bride.

Another wish came to Henry, then. That Julean was gazing at the moon that moment and that its light would bathe her in the glow of his love. He focused on that image, erasing all thoughts of Jenny and chastising himself for even thinking of her the night before his wedding.

Henry turned out the light and flopped onto the bed, begging for sleep to come quickly. Thinking of Jenny had uprooted old feelings, adding to his sadness at leaving home and the life he loved with his mom and dad.

It further conflicted with his excitement at getting married and getting on with his future, *their* future. He loved Julean so much. He didn't know how to handle this myriad of feelings. He put the pillow over his head, hoping his uneasy thoughts would be soothed by the soft feathers inside.

A NIMBUS OF LIGHT shimmered around the treasure chest and radiated outwards from the closet, easily passing through the wall of Mary and Bill's bedroom, leaving Henry's parents slumbering, undisturbed. Henry's bedroom brightened as the light hovered above him, asleep and dreaming. More than any other night, the light glowed with love and yearning.

In his dream Julean became Jenny. Henry stood and followed the light, searching for his long-lost love. He walked into his parent's bedroom, to their closet...where Jenny waited for him.

CHAPTER FIFTY-SEVEN

EDITH ARRIVED AT the airport at six in the morning. Traffic had been light because of the early hour and so she'd made good time. She picked up her tickets and marched to Gate C to catch Flight 384. She was on a mission. The same steadfast determination she'd shown in separating Jenny from Henry she now applied to bringing them back together. The guilt and remorse plaguing Edith and the constant dreams of Ted urging her to give Jenny the letter had motivated her to take drastic action.

She darted through the terminal, reviewing her strategy. When she landed in Regina at quarter to nine local time, she would go straight to the Pedersons' house. Based on her conversation with Mrs. Pederson, she wasn't sure she'd get much of an audience on the phone, especially since today was Henry's wedding day. Besides, her powers of persuasion were always stronger and more effective in person. She'd persuade Mrs. Pederson that Henry was marrying the wrong girl and the wedding must be stopped or, at the very least, postponed to allow Henry and Jenny time to sort things out.

Edith refined her argument in her mind, considering and planning responses to all possible objections Henry's mother might have. The heart of her argument would be that true love comes along only once in a lifetime and that those two were clearly destined to be together. Why, even the heavens were involved in sending the letters to each of them; they'd come out of nowhere, and each mother should have redirected the letter she had received to her child. And it should be Henry and Jenny—not their mothers!—who decided whether they were still in love and wanted to be together again. Those letters were an omen the women shouldn't have ignored, and Edith now recognized her actions might have devastating consequences for both their children.

Edith arrived at Gate C just as they announced boarding. Once seated, she forced herself to relax, taking deep breaths and letting them out slowly. In her purse was a vial of sedatives the doctor had prescribed for Ted towards the end of his life; her nervous fingers could barely undo the lid. She swallowed one, hoping it would help her calm down and perhaps get some rest. It was nearly a four-hour flight to Regina. She wanted to be alert, fresh and ready for anything. Her daughter's future was at stake. A future she had meddled with for far too long.

She was stunned when the stewardess woke her twenty minutes outside of Regina. She couldn't recall having fallen asleep.

Edith looked out the window as the plane flew over the Legislative Building and coached herself not to hold her breath as the landing gear came down and the plane descended. Her knuckles were white on the armrest as the plane hit the tarmac.

"Thank you, Lord!"

Her return flight to Ottawa was at seven that night so she hadn't brought a suitcase. She walked out of the airport and promptly hailed a cab. *No one will be at St. Mary's yet, so I should—* Suddenly she realized that she didn't know when the wedding was due to start! *Thank God it's two hours earlier here!*

The taxi slipped through the light Saturday morning traffic and, in fewer than twenty minutes, pulled up in front of the Pederson home. The place hadn't changed at all since they'd moved away. Fear gripped her as she cautiously approached the door. What if Henry answered?

If he does, maybe it will be for the best.

She stood on the front steps debating with herself for a moment, took a deep breath to settle her nerves, then rang the bell. Seconds later a man appeared in the screened doorway, half in and half out of a suit. An older image of the boy she knew.

"Hello? What can I do for you?" he asked through the screen.

"Yes, hello. Is Mrs. Pederson in?"

"Just a moment, please. Mary, there's a lady at the door for you."

A minute later, Mary came to the door. The mother of the groom wore a simple but elegant two-piece beige suit. Her brown wavy hair hung around her shoulders. From her expression, Edith knew Mary hadn't recognized her. But, then, they'd never even met face-to-face six years ago.

"Hello?" Mary said.

"Hello, Mrs. Pederson."

The moment she spoke the words, Mary's expression changed. "Mrs. Sarsky."

Edith noticed that Mary didn't move to open the door and invite her in. Instead she stepped out onto the porch and closed the inner door behind her. Obviously she wanted to keep their discussion as discreet and private as possible.

"What are you doing here?"

"I made a special trip to Regina in the hope that we might talk, oh, for no more than a half-hour. I have something very important to discuss with you."

"What is it you want, Mrs. Sarsky? As you can see, we're getting ready for the wedding."

"Is Henry at home?"

"No, he's at the church hall."

"Good. I'd much prefer to keep this conversation between us for the moment. It has to do with the wedding."

"What about the wedding?" Mary asked, her voice rising.

"Mrs. Pederson, I've come all this way to request that you postpone the wedding. I'm willing to share the costs of cancelling—"

"What! Are you serious?"

"Mrs. Pederson, please listen to—"

"Mrs. Sarsky, I'm afraid you don't understand. I am extremely busy. The wedding is scheduled to begin in a couple of hours. We still have to get all the food over to the reception hall. Postponing the wedding is just out of the question!"

"But, Mrs. Ped—"

"Mrs. Sarsky, I don't mean to be rude but I simply have to end this discussion right now."

"But, Mrs. Pederson," Edith repeated, "it's *imperative* that we—" Edith took a breath, reigned in her temper and calmed her voice. "It is imperative that we let Henry and Jenny decide whether or not they want to get back together. We have interfered in their lives for too long."

"*You* may have interfered in Jenny's," Mrs. Pederson retorted, "But *I* certainly haven't interfered in Henry's." Mary stepped so close that Edith feared she'd fall down the stairs. "We never stopped Henry from writing to Jenny. For three years my son yearned for a letter from your daughter, and then the only letter he receives arrives two weeks before his wedding. Two weeks! And now you want me to help break up another relationship?"

"I know now what I did was wrong." Edith hoped Mary would see that her contrition was real. "I have justified it all these years by saying that it was best for Jenny, only to realize that the one thing that *was* best for Jenny was the one thing, the one person, I kept from her."

Mary backed up and leaned against the screen door. After a moment she looked up. "Mrs. Sarsky. Henry is going to be married to his bride at eleven this morning at St. Mary's Church. He loves her very much. She loves him. I know Henry and Jenny had a very strong connection once, but Henry must be allowed to get on with his life. To stop this wedding would destroy him all over again, as well as his future wife, and I can't do that. There is nothing more you or I can do. Please go back to Ottawa." Mary disappeared into the house, slamming the door behind her.

Edith stood on the landing, utterly dejected. She'd thought for sure if she made the trip to Regina it would put pressure on Mrs. Pederson… No, this was all her own fault. *I'm the one who made the decision to keep them apart a long time ago. I'm the one who convinced Ted to destroy the letters. Now I'm just reaping what I've sown.*

Since she had dismissed the cab, having anticipated being invited in and having a longer discussion with Mary, she decided to go for a walk and work off some of her anxiety. She wanted so much to correct the wrong she'd done, but it seemed it wasn't meant to be. For the first time in her life she felt completely helpless, trapped by the results of her own manipulation.

Edith walked to the corner and headed up 13th Avenue towards Winnipeg Street where St. Mary's Church was located. She was surprised that she still remembered where the church was—she and Ted had only gone with Jenny a few times. Panic swept through her as she faced the front of the church. *Only a few hours…* She couldn't bear to stand there any longer and began to walk aimlessly ahead.

When they first arrived in Regina, she remembered, how happy they all had been—Jenny had immediately made friends, rather a friend: Henry. Edith had never seen her daughter so happy. But they'd grown so close so quickly, it was frightening.

Edith found a café on Victoria Avenue and ordered herself breakfast; she'd slept through the meal on the plane.

She examined Jenny's relationship with James, now—finally—fully realizing it was Henry who could bring back the sparkle and joy to Jenny's life. Ted had known from the start that what they were doing wasn't right, and in the end it had killed him. Her manipulations had killed her own husband. And to make matters worse, she had killed her daughter's spirit as well by encouraging a relationship with a man whose priority was financial gain. She had flown here hoping to somehow make amends for it all, but it was too late.

The clock on the café wall ticked ten-thirty and she knew

she had to start back towards the church. She wanted to at least see the woman who had taken Jenny's place in Henry's heart.

As Edith approached the church, she couldn't believe the number of cars and the number of people milling about. *Henry and his bride must really mean a lot to the community.*

One of the ushers greeted her when she entered the foyer.

"Good morning. Are you on the groom's side of the family or the bride's?"

How awkward! "Neither," Edith finally said, "Just a distant friend."

The usher was taken aback for a moment, then held out his arm and walked her into the church. As he guided her down the aisle, she noticed that the only room left was at the very back of the sanctuary. The usher led her to a space on the bride's side, the woman who was to take Jenny's place. She shuffled past the people already seated and took the space.

What seemed an eternity later, a heavy-set lady walked down to the altar and began to sing a love song, her full, beautiful voice rising above the congregation without accompaniment. It brought tears to Edith's eyes.

Love is what it is all about, and true love is so rare. Jenny had it and I took it away from her.

At precisely eleven the church bells pealed, announcing the commencement of the ceremony. The door to the sacristy opened and out came a priest followed by Henry and his two best men.

Edith recognized him immediately. *What a handsome young man he turned out to be.* Edith loved his dark hair and thick eyebrows. He had filled out, and his features were strong and mature. *Oh, if Jenny could only see him.*

The priest led the men to the front of the altar. They all turned and looked down the long aisle, anticipating the arrival of the bride.

Right on cue, as the organ piped out Wagner's "Bridal Chorus," the two doors at the back of the church opened. A young girl, perhaps eight or nine years of age, dressed in white and wearing a tiny veil, led the procession. The child carried a bowl of flower petals and began tossing pink and white blossoms as she walked along.

Edith didn't want to look but she had to. She just had to see who was replacing her daughter. *Oh, God, I can't bear to look...* Edith turned and gazed upon the bride. She was beautiful and, yes, she *did* have that inner glow, that inner sparkle. Jenny had had it once, too, but Edith had taken it away.

"Oh, Jenny," Edith whispered under her breath, "I tried, but it's just too late."

Edith could no longer look –at Henry as he beamed, at his lovely wife-to-be. Happiness was written all over them, but there was one thing wrong with the picture: it should be Jenny walking down that aisle.

Edith hung her head, trying to block out the words of the ceremony that seemed to scream at her, echoing throughout the church. Absorbed in her thoughts, Edith chastised herself over and over until the priest said something that gave her hope.

"If there is anyone among you who knows of any reason why these two young people should not be wed, speak now or forever hold your peace."

And here was her chance, her final opportunity. She *had* to speak up. Fear swept through her. She knew she would look like a fool, but she also knew she had to do it. Her guilt was so strong this was the only way to be free of it. It had killed Ted and now it was killing her and Jenny. Edith knew she had to be bold; she had to be strong.

She felt Ted's presence beside her, urging her on.

Deliver the letters. They were sent by God's messengers, His angels, but you wouldn't listen until it was almost too late. This is your last chance to redeem yourself—and me. Do it, Edith. Stop the wedding. Do it now.

The priest drew breath to continue the ceremony.

Do it before it's too late, Ted almost screamed in her mind.

"Father! Father, I know of a reason why these two should not be married!" Edith's voice was so dry it was barely audible.

She said it again. This time people several pews in front of her turned to look around. And then more and more members of the congregation turned to look at her as Edith, gaining confidence, shouted more loudly still.

The priest still did not hear her but he did look up to see what the commotion was all about.

"Stop the wedding," Edith shouted again. "Henry should be marrying my daughter!"

The ushers at the back of the church began to come down the aisle towards Edith. They weren't sure what to make of this. Was she for real? Did she really have a valid objection to the marriage or was she just some nutcase?

Unbelievably, the priest still hadn't heard her, didn't even see her, though several parishioners shuffled around and stood up to see who was yelling.

Edith continued to shout, Ted urging her on.

In desperation, Edith took off her shoes and stood up on the seat of the pew. She knew she looked foolish, but so what? She didn't mind being a fool for her daughter. Jenny's happiness was more important than any brief embarrassment. And who were these people anyway? Strangers, all of them. They didn't know her from Adam. By tomorrow she would be long gone.

Edith stood tall over the congregation and shouted again.

"Stop the wedding! Look this way!"

When she realized she *still* didn't have the priest's attention, she became nearly hysterical. She leaned forward and, shoe in hand, began beating the back of the wooden pew in front of her.

"Stop the wedding! Stop the wedding! This is all wrong!"

A hand gripped her wrist, but she fought against it.

"Stop the wedding!"

"Mom? Mom!" Jenny's voice broke through as she tried to restrain her mother from hitting the headboard with the heel of her slipper.

"Mom! Mom, what's wrong? Wake up, Mom—you're having a nightmare."

Jenny shook her mother, trying to snap her out of it.

Edith looked at her, completely confused and disoriented, then collapsed onto the bed, arms beside her. The slipper fell to the floor. Her nightgown was drenched in sweat.

"Oh, Jenny! Jenny, I'm so sorry. Please forgive me," Edith sobbed, bursting into tears.

"Oh, Mom, don't worry. It's okay. You didn't wake me. I was just going down the hall to the bathroom when I heard this awful pounding and you screaming, 'Stop the wedding!'"

"Jenny," Edith drew in a shuddering breath, "I'm not sorry that I woke you. I'm sorry about something else."

"What, Mom? What are you sorry about? And what on earth were you dreaming about? Whose wedding do you want to stop?"

But Edith was fully awake now. For a brief second, she'd let her guard down, leaving her temporarily vulnerable to the truth. But as her senses returned so too did her rationalizations and defenses.

"Oh, Jenny, I love you so. I want very much for you to be happy."

Jenny patted her shoulder consolingly, wondering what this was all about. "But I *am* happy, Mom. Don't be silly."

Edith was spent; she felt so helpless. Henry was getting married and there was nothing more she could do. She stared at her daughter standing at her bedside, tears blurring her eyes.

Oh, Jenny. If you only knew that today, this very morning, your first love, your one and only true love, will wed another. And I am responsible for it all. It should have been you, my darling girl, marrying Henry, but I had to meddle. I thought I knew best. Your father understood, he saw it all at the beginning. Oh, why didn't I see it then? Why was I so stubborn, so blind?

Edith turned onto her side.

She could no longer look at her daughter, frightened that Jenny would see in her eyes what she had done. Edith wanted only to sleep and never, ever wake up again.

CHAPTER FIFTY-EIGHT

T HE EARTH SPUN on its axis and the anxious sun could hardly wait to reveal the glorious day in store for Henry and Julean's wedding. The purple haze of the horizon kaleidoscoped to a rosy red, then pink and finally orange. Profiles of trees and buildings sharpened in the increasing light like the lens of a camera coming into focus. Then the dazzling sun peeked over the edge of the earth, chasing away the darkness in earnest. Shadows scampered in all directions with no place to hide. Brighter and brighter shone the light; sunrise in all its glory. The prairie landscape came alive as tips of standing wheat in the fields glowed golden. Lights came on in homesteads, dotting the land and adding to the sparkling light.

The joyous rays of the rising sun slipped silently into Henry's bedroom and grew stronger before he stirred under the growing warmth on his face. He was reluctant to awaken, but his dream could no longer hold him.

"What a strange dream," he muttered, rubbing his eyes then sitting on the edge of the bed. "Why would I be searching in my parents' bedroom closet for Jenny?"

Henry shook his head and stretched, shedding thoughts of

Jenny as he did. The clock on his night table read six-thirty. He jumped to his feet and went over to the window.

The sky was clear and blue, not a cloud in sight. He looked at the trees in the backyard; they were still. That was a good sign, too. Julean really wanted a nice day with no wind—something about her veil blowing off. So far, everything looked good.

"This is my wedding day," he said to himself, exhilaration surging through him. His spirits soared as he left his room.

"'Morning, Mom," Henry said as he walked into the kitchen. "Don't you look good."

Large cylindrical curlers covered his mother's head. "Culverts," his dad called them. She swatted at Henry with the dishtowel at his teasing.

"Darlene's coming over in an hour to do my hair and then you'll see quite a transformation," she countered.

"Mom, you look great just as you are. You're still the most beautiful woman in the world."

"Awww," she said, pulling him down into a hug and kissing his cheek. "Well, you'd better sit down and have breakfast if you want me to make it for you. I've got lots to do."

"Oh, it's okay, Mom. I can make it myself."

"But I *want* to make it for you! This will be the last time we have breakfast together."

"Don't make it sound so final! You never know, I just might come back every morning."

"I'm sure Julean will have a thing or two to say about *that!*"

They laughed.

"Well, if I had my choice, Mom, I'd like bacon and eggs and two slices of toast."

"Your order will be up in a minute," she replied, like a professional short-order cook.

"Make that two orders," said his dad, entering the kitchen. "And maybe I'll have a slice of that apple pie you baked last night. The smell of it lulled me right to sleep."

Mary smiled. "I'm glad it worked for you."

"Yeah, I slept real good. How about you, son?"

"I was a little restless. I dreamt I was looking for someone or something in your bedroom closet—"

Two eggs splattered across the floor.

Startled, Henry and his dad turned and looked at Mary.

"Why so nervous, Mom? *You're* not the one getting married!"

The thought of Henry discovering Jenny's letter today of all days sent a cold shiver down Mary's spine. The curlers on her scalp seemed to tighten. Unable to think of what to say to the two men staring at her, she forced a chuckle. But the uneasy tone, coloured by the redness on her face, betrayed her guilt.

The sound of the doorbell saved her.

"Who on earth would that be, so early in the morning?" Mary asked, thankful for the distraction.

"Oh, I bet that's the photographer," Henry said, jumping up.

"Oh no!" Mary wailed, "I look so terrible."

"No you don't, Mom," Henry called over his shoulder as he ran to the front door and opened it.

Flash!

For several seconds Henry saw only a bright light and then small spots. The photographer had propped the screen door open and moved back down the steps, ready to take Henry's picture as soon as the groom opened the door.

His mom and dad entered the hallway behind Henry and the photographer took their picture as well. His mom's hand flew up to her hair to try to hide the curlers.

"Oh, Mom," Henry said, "you look great, just relax. It'll be fun to catch what everyone's doing before the wedding."

Henry introduced the photographer to his parents then led the man to his room so he could take pictures of Henry's dress clothes laid out on the bed, and several before and after shots of Henry as he got ready. He spent about three-quarters of an hour with Henry and caught more candids of Henry's parents and of Aunt Darlene doing his mom's hair. The photographer then rushed over to Julean's place to do the same.

Henry tried to imagine the kinds of pictures the photographer would take over there. Probably something similar. Julean had said she wanted a photo revealing the garter on her leg. The thought aroused Henry and he wished he were the photographer to take that shot.

He emerged from his bedroom to hear his mom ask his dad to get her hat box down from the top shelf in the bedroom closet.

"Dad's in the bathroom, Mom. I'll get it for you."

She looked at him, her face paling. "Oh, that's fine. Your dad can do it when he gets out."

"Well, I'm here right now; I'll get it for you." Henry squeezed past his mom. Their big bed took up so much room it was difficult to get by her.

Mary held her breath as Henry stood on tiptoes and reached for the large Simpsons-Sears box. As his right hand brushed the treasure chest, inches away from Jenny's tender words of love, Mary cupped the palm of her hand over her mouth to hold back a cry.

"Oh, oh, thank you, Henry," Mary stuttered as Henry brought the box down and set it on the bed.

"I'd forgotten all about your treasure box, Mom, what all have you been hiding up there? I used to love to look through it when I was little."

Mary couldn't think. She was momentarily speechless. "I...I can't remember. It's been so long," she lied. The truth would have changed the destiny of the day.

Henry looked at her quizzically for a long moment. "Nervous about the wedding, Mom?"

Mary nodded, unable to speak.

Henry kissed her suddenly flushed cheek. "Don't worry. It'll be just fine, Mom."

Mary watched Henry walk out the bedroom. She felt hot and sweaty; the curls in her hair would begin to straighten. She went over to the window and opened it. The air was uncooperatively still and already hot, only adding to the heat of her searing guilt.

What a way to start my son's wedding day.

By ten they were all dressed and ready.

"You look great, Henry," Mary said, fussing unnecessarily with his tie. "My little boy has grown into such a handsome young man. Well, I guess you did have a good start." She winked at Bill. They laughed away some of the tension.

A car honked from the street.

"Travis is here," he said. "We better go."

"It's still pretty early, isn't it?" said his dad.

"No, we'd better go," Mary agreed. "We might have a flat or something. It's best to be early and know you're there, especially for a wedding!"

"Okay, okay. You win. Let's go then."

"Oh my, does the car ever look nice," Mary said.

Streamers of white and blue tissue flowers outlined their 1954 blue and white Oldsmobile, culminating at the front radiator where a huge floral heart was fastened. On the roof of the car was a large wedding cake, made completely of tissue flowers.

"'Mornin', Travis."

"'Mornin', Hank. Want to make a quick run for it while you still have the chance?"

They all looked at Travis and laughed.

As they drove away to pick up Eddy, Travis started honking the horn.

"No, no, Travis—we're not married yet."

"That's exactly why we should hoot and holler while you still have the chance!"

"You make it sound like he's going to prison," Mary tsked.

"Well, women can be pretty restricting, you know," Travis joked.

Mary leaned forward from the back seat and slapped his right shoulder lightly with her gloves. "Oh, you men!"

Eddy's 1962 pink Cadillac was parked in front of his parents' place. He'd told Henry to pick him up there.

"Wow, what a set of wheels!" exclaimed Travis as he pulled up behind the convertible.

"Some car, isn't it? Apparently Elvis has one just like it."

"Maybe I should change my career," reflected Travis as he honked the horn.

A minute later Eddy came to the door dressed in a brown suit, yellow shirt and a striped dark brown tie. The tie was loose and the top button of his shirt was undone. His pompadour looked a little higher and shinier than usual. The cigarette dangling from his mouth restricted his smile.

Eddy ambled up to the car, rested his hands on the window ledge and peered inside. "Hi folks! Big day, today. Well, lose a son and gain a daughter, isn't that the old saying?"

"Yes, it is, Eddy," Mary nodded.

Henry slid into the middle of the front seat to make room for Eddy. Eddy took a last drag of his cigarette, and true to his nature, flipped it into the air as he got into the car.

"Geez, I'm so excited I may pee my pants."

"Yeah, I'm pretty nervous, too, Eddy," Henry admitted.

"There's still time to make a getaway," said Travis, seizing the moment.

"Just drive to the church, Travis," said Mary with a chuckle.

A minute later they pulled up in front of the church.

As Henry and his best men walked down the long aisle to the sacristy, he marvelled at the thought that in an hour or so, he and his new wife would be walking down this aisle going in the other direction. They would be married, fully committed to starting a new life together as husband and wife. The thought sent a mixture of exhilaration and trepidation through his body.

"Hello, Henry," Mr. Engelmann said, breaking into Henry's thoughts. Mr. Engelmann looked like the Pope himself. His arms were crossed, his hands tucked inside the sleeves of his white vestment. He wore his trademark warm benevolent smile as he gazed tenderly at Henry. He looked just as Henry had imagined he would.

"Good morning, Father Engelmann," Henry said.

Mr. Engelmann pulled his hands from inside his loose

sleeves and held out his arms toward Henry. Henry leaned into him and gave him a quick hug.

"Good morning, Eddy. Good morning, Travis."

"'Morning, Father," replied both Eddy and Travis in unison.

"Well, Henry, this is the start of a new life for you, a very important day for you and Julean."

Henry nodded. As usual, Mr. Engelmann knew precisely what he'd been thinking.

"Come. Let us go and see Father Connelly. He has some instructions for you and the boys. Do you have the ring?"

"Right here." Travis raised his pinky.

Noise of the people entering the church and shuffling into the pews reached the sacristy and Henry's blood ran cold.

Mr. Engelmann patted his shoulder. "You are a very fortunate man to have the hand of such a beautiful young lady."

"Yeah, I know."

Father Connelly changed his black robe to a white vestment exactly like Mr. Engelmann's, and added a red stole around his collar that draped in front of him to almost his knees.

Fifteen minutes later, Father Connelly peered into the church.

"It's packed," he said. "I think everyone is seated now. Perhaps we should go out there and get ready to greet the bride!"

Henry's heart galloped in response to Father Connelly's words. Travis came up to Henry and took his arm.

"Come on, Hank. It's too late to run now."

Eddy grabbed Henry's other arm. "Yeah, let's get the show on the road, Hank."

Father Connelly led the procession, followed by Mr. Engelmann, then Eddy and Henry, and finally Travis. The boys were quite a trio. Henry's 5'11" frame smoothed out the huge difference in height between Eddy and 6'1" Travis. Henry smiled as he visualized them walking to the altar. He was surprised to see Mr. Engelmann stand at the centre and Father Connelly somewhat off to the side. Perhaps Mr. Engelmann was going to perform the wedding ceremony after all?

Margaret Tearhorst, accompanied by her friend Pat Kenton on the piano, began to sing "Love Me Tender." Pat played softly so that Margaret's beautiful voice would dominate and be fully appreciated.

After Margaret finished singing, many white hankies were visible. Even Henry had a hard time holding back tears. Margaret and Pat returned to their seats and Father Connelly nodded towards the organ in the choir loft.

As the unmistakable first notes of the "Bridal Chorus" rang out, Henry turned and looked down the long aisle towards the back of the church. Following her two bridesmaids were Julean and her father, Jack. Henry couldn't make Julean out yet from his vantage point, but as they proceeded, Julean's veil became visible from behind the bridesmaid in front of her.

The bridesmaid's blond hair seemed enclosed by Julean's veil, and reminded Henry of Jenny. There she was, walking down the aisle towards him. Henry blinked twice and shuffled from one foot to the other, trying to clear the image and repress the thought. Travis was looking at him and Henry knew his buddy was thinking he'd suddenly got cold feet and wanted to run out of there. Travis moved closer, but Henry turned away, trying to let him know all was okay. Rather than chastising himself for having entertained such a thought, he abruptly focused on the congregation and his mom and dad. They had their heads turned to the aisle, anticipating the procession and, of course, waiting to see their future daughter-in-law.

Henry turned to Vera, Julean's mom. She was staring at him rather than the procession coming down the aisle. Their gazes met and locked briefly. She feigned a smile then turned away. Henry wondered what was really behind her eyes. Wondered how Jack and she really felt about the marriage. Henry became increasingly uncomfortable as he thought about it. He knew in his heart they'd hoped their daughter would marry a doctor or pharmacist and definitely someone of their own faith. The feeling that they still hadn't accepted him strengthened as he stood at the altar.

Then Julean was suddenly beside him. God, she looked beautiful. The veil flowed loosely from the crown of her head and stopped short of her shapely hips. She wore a white satin knee-length dress and white satin high heels. Her dark hair and brown eyes sparkled as she stood there. Her smile radiated such a tender, warm love. Henry couldn't wait to hold her. He felt like the luckiest guy alive as she let go of her father then kissed his cheek. Jack turned to Henry, shook his hand and motioned Julean towards him. Henry would now watch over and care for his precious daughter.

Julean came over to Henry, kissed him on the cheek as well and took her place at his side. Mr. Engelmann beamed, his hazel eyes so wise and kind. Henry fully expected Mr. Engelmann to move aside for Father Connelly, but Father Connelly remained on the sidelines.

And then it happened. The surprise Mr. Engelmann had spoken of. Simultaneously Father Connelly and Mr. Engelmann made the sign of the cross and, speaking in perfect unison they started the wedding mass.

"In the name of the Father and of the Son and of the Holy Ghost. My dear Henry and Julean, you have come together in this church so that the Lord may seal and strengthen your love in the presence of the church's minister and this community. Christ abundantly blesses this love. He has already consecrated you in baptism. And now he enriches and strengthens you by a special sacrament, so that you may assume the duties of marriage in mutual and lasting fidelity. And so, in the presence of the church, I ask you to state your intentions."

Father Connelly's Irish accent had gone high against Mr. Engelmann's lower Austrian one. The combination was melodic and spellbinding.

"Henry and Julean, have you come here freely and without reservation to give yourselves to each other in marriage?"

"We have."

"Will you love and honour each other as husband and wife for the rest of your lives?"

Julean and Henry looked into each other's eyes and said in unison, "We will."

"Will you accept children lovingly from God, and bring them up according to the law of Christ and His church?"

Again Julean and Henry said most sincerely, "We will."

"Since it is your intention to enter into marriage, join your right hands, and declare your consent before God and His church."

Julean and Henry turned towards each other, gazed into each other's eyes and joined their right hands.

Then Henry began.

"I, Henry, take you, Julean, to be my wife. I promise to be true to you in good times and in bad, in sickness and in health. I will love you and honour you all the days of my life."

Tears came to Julean's eyes and Henry brushed a tear from her cheek.

"I, Julean, take you, Henry, to be my husband." She paused, her voice cracking. "I...I...promise to be true to you in good times and in bad. I will love you—"

Another tear rolled down her cheek, taking along with it a streak of black mascara. Once again, Henry gently wiped the tear away and, with the same motion, brushed away tears welling in his eyes as well.

"I will love you," she repeated, "and honour you all the days of my life." She then did something which had not been part of the rehearsal. She leaned into Henry and tenderly kissed him, and as she did, *ahhs* and *oohs* softly swept across the church like a warm summer breeze.

Julean stepped back slightly as Mr. Engelmann moved closer and looked into Henry's eyes, then Julean's. He took a deep breath and then once again in perfect unison with Father Connelly, said, "You have declared your consent before the church. May the Lord in his goodness strengthen your consent and fill you both with his blessings. What God has joined together let no one separate."

"Amen," replied Julean and Henry along with many in the congregation.

Mr. Engelmann then asked for the rings to be brought forward. Travis gave Henry Julean's ring, and Julean's sister gave Julean Henry's. Father Connelly stepped closer to Mr. Engelmann and they blessed the rings together, their hands moving over the rings in perfect harmony.

As they made the sign of the cross over the rings, they said, "Lord, bless and consecrate Julean and Henry in their love for each other. May these rings be a symbol of true faith in each other and always remind them of their love. We ask this through Christ our Lord..."

"Amen," Julean and Henry replied.

Slipping the wedding ring onto her finger, Henry said, "Julean, take this ring as a sign of my love and fidelity. In the name of the Father and of the Son and of the Holy Ghost."

Julean placed the gold band onto Henry's finger and said, "Henry, take this ring as a sign of my love and fidelity. In the name of the Father and of the Son and of the Holy Ghost."

Mr. Engelmann beamed like Henry had never seen before. In his excitement he raised his arms and for the first time without Father Connelly's assistance blurted out, "You are now man and wife!" And then waving his hands, he added, "Go on. Kiss each other."

JENNY SAT ON the swinging bench in the gazebo, surrounded by green shrubs and beautiful flowers. She had been tending to her mother off and on since her mother had woken from that awful nightmare. She had never seen her mother so distressed. She didn't seem to be getting over the nightmare the way people usually did.

Jenny had two books with her; one was a copy of *Gone With the Wind* and the other was her diary. She started to read another chapter in the novel but had difficulty concentrating on it. Besides her worry over her mother, she had something else on her mind.

She decided to write down her thoughts, hoping it would help dispel the uncomfortable feeling.

She opened her diary. It was a special one, with two parts to it. The first part did not require a key, it was held closed with a button tab, and Jenny wrote very general things and happenings in that part. However, there was a second section to the diary which required a key. There she wrote her secret, most personal thoughts. And it was that section she opened now.

September 9, 1962

While I love James, I still have so many recurring thoughts of Henry. Ever since I woke up this morning, Henry has been on my mind. I feel guilty thinking about him when in another year James and I will be married. I thought reading a favourite novel of mine would help me push thoughts of Henry from my mind, but they keep coming back. It's almost an eerie feeling I have, like something has come between us. I hope he is all right and happy.

A teardrop fell onto the diary page. Jenny made no effort to wipe it away. Rather, she gazed at the tear as it was slowly absorbed by the soft paper and disappeared, just like her first love.

Immediately following the wedding ceremony, the ritual of the mass took place. Mr. Engelmann and Father Connelly approached the altar, now with Father Connelly in the centre.

After the mass was over, Julean and Henry signed the register then walked down the long aisle and out into a beautiful, warm prairie day. A blizzard of confetti swirled around them as they mingled with relatives and guests.

Once Henry and Julean had talked to most of the people there, the newlyweds, best men and bridesmaids escaped into the waiting cars and sped off towards the photography studio, tin cans merrily bouncing and clanging against each other as they drove up and down 11ᵗʰ Avenue, honking horns and letting everyone know Julean and Henry were married.

The dinner meal at the reception was fantastic, the speeches both humorous and touching, and the dance that followed an exuberant expression of the joy they all felt. But perhaps the thing that stuck out most of all in that entire evening, besides being close to his new bride, was the single dance Henry shared with his mother.

When the music began with a very romantic waltz, Julean and Henry were the first on the floor. For the next song, they decided to dance with their parents.

As Henry approached his mom, she looked as if she would cry. He knew she was taking it hard and had been trying to put up a brave front for the past several weeks.

As they danced, they didn't say much, but somehow their hearts relayed the bond they shared. They knew that it would no longer be the same. Their bond would gradually, naturally fade a bit as Henry's new bride shared his inner world, but all the memories, the joys and sorrows, would never be forgotten.

For Henry, Mary would always be the woman who loved him first.

Everyone wanted to dance with Henry. And it soon became apparent that the guests felt it was their obligation to dance with the groom, to honour him in that way. However, he so desired Julean that he couldn't wait for each dance to end and hoped that the next one would be with his new bride.

Every time he got a chance, he held her especially close. Julean snuggled her head into his chest and he, in turn, lowered his head into the crease of her neck. He couldn't wait for the evening to be over so they could be alone in their bridal suite at the Hotel Saskatchewan.

As MARY WATCHED her son and Julean dance, so much in love, some of the guilt she felt for hiding Jenny's letter dissipated. All that day, beginning with Henry's dream and the hat episode that morning, thoughts of Jenny and Henry getting married had plagued her. Even as she visualized Jenny dancing with Henry at that very moment, it was overshadowed by the love Henry and Julean radiated as they looked into each other's eyes.

It was amazing how everyone lived in their own little world. How the choices people made shaped their reality. Everyone so unique and different. While others would see Henry and Julean dancing on the dance floor so much in love, Mary saw the possibility of Henry dancing with another love of his life; a possibility that she had denied.

Mary shuddered at the omnipotence. She shook her head, trying to shake the thought from her mind. She just knew he and Julean would be very happy together. She smiled at her son dancing by with his new bride.

Yes, I made the right decision.

Mrs. Fix grabbed Henry's shoulder, almost knocking him over. "You're not going to get away before you have one dance with me!" she barked, clearly a little tipsy. She was a big strong woman and easily had him under her control. She grabbed his arm, pulled him in and swung him around like a rag doll. Julean and others laughed as they went around and around.

Henry thought for sure he would throw up.

It was the final straw. When Henry next got close to Julean, he whispered to her that he wanted to go. It was only eleven-thirty and the midnight snack would be out soon. People would be more interested in eating than visiting—or dancing—with them. Julean whispered back that she was tired and would like to go, too, but didn't want to upset anyone.

"Leave it to me," Henry said. He climbed onto the stage and approached the band leader to tell him he wanted to make an announcement. After Henry tried to quiet everyone several times over the microphone, a hush eventually fell over the reception hall.

"Thank you, everyone, for coming to our wedding. You have made our day a very happy one, which we will always cherish. I have to be honest with you, I can hardly wait to be alone with my new bride, so Julean and I may be sneaking out in a short time."

Everyone cheered and *oohed* and there was a wolf whistle Henry suspected had come from Travis.

"Our band leader here says they'll play until there's no one left to dance. So, just because Julean and I will be leaving short-ly—"

More suggestive cheers went up. Henry blushed furiously.

"…so just because Julean and I may be leaving," he repeated, "doesn't mean that *you* have to. There's a terrific midnight lunch coming up and I'm sure you'll all want to stay for that. Please come by Julean's place tomorrow for a come-and-go lunch from eleven to four. All the gifts we received will be on display in the Carters' rumpus room, and Julean and I would love to thank you all again and say goodbye before we leave on our honeymoon."

Cheers went up again.

"So, thank you all again for coming!"

Henry raised a hand and waved to everyone.

The guests clapped and cheered as Henry walked off the stage and headed straight for his bride. He put his arms around her and kissed her tenderly. The clapping and cheering grew distant and then faded away completely as he lost himself in the bliss of the moment.

And then, just for them the band leader struck up Henry's request: "Save the Last Dance for Me."

CHAPTER FIFTY-NINE

ENRY AND JULEAN literally ran to their car. It had taken almost another hour for them to say their goodbyes and make it out of the hall. Unbeknownst to Henry, some of the guys had slipped a rope around the back bumper and tied the rope to a tree, so as Henry stepped on the gas to speed away the car jerked to a stop.

"Letting the clutch out too fast, Hank?" Julean asked.

"No, I'm sure it's not that." Henry stepped on the gas again, but the tires just spun. Henry smelled rubber as he got out of the car to check. He saw someone dash behind a nearby tree and immediately suspected something was up. He found the heavy rope looped around the end of the chrome bumper and tied to a huge elm tree.

"Those buggers," Henry muttered. He kicked off the end of the rope and held up his fist and shook it at the tree. He knew they were there. Muffled laughter followed his weak threat.

He started the car again and slowly pressed the gas to silently steal away, but Henry's stealthiness was shattered by clanking that came from behind them.

Henry and Julean looked at each other.

"Did you hit something?" Julean asked.

"I don't think so." But the faster they went the louder the noise became. Henry stopped the car and got out, more than a little perturbed, and there on the other side of the bumper was another rope with dozens of tin cans attached.

Once again, Henry shook his fist into the darkness. "You buggers!"

Giggling and laughter surrounded him and yet he couldn't see anyone. He stomped back to the car.

"Well, I hope that's the end of it," Henry said sternly. As he was about to pull away, he quickly put the car into neutral and jumped out, hoping to catch those rats red-handed. He ran to the back of the car, fully expecting to catch at least one of them.

But they had fooled him again.

"I'm warning you guys!" he shouted into the night. "I know you're there. Enough is enough."

He looked at Julean and they both burst out laughing. Henry held his breath as he stepped on the gas, not sure now what to expect. The car went forward unimpeded.

As Henry approached the corner, however, there was a blockade across the road, with a sign that read ROAD CLOSED.

"Road closed? Impossible, we all came this way earlier, when we went to the hall. What on earth could have happened?" Henry stopped the car and got out to look for a broken waterline or something. He walked at least fifty feet down the street. There was absolutely nothing wrong up ahead as far as he could see.

As he walked over to remove the blockade, Henry suddenly froze as a geyser of water gushed out of the hydrant at the corner like a tidal wave directed at him. Henry stood there, at its mercy, its full impact knocking him back. He stumbled and fought against the blast, trying to regain his feet and move out of the way of the full stream.

Julean witnessed it all. She'd seen someone at the hydrant and reached over to the horn to alert Henry. But it happened so fast she hadn't made it in time. She gasped and put her hands to her mouth as the huge stream of water hit Henry square in the chest. All she could think was if that didn't cool him off, nothing would. She chuckled, hoping that he was all right.

Henry stood there, soaking wet and gasping for breath as the ice cold water streamed by him. He didn't know whether to cry, scream or run into the darkness after them.

"How could those guys do this to me?" Henry mumbled under his breath. "On my wedding night! Those buggers."

Henry moved the barricade and got back into the car. Julean wanted to laugh but didn't dare. As they drove off, the distinctive clattering of tin cans—no doubt reattached to the back bumper—followed them. Henry hit both hands against the steering wheel.

"It's unbelievable! Things couldn't be working out more perfectly for those guys."

He didn't dare stop. "Cans or no cans, clanging or not, we're heading to the hotel," he said to Julean. "If I stop, God knows what they might do next!"

When they finally arrived at the hotel. Henry was too embarrassed to pull up front. He had some clothes in his suitcase but he'd dropped it and Julean's off at the hotel the day before.

"Oh, let's just go in the way you are," said Julean. "Who cares! It's our wedding night. Anything can happen, you know."

"Yeah, okay."

They parked in back of the hotel and went in the guest entrance. Two other guests were lounging in the lobby and a hotel attendant stood behind the registration desk.

"Why don't you go get the key to our room, Julean. I'll wait here by the elevator."

Julean looked at him and could no longer contain her laughter. "Sorry, Hank, but you look hilarious." She laughed so hard the other people in the lobby turned their way. Julean's gown immediately gave them away as newlyweds.

The other hotel guests smiled and Henry heard one of them comment, "Well, she sure cooled him off!"

While Julean picked up the key, Henry pressed the button for the elevator, which, much to his delight, opened immediately. The doors slid closed, cutting off the laughter from the lobby.

"Well, you have to admit we do look funny," Julean said, diplomatically, using the term "we" when both of them knew who the funny-looking one was.

In less than thirty seconds, the elevator bounced to a stop on the third floor. Julean gave Henry the key and he opened the door. And just as she was about to walk in, he picked her up in his cold, wet arms.

"Oh, Hank, you're so wet!—I mean, *wonderful.*"

"I love you," Henry responded as they entered their honeymoon suite.

A fire burned in the fireplace and several lit candles created shadows that danced across the walls.

The room smelled of lavender. A bottle of champagne in an ice bucket sat on a counter. Dozens of roses filled the room, Henry's were among them. A card was propped up on the counter beside the glasses from the hotel management, congratulating them and informing them that the hotel staff was completely at their beck and call.

Everything looked incredibly romantic and sensual. Henry kissed Julean again, then put her down. She turned, put her arms around him and kissed him tenderly.

"I'm going to take a shower and get changed," Julean said. "Why don't you take off your clothes and wrap a towel around you until I'm finished?"

"Yeah," Henry replied. "I can hardly wait to get out of this wet suit."

Julean walked toward the bedroom where their suitcases were. She gasped.

"Oh, Hank, you have to see this."

Four pillar candles sat on the end tables, and two large bouquets adorned the dresser. Their bed was turned down, and a Belgian chocolate rested on each pillow. Across the foot of the bed lay two white robes with the words *bride* and *groom* embroidered on them in blue and pink stitching.

"Look, Hank," Julean said. "There's a robe for you. That'll keep you warm until I get back."

"Boy, they sure do it up right," Henry said.

"Yes, they certainly do."

After he heard the shower go on, Henry picked up his robe and went out into the living room area to take off his damp clothes. The warmth of the fire felt good. He put on another log, then sat down on the chair beside the fireplace and watched as it caught fire.

As the flames danced in front of him, a smile spread across his face as he thought about Julean. Now, on their wedding night, he was glad he and Julean had waited. What a perfect way to begin a marriage, with all the discovery and excitement of each other still to come. And along with this fresh thrill and anticipation of the journey, a freedom, security and peace surged through him. They were now truly ready to give the ultimate gift to each other: their total and complete selves in an atmosphere of love and commitment.

He put on the robe, went over to the stereo and turned it on. The record player had a stack of four long-playing records on it. He pressed the button, anticipating some romantic music. He wasn't disappointed. The first record was by Nat King Cole, the second by Perry Como. After that he no longer cared. He went over to the counter to the bottle of champagne and started to open it, but then decided to wait for Julean.

As he put the bottle back in the bucket, Julean emerged wearing low-heeled white slippers and a knee-length diaphanous gown, a picture of pure beauty. As Henry's gaze travelled up, he discovered that he could almost see her breasts through the semi-sheer material. His desire for her grew almost uncontrollable. The soft light of the candles cast a warm glow on her luminous skin and voluptuous body. Her eyes sparkled with an intoxicating gleam.

Henry drew near to his lovely wife. Their gazes locked as he reached out for her, and she leaned into him. Henry kissed her then, lightly, knowing full well that if he didn't take a shower right then and there, he would never make it.

"I can't believe I'm doing this, but I'm going to take a shower."

"Okay, I'll be here when you get back," she winked.

"You better be. I've had too many pranks for one night."

Henry rushed into the bathroom. It was large and spacious and still steamy from Julean's shower. He showered just long enough to get clean and fresh. He couldn't wait to get out. He was too self-conscious to walk out in the nude, so he put on his pajama bottoms.

Julean was on the bed, propped up by a pillow, her legs curled under her. Henry ached as he looked at her; he desired her so much. She waved an empty glass at him, suggesting he get the champagne.

Henry got the bottle from the living room and filled her glass, then his. He sat beside her on the edge of the bed, and as Henry raised his glass towards her, she raised hers to his.

"Here's to you, honey. I love you."

"And here's to you, Hank. I love you too—with all my heart."

As they sipped their champagne, listening to Nat King Cole's "It Had to Be You," Henry took the glass from Julean's hand and set it on the table. Julean slid down on the bed as he moved over to her. He put his arm under her head, and she leaned into his chest. He had never felt such an urgency to hold someone before. The words of the song, candles and the faint smell of her perfume intoxicated him.

Henry tipped Julean's chin up and kissed her hard and long and then again. All the months of waiting and holding back disappeared with each passionate kiss. He could finally feel the release of their total love for one another pass through their bodies, their spirits, their souls. They had become one in mind, in purpose, in flesh.

HENRY LAY BACK and raised his arm as Julean snuggled closer, closed her eyes and buried her head into his chest. They were both exhausted from the day; the gamut of emotions; the giving of themselves.

Henry kissed Julean's forehead softly, tenderly. He heard a Johnny Mathis song playing and the crackling of the fire, which was dying out. He briefly watched the shadows of the candles dance to the music on the ceiling. Henry held his new bride in his arms, feeling the warmth of her body, his eyes flickered like the candles and then closed as he dreamt he had just made love…to his first love.

HENRY WAS SURPRISED by the number of people who showed up at Julean's house to see them off. A caterer had brought in a bunch of hors d'oeuvres and kept them warm in chafing dishes. When Julean and Henry arrived, people were everywhere. The gifts were laid out on the tables Julean's parents had rented and set out around the perimeter of their rumpus room. Henry couldn't believe the number of things they'd received.

Around three o'clock, Julean and Henry left to drive to Estevan, a town near the border. From there they would drive to Minot in the morning. "JUST MARRIED" had been printed on the back window of Henry's car with bright red lipstick. "LOVE BIRDS" and "DON'T KISS AND DRIVE" were written on both sides of the car. In smaller writing were little private notes, written everywhere. Some were naughty enough that Henry was glad you had to be up close to read them.

Everyone laughed.

As they got into the car, people waved and shouted their best wishes. Henry turned the ignition, and the Chevy sprang to life. He crouched down and waved to as many people as he could see and they sped off, honking the horn for at least half a block.

CHAPTER SIXTY

"HI JEN, HI James. This is a pleasant surprise!"

"We were just on our way home and decided to drop this off for Chloe."

"Oh my gosh, what did you buy her now?"

"It's a dollhouse. James is good at putting things together so he said he'd set it up for Chloe."

"Is Auntie Jen here, Mommy?" Chloe called out as she came out of her bedroom.

Jenny ducked behind a door. "I'm over here, Chloe."

Chloe ran out into the living room, "Where's Auntie Jen, Mommy?"

"I'm over here, Chloe!"

And as Chloe crept up to the door, Jen snuck out and ran into the kitchen.

"There she is, it's Auntie Jen!" she shrieked and she ran after her.

Jen ran through the kitchen and back around to the living room. When Chloe ran in, Jen was on her knees with open arms and Chloe ran right into them for a big hug.

"Oh Chloe, I love you so much!"

She laid Chloe on the floor and tickled the little girl until she was laughing hysterically.

"Jenny, I don't know who the bigger kid is," James said.

"Look what Uncle James has for you, Chloe." Turning to James she added, "Maybe set it down here, James."

"Look Chloe, look at the picture on the box. It's a dollhouse!"

"Open it!" the little girl demanded, nearly dancing with glee.

James knelt down and began opening the box.

"Hurry up, Uncle James."

"I'm going as fast as I can, Chloe."

James began tearing at the box more aggressively until the flaps were open. He reached in and brought out a folded cardboard dollhouse, along with several packages containing parts and instructions.

"Well, Chloe, you help Uncle James put the dollhouse together while your mommy and I visit. Okay?"

"Here, Uncle James!" Chloe said, handing him one of the packages.

"Thanks, Chloe." James took the package and set it down and began opening up the dollhouse and looking at the instructions at the same time.

"Can I get you a drink, Jenny?" Tammy asked as she made her way into the kitchen.

"A glass of orange juice if you have it?"

"I do. How about you, James?"

"Not now, I'll spill it all over for sure."

Tammy handed Jenny her drink and noticed the huge diamond ring she was wearing. "Oh my, Jenny, is that an engagement ring?!"

"Yes," Jenny smiled, tilting her hand in the light until the diamond flared, "James proposed to me last Saturday when we went out for dinner."

"Why didn't you tell me!? My gosh, look at the size of that rock! It's three times the size of the one Robbie gave me."

"Oh, Tammy, an engagement ring is an engagement ring— it's the love behind it that's important."

Jenny herself wondered why she hadn't phoned Tammy like Tammy had when Robbie had proposed to her two weeks ago. Tammy had almost flown through the phone in excitement. The sparkle of the huge diamond had made Jenny happy when she first put it on and yet the initial happiness seemed to have faded. She shook her head. Why was she thinking this way?

"Do you mean, you haven't told Tammy our news that we're getting married next May?"

Jenny was momentarily embarrassed. "I was waiting until we saw her in person to break the news—and now you've spoiled my surprise."

"Well, congratulations!" Tammy gushed. "I'm so happy for you, Jen! For you both, I mean." Tammy set down her drink and rushed over to give Jenny a hug.

"Maybe I should convince Robbie we should delay our wedding at Christmas to the spring as well and we can have a double wedding! Wouldn't that be something!?"

"Yes, that would sure be different."

"I don't think Robbie would hear of it, though—he called last night and you'll never guess what he's done. He joined some athlete's group for Jesus."

"He what?" asked James, looking back at the two girls sitting on the couch.

"He's turned his life over to Jesus, and he was so excited about it. He said it all started when we began going to church together. It made him think about family and when he saw some of the guys he plays with get down on their knees and pray before and after a game he got interested."

"That's wonderful, Tammy."

"Sounds to me like he's losing it, if you ask me."

"Oh, James, it's great that he's turning his life over to God. Maybe you could take a lesson from him."

James grunted under his breath and then asked Chloe to hold something for him. Jenny watched him working with the little girl and it made her heart happy. Perhaps there was hope for this business-minded man of hers.

"So, tell me more, Tammy? What happened next?"

"Well, he said he attended one of the Campus Crusade meetings two nights ago, gave his life to Christ and now he's a born again Christian."

"A what?" James blurted, startling Chloe.

"He's become a born again Christian. You know, he's made a personal commitment to Jesus and received His Holy Spirit."

Once again James stopped what he was doing and turned to Tammy. "What the hell is a Holy Spirit?"

"Watch your language in front of Chloe," Jenny mouthed to him.

He frowned at her and waved a hand dismissively, wanting to hear Tammy's explanation.

"Well, James, the Holy Spirit is the third Person in the Holy Trinity and—"

"Forget it, Tammy, you've lost me…hand me that, Chloe."

Tammy turned back to Jenny. "He sounded so different when he called. He apologized over and over for the way he treated me and for his lack of support, and he begged me to forgive him." Tammy's eyes began to tear up.

Jenny reached over and took her dear friend's hand. "Oh, Tammy, that's so wonderful."

"He said he doesn't want to wait until Christmas to get married. He wants to come home at Thanksgiving and get married then and take me back with him. He said that he's neglected his responsibility for too long and that it's unfair that I should be raising Chloe alone."

Tammy began to cry.

"Why is mommy crying?" Chloe wanted to know.

Jenny got up and knelt down in front of the little girl. "Because she's so happy that she has you and daddy." Jenny sorted through all the plastic bags. "Boy, Uncle James is doing such a good job! It's almost done and then we can set up all the furniture in the different rooms."

Jenny tore the top off one of the clear plastic bags and poured the contents on the rug. "Here, let's put this chair in the living room. Now, where should we put this bed?"

"In the bedroom."

"That's right Chloe! Where is the bedroom, here?"

"No, silly! That's the *bath*room. *There's* the bedroom," she said, pointing her finger.

"Well, you know better than me. Okay, you and Uncle James put the rest of the furniture in the rooms."

Jenny returned to the couch. "So what did you decide Tammy? Are you going to be married at Thanksgiving?"

"No, I'm halfway through my last year of nursing. And it's just too complicated to move now. It took me over an hour to convince him to wait until Christmas. I'll be finished then and there will be more time to move and everything."

"It looks like your wish on the shooting star has come completely true, Tammy. You and Robbie are getting married!"

"See? I told *you* to make a wish too." Tammy looked pointedly at James and then back at Jenny as she recalled the wish Jenny held in her heart.

"Well, Chloe, time for bed! You'll have the whole day tomorrow to play with the dollhouse."

"No, mommy, please let me stay up a little longer, *please.*"

"Well, we should be going, Tammy, it's a long drive home and then James has to drive all the way to his place."

"It was so nice of you both to drop by! And thank you, James, for setting that up."

"You're welcome, Tammy. Do you want me to carry it into Chloe's room?"

"That's okay, Chloe will probably want to play with it out here tomorrow. How are classes coming along?"

"Actually, I dropped out. Dad isn't doing too well and I know most, if not all, the stuff they're teaching already."

"But you were so close to getting your degree!"

"A degree doesn't mean much in our business, it's just something to hang on the wall and collect dust."

"Maybe for you, but I can't wait to get mine. Have you started your practicum yet, Jenny?"

Jenny nodded. "Yes, two weeks ago we were assigned our high school. I just love working in the library. The students can be a challenge at times, though."

James grunted again. "The boys all want to take her out. Probably half of the male staff does too."

"James, that's ridiculous."

But it wasn't ridiculous; James' perception was dead on. Jenny had to be very firm with the students and graciously decline all the approaches made by several of the teachers, even though her large diamond engagement ring flashed very visibly.

"Come and give Auntie Jen and Uncle James a big hug and kiss."

Chloe ran into Jenny's waiting arms and squeezed her tight, smothering her in kisses. She gave a quick peck to James.

IT WAS LATE when James dropped Jenny off at home. Her mom had gone to bed and the house was big and quiet. It seemed empty without her dad and Jenny missed him very much. Often he would still be up when she got home and they would sit and chat. She relished those visits and talks, especially when she was confused about something, like now.

She looked at the huge engagement ring on her finger. The sparkle that had made her so happy the night James had given it to her had long since faded, just like their relationship.

What would her father think of their engagement? He liked James but had strongly encouraged her to go out with other boys. *I know Dad was trying to tell me that James might not be the best choice. But there was no one else but him and...Henry.*

I so wish Daddy had met Henry in Regina, perhaps things could've been different somehow. He only saw Henry through Mom's eyes and her concerns.

Jenny saw the same concerns about her relationship with James that her father had seen, but over the months and years she had begun to accept them. In part due to her accepting nature and in part because she assumed it was just James' character, simply part of him and therefore their relationship.

Jenny had learned to live with it.

And, now that she thought about it, James' traits and idiosyncrasies actually didn't seem so unsettling anymore; they only spent a few hours a week together anyway. And that's what was bothering her now. James spent so much time at his father's business. He kept promising it was only for a little while until he corrected some of the problems his father had overlooked, or until he'd helped with the next merger.

The way things were right now, Jenny felt as though she had to make an appointment to see her fiancé.

Still, she loved the way he'd helped set up the dollhouse for Chloe tonight and the way he'd talked to the little girl. Underneath all that business stuff and all the rest of it, James was a loving man. *I just wish I saw it more often.*

Shaking her head to rid herself of these thoughts, Jenny decided that she felt lonely because James was so preoccupied with work and that was the only reason her mind still swung back to Henry. Soon, James would have the business in order. And things would be different after they were married, she was sure. They'd have more time together. They'd raise children and go on vacations to exotic places around the world.

Jenny made her way to the kitchen, guided by the luminosity of the clock on the range. The dim light complimented her mood so she didn't turn on the lights. The radiance of the full moon further added to the light in the kitchen. She went to the patio doors, slid open the door and stepped outside.

It was a beautiful fall night. The air was warm and filled with the scent of the herbs and flowers that were still in bloom. The heavens were adorned with millions of twinkling stars. She looked to the east but her star no longer stood out. It was there, snuggled in amongst the rest of them, but its shimmering rays no longer embraced her like they used to.

She wondered about her first love. Had Henry gone to college and if so, what had he taken? It would be business or art, for sure. But he was so kind and considerate he might have chosen education and taught art like she suggested he might.

What could have possibly happened to that last letter she had sent to him? The one with the pewter angel inside? Surely it couldn't have just disappeared. But why else wouldn't he have answered?

Jenny, she said sternly to herself, *enough of this foolhardy talk and thinking! You're just getting yourself upset and living in the past. It's all just a memory. For God's sake, it's James you're going to marry, not Henry!*

But the thoughts would not leave her. She knew he had met someone else, she felt it now all the time and their star told her it was true.

It had all started again that day her mom had woken from that awful nightmare, shouting for someone to stop the wedding. It was so real to her mother, the memory of the fright in her eyes still sent shivers up Jenny's spine. And later that morning as she wrote in her diary, she'd had the strong premonition that something was happening to Henry. She'd felt a detaching of their love. It was like a receding tide pulling away from the shore of her heart. Each night she prayed for the tide to return, but the dawning of a new morning never brought the waves to the shore.

Jenny gazed into the celestial heavens in search of the star of the east once more, but it was nowhere to be found. She whispered the words anyway, knowing it would be received by their star: "Even though we are far apart, you are forever in my heart."

And just as Jenny turned to go back into the house, a shooting star blazed brightly across the heavens and Jenny sent out her long-held wish.

She felt its warmth settle in her heart and her sparkling, tear-filled eyes were soothed with wonder...and hope.

COMING SOON

THE ANGELIC LETTERS SERIES

— ✴ —

ANGEL OF THANKSGIVING

1963-1982

Discover just how powerful love can be.
Your heart will never be the same again.

HENRY K. RIPPLINGER

The following is a preview of Chapter One

CHAPTER ONE

THE NEWLYWEDS HAD just settled into their third year of university in Saskatoon when Julean suspected something she could no longer keep to herself.

She lay in bed one night, Henry's breathing having long since grown deep and rhythmic. Julean turned over and under the light of the moon shining through their bedroom window she could just make out the back of his shoulders. She ran her fingers up and down his back. He moaned and groaned a bit, but kept sleeping. She pushed a little harder.

"Come on, honey, go to sleep." Henry lifted the blankets over his shoulder and rolled slightly away from his playful wife.

She moved closer and, knowing how ticklish her husband was, slowly moved her hand to his side and dug in with her fingers.

The blankets flew as Henry jumped in the air and rolled over at the same time. "What's *with* you?"

"What's with *you*, you mean? You never turn down my advances."

Henry opened one eye. There was just enough light to see his wife's face in front of his. Her eyes and white teeth glistened in the light. "Well, I could be persuaded with a little more en-couragement, I guess."

"Since when do you need persuasion?"

Henry grabbed Julean and drew her in, hard. "I guess I'm persuaded enough." He moved to kiss her.

She quickly brought her hands up and pushed him away.

"What's going on? First you want me and now you chuck me away?"

"Honey, I've got something to tell you! I haven't had my period for over two months and I think I may be—"

"Are you pregnant?" Henry sat up and looked at her. He couldn't read her expression in the darkness. He felt more than saw her nod.

"I'm pretty sure. I made an appointment to see the doctor on Friday for confirmation."

"Oh, honey, that's wonderful! I can't believe it! We've only been married a couple of months."

"It only takes once, you know."

"Well, I guess we *have* done it a couple of times," Henry chuckled as he settled back down into the bed. He looked into his wife's eyes and murmured, "I love you, Momma."

"I love you too, Daddy."

Henry drew Julean in gently and caressed her. Within moments their lips found each other in the moonlit room. They made love, falling asleep in each other's arms.

Around three in the morning, Julean felt Henry's fingers run up and down her back. She turned over to face him.

"Why am I not surprised?"

"Oh, Mommy, you're just *toooo* irresistible."

WITH EACH PASSING day Henry and Julean got more excited about their baby. They had called home and told each of their parents. Henry's mom and dad welcomed the news with joy, but Julean's had reservations. Would this affect their daughter's education? Julean assured them that she would definitely complete her degree but also told them she wouldn't be able to work in her father's office next summer.

Henry and Julean loved their basement suite apartment. It was only four blocks south of the university and they walked back and forth to classes every day. They even came home for lunch. Some days they skipped lunch altogether and made love. That often happened when Julean slipped Henry a note just before they separated for their respective morning classes. The notes were always filled with much love and seductive luring. It seemed a little out of character for Julean, but Henry loved it and some days couldn't get back to their apartment fast enough.

What they liked about their suite was that it was only four steps below ground level and so didn't even seem to be in a basement. The windows were large and let a lot of light into the small kitchen and spacious living room. The landlady had fixed it up real nice with frilly curtains, and every room was painted a pale yellow so it seemed like the sun was shining all the time. It had two bedrooms; one of which was for them, of course, and the other Henry and Julean used as their study room. There was just enough space for two desks and a bookshelf.

The landlords welcomed the news too. They had four children of their own, the youngest was a boy, four years old, who often came down to visit them. Sammy and Julean hit it off immediately. But then Henry had already known that Julean was going to be a wonderful mother.

Helen, the landlady, said it would be okay if Henry and Julean wanted to repaint the second bedroom of the basement suite and turn it into a nursery. She also, quite kindly, offered to lower the rent a bit the following year when they returned to complete their last year of university.

Ever since Julean had told Henry they were expecting, Henry had felt a sort of roiling anxiety in the pit of his stomach. It was a familiar feeling; he'd felt the same way a long time ago. At first he couldn't recall when until one day, while walking to university with Julean, he remembered it was the same feeling he'd had in Grade 9 when he'd had the ridiculous notion that Jenny might be pregnant. The feeling had stayed with him for days and then months, just like now. Henry knew Julean sensed his nervousness by the way she looked at him at times.

It sort of came to a head one night. Julean lay on the bed in her nightgown, reading a book. Henry had finished studying for a midterm exam and came to the edge of the bed to sit beside her. He placed a hand over Julean's growing belly.

"I can't wait for our little one to be born, Julean."

She put down her book and looked at Henry lovingly.

"I can't wait, either. I wonder what it is? I have a feeling it's a girl."

Henry put his head to her stomach and listened for the heartbeat. "I still can't hear anything. Well, it's only three months old, right?

Julean nodded. "Yes, I think I became pregnant while we were on our honeymoon and November is just about over."

Henry did some quick calculations. "So we should expect our first addition in June sometime."

Henry lay back on his side with his head resting on Julean's belly and stared dreamily at his lovely wife. His anxiety ebbed away as it usually did in moments like this.

Julean reached out and touched Henry's face and gently stroked his cheek. Her eyes misted as she spoke in a very soft but deliberate voice. "Hank...?"

"Hmm?" Henry's eyes were closed, reveling in the warmth and tenderness of his wife's touch.

"Do you love me? I mean really, *really* love me?"

Henry opened an eye and took Julean in to see if she was serious, then quickly sat up and met her gaze head on. When he read Julean's earnestness, his brow wrinkled, his jaw dropped and his eyes focused even more intently on his dear, sweet wife.

He was stunned, momentarily speechless. "Of *course* I do, Julean, what a silly question." Henry shook his head in disbelief, "Why would you ask such a thing...are you serious?"

Julean felt somewhat embarrassed, and yes, it was foolish. It's just that her instincts played upon her feelings every now and then…and there was *something,* a part of Henry that she couldn't explain. She'd felt it occasionally when they were dating; that his heart was divided. Divided between her and…?

Oh, I'm being ridiculous. Julean's concern softened into a warm smile. "I'm sorry, Hank, it's just that I love you so much. I never want to lose you."

Henry came to Julean's side and put his arm around her. "Julean, I love you with all my heart. Please don't let any other thought ever enter that pretty mind of yours." And placing his hand upon her rounding tummy, he added. "And I love our baby too. I can hardly wait until he or she is born!"

AROUND THE FIRST week of December sitting in class listening to a lecture on classroom discipline, the nervousness that Henry had been feeling of late suddenly skyrocketed, sending him into a panic. He shuffled in his chair as his stomach churned and then a rush unlike anything he'd ever experienced before swept from the pit of his stomach to the top of his head. His heart began to palpitate uncontrollably. He thought he was having a heart attack. He could feel the heat overtake his face and the sweat running down his armpits. He could no longer sit still as the threat of some sort of impending doom overtook him. He was embarrassed to get up and leave, but he had no choice, the fear gripping him was overwhelming

He hurried outside, his heart still pounding wildly; nausea threatening. How much longer could his heart beat this fast without giving out? he wondered. He walked slower, trying to control his racing heart. Finally, he inched his way to a bench and collapsed on the seat. He took in deep breaths of cool air hoping to calm down. His heart continued to gallop. He wished Julean was there so he could tell her how much he loved her just in case he didn't make it. He was supposed to meet her at the Faculty of Agriculture building. It was halfway between their respective colleges.

Henry checked his watch. They were supposed to meet in another thirty-five minutes. Would he last that long?

Please dear Jesus, don't let me die.

Suddenly the palpitations stopped and relief swept over him. Even though it was cold and there was snow all around him, he felt like a furnace inside. The perspiration covering his face gave testimony to the internal combustion he felt. Slowly Henry regained control and his worry subsided somewhat. What on earth had just happened? Was his heart starting to give out?

Another fifteen minutes until he met Julean. He decided to make his way to their meeting place. Although his heart rate was now under control, his anxiety wasn't. He could still feel the steady churning of his stomach.

Henry was relieved to see Julean waiting for him at the corner. Her warm, welcoming smile relaxed him and the anxiety fell away from him in a rush. As they walked home, Henry shared with her what had happened.

"I don't think it's your heart, Hank, maybe it has to do with the pressure of university and the added responsibility of being a father and all." Julean was going to add another possible explanation but decided not to—it had to do more with her feminine intuition that Hank was clinging to something in his past, something that could come between them. *Oh it's too foolish to discuss,* Julean said to herself. *And he's already feeling the pressure.*

"Yeah, that might be it," Henry agreed. "But it sure felt like I was having a heart attack, Julean. It scared the hell out of me."

Julean took his hand and they walked back to their apartment.

That evening, right after dinner, Henry had another attack.

Julean came to his side and felt his chest.

"My gosh, Hank, your heart is just racing. Do you want me to phone my dad and get his advice?"

Henry wasn't sure what to do or whether he should bother his father-in-law with it. He already felt his in-laws didn't like him much.

"No, that's okay, hon. I'll make an appointment to see a doctor first thing in the morning."

Henry was relieved when the doctor told him his heart was fine. The doctor repeated much of what Julean had suggested; the pressure of university, perhaps his impending fatherhood. But he did add that these attacks could also be a culmination of past concerns adding to present ones. It reminded Henry of his worries over Jenny and what had happened to her—and the guilt he sometimes felt when his thoughts drifted to his first love.

The doctor prescribed sedatives, which Henry was reluctant to take. But once he did, the medication quickly alleviated his apprehensions and seemed to stop what the doctor called anxiety attacks. But Henry felt that the medicine was only treating the symptoms. There was something at the core of it all that he didn't totally understand. Yet.

THE YOUNG MARRIED couple could hardly wait to get home for the Christmas holidays. Julean's expanding belly was visual proof to family and friends that she was having a baby. She was looking more and more radiant with each passing day.

Since the Carters had extra room, Henry and Julean stayed at her parents' place. Although Mr. and Mrs. Carter were friendly, Henry felt an undercurrent of not being accepted. Julean told him not to worry himself over it, that he was married to her and not to them. She further stressed that time would make everything right. Henry wasn't so sure; he'd thought the same would happen with Jenny's parents but it never had.

It was great to see Mr. Engelmann, though. Neither Henry nor his parents could believe how much younger Henry's mentor looked each time they saw him. It was as if he were taking some sort of youth pill. Wrinkles that had covered his face and circled his eyes had diminished—some even seemed to have disappeared. The slight paunch that prevented him from closing his vest all the way had all but vanished, the vest hanging so loosely it didn't even seem to fit him anymore. It seemed his new vocation had given him a new lease on life. He was prepared to serve his Lord in his new capacity as a parish priest.

IN THE SEVENTH month of Julean's pregnancy the doctor noticed that the baby was in the breech position.

"The head is supposed to be down, not up," said Dr. McCall.

"I guess he wants to come out running," quipped Julean.

The doctor, however, didn't see it as a joking matter. He worked for over twenty minutes and was finally able to turn the baby into the correct position for delivery.

Julean understood the doctor's concern: the breech position and turning the baby to the correct one could cause the umbilical cord to become entangled around the baby's throat.

"Well, now that we've got this little guy or gal in the right spot, I hope he or she stays there," Dr. McCall smiled at Julean. "See you next month."

"Yes, that'll probably be the last time; we're going back to Regina for the summer."

"That's right. Have you decided on a doctor there?"

"My father, Dr. Carter, is making arrangements for that and either he'll notify you or I can tell you when I see you next month."

HENRY COULDN'T GET over how huge Julean was.

"My God, Julean, I'm amazed how much skin can stretch! And it's only seven and a half months; you still have nearly two months to go. How on earth will that baby come out?"

Julean laughed, "Well, nature has looked after it all so far, Hank. The cervix does dilate quite a bit once labour starts."

Henry was always amazed how easily Julean spoke of sex and anything else that might cause others to blush. Clearly it was a part of her upbringing, something Henry hadn't experienced in his own family. He was getting used to it, though, and was glad their children would be raised with that kind of openness.

With the landlady's permission, Henry and Julean started to plan the nursery. They moved their desks out into the living room, and instead of painting they decided to wallpaper the room in a nursery theme that would welcome either a boy or girl. The landlady also gave them a crib, change table and baby carriage her children had outgrown. The time was getting closer and the two of them could hardly focus on their final exams. Henry still felt an undercurrent of anxiety though; it permeated his joy.

When Julean went to see Dr. McCall for her eight-month check-up, he was dismayed to note the baby had turned breech again.

"This is my last appointment with you, Dr. McCall. I wish we were staying in Saskatoon so that you could deliver the baby."

"Well, I'll forward your files to your new doctor in Regina after today's examination. Now, let's see if we can turn this little bundle of joy."

Julean smiled at the doctor's words and then began to squirm as the doctor pushed and pulled on the hard wall of her womb.

"Everything's packed and ready to go, Julean. I'm not sure you'll fit in the car though!"

"Henry!" Julean smacked him playfully, then said, "yes, I can feel the strain on my back. Oh well, the baby will soon be here."

"And I'll be one very proud father!" Henry came over and kissed Julean tenderly. She held onto him for a few moments longer and gazed into her husband's eyes.

Yes, she thought, *our baby will truly unite us. And it will take away all my foolish thoughts.*

Henry kissed his wife once more, then led her into the nursery. "The room sure looks nice the way you've decorated it, Julean."

Julean cradled her belly in her hands. "Yes, I just love it too Hank. It was so nice of Helen to give us all her baby things. We're ready to bring home our beautiful little angel!"

About the Author

Henry Ripplinger is the bestselling author of *Pewter Angels,* the first in the six-book series "The Angelic Letters." The overwhelming response by readers to *Pewter Angels* gives testimony to Henry's gifts as an author to write books that touch human hearts and offer direction to their lives.

Henry's empathetic abilities, combined with his lifelong experience and eclectic career as a high school teacher, guidance counselor, professional artist and businessman, prepared him to craft this inspirational Christian romance series and indirectly realize his aspirations of writing a self-development book.

Henry is also one of Canada's foremost prairie artists. His work is on display at private and corporate collections across Canada, most notably in Saskatchewan, his home province, and can be seen in the critically acclaimed book, *If You're Not from the Prairie.*

He resides with his wife in the panoramic valley setting of Lumsden, Saskatchewan, Canada.

To contact the author and for more information on "The Angelic Letters Series," visit his website at: **www. henryripplinger.com**

ALSO BY HENRY RIPPLINGER

If You're Not from the Prairie, written by David Bouchard and illustrated by Henry Ripplinger, is a poetic and visual journey depicting the prairies and the people who have made this diverse land their own...a treasure for the mind and soul.

For further information about this book as well as other artwork, limited edition prints and other products, please visit:

www.henryripplinger.com

PEWTER ANGELS: BOOK ONE OF THE ANGELIC LETTERS SERIES

*"He hath given his angels charge over thee; to keep thee
in all thy ways…In their hands they shall bear thee up:
lest thou dash thy foot against a stone."*

PSALM 91:11-12

…Suddenly, she turned to Henry as if to speak, catching him off guard. He didn't have time to pretend he wasn't staring at her. He'd been caught. Their eyes met now for a second time and although he felt his face warming again with a blush, this time he couldn't turn away. Her gaze locked with his and his with hers. They rose from their knees simultaneously, as if lifted, and were at once standing, facing each other.

Nothing existed except this moment and this place.

A charged, earthly attraction united their hearts while a spiritual energy traveled the length of the gaze they shared, drawing their souls from their bodies and joining them at the halfway point. The aura around them brightened…enclosing both in the surrounding glow of their celestial connection.

Time stood still…

Pewter Angels will grab your heart, squeeze it
and hold it to the very last page.

For more information, please visit: www.henryripplinger.com